Tara and E............. love and could not take their eyes off each other in public or in private. Their sexual greediness was plainly obvious to everyone and the town's gossips dubbed them the Golden Couple. They were so young, so beautiful and so much in love that everyone wanted to be around them. They radiated charm wherever they went and friends and strangers alike were drawn to them. They made one want to smile a lot. But Eric and Tara noticed none of this. They were alone in a room of a thousand people. Their tender glances were only for each other.

It was a revelation to Tara. She had never thought much about love before and was completely entranced with Eric Marlowe. She was absorbed by him, captivated by his gaiety and charm, his love-making, his genius as a director. She followed him about, her eyes filled with love and wonder, constantly astonished by him.

They made love everywhere . . .

And they were so in love that when dark secrets from the past drove them apart, everyone felt their pain . . .

Love
AND Dreams

AN INTIMATE NOVEL BY
NANCY BACON

BALLANTINE BOOKS • NEW YORK

Library of Congress Catalog Card Number: 80-80921

ISBN 0-345-28767-3

Manufactured in the United States of America

First Edition: August 1980

PROLOGUE

TARA WOODHAUSER hurried along the darkened street, her arms piled high with books. Her head was wrapped in a wool scarf that also covered the lower part of her face. She paused in front of the ugly gray building where she lived and looked up to the top floor, trying to see if there was a light burning. The windows were so filthy she could not see inside. Caravans of cracks, horizontal and vertical, ran together unevenly and bisected in the center of the tall brick wall. A piece of cardboard replaced a broken pane, with the words *fuck you* scrawled across the middle.

"You thinkin' of pullin' a heist, kid, casin' the buildin' that a way?" The deep baritone wheeled her around and she almost slipped on the frozen snow.

"Oh, hi, Calhoun," she said, looking up at the big, beefy policeman.

"*Sergeant* Calhoun to you, me girl," the big cop growled, but there was a crooked grin on his homely face and he gripped her shoulder warmly. He hooked his nightstick in the cuff of his blue uniform and pulled it back, looking down at his wristwatch. "Ain't it kinda late for you to be out on the streets?"

"I'm just going in now," Tara said and took a tighter grip on her armload of books. "I've been to the library and I didn't realize how late it was until they kicked me

out and closed up." She smiled, inviting his, and he gave
her a wink and a little push toward the tenement steps.

Balancing her books in one arm, she pushed open the
paint-blistered door and started up the three flights of
stairs, paying no attention to the familiar sounds and
shrill voices that came through the thin walls. Odors of
food mixed indiscriminately with one another, but the
strong odor of garlic predominated. She felt a hollow rum-
ble of hunger in her stomach and hoped that her mother
had left something to eat.

The apartment was silent as she entered, a naked
light bulb glaring harshly against the aged ceiling which
was stained in round patterns of rust amber. Each circle
marked a past rainfall that had seeped through the loose
roof, staining the old plaster of the interior. A clumsy
attempt at painting had only added to its indignity, for
the once white paint was now yellow with age and chipped
off in places. The ceiling seemed to sag, bowed by the
weight of neglect. A thin haze of smoke drifted through
the open kitchen door, and Tara dropped her gunnysack
and books and rushed inside.

The table had been set for three. Water glasses had
been filled and a half loaf of sourdough bread lay harden-
ing in a saucer in the center of the table. A brown bag
on the sink held groceries, and there was the strong odor
of rum in the dense air. She turned off the gas under a pot
of spaghetti that had cooked itself dry. Mama's been trying again, she thought wearily as she stared at the burned,
crusty mess in the blackened pot. Some day she would
burn the building down with her feeble attempts at playing loving mother. She opened the icebox and scanned
the almost barren shelves, taking out a jar of blackberry
preserves and a jar of peanut butter. She tore off a piece
of the day-old bread and spread it generously with peanut
butter and preserves. Music was playing in the living-
room, competing with the whining static, and she took a
bite of her sandwich and walked toward the door. She
wondered if her mother was dead—or just dead drunk.

Tara stepped into the living room and stood looking
down at her mother. Belle was lying on her back on the

couch, her arms almost primly at her sides, her legs
spread wide. She wore no panties but a tattered slip clung
to her, sticking to the cleft between her breasts where she
had perspired. The room was filthy. Her rumpled flowered
robe was bunched under her body. An empty rum bottle
lay next to her head, its contents soaked into the dirty
cushions. Dried spittle clung to her cracked lips, and a
thin snake of ashes curved close to one hand where a
cigarette had burned itself out between her numb fingers.
Two transparent skin blisters bubbled on either side of
the now extinguished butt which still reeked from the
smoldering filter. The fetid air in the small closed room
was permeated with the stench of cheap booze, cigarette
smoke, body odor and sex.

Tara gasped aloud and dropped her sandwich as she
stared at her mother and the young boy who lay asleep
between her naked thighs. She stumbled toward them, her
hip bumping into a table and knocking it over, spilling
its litter to the floor with a loud crash. The boy sat up in
one swift movement, his eyes large and frightened as he
stared dumbly about. He saw her and jumped to his feet,
fumbling with his trousers as he quickly jerked them up
and buttoned them. He wanted to say something to the
girl, say anything to make her stop staring at him like
that. Her brown eyes had grown black with rage and
shock, and her small nose grew pinched and white before
his eyes. Her little fists clenched and unclenched as she
moved toward him.

"Get out! Get out!" she screamed and her whole body
shook violently. She began to pant and her thin chest rose
and fell with each deep spasm that shook it.

"I'm—I'm sorry—I—" Eric made a wide circle around
her and jerked open the door, half falling into the hallway.

"Get out, get out, get out!" Tara cried, and then her
eyes fell upon the wire coat hanger that held the scuffed
brown shoes and she jerked it off the nail and flung the
whole thing at the boy's retreating back. The shoes hit
him on the back of the head, and he cried out and bent
quickly to pick them up. She flung his patched and tat-

3

tered jacket in his face, slamming the door as hard as she could.

Tara stood trembling, leaning against the door and staring at her mother's obscenely sprawled figure, and she screamed, "Wake up, Mama! Wake up, damn you!"

With a groan that was almost a whimper of pain, Belle Woodhauser pushed herself to her elbows and stared fuzzily at her daughter. She lowered her head, trying to focus on the blurred and trembling figure. Her parched lips parted as if she would speak, then, wordlessly, she fell back.

Tara burst into tears and rushed from the room into the kitchen, her fists beating impotently against her knotted stomach muscles. "Why, oh God, why does she do it?" she cried aloud to the stinking, smoke-filled kitchen. She sank into a chair at the table and picked up a glass and gulped a few swallows of the now tepid water that her mother had poured earlier. She stared at the three plates and wondered if her mother had intended to invite her new young lover to dine with them. She certainly could not have been expecting Charles for dinner. Her older brother hardly bothered to come home at all these days unless he had dirty laundry to leave.

The static on the ancient radio crackled and hissed and then sweet music blared forth, and Tara buried her face in her hands and cried bitterly. She wished she had never been born. Oh, God, why could it not be like in the books and movies with pretty clothes and lovely homes and kind mothers baking cookies for their dear little daughters?

She gave in to self-pity for only a moment, then she raised her head, sniffed loudly, wiped her runny nose on the sleeve of her sweater and brushed the tears from her face. She walked into the living room, sighing heavily. Her mother lay where she had left her, snoring serenely, her nakedness still exposed, and Tara went to her and pulled the flowered robe over the blue chilled flesh.

Sighing, stubbornly fighting back tears, she bent to retrieve her sandwich and brushed the bits of hair and dirty fuzz from it. The library books were on the floor near the doorway and she picked one up, fondling it, and went back into the kitchen. Settling herself at the table she took a bite of her sandwich and began reading, "Once upon a time, there was a beautiful little princess who lived with her father and mother, the King and Queen of a great palace . . ."

CHAPTER
ONE

TARA sat at her typewriter in Jim Glasser's office, staring at the telegram in her hand. The message was brief: HI, SIS. DECIDED TO MOVE TO SUNNY CALIF. & OPEN BUSINESS CALL—and there was his telephone number. Charles. Her gay brother who had caused her such suffering as a child. How in the world had he found her? She had not spoken to him in six or seven years. Not since the Christmas Eve she had gone looking for him to beg him to please have dinner with her and Mandy, like a family should on special holidays. And he had laughed, and told her that she could not afford him for a dinner date. And besides, she was the wrong sex. How had he known she had moved to Los Angeles? Then she realized he must have seen her name in a magazine or newspaper recently. In the past few months her byline had been appearing regularly in the fan magazines and tabloids. He obviously had seen it and decided to torment her further. She remembered how he used to flaunt his gay friends and johns in the neighborhood, making them wait in front of the shabby apartment building for the whole world to see and whisper about. How he had dropped out of high school to become the lover of a local businessman, almost driving Tara out as well to escape the cruel taunts of her classmates. And when their mother had died, leaving the baby, Mandy, to be cared for, Charles had not even bothered to inquire how Tara would manage. Well, she *had* managed. And without anyone's help. She made a place for herself and Mandy and she wasn't about to let anyone disrupt it.

I should change my name, she thought grimly, staring down at the block letters spelling out T. Woodhauser. She glanced down at her typewriter and the word Remington seemed to leap out at her. "Remington," she said aloud, liking the sound. "Tara Remington." She repeated it to herself a couple of times and then typed it out in all caps: TARA REMINGTON. It looked good, classy. Woodhauser had always sounded rather tacky to her and she was glad of an excuse to change it. Now, not only would Charles be less likely to find her, she also would not be connected to anything he might become involved in. And with Charles it was almost a certainty that he would choose something sordid.

A crash of thunder boomed near the window and the already dark and dreary day turned even grayer. Tara shivered and pulled her sweater more snugly about her. God, what a lousy day to go Christmas shopping, she thought as she covered her typewriter and prepared to leave for the day. It was Christmas Eve, and she stared down at the telegram a long moment before crumpling it in her fist and tossing it into the wastebasket. How ironic that the last time she and Charles had spoken was on that Christmas Eve so many years ago. Too bad he was such a skunk. She would have invited him to dinner tomorrow. As usual, Tara would be cooking Christmas dinner for her "Hollywood orphans"—those transplanted Easterners, recent divorcees and assorted strays who were at loose ends during the holiday season. Jim had given her a fifty dollar bonus and she had been looking forward to her shopping spree. Now this damn telegram from Charles had upset her so much she did not feel like going. She did not want to remember all that crap from her childhood, but just seeing his name had brought it all back. The gray day and the fact that it was Christmas Eve seemed to sink her lower into gloom, and she forcibly pushed herself away from her desk and went to the closet for her coat.

A brisk wind whipped past her face as she pushed open the heavy glass doors and stepped onto the sidewalk. Sunset Boulevard was packed with bumper to bumper traffic, headlights glowing dully in the misty rain and haloed in pale yellow. Tara hunched her shoulders, sinking her face deeper into the turned up collar of her coat, and made a dash for the parking lot. The wind soaking her through as she tugged at the door of her car. Sliding swiftly behind the steeering wheel, she shook the rain from her hair and started the motor. God, it was cold! She grinned, thinking of Charles and his recent move to "sunny California." Served him right, she thought grimly, for screwing up my shopping trip. She backed out of her parking space and eased her baby blue Corvair into the slow-moving traffic. She reached into her purse for a cigarette and her fingers felt the cool plastic bottle of Dexedrine. Why not? She shrugged and loosened the cap and shook a pill out into her hand. She needed a pick-me-up, had a lot of shopping and cooking to do. She popped it into her mouth and swallowed several times to get it down her dry throat.

Making a right turn on LaBrea, Tara shrugged away the tiny annoying tug of guilt. One little Dexie was not going to hurt anything, she thought, rather defiantly. Everyone she knew took some kind of an upper. In this crazy business you almost had to. And she only took the prescribed amount. She would not allow herself to fall into the pill-booze-cocaine-marijuana-upper-downer trip like so many others she knew. She was only vaguely aware that, like so many others, she was good at rationalizing.

By the time she had fought her way through the crowd at The Broadway, the Dexie had hit and Tara was fairly buzzing about the huge, sprawling department store, her brother's telegram all but forgotten. She just had Barry Wilde left on her list but she had no idea what to buy him. Barry was so crazy she had to find a suitably crazy gift. He and Tara always tried to out-do one another in the whacky gift department. Last year it had been a seven-foot-long, bright green, stuffed crocodile from Barry—and Tara had reciprocated with a huge wristwatch, the face two feet in diameter, the wrist band at least four feet long. She was shoved rudely from both sides by a tight little group of women who seemed determined to walk right through her if necessary to get to the sales table piled high with holiday aprons. She headed for the exit. The Broadway probably wouldn't have anything bizarre enough for Barry the Bear, anyway.

An hour later Tara was sitting in her apartment on Franklin Avenue, wrapping gifts, sipping an eggnog and listening to Frank Sinatra albums. Ole Blue Eyes was crooning about the joys of love "The Second Time Around" and Tara swayed with the soft, gentle strains, humming along. A warm flush crept up her cheeks and she felt a sudden thrill shoot through her belly, leaving her weak with its intensity, and she recognized the familiar ache in her groin. God, it had been ages since she had had a good love affair. She was more than overdue, she told herself with a wry grin, if just listening to a love song made her horny! This Most-Famous-Novelist-in-the-World business was hard work! She hadn't had a week-end off in over three months. When she wasn't doing some assignment for Jim Glasser, she was working on her own freelance writing. The long hours at the type-writer had paid off, however, and her byline was appear-ing more and more often in the fan magazines—"written by" or "as told to Tara Woodhauser"—then she remem-bered. "No more Woodhauser," she said as she got to her feet and carried an armload of gifts to the tree. She placed them under the decorated branches and walked, a little unsteadily, into the kitchen. "Tara Remington," she said gaily as she dipped herself another eggnog from the punchbowl on the table. "Merry Christmas, Tara Remington." She toasted herself and took a sip, then placed the cup on the cabinet. Humming, feeling the effects of the Dexie and eggnog, she began chopping on-ions for the dressing.

She glanced at her watch. Barry should be here any

minute with the turkey. He always supplied the meat at Christmas, Easter and Thanksgiving, making it a tradition over the years they had spent together. Tonight he would be working Sunset Boulevard with his "Xmas scam," so he might be a little late. She grinned as she thought about it. He had somehow conned a zoo keeper into letting him borrow a reindeer and, armed with his trusty Polaroid, he had set up shop on the sidewalk. A vividly painted sign proclaimed: HAVE YOUR PICTURE TAKEN WITH SANTA'S REINDEER—ONLY ONE DOLLAR. And there was Barry dressed in a Santa suit and thrusting lollipops at children as they were dragged past by holiday-frazzled parents.

Tara went to the window and looked out. The rain had stopped, finally—it had rained for three days straight —but it was still cold and bleak outside. She hoped Christmas Day would be clear and sunny. She liked the rain, but only when she was curled up in front of the fireplace with a good book or a good lover. Parties called for cheerier weather. A knock sounded and Tara rushed to the door and threw it open.

"Merry Christmas, Bear!" she said as she stepped back to let Barry inside. He was loaded down with bundles and she could hardly see his face as he staggered through the door, swearing.

"Jesus Christ, let me get rid of this stuff!" He dropped the bundles onto the dining room table and grabbed her, hugging her close. "Merry Christmas, babe. God, that damn turkey weighs thirty pounds!"

"Thirty pounds? You've got to be kidding!" Tara peeked into the limp sack at the huge turkey. "My God, Bear, that will take all day to cook!"

"Put it on tonight. I'll help with the dressing." He shucked off his heavy coat and tossed it across the back of a chair. "Hey, the tree looks great. When did you have time to get everything decorated?"

"I've just been working mornings at the office this week. I told Jim I had a couple of freelance magazine articles to get out, so he gave me some time off. He always does, to 'pursue my career,' as he calls it." She went

11

to the punchbowl and dipped the ladle in, stirring the nutmeg in a round pattern. "Want a little Christmas cheer?"

"I'll have a *lot* of Christmas cheer. Christ, I damn near froze my balls off standing out there in the street all night." He rubbed his hands together before accepting the mug of eggnog, then raised it to his lips and drained it quickly. Tara raised an eyebrow at him when he held out his mug for a refill. "Ahhh, that's good." He watched her ladle the rum mixture into his cup and took a small sip before adding, "But I did make sixty-two bucks tonight. That ain't bad for a bear and a reindeer." He laughed and threw his arm around his shoulders, hugging her close for a moment. He looked down at her, his blue eyes warm with the love he felt for her as they traveled over her body. She was beautiful, but for some strange reason he wasn't sexually attracted to her. She was more like a lovely kid sister he wanted to protect and shield from the realities of life. He had met her fresh off the bus, a scared, skinny little kid but with more determination, guts and just plain stubbornness than anyone he'd ever met. She had taken care of herself and her mentally retarded sister with no help from anyone that he knew of. He had never known her to borrow so much as a dollar from anyone, and yet he knew that there had been many times in the past four years when she could have used a few extra bucks. She laughed up at him and poked him in the ribs.

"Well, I guess it beats doing army training films in a gorilla suit," she said with a wink, reminding him of the time he had made a ludicrous minimovie about transporting dangerous cargo aboard an airplane. Before he could give her a slap on the fanny, she had whirled away and gone to the dining room table where he had piled his packages. He watched her pick up a brightly wrapped box and shake it, laughing at him and looking incredibly beautiful in the soft glow of the candle-lit room. Her dark auburn hair fell to just below her shoulders, parted in the middle to frame her perfect oval face. Her eyes were a strange combination of green, gray

12

and brown, and when she was angry or sexy or high they turned a deep emerald green. It was the weirdest thing Barry had ever seen but when he commented on it, Tara seemed not at all impressed, insisting that her eyes were "just plain hazel." Her mouth was full and pouty but it could tighten into stubborn determination. He let his gaze travel down her body, taking in the high, firm breasts, large for a girl her height, braless now in the clinging jersey hostess gown she wore. Tara was one of those women who looked elegant in a man's oversized shirt, he thought as he watched her carrying the packages to the tree. She bent to place them with the jumble of gifts already there, and Barry whistled appreciatively at her high, rounded fanny. "Sassy," he said, walking over to pat it fondly.

"What?" Tara straightened and went to find her eggnog. She lit a cigarette and fell into the soft cushions of the sofa with a huge sigh.

"Your ass," Barry said, flopping down beside her. "It's sassy."

"Is that a fact?" she said dryly.

"What's the matter, babe? Got problems?" Barry pulled her into the curve of his arm, stroking her hair back from her face.

"Nothing big. Just the same old bullshit." She dragged deep on her cigarette and rested her head against his shoulder, wishing again that she could love Barry as a woman should love a man. He would be a perfect mate for her, they were so much alike in so many areas, and there was no denying his good looks. Every girlfriend she'd ever had had flipped for Barry and wound up in his bed. But somehow the sex thing hadn't clicked between them and she doubted that it ever would.

"You mean, as in money, money and money?" Barry gave a snort of laughter. "Hell, what else is new?"

"Damn it, Bear, I'm getting so—so—" She groped for a strong enough expletive. "—*fucking* tired of being broke!" She hit the arm of the sofa for emphasis and he laughed, hugging her close.

"Like I said—what else is new?" He drank some egg-

13

nog, looking at her over the rim of the cup. "You know, if you had any brains you'd be modeling or acting—not knocking yourself out at some office, typing Glasser's junk. Christ, Tara, I'm around the studios all day, all week, all year—" He made a face and took another swallow of his drink. "And you're a hell of lot prettier than the chicks I see on the lots." He patted his pants pockets, then his shirt pockets, looking slightly perplexed. "Can I bum a cigarette? I'm trying to quit, so I don't buy them anymore." He reached for her pack, shook one out and lighted it. Tara smiled at the familiar dialogue. Barry was always trying to quit smoking and therefore was always smoking someone else's cigarettes. They had figured it out once. Barry had about a two and a half pack a day habit and yet he never spent a nickel on tobacco. "But, no, you won't listen. It's like talking to a brick wall." He dragged deep on the cigarette and let the smoke trickle out in its own time. "I told you about that producer at Universe Studios who saw you the day you picked me up. He really flipped. No kidding, babe. You could probably write your own contract if you'd just go out and meet him. He asks me every time he sees me if I've given his message. Hell, I don't know what to tell the guy, ya know? I mean, he's used me in a few things and I'd like to keep the door open."

"Then you'll have to use your own ass to do it. I don't sell mine for anyone or anything." She tossed off the rest of her drink. "Really, Barry, you know his reputation. My God, the old lecher isn't satisfied just getting *his* cock sucked, he takes the girls home to his wife, yet!" She handed him her mug. "Get us a refill, okay? Then I guess we'd better get that mammoth turkey stuffed and in the oven or we'll be eating Christmas dinner at midnight tomorrow."

Barry got to his feet and started toward the kitchen with the mugs. "Oh, come on, Tara, that's not the reason. Hell, I've seen you handle guys twice as lecherous as ole Al when you wanted a particular writing assignment." He ladled eggnog into the mugs, adding, "But I suppose that's different."

"Yes, it is different. For one thing, most of the guys in publishing who would try to ball me live in New York and I'm able to keep a healthy distance between us. I only see them a couple of times a year and I'm very good at being evasive. I can handle flirting long distance, but with Al-baby I'd be right there within his reach." She took the mug as Barry sat down next to her. "And from what I hear, his reach is pretty damn long."

"Admit it. You don't think you'd make it as an actress and you couldn't stand the failure," he teased, giving up trying to talk any sense into her.

"Yeah, that's it, Bear," she said solemnly. "I just don't have what it takes."

"Tara, You know so many people in the industry and they all like you. Why don't you use them to open a few doors?"

"Did it ever occur to you that the reason they do like me is because I *don't* use them?" Tara got to her feet and took his hand, pulling him up with her. "Come on, Bear, no more show biz talk. The turkey awaits."

"Stubborn broad," Barry muttered, allowing himself to be pulled into the kitchen, where Tara handed him a knife and a large green bell pepper.

"Here, cut this up, please, while I wash out the bird and put the giblets on. Daisy loves the liver and neck and I hate it, so it works out great." Hearing her name, Daisy raised herself in a lazy stretch, then padded over to stand next to Tara, her pink nose twitching with the smell of raw meat.

"What? You mean you cook the giblets and then feed them to that—that *animal?*" Barry cried in mock horror. "You've got to be kidding!"

"No, I'm not. I always feed her the giblets. After all, she's a member of the family, too. Aren't you, sweetie?" she cooed at the big, shaggy calico as it purred furiously and rubbed back and forth against her legs.

"Speaking of family, it's too bad Mandy can't be here with us tonight, isn't it?" He chopped the green pepper into small chunks and tossed them into the bowl of dressing mix.

"It really isn't that she *couldn't* be here, it's just that I don't feel right about having her visit me in the apartment. There're too many people around." Tara placed a cube of butter in a small skillet on the stove, turning up the flame and stirring it as it melted swiftly. She reached into the refrigerator with her free hand and took out two eggs, handing them to Barry. "Here, Bear, break these in the bowl, will you?" She turned back to the melting butter, stirring it absently. "I've taken her out a few times this year, but she still gets so frightened of crowds that I really hate to put her through all that trauma. She actually shakes with fright and hangs onto me for dear life whenever we go to a movie or even out to lunch. The doctors don't know why she is so scared of people. There's been nothing in her past that had anything to do with large crowds. In fact, she's been very sheltered all her life."

"Maybe that's why she freaks out when she's around people," Barry said with a short laugh. "God knows there's enough loony birds out there running around loose to frighten anybody."

"Well, I plan on moving into a house as soon as I can possibly afford it and then I'll have Mandy live with me all the time." She poured the melted butter over the cornbread crumbs, onions, eggs and bell pepper and stirred it briskly. "I want a house out in the San Fernando Valley with at least two acres of land, so Mandy can have a pony and I can have a garden. I've wanted a garden all my life, and you want to know something strange? I've never even *seen* a real garden except in magazines." She added several dashes of various spices and then motioned toward the turkey. "Grab that big varmint and hold it in the sink for me, will ya, Bear?"

Barry held the turkey upside down in the sink, spreading its legs apart while Tara spooned the dressing into the cavity. "The Valley? Are you crazy?" he said. "There's nothing in the Valley but orange groves and horse shit." He took a pinch of the dressing and Tara slapped his hand.

"I swear, Barry, you're going to get worms the way you eat everything raw." He had a habit of standing over her when she was cooking, snatching bits of raw hamburger, steak or even potatoes if he could catch her peeling them.

"Nag, nag, bitch, bitch," he grinned at her, giving her a pinch on the fanny.

"Ouch, that hurt!" She flinched away and gave him a stern look. "When are you going to stop treating me so damn rough? Didn't your mother ever tell you it wasn't nice to pinch girls?"

"Yeah, but luckily I found out at an early age that she was lying." Barry laughed and grabbed her around the waist, tickling her until she begged him to stop, tears streaming down her cheeks.

It was two in the morning when Tara finally fell into bed. Barry had stayed until midnight, helping with various chores, but after he had staggered off into the night singing "Here Comes Santa Claus" in a drunken baritone, Tara had gone back into the kitchen to make his Christmas gift. The Bear's one weakness was divinity candy with walnuts and maraschino cherries and she was going to make him five pounds worth. Every holiday for the last four years she made divinity and Barry always somehow managed to arrive early and consume the entire dish of candy before the other guests even got a look at it. They had a running battle over Tara's famous divinity, she hiding it before Barry arrived and he cursing her as he searched every cupboard and cabinet. She hoped he ate enough this year to make him sick for a month.

Christmas morning dawned bright and clear. Last night's rain had cleared away the smog and a sweet, crisp breeze was just barely ruffling the fronds of a tall palm tree outside Tara's kitchen window. Bright sunlight spilled through the sliding glass door, laying like a pale scatter rug on the floor and bathing the sleeping cat in its warmth. Tara stooped down and ruffled the thick, multicolored fur, saying, "Merry Christmas, Daisy—rise and shine." She placed a dish of dry Friskies next to the cat. "That should hold you until we cut the turkey and then, as you well know, everyone will be feeding you from

17

their plates." Daisy gave her an innocent stare from huge, round yellow eyes and deliberately yawned as if she had no idea what her mistress could possibly mean. "Spoiled brat," Tara grinned as she plugged in the coffee pot and measured water.

The fragrant odor of roasting turkey filled the small apartment as Tara wandered through the combination living and dining room, checking decorations. Daisy still thought the tree and all the bright ornaments were hers alone to practice her hunting skills on; she put out hors d'oeuvres, ashtrays, holiday matches and napkins. She jumped when the doorbell rang and glanced at her watch. She wasn't expecting anyone for at least four hours and she wondered who could be here so early as she called out, "Who is it?"

"Open the fucking door!" a loud voice demanded and Tara laughed and threw it open, her arms outstretched.

"Jim—Merry Christmas. Come in—what in the world are you doing out so early?" She pulled him inside, shaking her head when he staggered against her and breathed strong liquor fumes in her face. "Whew," she gasped, stepping back a little as she guided him to a chair. "Where in the world have you been to get so sloshed so early in the morning?"

"Not early—late," Jim mumbled with a mischievous giggle. He reached out for Tara and almost lost his balance when she deftly side-stepped his embrace. He righted himself, sank into a chair and fixed her with a pathetic look. "Haven't been home yet—Frances will kill me." He looked up at her with a suddenly pleading, hang-dog expression in his usually twinkling blue eyes. "You gotta help me, Tara, honey. You call Frances and tell her I spent the night here—working—working on—on—oh hell, tell her anything. Tell her we were screwing all night." He laughed loudly, staring boldly at Tara's thin beige satin nightgown and half-exposed breasts. "Get me a drink before I lose the habit," he suddenly demanded. "I don't want to talk about Frances anymore—don't want to even think about Frances anymore . . ."

Tara filled a large coffee mug with eggnog left over

18

from last night and took it to him. She would have to make a fresh batch before her guests arrived. "Jim, you know you have to go home, so don't talk dumb. Even if you don't give a damn about Frances, and I don't blame you in the least, the kids will be expecting you and you can't disappoint them."

"Yeah, yeah, I know." He took the mug and drank deep, wishing Tara wouldn't stand so close to him in her half-dressed state. He had trouble concentrating when she got that close. All last night he had thought about her and had fought the desire to drop by her apartment. He had gotten very drunk and had finally picked up a young hooker who looked a little like Tara, in a hotel lounge and he had screwed her until dawn, whispering Tara's name. At least a thousand times since Tara had gone to work for him he had wanted to grab her and tell her how much he loved her, desired her, wanted to be all things to her. But he was afraid she would laugh at him. The fair Tara, so young and beautiful it almost hurt to look at her. So innocent and untouched by the world—and so eager to have it touch her, it made him heartsick. He had seen the restlessness in her, the awakening of sexual awareness as she grew almost before his eyes. She had been just eighteen when she had come to work for him, now she was almost twenty-one, a gorgeous, sensual young woman whose face and figure were going to get her into a lot of trouble if she stayed in this business. Why the hell she wanted to be a writer when she could make a fortune off her looks, he would never understand. But he admired her for it. He glanced at her as she perched on the arm of his chair, her lush curves dimly outlined beneath the sheer fabric of her gown, her auburn hair falling around her shoulders. Then he chuckled softly when he saw her slippers—big, fuzzy pink things with a clown's head on the front! His little Tara wasn't completely grown up yet, and the thought comforted him.

"Want me to fix you some eggs or something?" Tara asked. "You really should have something to eat, you know." She looked at him anxiously. His light blue eyes were bloodshot and puffy, his usual laughing mouth lax

19

with drink and fatigue and his day-old beard was spotted with gray, giving him a raggedy look. She felt her heart move with affection for him and she leaned over and placed her hand on his shoulder. "At least a cup of coffee, Jim—okay? I have a fresh pot on and it'll make you feel a lot better. I promise." She gave him a little shake and grinned, encouraging him. "Have I ever lied to you?"

"Hell, yes!" Jim roared. "All the fucking time!" Then he laughed, for the first time looking like his old self— the mischievous Irish leprechaun. "Okay, okay, I'll have coffee. Christ, you'll nag me to death if I don't—" He pretended anger but his eyes looked a little better, and Tara dropped a kiss on his cheek before moving away. She heard him yell to Daisy, "Hey, come over here, you rotten bastard, and give your old Uncle Jimmy a Christmas kiss!" Tara laughed as Daisy flicked her bushy tail in contempt and leaped upon a chair across the room from Jim, paying him not the slightest attention. "Spoiled bastard," Jim muttered but he got to his feet and stumbled over to scratch Daisy's ears. The calico purred and pushed her head closer, loving the attention and the fact that she hadn't had to go out of her way to receive it.

Tara had just poured a cup of coffee when Jim lurched into the room and jerked open the cabinet door where he knew she kept the liquor. "Got any whiskey in here?" he demanded as he pawed through the bottles. "That damn eggnog's too damn sweet—makes me wanta puke!"

"Jim, at this point anything would make you barf—and the last thing you need is another drink. Here, just drink your coffee—" Tara firmly closed the door.

"God, you sound like Frances," he growled and jerked the cabinet door open again and grabbed a bottle of Jack Daniels. He poured half of his coffee into the sink and filled the cup with whiskey, his eyes glittering with hate.

Tara moved away and quickly bent to check the turkey, keeping her back to him. She had seen that expression before and she couldn't help but get a shiver of fear. She had seen Frances more than once with black eyes, swollen lips, her neck bruised as if someone had tried to

20

strangle her. She knew that Jim was considered a "bad alcoholic" when he went on one of his binges and, even though she really didn't think he'd ever hurt her, she wasn't brave enough to put it to the test. She basted the turkey in its own bubbling juices, breathing in the aroma, and called to Jim over her shoulder, "Smell that, Jim. Isn't it heavenly?" She replaced the foil over the browning bird and closed the oven door, standing to face him, a smile ready. "Hey, why don't you make me a Bloody Mary? I may as well join you in a Christmas drink." With relief, she saw that the ugly snarl was gone from his face and he was back to looking haggard and beaten. She gave him a pat on the shoulder and a wide grin. "The fixin's are in the fridge. I'm going to slip into something a little more respectable while you do the honors—okay?"

"Oh, please, don't go to any trouble on my account," Jim said broadly, leering at the thrust of her breasts through the sheer fabric.

"You old lecher," Tara laughed and blew him a kiss before making her exit.

She returned in less than five minutes dressed in Levis and a black turtleneck sweater, her feet still in the fuzzy pink slippers. He handed her the drink and raised the coffee cup in a toast. "Bah, humbug," he said.

"To a very merry Christmas and all that good stuff," Tara said and took a big swallow, grimacing when the strong vodka hit her empty stomach. "God, Jim, that's a healthy drink!"

"Oh, shit, I almost forgot. I've got your present in the car. Wait right here—okay?" He drained his cup and headed for the front door.

"What? Oh, Jim, I—" But he was already gone, slamming the door behind him. She shook her head, wondering what Jim had gotten her this year. Every year he bought her something outrageously expensive—as well as outrageously personal. For her last birthday he had given her several pieces of intimate lingerie, crotchless panties, bras with lace-trimmed peek-holes for her nipples and assorted baby-doll nighties. She had exchanged them for a ski jacket and asked him to please refrain from living his fantasies through her. She just had time to dig his package from her out of the jumble of gifts under the tree before he was back, bursting through the door in a gust of damp, chill air. He was half hidden behind a huge, gaily wrapped box, which he dropped with a loud *thunk* on the dining room table.

"My God, Jim, what is it?" Tara advanced closer, staring at the gigantic box. It was clearly too large to be anything *too* intimate and she relaxed a bit. She opened the card Jim was thrusting at her and read aloud, "To the best selling writer of 'Seventy-three—I love you, kid—Jim." She began tearing off the wrapping paper, laughing, "You crazy Irishman, you must have been stoned like a statue when you wrote the card. It's the brand new year of 'Seventy-one—*not* 'Seventy-three!"

"My dear young child," Jim said with great patience. "Even a best-selling writer must wait until the book is published and on the stands. I figured if you write that book now, it'll be out in 'Seventy-three—hence, the gift. Open it, for Christ's sake!"

"Ohhh," Tara cried as she tore off the top of the box and revealed an electric typewriter, creamy beige in color, big, square and sturdy. And it was a Remington. "Jim, I didn't tell you, did I? Oh, wow, this is too much. Just yesterday I changed my name to Remington and now"—She gestured at the typewriter, her eyes brimming with tears—"now this!" She threw her arms around him and gave him a quick kiss.

With a groan, Jim grasped her tighter, his mouth hot and demanding upon hers, his tongue forcing its way between her lips. She pushed against him, trying to pull her mouth away but he held her closer, forcing her to kiss him. His body was hard and hot against hers, and she could feel him getting an erection. She jerked her mouth away and pushed as hard as she could against his chest, crying, "Jim, stop it! What the hell do you think you're doing?" She felt his lower body shove hard against her belly, almost knocking the wind out of her and she was suddenly frightened. "Jim," she said, slowly, a little shakily. She took his chin in her hand and brought his

22

face around so she could look into his eyes. They looked angry and ashamed. She smiled brightly. "Hey, come on, Jim, let me examine my fantastic new typewriter, for God's sake! Jeez, I get one look and then you're all over me like an octopus!" She laughed, keeping it light, and a little reluctantly Jim laughed with her. She reached behind her for his gift and handed it to him. "Hope you like it, my good friend."

"Christ, what did you go and get me anything for?" Jim growled, his expressive Irish face screwed up in a Wallace Beery grimace. "God, I hate gifts!" He tore at the curling red ribbon as if it were the enemy, tangling it all around his fist and jerking the whole thing off, paper and all. Then he stopped, his eyes softening as he looked down at the leather bound copy of Omar Khayyam's *Rubáiyát*. "Hey, Tara—hey—" Jim whispered as he picked the book up tenderly, feeling the soft leather, his fingers tracing the raised gold lettering. "Somebody borrowed my copy years ago and never returned it. I just never got around to buying another one."

"I know." Tara smiled and patted his arm. "Come on in the kitchen and talk to me while I baste the turkey and get started peeling potatoes, okay? You can fix us another drink if you'd like. A little milder this time, please. I have to cook dinner for fifteen people in less than three hours!"

Jim carefully tucked the book into his overcoat pocket before following Tara into the kitchen. The aroma of roasting turkey filled the small room and both Tara and Jim laughed out loud when they saw Daisy sitting as close to the oven door as she could get, her plume-like tail swishing gently.

Barry Wilde lay sprawled on the floor, his back propped against the sofa and Charlotte's legs. Christmas carols played softly in the background and the only light in the room came from the tree and several small holiday candles. Charlotte moved her legs from behind the Bear's back and stood, stretching up on her toes. "Umm, I'm so stoned, Tara, I don't think I can make it home tonight. Mind if I borrow your couch?"

"Not at all," Tara murmured. She lay on her stomach on the floor, her head cushioned by her arms, one finger moving in time with the music. A half-filled glass of champagne stood near her head and the floor around her was littered with overflowing ashtrays, empty eggnog mugs and glasses of all description. Plates with the remains of turkey dinner were scattered over every surface in the room. She shuddered and closed her eyes.

"What's the matter, luv?" Barry teased, catching her expression. "Isn't the maid coming in tomorrow?"

"No—unfortunately it's her day off," Tara answered dryly, sticking out her tongue.

"Don't fight, children," Charlotte called over her shoulder as she carried a few plates and glasses into the kitchen. "I'll stay tomorrow and help wash dishes, and you, friend Bear, can come over and give us a hand."

"What's this 'come over' jazz?" Barry snorted. "I'm staying right here, ladies. You couldn't *pay* me to get out on the road tonight with all the crazies driving home full of Christmas cheer! Besides, I've had a little too much Christmas cheer myself." He burped delicately, stood, kicked off his shoes and loosened his belt. "Just throw a blanket over me and wake me when the coffee's ready or you want the garbage taken out. Whichever comes first." Crawling onto the sofa, he turned his back to them and curled up, preparing for sleep.

"How do you like that?" Charlotte laughed as she came back into the room carrying a fresh bottle of champagne. "Hey, Bear, get your ass off my couch! I'm sleeping there tonight."

"Oh, leave him alone, Charley. Let him sleep." Tara held out her glass for a refill. "He's had a lot to drink and really should sleep it off. You can sleep in the den. The sofa in there makes into a bed."

"Okay, whatever's fair." She sank down on the floor next to Tara and raised her champagne glass in a toast. "To a super Christmas, Tara—the dinner was superb!"

She took a long swallow, sighing, "And so is this champagne. Who gave it to you again?"

"Thorton Kennedy, you met him, the tall, scholarly looking chap who kept saying 'quite frankly' and eyeing the ladies. He gave me a whole case of champagne, everything from pink to cold Duck to Very Cold Duck. He does the same thing every year."

"You're kidding? Why haven't I heard more about him?" Charley sipped her champagne, enjoying the quiet after the noise and exuberance of the party.

"I don't know—just missed each other, I guess. Thorton's an agent and one of the last living 'star makers' in Hollywood today. He discovered a lot of big stars in the Forties and Fifties, but when television reared its ugly head, there was no longer a star system—and Thorton's talents became obsolete. He still has one actress under personal contract, but he mostly does PR work for the big hotels in Vegas and Chicago and like that. I really dig Thorton. He keeps telling me he's going to make me the first 'star' of the literary world. The number one Queen of the Best Sellers!" Tara flung her arms out in a broad theatrical gesture, giggling. "That's what he says, anyway." Then, suddenly, "Hey! it *was* a good party, wasn't it?" She looked at Charley sitting curled up on a pillow on the floor and was reminded of a small cuddly kitten. Her blonde hair curled softly about her face in childish ringlets and her big baby blue eyes always managed to look slightly surprised at everything. She was roundly curved, a couple of inches shorter than Tara and leaned toward very feminine clothing: ruffles, flounces and yards of billowing chiffon. Her weakness was expensive champagne and tall, arrogant men—and she never wanted for either one.

"Yeah, it was really terrific, babe," Charley murmured and poured more of the bubbly wine into their glasses. "And I love your new typewriter. What a super thing for Jim to do." She leaned her head against the side of a chair and stretched her legs out in front of her, wiggling her bare toes. "Now you have no excuse not to write that novel. You always said if you had an electric typewriter

25

you'd be able to knock it out in a couple of months. Remember?"

"Did I say that?" Tara asked innocently. "Toss me a cigarette, will ya, Charley?"

Charlotte took a cigarette from her pack, lit it and handed it to Tara. "Don't try to change the subject, Woodhauser—"

"Oh, I didn't tell you!" Tara squealed, interrupting her. "I changed my name to Remington—Miss Tara Remington, authoress."

Charlotte jumped, almost upsetting her wine. "Jeez, you scared me to death! Don't scream like that so close to my booze-laden head. Now, start over and slowly—" She struggled to a sitting position and poured more champagne, giggling, almost toppling over.

"Charley, you're drunk," Tara giggled, and suddenly it seemed very funny that she was a new Remington *with* a new Remington and she laughed and laughed, rolling over and clutching her stomach.

"*I'm* drunk?" Charley laughed, pointing. "And you're the one rolling all over the floor." She poked her and tickled her until Tara straightened up and composed herself. "Here's your drink—gotta keep up with the kid. Now, tell me again about your name."

Tara told her about the telegram that had arrived the day before, and when Charlotte heard Charles' name she cursed softly under her breath. She knew all about Tara's past and the part her brother had played in that sordid drama.

"I like it," she said when Tara had finished speaking. "It sounds sophisticated and sorta blue blood—you know, like the jet setters—Vanderbilt, Rockefeller, Kennedy, Radziwill, Remington—"

"Right on," Tara laughed. Her head spun suddenly and she sensed the room swirling madly around her. She opened her eyes wide and pushed herself into a sitting position, giggling at the effort it took. "Hey, we'd better go to bed before we pass out, Charley ole pal, don't 'cha think?"

"Oh, I do indeed, Miss Tara Remington, ole pal."

Charley stood, swaying, and offered Tara her hand. "May I give you an assist, ole pal, ole chum?"

"I certainly wish you would, ole buddy, ole comrade." Tara giggled and put her finger to her lips. "Oh oh, ole pal, we forgot something." She pointed to the sofa where Barry lay curled in the fetal position, his hands tucked between his thighs for warmth. "We forgot to cover up our other ole pal, the Bear." Giggling and stumbling into each other they found a blanket in the hall closet and clumsily spread it over Barry's sleeping form.

Tara helped Charley with the sleeper sofa in the den then stumbled into her own room and slipped into a warm flannel nightgown and fell into bed. Her head was still spinning but sleep was so near it did not make much difference. She pulled the cool sheets up to her neck, turned on her electric blanket and listened to Sinatra's voice drifting from the hi-fi in the livingroom. She was too tired to get up and turn it off, so she hummed along for a moment thinking of the day. It had been a good party. She snuggled deeper into the warm blanket, thinking about her shiny new Remington electric typewriter and the destiny it would fulfill. What a sweetheart her crazy Irish boss was. She had had a hard time getting rid of him, however, she remembered with a drowsy smile. He had killed the bottle of Jack Daniels and had seemed determined to spend the rest of the day and possibly the evening in his favorite chair near the fireplace. She had finally resorted to shaming him into going home by telling him how disappointed his three kids would be if he wasn't there to play Santa Claus. She knew that he still had all their presents in the trunk of his Lincoln, as he had not been home for the past three days. "Frances will kill me," he kept repeating as she shoved him gently outside.

Then Charlotte had arrived at noon to help with the dinner and together they had gotten it on the table in record time. Barry arrived with a big-breasted starlet on his arm, Jody something or other, who had gone immediately to the punchbowl and hors d'oeuvres table and remained there most of the evening. Then when Johnny Raggio, a young actor friend of Thorton's, had left a little before midnight, Jody had gone with him, a bottle of champagne in one hand, a napkin filled with canapes in the other. Tara smiled drowsily, then suddenly opened her eyes wide and said aloud, "Oh no, I promised Thorton I'd go to a party with him tomorrow night! I'll never make it." Sighing, she turned over on her stomach and hugged the pillow with both arms, burrowing her face deep into the warmth. A moment later she was sound asleep.

CHAPTER
TWO

THORTON KENNEDY eased his long Cadillac up the narrow drive, bringing it to a purring halt at the top. Four red-jacketed parking boys rushed forward to help Thorton and Tara from the car, giving them bright smiles and a cheery "Merry Christmas" as they showed them up the walk. Tara frankly stared at the huge, sprawling mansion on the hill. It was the largest private home she had ever seen. The enormous rolling lawn was decorated like Santa's Village, holding animated figures of elves, reindeer, toys and Santa Claus himself, all lit up with hundreds of brightly colored bulbs. At least fifty giant candy canes edged the walk leading up to the front door, on which was a gigantic wreath of holly, berries and pine boughs. The red carpet reached halfway out to meet them as they neared the double doors, which were tied with an enormous red ribbon. When Thorton opened the door the ribbons parted, covering them with a shower of crisp cellophane wrapped candies.

"Thorton, I don't believe this," Tara whispered as they stepped inside. "Who did you say was throwing this party —Frank Sinatra?"

"No, baby, Dick Wilson, the most successful independent recording executive in the business. Everything he touches turns to gold, or platinum."

She stared with open awe at the lush surroundings. A

pretty young girl, no more than sixteen, was sitting behind a desk which had been decorated to resemble a huge Christmas gift. She was encircled in a heart-shaped wreath of mistletoe, and her elf's costume of red and green was skimpy beyond belief. Her pert nipples were plainly visible beneath the sheer fabric, and the tiny bikini bottom could have passed for a G-string. She stood, smiling broadly, and went to them to take their coats. Her long legs were encased in knee-high red boots—the only item of her costume that was much larger than a postage stamp. The sexy elf gave Thorton a dazzling smile, all but ignoring Tara as she asked them to sign the guest book. She leaned suggestively against Thorton's side, peering over his shoulder to watch him sign his name, hoping, no doubt, that he was someone important enough to merit her attention—or arrange a screen test for her.

Before Thorton could notice her, a youngish sandy-haired man slapped an arm about his shoulders, hugging him and simultaneously shaking hands. "Hey, Thorton, you old bastard! Merry Christmas! Come in! Come in!" He turned to the clinging elf and gave her a slap on the fanny. "Christ, Cissy, let the man have a drink before you jump him!" Laughing, he began leading Thorton toward the main room, then stopped, staring hard at Tara. "Well, hello, and who is this gorgeous young thing?" His pale eyes raked her body as he stepped forward to take her hand. His palms were moist and he squeezed her with his gaze as well as his hands.

"Tara Remington—Dick Wilson," Thorton said, his gaze on Cissy who leaned provocatively against the desk. Her exposed buttocks were baby pink through the sheer pantyhose, and he thought he could detect the shadow of pubic hair at the edge of the small bikini. He would have to look into that possibility later in the evening.

Dick Wilson still held Tara's hand, his pale blue eyes going slowly over her body. He wasn't much taller than Tara, even though the boots he wore had well-disguised high heels. Suddenly he drew her into his arms, kissing her with a passion that both shocked and frightened her. His tongue filled her mouth and she jerked her head away,

30

pushing hard against his chest, ready to tell him to go to hell—no matter that he was obviously their host, when he grinned and pointed up. "Mistletoe," he said with a short laugh. He was perspiring and his eyes had a glazed look in them. "Works every time."

Tara followed the gesture and saw a mammoth bouquet of mistletoe directly above them, bright ribbons cascading in a jumble over the pale berries and leaves. "Oh," Tara said faintly. She offered a small smile, but Dick Wilson's unusually bright eyes made her uncomfortable.

"Hey, Dick, where's that drink?" Thorton said and Tara let out a sigh of relief, feeling as if she had somehow been rescued. But from what, she wasn't sure. She went quickly to Thorton and looped her arm through his.

Dick followed, taking Tara's free arm and pulling her close against his side. "I've got something a whole lot better than a drink for you, honey," he stage-whispered as he led them toward the vast living room. "How would you like a little something for your nose?" He gave a wink and made a sniffing noise.

"What's the matter with my nose?" Tara asked, baffled, but Dick was being pulled into the crowd by several pairs of hugging arms and Tara heard him call, "Meet me in the master bathroom in—" the rest was lost as he was swallowed up in the mass of party-goers.

"Come on. I think the bar's over this way," Thorton yelled to be heard above the crashing din of rock music. They plunged into the dancing, shouting crowd and Tara looked eagerly about, trying to take in as much as she could of the fabulous room. It seemed to reek with wealth. Everything was white and gold—white carpets and furniture, gilt mirrors, gold and crystal chandeliers that dripped their icy teardrops of brilliance upon everything below. The guests seemed to fit perfectly into the scene, elegant, beautiful, aloof, rich, they mated well with their gold and white surroundings. An enormous Christmas tree, easily twenty-five feet tall, rose majestically in the very center of the room. It was flocked white and laden with glittering gold ornaments. The living room itself was the largest Tara had ever seen in a private home. The beamed ceiling was vast and was hung with three enormous crystal chandeliers.

"God, Thorton, maybe I should go into the music business if this is how they live," Tara said when they finally reached the bar.

Thorton grinned and ordered two margaritas, handing one to her. "Well, here's looking at you, kid— Happy New Year!"

"Same to you, fella," Tara grinned, returning the toast and taking a sip of her drink. Thorton always drank margaritas, no matter what the occasion, but she would have preferred a gin and tonic. She shrugged, took another sip and turned, leaning against the bar to watch the dancers gliding by on the immaculate white marble floor. At first glance they seemed lost in their own private world, but as Tara looked closer she saw their eyes darting around the room, seeking, searching, ever watchful for whatever it was they were looking for. With something of a shock, Tara realized she recognized almost everyone in the room. Near-naked starlets writhed suggestively against the quivering paunches of sweating movie producers and directors. Married movie stars whispered promises and propositions into the ears of other married movie stars. She saw a clean-cut, broad-shouldered western hero of a popular television series dance methodically with his sexily clad date, but his eyes sought and held those of a handsome young waiter as he glided by, balancing a tray of drinks. The waiter caught the glance and twitched his hips in acknowledgment. It would just be a matter of time before the broad-shouldered hero made arrangements to meet the waiter in one of the upstairs bathrooms.

Tara tossed off the rest of her drink, shaking her head and smiling a little. Boy, she sure could get a lot of dirt for the fan mags tonight! She quickly ordered a gin and tonic before Thorton could ask for more margaritas. She smiled at the good-looking bartender, glancing admiringly at the long stretch of polished bar. It was easily large enough to seat twenty people, and once again she

was awed by all the wealth. She saw Dick Wilson dancing with a beautiful redhead, their bodies so close it seemed
in another moment they would be making love. She suddenly remembered his reference to her nose and turned
to Thorton, asking, "Hey, is there something the matter
with my nose?"

"What? Your nose? What's wrong with your nose?"
Thorton adjusted his glasses and peered at her near-
sightedly. He was vain about his looks and hated the
thick glasses but for some reason known only to himself,
he refused to wear contact lenses. Tara explained what
Dick had said and Thorton burst out laughing. "My dear
innocent," he said gravely. "You were just asked to in-
dulge in what the jet set calls 'nose candy'—better
known to the LAPD as cocaine."

"You're kidding?" Tara gasped. "You mean just like
that? He doesn't even know me! What if I was an under-
cover cop or something?" She took a cigarette from a
filigreed gold box on the bar and leaned forward, accepting the quickly held match from the bartender.

"I hope you told him to go to hell, Tara," Thorton's
voice was stern. "I don't want to see you messed up in
the drug scene."

Tara showed him her cigarette, grinning. "This is my
only vice, I'm afraid. Gosh, I haven't even tried marijuana yet." She frowned. "In fact, no one's ever asked
me to try it."

"You just haven't met the right people—yet. I have a
feeling you will tonight, however. Dick Wilson is Hollywood's newest millionaire, so he'll be the host with the
most for a few months until some other boy genius
knocks him off the charts."

"What is he exactly?"

"A thirty-year-old record producer and a bloody millionaire already. He produces the Moonstones—"

"The Moonstones?" Tara interrupted. "Wow, they just
knocked the Beatles off the charts with their new single
Pearls. He must be loaded." She looked at Dick Wilson on
the dance floor, still wrapped around the redhead. His
hands were lovingly cupped about her buttocks and he

was slowly and sensually grinding his pelvis against hers.

"I knew him when he was with Liberty Records." Thorton licked some of the salt from the rim of his glass, pursing his lips. "Dick's okay, I guess. He's sure having a hell of a ball spending his money—as you can see." He gestured with one hand, taking in the lushness. "The first year he broke a million he divorced his wife and bought this place. I think it once belonged to Errol Flynn. You should see his den, autographed pictures of everyone from Frank Sinatra to President Kennedy. Like I said, Dick's the hit of the season. Next year somebody else will be on top."

Tara nodded and glanced toward the dance floor again. A huge, many-faceted glass ball hung from the beams, revolving slowly and casting the dancers in multi-colored lights, like an old ballroom in the Thirties. She saw the Smothers brothers, Tom and Dick, standing at the edge of the dance floor. Tara recognized Dick's wife, Linda, from the fan magazines but Tommy was with an unidentified brunet. She wished she had the nerve to approach them and ask for an interview. Their new show was the hottest thing on television and every writer she knew was trying to get to see them. Maybe if she had a couple more drinks she would ask Dick Wilson to introduce her. She tossed off the rest of her gin and tonic and slid the glass across the bar. The bartender smiled, his white teeth flashing, when she told him to make it a double.

An hour later she was on her second double, still leaning against the bar, watching the crowd. Several men had approached her to ask her to dance or have a drink with them, but she had declined. She felt utterly out of place at this swinging, glittering party, almost like an eavesdropper peering over the shoulders of the rich and famous. Someday she would belong at a party like this, she told herself, her eyes lingering on the richly gowned and expensively coiffed women. She glanced down at her own gown. It was emerald green velvet, strapless, falling straight from her breasts to the floor, soft folds forming to the curve of belly and thigh. She had thought it the most elegant gown she had ever seen—until tonight. Now it looked like it had cost forty dollars on sale at The Broadway. Which it had. She gulped down half of her drink, determined not to get depressed. Holidays had always left her feeling melancholy, but she had been forcing herself to enjoy this party. She wanted this kind of life so intensely it was like a knife in her side. She wanted to look as glamorous and worldly as the women milling about the luxurious room, chatting with famous politicians and actors alike with such ease. She felt her stomach lurch and was not sure if it was envy or the double gin and tonics she had consumed.

"There you are, Green Eyes!" Dick Wilson grabbed her from behind, letting his fingers brush her breasts as he hugged her. He leaned in to kiss her and she wrinkled her nose at the sour smell. The pupils of his eyes were contracted to pinpoints and his face was florid and sweaty. "Been looking all over for you, you pretty little thing! Where in hell you been?" His words slurred together and he stumbled against her, almost upsetting her drink.

"Right here—holding up the bar," Tara smiled, pulling away from his moist hands. His black bow tie hung from one side of his open collar and his face and shirt front were covered in lipstick stains. He was hanging onto a lush blonde whom Tara recognized immediately as Doe Kingston. "Want you to meet somebody," Dick slurred, his eyes trying to focus on Tara and failing. He turned, stumbled against Doe, apologized, stepped back and bumped into the man standing behind her. Doe smiled tolerantly and drew the man forward, her hand gripped possessively on his arm.

"Hello, Miss Kingston, of course, I recognize you—" Tara stammered, embarrassed and a little in awe of the glamorous star.

"Sure, Miss Big Tits of 1970!" Dick laughed loudly and squeezed Doe's bare arm. She gave him a flinty smile and stepped back, shaking off the hand. "Thought you might want the scoop on the romance of the year— Thorton said you were a writer—" He clapped his arms around both Doe and her escort, ignoring their attempts to dislodge him. "And now, may I present the other half of the romance of the year, the illustrious Eric Marlowe, King of Smut!"

Doe gasped and Tara saw Eric's hand clench into a fist at his side. His lips went white and Tara couldn't take her gaze off his bright blue eyes as they glared at Dick Wilson's foolish face. They grew darker, a glittering cobalt blue, cold as ice, then suddenly he smiled, shrugged his shoulders causually and murmured, "Pleased to meet you, Miss—?" He gave her a warm smile, extending his hand.

"Remington," she breathed faintly, unable to pull her gaze away from his face. "Tara Remington."

Eric Marlowe bowed slightly, his eyes mocking. "Miss Remington—I always bow before the power of the press. What sort of things do you write?"

Before Tara could reply, Doe stepped forward, drawing Eric back beside her and purred, "Eric, darling, order me a drink. It's becoming quite close in here." She threw a meaningful glance in the direction of Dick Wilson, who was leaning heavily against her shoulder. "I thought cocaine woke you up—not put you to sleep!"

"Not when you mix it with two quarts of bourbon," Eric laughed, his eyes still on Tara. "Did he offer you a snort the minute you walked through the door or was that our privilege alone?"

Tara laughed. "No, I'm afraid I shared that dubious honor as well."

"Eric, please, my drink." Doe fanned herself with her hand and gave Dick a sharp poke in the side. He grunted, said, "Wha?" and straightened up a little, swaying away from Doe and into Tara. "Where's my drink?" he mumbled.

"In your hand, Dickie-pooh," Doe purred, her magnificent topaz eyes flicking over him as if he were a bug. She turned to Tara, dazzling her with her famous movie star smile, but the amber eyes were narrow slits in her smooth face. "So you're a writer, dear? Not, I hope, one of those dreadful fan magazine hacks?" She accepted a drink from Eric with an equally dazzling smile.

"Uh, well, not exactly," Tara stammered, taking a hasty swallow of her drink. Doe's cool eyes unnerved her and she looked wildly about for Thorton.

Dick had discovered his drink and raised it to his mouth spilling some down the front of his already soiled shirt. "Where the hell's Thorton?" he demanded, swaying toward Tara. "Wanna let him in on that hot little number at the door." He giggled and pointed his drink at Tara. "Cissy'll do *anything* for a mention in the columns. Maybe you should get together with her—if you're 'that way'—" He winked lewdly and Eric took him firmly by the arm and pivoted him around, facing the crowded dance floor.

"I saw him over by the band," Eric said, as he gave the drunken young man a gentle push away from Tara. He smiled down at her shocked expression. "I gather you don't know Dick very well. He takes some getting used to."

"I just met him tonight," Tara answered, holding her empty glass like a shield in front of her breasts. Where *was* Thorton? She was feeling a little ill and definitely lost.

"May I get you another drink?" Eric asked and she felt her heart flutter helplessly at his nearness.

"No—no, thank you—I, uh—I feel a little woozy—" She smiled faintly, moving a little away as she caught Doe's cool gaze. "Maybe I should have something to eat. I suppose there's a buffet?"

"The biggest and best money can buy," Eric said. He set his glass on the bar and took her hand. "Come on, food sounds like a good idea."

"Oh, Eric, darling, not now," Doe said plaintively. "We've just found this spot at the bar and I for one do not want to lose it." She spoke to him but her long golden eyes were on Tara's flushed face.

"Then you stay and hold down the fort. I'll bring you a plate." He took Tara's elbow and steered her into the milling crowd.

They pushed into the dining room, a huge room of pale green and sunny yellow with elaborately flocked wallpaper and heavy patterned drapes. Long tables were set up against three walls in a horseshoe pattern, laden with more food than Tara had ever seen at one time. Three huge turkeys, roasted to a crisp brown, dressing spilling from their cavities, stood on one side next to a platter of giant lobsters and three whole Virginia hams. More silver trays held mammoth mounds of jellied meat that looked like tongue, and next to them stood whole broiled salmon, steamed clams and oysters on the half shell, all mixing their odors indiscriminately. Down the immense stretch of snowy tablecloth were silver dishes with every kind of vegetable imaginable, some hot and steaming, others cold and jellied. Four huge silver bowls held salad, and many more smaller serving trays were laden with celery, olives and condiments. Five white-coated men stood behind the U-shaped table, their tall chef's hats starched to perfection, their fingernails shiny with clear polish and their skin as pink and clean as the food they served. The entire table was decorated end to end with blazing red candles and bright bowls of poinsettias and roses. A sideboard held dozens of cakes, pies, pastries and holiday cookies and candies.

"Good heavens," Tara breathed, pressing close to Eric's side in the moving mass of humanity. "I've never seen anything like this before." She stared in awe at the gigantic ice sculpture of a swan, ringed with parsley and fresh fruits, now melting in shimmering pools of water in its silver tray. There was a long line of people chatting and clinking glasses and silverware, shoving and crowding around the table. "How on earth will we get anything to eat in this crowd?" she asked, looking up at Eric for the first time since they had left the bar. She found it easier to speak when she was not looking directly into his dark eyes.

"Follow me," Eric said, elbowing his way in front of a small group of men and women. "Excuse us," he smiled warmly, "but we were ahead of you." He pulled Tara after him, grinning, murmuring, "Excuse us, please—excuse us—we were ahead of you—" The guests showed not the slightest annoyance but smiled, stepped back, and continued chatting and sipping their drinks. Giving her a grin of triumph, Eric grabbed silverware and plates for both of them.

"Aren't you getting something for Miss Kingston?" Tara asked shyly, her eyes not quite meeting his.

"Oh, yeah." Eric took another plate and set of silver. The tangy aroma of curry drifted to them from a large silver dish and Tara felt her stomach lurch slightly. The drinks, the closeness of the room—and Eric—all spun together rapidly in her head and she swayed against him, closing her eyes. "Hey, are you all right?" he asked anxiously. "Don't pass out on me."

"Oh no, I won't—it's just—just so warm in here, don't you think?" She tried a smile, but it failed miserably and she ducked her head so he wouldn't see her sick expression. She knew she was going to throw up and looked wildly about for some escape.

"Here—drink this." Eric held something cold to her lips and she dutifully swallowed, shuddering as it hit her queasy stomach. She had to laugh.

"Milk? I don't believe it!"

Eric gestured toward a large silver coffee urn and several smaller cream and sugar servers. "Nope. Straight cream. It'll coat your stomach and help you make it through the night." He was laughing, but his eyes were grave as they gazed into hers. He felt an overpowering desire to take her into his arms and protect her from this sophisticated crowd of jades and degenerates. She seemed so tiny and frail in this huge clamoring crowd and he found himself wishing they were anywhere else in the world. Then he remembered Doe and turned back to the table with effort.

"Thanks," Tara said in a stronger voice. She licked the cream off her upper lip with a dainty pink tongue. Grinning, she held her plate while he piled it high with turkey and dressing, protesting at the amount.

"Get it while you can," he said as he elbowed past a couple debating the aphrodisiac powers of curry. "It'll be nothing but a pile of bones in twenty minutes. God, have you ever seen so much food in your life?"

Tara laughed that she hadn't, suddenly enjoying the warmth and closeness of the crowd as it pressed her even closer to Eric. "Oh, may I have some ham? I simply adore it—even though it's terribly fattening." She held her plate out for the chef to serve her a thick succulent pink slice studded with cloves and topped with a pineapple ring.

"I don't think you have anything to worry about," Eric grinned down at her. "In fact, you look like you could use a couple of extra pounds. I hate women who are always dieting." Tara immediately scooped a helping of mashed potatoes and gravy onto her plate, and he said, "Good girl," making her feel warm all over.

Laughing, they broke through the crowd at the door and made their way toward the bar. Doe sat where they had left her, long legs crossed, one foot bouncing impatiently as she peered into the crowd. Her face brightened when she saw Eric and she moved her purse from the bar stool next to her, making room for him. There was no other empty stool and Tara felt her cheeks flush with embarrassment. She plainly was not wanted. Eric set the plates on the bar and took Tara's elbow, helping her upon the tall stool. "Sit here," he murmured. "I'll stand and guard the rear."

"Oh, Eric, darling, do sit down and eat your dinner." Doe opened her napkin and spread it out in her gold lamé lap, patting the place next to her.

"There are only two seats, Doe," Eric said in a low voice but Tara heard and blushed even more. She wished she had the nerve to get up and walk away from Doe's cool gaze, but she was too frightened. She knew no one else in the room, having no idea where Thorton had disappeared to, and she wasn't about to let Eric out of her sight. Tossing her head, she slid onto the stool and took up her silver.

"Umm, smells heavenly, doesn't it, Miss Kingston?" she said brightly. "You should have seen the spread in there —simply outrageous!"

"I'm sure," Doe said dryly, eyeing Tara's plate as if it

were full of worms. "My dear, surely you aren't going to *eat* all of that?"

Laughing a little recklessly, Tara said, "I don't know what rich movie stars do at Christmas banquets but poor freelance writers eat all they can get!" She raised a fork-ful of food to her mouth, watching Doe's face as she chewed. "Umm, fantastic! Here, Eric, try some." She forked another portion onto her fork and held it to his mouth, laughing silently at Doe's angry expression when Eric covered her hand with his to guide the fork.

"Hey, there you are! God, what a madhouse!" Thorton pushed between Tara and Doe, mumbling "Excuse me" and then doing a double take when he recognized her. He slid his plate and silver onto the bar next to Tara's. "I see you found the dining room all right." He had lipstick smears on his mouth, and his usually calm blue eyes seemed very animated. He glanced questioningly at Doe and Eric, and Tara quickly made the introductions.

"Eric has been kind enough to entertain me in your absence," she said, ignoring Doe's murderous glare. She was finally feeling the excitement of the party, as well as the closeness of this incredibly good-looking man. She did not give a damn what Doe thought. Obviously, Eric would have preferred to be with her. "Come on," she said to Thorton, "you can crowd in here next to me." She moved her legs, nudging Doe's out of the way and caught Eric's amused smile. Their eyes met fully for the first time since they had been introduced, and Thorton would swear later that he could actually see the sparks between them.

"Do I still hear music?" Eric asked softly. He led Tara away from the bar, tightened his arm about her waist and drew her close. They held one another until the throng of dancers leaving the floor forced them apart. Reluctantly they returned to the bar, and Doe and Thorton.

Tara avoided Doe's icy stare and turned her attention to the tall young man engaged in animated conversation with Thorton. She recognized him immediatly as Zock McBain, California's answer to the Beatles, and Elvis Presley all rolled into one. He was handsome to boring perfection, dark blond hair carefully mussed in a tousled, just-bedded effect, expertly sun-streaked by a top Beverly Hills stylist for that golden youth, surfer look. His penis was clearly outlined beneath the burgundy sheen of his trousers, and his body-hugging satin shirt was opened precisely the proper number of buttons. A gold disc the size of a saucer hung from a gold chain about his neck, stating in diamond-studded letters that he was an Aquarian. A Gucci morocco leather handbag was slung casually over his shoulder, and he towered above her in shiny, high-heeled boots the same shade as his trousers. Thorton made the introduction and Zock swiftly appraised Tara with a practiced eye.

Apparently finding her worthy of his attention, he took her hand and exclaimed dramatically, "I think I'm in love!" He crushed her fingers to his lips, and his intense blue eyes seemed to strip her of the green velvet gown. "If your taste in music is as good as your taste in chicks, we might do some business, old man!" He spoke to Thorton but kept his bright, hard gaze on Tara.

Thorton winced at the "old man" as he helped Tara onto the bar stool. Zock moved in with her, dropping an arm possessively around her shoulders, his hip thrust familiarly against her side as he continued to smile into her face. She did not know where to look to avoid that intimate stare, and he was plainly making her nervous. Each time she moved away from him he just widened his grin and leaned closer still, maintaining the body contact. His hand had begun to massage her bare shoulder and she looked quickly up at Thorton, but he was questioning Zock about his recent concert tour in Japan and had not noticed her plight. Zock's hand slid down, the fingertips just brushing the tops of her breasts. She was trapped against him and the bar, her left breast crushed against his bare chest, his groping fingers seeking to claim the right. She ducked her head to one side, desperately seeking Eric's eyes and mouthed a silent, "Help!"

"Excuse me," Eric said and stepped forward to place his hand on Zock's shoulder. His smile was guileless as he gently moved the rock star back a little and leaned toward the bar. "Just want to get my drink." He grinned apologetically, leaned in closer and forced Zock to step away from Tara. Taking a quick swallow of the first drink he picked up, Eric made a face and leaned back toward the bar. "Wrong one," he said and handed the drink to Tara. "I believe you were drinking gin and tonic, weren't you?"

"Yes, thank you." Tara took the glass, her eyes laughing into Eric's as he leaned forward again and ordered a Jack Daniels.

"What the hell, man? You interrupted me here," Zock said belligerently, his expression shocked that anyone would dare move him aside, however gently. And just when the chick was warming up to him, returning the pressure of his leg against hers.

"Sorry." Again Eric flashed the apologetic grin, but his eyes were cool as they leveled on Zock's indignant face. Pompous little ass, he thought savagely, he would like to bust him right in his expensive, dazzling caps! He was slightly surprised at his reaction to the rock star's pass at Tara. It had sent a swift, sudden rage through him when he had seen Zock casually touching Tara as if she were his for the taking. Eric supposed Zock McBain had gotten used to groupies being available 24 hours a day, but Eric had found himself hoping that Tara was not that type. She had a majestic bearing that set her apart from other women. A quiet intelligence glowed from her dark eyes, and there was about her an innocent sexuality that seemed on the verge of bursting into flaming passion. That she seemed unaware of it herself only added to her appeal. And when she had sought Eric's eyes in a silent plea for help, his heart had swelled with pride and triumph that he had been right about her.

Immediately suspicious of Eric's closeness to Tara, Doe tapped Zock smartly on the shoulder. "Excuse me, please, but you must step back a bit. I'm being suffocated in the crush." She spoke in her loud, crisp voice used to commanding an audience and Zock quickly stepped back, giving her room. She fluffed her blonde hair into place, smoothed the shimmering gold lamé over her hips and dazzled him with her famous, pouty smile. "Thank you, darling," she purred. "That's *so* much better." Her heavy-lidded eyes raked his lean frame, resting briefly upon the bulge in the carefully cut trousers, and her smile broadened.

Zock found himself on the outside of the group at the bar, not knowing quite how he had gotten there. He glanced at Eric's back and then turned his attention to the blonde movie star. Doe Kingston, sex symbol, was no stranger to him, even though this was the first time he had ever seen her in person. As a boy he had clutched her picture in one sweaty palm while masturbating furiously and hurriedly in a dark corner of the garage. He had grown up spending his Saturday afternoons in the neighborhood theater with other boys his age who had giggled and poked one another in the ribs as Doe Kingston gyrated seductively on the screen, their horny, pubescent minds conjuring up all sorts of fantasies. He thrust his hip forward, ran a hand through his already mussed hair and readied his perfect smile.

But Doe had quickly dismissed the sulky young man and had turned her attention back to Eric, who was talking quietly with Tara. They looked so intimate together that Doe actually hesitated a moment. Then anger flashed in her topaz eyes, turning them yellow as a cat's, and she curved her hand possessively about Eric's arm, drawing him to her. "Eric, darling, you're neglecting me," she pouted. Her voice was as light as a soufflé, but there was an unveiled warning in her yellow eyes. "Besides, you assured me absolutely that if I came to this boring affair with you, we would leave soon after midnight." She lifted a slim wrist, glanced at her diamond-clustered watch and made a little move with her mouth. "Good heavens, it's two-thirty! Darling, you *know* I have a five o'clock call tomorrow." She slid off the bar stool and gathered up her cigarettes, lighter and handbag. "Eric, please." Her voice was slightly authoritative, a harried but patient mother gently reprimanding her child in public.

Tara saw the muscle tighten in Eric's jaw as he deliberately raised his glass and finished his Jack Daniels. Just as deliberately, he took a last drag of his cigarette, crushed it out thoroughly and shook hands with Thorton and Zock. He leaned over to kiss Tara's cheek, lingering a moment to whisper something in her ear. They laughed together, then he turned and took Doe's arm, asking pleasantly, "Shall we go, my dear?"

Tara looked after him until they were swallowed up in the pulsating crowd, a soft smile curving her lips. When he had kissed her goodnight, he had whispered, "I'll get your number from Thorton and call you tomorrow."

Diahann Carroll perched on the edge of a tall stool, one long, luscious leg stretched out *à la* Marlene Dietrich, and sang about the man that got away with such sweet sadness that Tara felt a lump rise in her throat. She squeezed Eric's hand and he returned the pressure at once, leaning over to whisper, "Would you like anything else?"

Tara smiled and shook her head. "No, I'm stuffed. What about you?" They had dined leisurely at The Cloister on Sunset Strip, lingering over coffee and brandy as they listened to Miss Carroll's husky voice bemoan lost loves. More than once Tara had glanced at Eric to find him staring at her with such intense passion that she had been shaken. He seemed to be waiting, as she was, for the moment they would be alone.

"Completely stuffed," Eric sighed. He glanced at the check and then placed it with his American Express card in the silver tray. A waiter materialized out of the shadows and silently whisked it away. Lifting his brandy snifter in a toast, Eric smiled. "To a very special evening, Tara. I really enjoyed being with you tonight."

"Me, too, I mean—so did I—I mean—" Tara stammered idiotically and ducked her head to hide her flaming cheeks. She quickly swallowed the rest of her brandy although she already felt rather woozy from all the champagne she had consumed before and during dinner. She

45

gathered up her bag and cigarettes while Eric signed the
check, praying fervently that she would not knock anything over when she stood. Her new black strapless sheath
was skin tight, the narrow slit at the hem barely enabling
her to rise without assistance.

"Shall we go?" Eric stood and took both her hands,
pulling her to her feet easily and gracefully, then slipped
his hand beneath her elbow and guided her through the
crowded room. He noticed heads turning as they passed
and felt a certain pride at the admiring glances men lav-
ished on Tara. He tightened his hold on her arm and
pulled her closer to him.

"Oh, God, baby," Eric moaned, his lips brushing her
hair and cheeks, nibbling at her neck as he ventured
down to the deep cleft between her breasts. "You're so
beautiful—so soft and sweet—like a baby—" He kissed
the tops of her breasts, his lips nuzzling the fabric of her
gown further down. "A sweet, sexy baby . . ."

"Eric, I—" Tara struggled weakly beneath him, knowing that she should stop him, push him away before he
succeeded in removing her gown. But her arms still clung
to him, and her body arched against him of its own ac-
cord. His hands seemed to be everywhere at once, stroking her back and hips, sliding around to cup her buttocks
a moment, then moving back to her breasts which he had
succeeded in freeing.

"Oh, baby, you're so beautiful," he whispered close to
her ear, and his warm breath sent shivers of delight dancing up her spine. His hands were tugging gently at her
zipper and his hot lips moved down to claim her nipple.
She knew she should speak, stop him now before it was
too late, but she couldn't utter a word while he was kissing her naked breast like that. "Let's go to bed, darling,"
he murmured huskily and pressed his erection against her.

"Oh, Eric, I can't!" Tara wailed and turned her head
away, pressing her face into the cushions of the sofa.
"Please don't—don't—" She drew her legs together, forcing him to lift himself off her, and then quickly sat up.
"I'm sorry," she whispered miserably

46

Eric stared at her with surprise. She was on the verge of tears and looked so pathetic that he took her into his arms and held her tenderly. "What is it, baby? What's the matter?"

"I—I don't usually behave this way on a first date," she blurted, shamefaced. "And—and I shouldn't have led you on—because—because I probably led you to believe that I was—was—you know—like *that*." She kept her eyes averted and wished there was something she could do with her hands. They seemed gigantic just lying there in her lap. She took a shuddering breath and just barely whispered, "I'm not a—a C.T."

"Well, I'll be goddamned," Eric said softly. Then he let out a boom of laughter and grabbed her, hugging her so tight she thought he would surely crack her ribs. He kissed her soundly upon the mouth and laughed again. "An honest to God old fashioned girl in this day and age! And in Hollywood! Who would've believed it?" He thought of her comparing herself to a "cock tease" and burst out laughing again.

Tara's cheeks flamed and she would gladly have disappeared through a hole in the floor if one had been available. "It's not that funny," she mumbled in a sulky voice, suddenly hating him for his sophistication and obvious sexual experience.

"Oh no, no, darling, it isn't funny at all! It's marvelous! Glorious! Wonderful!" He grabbed her again, and this time when he kissed her she let herself respond just the tiniest bit. Eric took her arms and placed them around his neck as he kissed her, and she stiffened and drew back. "You aren't a virgin, are you?" he asked suddenly, something close to shock in his voice.

"Of course not," Tara replied indignantly. She straightened up on the sofa and reached nervously for her cigarettes, tapping one out before he could help her.

Eric smiled, more convinced than ever that he had discovered a rare find—a natural innocent in Hollywood —and just as convinced that he was the man to change all that. But not tonight. He did not want to frighten her away by moving too fast. This one would take some romancing before he could get her between the sheets. He smiled as she quickly stuffed her breasts back into her gown and tried to straighten the tangled mess of her dress. Her auburn hair tumbled over her bare shoulders like a wanton gypsy wench, and he thought how satisfying the plucking of the cherry blossom would be. The fact that she was not technically a virgin meant nothing. Her every blush and gesture proved her innocence. Yet she had responded instinctively, even eagerly, when he had first taken her into his arms and kissed her.

"A guy would be nuts not to fall for you, Tara." He leaned forward and kissed her softly. "Well, I'll be running along." He straightened his tie and stood, hoping she would ask him to stay. He slipped into his overcoat and walked slowly toward the door, still hoping that she would call him back. With his hand on the door knob, he turned back to her. "Well," he said cheerfully, "goodnight. I'll give you a call sometime next year."

"Next year?" Tara cried before she could stop herself. Then realizing his attempt at lightness, she forced a tiny smile. "Oh, sure—next year." She plucked at a loose thread on the arm of the sofa, not looking at him. "Well, Happy New Year."

He was across the room in three steps, scooping her up into his arms, kissing her eyes, nose and lips, laughing, "You silly little goose! What am I going to do with you?"

Love me! Tara wanted to scream. Just *love me and hold me and protect me from everything that scares me.* Instead she laughed up at him, relief flooding her that he was not angry. Before she could reply he kissed her again, taking her firmly into his arms and holding her with tenderness and passion as he parted her lips with his tongue and found hers trembling inside. She swayed against him, her head reeling, pulses pounding wildly at his nearness. Then abruptly he released her and strode to the door and opened it. "I'll call you," he said, and then he was gone before she could even tell him thank you for the evening.

She hurried to the kitchen window that overlooked the

street and watched him get into his car and light a cigarette. The flame of the match illuminated his handsome face, and she felt a surge of desire so violent it left her knees weak. She sank into a chair and watched him until the tail lights of his Cadillac were mere red dots in the far distance.

CHAPTER THREE

⬥━⬥━⬥━⬥━⬥━⬥━⬥━⬥━⬥━⬥━⬥━⬥━⬥

DURING THE MONTH of January, 1972, the courting of Tara Remington by Eric Marlowe was the talk of all Tara's friends. Doe Kingston and Eric's friends were inclined to call it the pursuit of Eric Marlowe by Tara what's-her-name, that cute little writer. But to Eric and Tara it mattered not in the least what others thought. They were madly, passionately in love with one another —although it would be several weeks before either of them admitted it.

After that first date, Eric had not called Tara until the second of January, five long days in which Tara alternately cursed and cried, hating him for being able to forget her so quickly and sobbing in her bed at night from wanting him. Then he had called and they had gone to Au Petit Jean's, an intimate, exclusive little bistro in Beverly Hills where the maître d' had tucked them into a secluded corner booth and then had left them discreetly alone. Tara had sat in awe most of that evening, gazing rapturously into Eric's handsome face, completely captivated by this charming, sophisticated man who seemed to know everything about everything. She had felt such a strong physical reaction that she had been convinced that he could see the naked desire on her face. Later, she could only remember the evening passing in a warm, hazy blur as she listened to Eric's deep voice and watched his

...ce as he spoke about his new ... only vaguely aware that his "proj- ...rking with Doe Kingston. He seemed to ... exciting, glamorous life that she felt some- ...Cinderella must have felt trying to make conver- ...n with Prince Charming while dancing that famous waltz.

Eric looked at Tara and saw not only youth and beauty, but a quick, intelligent mind, sharp wit and an unawakened passion that he took as a personal challenge. It was a heady, glorious time for them both as they realized they were falling in love.

Eric showed Tara a Hollywood and Beverly Hills that she had only dreamed about—and written about. It was an exotic, fast-paced world, and she felt as though she had been born into it. She loved the gaudy trappings of show business people, the almost vulgar jewels of the women and lavish Rolls Royces of the men, the outrageously expensive restaurants and nightclubs, the intricate games that these Beautiful People played and the mind-boggling details one must keep straight regarding their various affairs, marriages and business dealings if one wished to be accepted in the "A" group. She loved the worldliness and affluence of these dazzlingly beautiful men and women she had only seen in the movies until now. She loved being seated at the best table and being swept past the velvet rope that held back screaming fans as Eric guided her up the red carpet and into Grauman's Chinese Theater for some fabulous premiere. But most of all she loved Eric Marlowe. His every glance sent shivers of delight up her spine, and when his hand brushed hers she felt herself grow embarrassingly moist with desire.

But Eric had not tried to make love to her since their first date. He would walk her to her door and kiss her goodnight, holding her in that rib-crushing embrace of his, then abruptly hurry away. Tara would toss and turn in her bed, raising and lowering the temperature of her electric blanket as waves of hot passion and cold despair swept through her. She would lie awake for hours, wrack-

ing her brain for the exact words they had spoken to one
another since they had met, trying to find the flaw that
had obviously turned him off. She knew that he had been
attracted to her that first night at Dick Wilson's party and
again when he had tried to seduce her on the sofa. What
had happened? Was he merely amusing himself with her
while saving his physical love for the sultry Doe Kingston? She knew that he saw the blonde star almost as often
as he saw her, according to Jim Bacon's column. And
the gossip columnists had the two of them practically
married. How could she show Eric that she was a woman
grown, ready for love?

She took her problem to Jim Glasser, but his curt bit of
advice had been disappointing. "Tell the prick to take a
hike," he had grumbled. "The bastard's interfering with
your work."

Wondering why she had not thought of it before, she
called Barry Wilde and invited him for dinner, telling him
that she had a special problem that only he could help
her with.

"Okay, shoot," the Bear said after he had devoured two
helpings of her homemade chili and a half-gallon of milk.
"What's the problem?"

"How can I get a guy to take me to bed?" she blurted,
then blushed and looked down at her plate. "I mean, how
can I make him think I'm sexy and, you know, ready?"

Barry looked at her beautiful face, furrowed now with
anxiety, and her lush figure beneath the white turtleneck
and tight blue jeans. "Offhand, I'd say just stand in front
of him for about five seconds. Any chick who looks like
you do shouldn't have any trouble in those areas—unless
the guy's a fag." He went to the refrigerator and opened
another quart of milk, taking a swig directly from the
carton. "Who is this dude, anyway?" he said as he sat
down and placed the carton of milk in front of him.

"Eric Marlowe," Tara sighed. "I've been seeing him
ever since that Christmas party Thorton took me to at
Dick Wilson's. You remember—I told you all about it."

"Oh yeah, Eric Marlowe. I thought he was going hot
and heavy with Doe Kingston?" He patted his shirt

pocket absently, then reached for Tara's cigarettes and shook one out, a question in his eyes.

"Yeah, yeah, I know—you're trying to quit, so you don't buy them anymore." She smiled wanly. "Go ahead, have one." He lit two and passed one to her. "Thanks. Tell me what to do, Bear. I know he likes me or he wouldn't take me out all the time. My gosh, he takes me everywhere and introduces me to all his friends and treats me like some kind of porcelain princess. But when we get home he just kisses me goodnight and leaves! It's driving me crazy, Bear! I don't know what to do. Am I different from other girls, or what? Why does he ball Doe Kingston and not me?"

Barry drew thoughtfully on his cigarette, stalling his answer. Tara's innocent face, now free of makeup, looked even younger than usual. Next to Doe Kingston's sultry looks, she could pass for a child of fifteen. He reached across the table and took her hand, squeezing it fondly.

"Honey, some guys are just attracted to the really obvious dames, like Doe. Maybe Eric thinks you're too young and inexperienced for him. You have to remember that he started out in the skin flick business and has probably seen more ways to get laid than you or I ever thought possible." He lifted the milk carton and drank. "Christ, the guy's gotta be on fucking terms with every hardcore porno gal in the business." His voice was slightly envious. "I don't see why you're even interested in a guy like him—"

Close to tears, she wailed, "I love him, Bear! I think about him all the time and—and I want him to love me, too!"

"Then seduce the bastard, plain and simple. When are you seeing him again?"

"I don't know—not for a couple of weeks." She sniffed and wiped her nose on the back of her hand like a child. "He's in Mexico—with Doe Kingston. I know they're doing that movie together, but, oh, God, Bear, I just *know* they're probably sleeping together every night!" She looked so utterly miserable that Barry leaned over and kissed her on the cheek, patting her shoulder in an effort to comfort her.

"Come on, don't go weepy on me, babe. Let's plan this out, okay?" He took her chin in his hand and lifted it, forcing her to look at him. "You gotta make him think you're the greatest thing in the sack since Mae West. Vamp him, shock the shit outta him, ya know what I mean?"

She shook her head and sniffed again. "No, I don't. I guess that's the problem, huh?"

"Yeah," Barry grinned. "That's the problem." He pushed away from the table, pulled her to her feet and led her to the sofa. "Come on now—no more tears. Let's get serious and plan the seduction of Eric Marlowe." He grinned and touseled her hair as one would a small child's. "I'll give you the benefit of my years of the sexual experience."

It was seven-thirty when the firm knock sounded on Tara's door and she jumped nervously, glancing quickly at her reflection in the mirror. She was wearing a sexy hostess gown, black and low-cut, the soft folds clinging to her breasts and hips. She reached shakily for the half-filled glass of gin and tonic and swallowed the whole thing with a shudder. It was her third one of the evening. Barry had told her that it was "gin, gin, gin, that made ya wanna sin," singing it in a falsetto that had made her giggle. "Get a few stiff drinks in you before he shows up," he had advised.

The knock sounded again and she quickly sprayed her mouth with Binaca before hurrying to open the door. Eric stood there dressed in an impeccable dove gray suit, silk paisley ascot and a dark raincoat thrown casually over his shoulders. He held a large paper bag in his arms which almost obscured his face.

"Eric! Hello! Come in!" Her voice sounded high and unnatural, and she swallowed nervously as he followed her inside.

"Happy Valentine's Day," he said around the bag, then stopped short, staring at her. Slowly he lowered the bag onto the dining room table, not taking his eyes off her. "Happy Valentine's Day to *me*," he said softly as his vivid blue eyes traveled slowly over her body in the revealing gown.

"Hi," Tara said inanely, wondering why she had ever let Barry talk her into this blatant sexual display. She smiled and played with her ring, twisting it around and around on her finger as he still stood staring at her. "I—I thought we'd stay in tonight and—and—"

"Good idea," Eric grinned. "You're not exactly dressed for Ciro's." He closed the space between them in three long strides and took her into his arms. "God, I missed you! It seemed more like two months instead of two weeks!" Then he was kissing her and she sighed and closed her eyes, letting her lips and body answer him. Eric tasted the gin on her breath and drew his mouth away, smiling gently. She obviously had had to fortify herself for this evening with him and it made him feel even more protective toward her.

"Come on and see what I brought you from exotic Mexico," he said, taking her hand and leading her to the table. He reached into the paper bag and brought out a dozen red roses and a long, black velvet box which he handed to her. "Happy Valentine's Day," he said again.

Not trusting herself to speak, she opened the box and looked down at a gorgeous turquoise necklace nestled in white satin.

"I understand turquoise is the latest 'in' jewelry of the jet set," he said. When she still did not speak, he took the necklace from the box and clasped it around her neck. The large, chunky turquoise nuggets were far too bulky for her slim throat and it hung down to the tops of her breasts.

"Well, maybe you'll grow into it," he said lightly, unclasping it and returning it to its white satin nest. He reached into the bag again and brought out a huge red satin heart-shaped box of candy, presenting it to her with a deep, courtly bow. "For you, Madame," he said gravely, then reached into the bag once more and pulled out a bottle of champagne. "Dom Perignon, 1933," he said. "And—" digging into the seemingly bottomless bag, he withdrew two tins of caviar.

Finding her voice at last, Tara giggled, "Oh, Eric, you're too much." She was feeling the three quickly gulped drinks and a warm glow had replaced the icy panic.

"Wait—there's more." Again he reached into the bag and this time produced a box of elegant little crackers to go with the caviar. He grinned and kissed her nose. "See? I also planned on staying in tonight and—and—" He left the sentence unfinished as she had earlier, and they both laughed.

Tara showed him where the kitchen was and watched intently as he expertly unfurled the gold foil, snapped off the wire and then popped the cork. Not a drop of wine was spilled as he flourished the bottle over the two glasses and filled them to the brim.

He then took her hand and led her into the living room. "Sit," he ordered, pushing her gently down upon the sofa. "I am here to serve and satisfy. Tonight you don't lift a finger."

He went to the drapes and pulled them open, exposing the lighted, kidney-shaped swimming pool in the courtyard and the shadowy outlines of trees and shrubs, high-lighted by amber, red, green and blue lights subtly hidden in the foliage. A light rain was falling, glistening in misty, colored drops upon the tall palms and tamarisks. The pale drapes seemed to frame the scene like a Hollywood backdrop, and the rain streaked the windows like a woman's tears.

Eric bent over her stereo, humming tunelessly as he pawed through her records, then the soft crooning of Frank Sinatra floated to her and she smiled when she recognized his album, *For Lovers Only*.

A moment later he was beside her with the crackers and caviar attractively arranged on a plate, the champagne chilling in a deep cooking pot which he had filled with ice cubes. She was embarrassed at not having wine glasses and silver serving trays, but he silenced her apologies with a kiss.

They sat side by side, almost formally, munching caviar and crackers, sipping icy champagne as Eric regaled her with stories of filming on location. Suddenly he stopped speaking and kissed her. He did not touch her, just leaned forward and pressed his warm lips against hers. Her arms went around him and she pulled him close with a small moan of pleasure.

"Tara, Tara," he murmured against her lips as his arms went around her and pulled her close. "Darling, I've dreamed of this moment for weeks. I want you—and you want me. No, don't deny it. I know you do!" He kissed her again, holding her so close she could not have struggled even if she had wanted to. She felt his hands moving urgently against her breasts, slipping beneath the sheer fabric, and all the resistance went out of her. She clung to him, breathing rapidly, feeling his warm, large hands capture her now-naked breasts, draw them out of her loose gown, then his lips were upon them, kissing the suddenly rigid nipples.

"Eric—I—" She tried to draw his head up, but her arms seemed to have lost every vestige of strength.

"No, darling, don't say it," he murmured against her breast. He raised his head and gazed into her eyes, but his fingers still caressed her, tracing the rosy nipples nestled in a larger circle of light brown. He bent his head and kissed them, one at a time, tenderly. "Don't say anything to spoil this moment," he whispered huskily.

"Oh, Eric, I love you!" Tara cried and her arms tightened around him, embracing him with a passion that screamed her long-suppressed desire for him. She drew him to her fiercely, pulling him down on top of her as she fell back upon the sofa.

Seconds later they were naked and Eric caressed her trembling body, finding it more perfect than he had imagined. Her legs were long and strong, vibrating with desire as he gently raised them and placed them around his waist. She said his name softly as he entered her, then she seemed to explode beneath him. Her arms clung and her legs locked so tightly about him that it was difficult for her to draw a full breath. He eased them open a little, raising himself to gaze into her face a moment before plunging deep within her.

"Darling, darling, darling," she whispered softly. Just that one word repeated over and over again as she opened herself for every pulsating inch of him. Her glowing auburn hair was a tangled mass about her face, her eyes passion-dulled and glazed, her full moist lips repeating again and again, "Darling—darling—"

With an intensity that surprised him, Eric spilled into her and felt her lift herself beneath him, matching his premature climax with her own.

Then she lay trembling under him, her heart beating wildly against his, her deep breathing as labored as his own. For the first time in his adult life, Eric did not know what to say to a woman he had just made love to. He held her with her face buried against his neck, not ready to face her dark, love-filled eyes. Minutes passed as he tried to think of something to say, some apology for his adolescent ejaculation.

Then, timidly, but with an unmistakable teasing note in her voice, she asked, "Does this mean I get my screen test, Mr. Marlowe, sir?"

He laughed out loud, hugging her with relief. Then he began kissing her and when he felt himself grow hard again inside her, he was ready for her eager response.

Then came the happiest days either of them had ever spent, the sweet, glistening, crisp days of spring, the hazy, golden days of summer—and the heated, love-filled nights. Thorton kidded them about holding hands more than any other lovers in history, and Don Rickles threatened to throw cold water on them unless they stopped necking during his act.

They were wildly, deliriously in love and could not take their eyes off each other in public or in private. Their sexual greediness was plainly obvious to everyone and the town's gossips dubbed them the Golden Couple of 1972. They were so young, so beautiful and so much in love that everyone wanted to be around them. Photographers followed them from restaurant to theater to nightclub, shooting them simply because they were so incandescently vital and beautiful. They radiated charm wherever they went and seemed the only couple in the world ever to be so much in love. Friends and strangers alike were drawn to them, wanted to sit next to them at restaurants or merely eavesdrop from a nearby table. They made one want to smile a lot. But Eric and Tara noticed none of this. They were alone in a room of a thousand people. Their tender glances only for each other.

It was a revelation to Tara. She had never thought much about love before and was completely entranced with Eric Marlowe. She was absorbed by him, captivated by his gaiety and charm, his lovemaking, his genius as a director. She was convinced that he was the most brilliant man in Hollywood—possibly the world—and never once did she doubt his superiority. She followed him about with her eyes filled with love and wonder, constantly astonished by his uniqueness, his intelligence.

They spent sunny summer days on picnics with Mandy, Eric gently drawing her out, making her laugh with delight. They took her to Disneyland, and the large crowds and rather intimidating figures of Mickey Mouse and other Disney characters did not frighten her as Tara had feared. She clung to Eric's hand, her large blue eyes trusting, as he lifted her onto the brightly painted carousel pony. She clung to him, hiding her face against his shoulder, as the three of them screamed in unison on the wildly hurtling Matterhorn. She allowed Eric to coax her into the ocean and teach her to swim and not be frightened of the high waves that crashed about them. And she dutifully fell asleep in a wind-sheltered cove, while they made love a few feet away.

They made love everywhere. On the shoulder of Mulholland Drive while cars sped past, honking knowingly at the steamed-up windows of his white Cadillac. Swiftly and urgently beneath the shade of a tree, while Mandy picked flowers a few yards away. On the floor in front of Eric's huge fireplace. Even on his pool table, and in the kitchen when passion overcame them.

Mandy clearly adored Eric and he seemed to return the feeling. Hardly a week went by without him suggesting some new way to please the little girl with the

solemn blue eyes. But as the months passed, Mandy became less solemn and Tara began to hope that she would
soon be able to take her home to live with her.

The only discordance in Tara's otherwise completely
happy life was the fact that her novel had suffered
greatly. She did not seem to be able to sit at her typewriter as she once had. She would hurry home from Jim
Glasser's office, waiting impatiently for seven o'clock,
when Eric would be through shooting for the day and
they would be together. She was too happy to even think
about writing.

On her twenty-first birthday in August, Eric hired a
plane and had the pilot sky-write "I love you" across a
cloudless blue slate. That night after a sumptuous dinner
at Romanoffs, he had presented her with a six carat diamond ring, one carat for each month that they had been
in love. They had fallen in love February 14th and
Tara's birthday was August 16th, so he had added two
perfect baguettes to set off the solitaire diamond.

They spent hours in bed, making love, talking quietly
or simply gazing at one another. Tara soon discovered
that two or three hours' sleep was more than enough for
a woman in love, and she laughingly told Eric she now
regretted all those wasted hours she had spent in bed just
sleeping.

In September, Eric's film was premiered and Tara was
more convinced than ever that she had had the good
sense to fall in love with a genius. She had made her
peace with Doe Kingston some weeks before, stammering an apology for falling in love with Eric when she
knew that Doe was still dating him. Surprisingly, the
blonde star had shrugged and said, "That's okay, honey,
but don't forget, you owe me one!"

Tara had repaid her on premiere night by arranging for
Barry Wilde to escort Doe to the filming and party after.
The next morning, Doe telephoned to sigh happily, "What
a stud! What a cock! Now I can die happy!"

Christmas that year was everything Tara had always
dreamed it should be. She cooked her usual dinner for her

"Hollywood orphans," but this year at Eric's house. And Mandy was with them, happily chattering as she helped trim the tree and hang the mistletoe. Even the boisterous holiday guests did not intimidate her as Tara had feared. She was, in fact, the hit of the party as everyone tried to outdo the other in pleasing the little girl. She was showered with more stuffed animals than Tara had ever seen outside of a department store and was predictably suffering from a tummy ache by early evening from all the treats the holiday-spirited guests had pressed on her.

Eric carried her into the guest room, and he and Tara undressed her and put her to bed. She was half-asleep by the time Eric bent to kiss her goodnight and Tara had tucked a few of the smaller stuffed animals into bed with her.

They stood looking down at her for a moment, hands tightly clasped, and Eric whispered, "If I'm ever lucky enough to have a child, I hope she's as beautiful as this little one." And Tara's heart swelled with love for both of them.

It was after midnight by the time the last guests had departed and Eric and Tara were alone. She began carrying dirty ashtrays and empty glasses into the kitchen, but Eric stopped her. "Leave it, honey. Maria is coming in tomorrow." He took her hand and led her to the sofa in front of the fireplace.

"How in the world did you get a maid to come in to work the day after Christmas?" she laughed as he pulled her down upon his lap and began kissing her neck.

"She's crazy about me," Eric mumbled through the thick mass of her hair as he nibbled her ear. He slowly unzipped her gown, kissing each new area of flesh he exposed. He pulled the gown off her arms and pushed it down around her waist, kissing her bare shoulder, murmuring, "Have I ever told you what incredibly soft skin you have?"

"Umm, several times," Tara sighed, leaning back against him and raising her hips for him to slip the gown all the way off. She turned in his arms, her fingers quickly unbuttoning his shirt, then furrowing through his thick chest hair. She caressed him a moment before unzipping his trousers and pulling him free.

"Wanton hussy," he said. "You're just after me for my body." He lay back with a sigh as she tugged his trousers off.

"Of course, darling, I thought you knew that." Tara leaned forward and kissed his navel where the dark hair curled in tight little rosettes. Her lips brushed down the hard, flat plane of his stomach, then she took him into her mouth and heard his moan of pleasure.

She manipulated him lovingly for a moment, then his hands went under her arms and he pulled her up, crushing his lips to hers. She could feel him hard and impatient against her stomach, and she quickly slipped under him and drew him down on top of her. "Oh, Eric darling, love me," she whispered against his lips. Her legs opened for him and her hand gripped him, guiding him. But he held back, quivering.

"Not until you say you'll marry me," he whispered huskily and she felt his penis bucking against her, wet with love juice.

"Oh, God, Eric, yes! Yes!" she cried and wrapped her legs around him, heels pressing urgently into his buttocks in an attempt to force him inside her. With a groan he crushed her to him, sinking deep within her and their gasps of love mingled together in the still night.

Tara snuggled deeper into the blankets, dozing, putting off getting up until the last moment. When the telephone rang she cursed softly, pushed herself out of bed and hurried into the kitchen. Wondering who could be calling so early, she picked up the receiver and mumbled, "Hello?"

There was heavy breathing for a few seconds, then a low, husky voice whispered, "Tell me what you're wearing, baby—are you naked—your body aching for a good hard—"

Tara leaned against the wall and listened for a few seconds, grinning, then said, "Look, chum, if this is an obscene phone call, get to the point. I'm horny."

Eric laughed. "Insatiable bitch. I just left your bed two hours ago."

"Umm, and I miss you already." She glanced at her watch. Nine o'clock. "Thanks for calling to wake me, darling. I would have slept the day away."

She stretched the phone cord behind her as she moved about the small kitchen, measuring water and coffee into the pot, making the appropriate sounds as Eric complained about yet another delay on his current movie, *The Savage Desert*. His second teaming with Doe Kingston. She opened a can of Kitty Queen for Daisy and lit a cigarette.

"So what's the problem this time?" She smoked silently as he explained something about Sandra Sinclair's costume having to be altered and that it would screw up the whole day's shooting as she was in every scene. Sandra Sinclair was the ingenue lead, with Doe Kingston playing her older sister. She was a pert, bright-eyed child star who had just recently moved into more adult roles. Her promiscuity was common knowledge in Hollywood, and rumor had it that she had gotten pregnant no less than three times while still in her pinafore and Mary Janes. Eric had suddenly found himself with a free afternoon. Would she like to have lunch?

"Love it. I'll take the day off. What's with Sandy, anyway? Costume too large or too small?"

"Too small. Dumb cunt is pregnant. Again."

"Any idea of who the proud papa might be?"

"The prospects are too numerous to mention." He chuckled softly, intimately. "But I do know whose it isn't."

"So do I," Tara replied smugly. She had kept her handsome fiancé well satisfied these past months and knew for a fact that even if he had wanted to stray he wouldn't have had the strength! She giggled, then sobered suddenly. "That poor kid. How's she taking it?"

"Pot, downers and a string of young studs. She said she read somewhere that if you do a lot of screwing it can bring on a miscarriage." He gave a snort of laughter. "She'd better hop to it—she's already got a belly on her that would make Jackie Gleason look downright svelte. Wardrobe said she couldn't even begin to zip up her costume. Christ."

Tara smiled, listening to the familiar tirade against dumb actors, drunk directors, stupid producers and Hollywood in general. Since entering Eric's world, she had gotten used to everyone in show business bitching about some aspect of it. From the lowliest stripper to the mightiest producer: "It's a heartbreaking business"—"It's a fucking pornographic jungle"—"It'll suck you in when you're young, ripe, juicy, then use you up, baby"—"It'll drain ya, man, devour your talent"—"Nothing but phonies and pricks in show business; don't trust anyone unless they have their own printed cards and a secretary, man." She had asked Eric why they didn't get into another line of work if they hated it so, and he had quipped, "What? And give up show business?"

They agreed on a time, then Tara put a call through to her office, telling the secretary that she was taking the day off. She felt a thrill of pleasure when the girl called her *Miss* Remington in the reserved tone used for celebrities and top brass. Tara still was not used to her new celebrity. She had been writing a column for Jim's trade paper, *Beverly Hills Beat,* for several weeks and suddenly it seemed to be catching on. There was suddenly no waiting for a table at her favorite lunch spot, and the fresh receptionist at the office had switched from "Morning, kid" to a respectful "Good morning, Miss Remington."

Tara poured a cup of coffee and carried it into the bathroom while she ran her tub. She had wanted to quit work at once when Eric had proposed to her last Christmas, but it had not been in the cards. Eric was clearly too busy with *The Savage Desert* to take any length of time off, and neither of them wanted a rushed honeymoon. There had been the usual minor problems. The usual delays. There would be a lot of editing to cut the lengthy monster down to a hundred and twenty minutes. Promotion to get out. Then the big premiere in November. What he had in mind was a December wedding—she could pick the date—then a month-long cruise around the islands. Just the two of them. A lovely, leisurely holiday honeymoon cruise.

Tara had agreed enthusiastically. She wanted him all to herself. Perhaps to prove that he was finally hers alone. She certainly did not want him worried about the hassles of movie making on their honeymoon—or the sight of Doe Kingston on the set every day. Not to mention the precocious Sandy Sinclair.

Finding herself still employed and single, but also living in a sort of marital state, Tara had thrown herself into her interviews and her column. On the rare occasions they did not go out, she would rush home early and prepare dinner and herself before Eric arrived. Weekends were spent in Eric's sprawling bachelor home in Benedict Canyon, often with Mandy staying over as well. Several times a week, Eric was obliged to attend this dinner or that private screening or some such function and he naturally expected Tara to accompany him. Which meant a frantic search for the proper outfit and a hurried trip to the hairdresser, who always managed to work Tara in no matter how many other ladies were ahead of her. Then after the screening or business meeting, they would have a late dinner, often not getting to bed until well after midnight, and make love until dawn, still unable to get enough of each other.

After a few months the strain began to show on Tara. She would rush to the office, late, dark circles under her eyes, hair hastily brushed out from last night's elegant style and wishing she were still in bed. She did her work automatically, keeping one eye on her watch, and precisely at five o'clock she would stand and cover her typewriter. Everyone in the office had begun setting their watches by her, until she started leaving five minutes earlier, then ten, then fifteen. When she had stood and covered her typewriter one lovely summer afternoon at four-thirty, Jim had called her into his office.

"All right, let's talk." He sat down behind his desk, clasped his hands behind his head and fixed her with a stern, Spencer Tracy glare. She sat meekly on the edge of the sofa, waiting. It was not a long wait. "You haven't been worth a shit around here lately," he said in a low, almost pleasant voice. "You come dragging in late, then spend the rest of the morning at the coffee machine trying to wake up. You meet that prick for lunch and spend two fucking hours doing God knows what. Your editing is sloppy as hell and the last two articles you turned in could have been done by a high school kid." His voice rose and he shouted, "Then I'll be damned if you don't have the fucking balls to walk out of here at four-fucking-thirty in the afternoon!" Both hands came down with a loud smack on the desk top, sending the ashtray bouncing a foot in the air. "Just what hours would be more convenient for you, *Miss* Remington? Would ten to four suit you better? Or perhaps eleven to three?" All ten fingers were splayed and rigid, braced on the desk as he glared at her.

"Oh, Jim, I'm sorry." Tara went to him and placed her hand on his shoulder, looking properly contrite. Then her expression became suddenly angelic and she said, "You're not really mad at me, are you?" She smiled winningly, squeezed his arm. "After all, I learned everything I know from you. You raised me from a pup, remember?" He was almost grinning but still not ready to let her off the hook. She tickled him. Kissed his ear. "Come on, you old cocker, I'm just doing what you taught me. Living life to the fullest."

"*I* taught you?" He clasped a hand over his heart, pretending to stagger backwards. "You must be doing a hell of a lot more than *I* taught you if you drag in here every morning looking like you haven't slept for a month!"

"That's because I haven't." She gave him a lewd wink and he finally smiled. "I'm sorry, Jim, honestly I am. I promise I'll try to be here on time every morning." She tweaked his cheek, then frowned and perched on the arm of his chair. "Gee, I see Joyce Haber, Army Archerd and Jim Bacon out late just about every night. How do they manage to get up and write a column the next day?"

"They don't go into the office until late afternoon," he grumbled. He was still sore at her and wondered how the conversation had taken such a friendly turn. She perched on the arm of his chair, one hand resting lightly on his

67

shoulder, her leg swinging absently. "Or they work at home—or drop by the office and knock out their columns before they go to bed—how the hell should I know? Christ, what difference does it make as long as they get their columns written?"

"Just wondering."

"Well, wonder about how you're going to get your ass out of lover boy's bed and into my office by eight-thirty!"

"Jim, I have the most terrific idea! Why don't you let me write a column for *this* paper, then I wouldn't have to worry about coming in so early!"

And that's how it started. He had grumbled at first, but Tara soon convinced him that she could do it. Who was better qualified than herself to write a gossip column? Wasn't she out among the stars almost nightly? Didn't she know most of them on a first-name basis? Wasn't she a good enough writer? She had no desire to compete with the old-fashioned dragons, nor would she get into anything too heavy. She wanted to do a light, frothy piece of fluff once a week, more or less kidding the stars in particular and the Hollywood scene in general. She called it *Hoots 'n Toots from Tara* and it appeared every Friday on the inside front cover.

To Jim's surprise, Tara's witty, tongue-in-cheek style caught on, and it wasn't long before the regulars at Schwabs Drugstore and the Polo Lounge were passing the paper between them. And just-getting there actors slumped over their coffee at the counter, grinding their teeth in near agony: "It says here Clint Eastwood's set for that new Western at Fox. The deal was made at a dinner party given by Eric Marlowe—and this Tara-chick is his old lady. Jeez, I *gotta* get a mention in her column, man!" And Tara didn't miss a chance to plug her brilliant fiancé whenever possible: "Tagged along with that young genius Eric Marlowe to a sneak preview of his smashing new film, *The Savage Desert* . . . this one looks like an Oscar contender . . ."

Tara stepped out of her robe and into the tub, lowering herself gingerly into the hot water. She felt no guilt at

taking the day off. Since beginning her column, she found
she only had to spend a couple of days a week at the
office. Writing the column itself posed no time problems,
but there were always items to be checked out to protect the paper from possible lawsuits. Jim had hated the
thought of seeing her only twice a week but had to admit
that since *Hoots 'n Toots* had been appearing in *Beverly
Hills Beat,* the sales had doubled.

Tara soaked leisurely, lying back so that the water
enveloped her to the neck. Outside a light rain had begun to fall. The weather had been alternately bright and
sunny and then gray and damp for the past two weeks,
and she wished it would settle down to a good hard rain
and get it over with. She had become accustomed to
California's weather these past few years and knew to
expect a heavy downpour every spring and fall. With her
wedding only a month away she wanted everything, in-
cluding the weather, to be perfect.

It was funny how everything good seemed to happen
to her around the holidays. She had met Eric between
Christmas and New Year's, had become engaged to him
a year later on New Year's Eve and they would be married this December 20th. She would start out the new
year of 1974 as the new Mrs. Eric Marlowe. They planned
on spending Christmas with Mandy and a few close
friends, then fly to New York the next day to catch a couple of shows before starting the month-long cruise of the
islands. And when they returned they would bring Mandy
home to live with them. Everything would be perfect.
Even Mandy was perfect. Or almost. At least she was
not retarded or brain-damaged, as Tara had mistakenly
believed all these years.

After being around the child for a while, Eric had
asked Tara just what the problem was, why Mandy had
spent all those years in a home for problem children
when she seemed as bright and healthy as anyone else.
Tara confessed to not knowing the exact name of her
little sister's affliction but had been told by several doctor's that the child suffered "mild brain damage." Eric
had immediately gotten his secretary to check on doc-

tors in the Los Angeles area who specialized in such disorders, and after an exhausting round of appointments and tests it was discovered that Mandy was merely "traumatized" and suffering from a mild psychological disturbance. She was slow to learn but only because of her suspicion of people, not because she lacked the necessary skills. She was painfully, almost tearfully, shy, unable to utter a single word when interviewed by visiting psychotherapists, and these well-meaning but overworked doctors had simply stamped "mild brain damage" on her report before hurrying on to the next case.

The past two years had shown a remarkable change in the child, however. She had responded easily to Eric and seemed to sense that her sister and this big, laughing man with blue eyes so like her own would make a family for her. When they picked her up for weekends, she would be packed and waiting, her small face both eager and frightened. Even though they had never once broken a promise to her, she seemed to have a deep dread that something awful would happen. They would be killed on the freeway and she would be doomed to spend the rest of her years in loneliness and fear, as she had spent the last six. She loved Tara with all her heart, but deep inside her uncomplicated child's mind she did not understand why they could not be together all the time. Visiting days and weekends were met with dread and excitement as her heart pounded, waiting for Tara to show up, and her mind whispered that if her sister really loved her she would find a way for them to be together. She understood nothing of money and the responsibilities of raising a child when you were a single woman, even though Tara had often tried to explain.

With the appearance of Eric Marlowe in her life, she was at last able to hope. And with the hope came the old fears that something dreadful would happen to keep her forever a prisoner in the sunny yellow room she had grown to despise. She had never put her thoughts into words, but Tara had somehow guessed and had constantly reassured her. The only person in the whole world whom she could honestly pour out her darkest secrets was

Uncle Bear. With him she felt like a fairy princess, and he was so funny and handsome that she loved to show him off to her friends at the school. She had a secret dream that he would someday marry Tara and they could be a real family like the kind she saw on television. Therefore she had hated Eric and blamed him for taking Uncle Bear's place on the weekend visits. Uncle Bear had been the only man in her life until then and she didn't like things changed around. It angered and confused her. She had not wanted to like Eric, but it was impossible to be around him and Tara without picking up some of their happiness. And as the weekend visits piled up, it seemed that it had always been this way: Eric, Tara and Mandy.

Tara stepped out of the tub and wrapped herself in a towel, thinking perhaps she should ask Eric if they could pick Mandy up and take her to lunch with them. She still felt a little guilty at leaving her during the holidays, but she also recognized her own selfish desire to have Eric all to herself for as long as possible. Surely she was entitled to a honeymoon all her own. Mandy would just have to understand. Eric had told Tara to start looking for a house when they returned, and she planned on taking Mandy with her so the child would have some voice in the selection of her new home. Tara knew she wanted to live in the San Fernando Valley, even though it was considered less than fashionable to do so. She wanted a big back yard for Mandy and the puppy and pony she had promised her years ago. Pets were not allowed in the school, and Tara knew how much Mandy wanted her very own. She hoped they could find such a house close to an elementary school and with a neighborhood filled with children. Dr. Moss had told her that all Mandy really needed was love and a solid home life. In short, security. "Doesn't everyone?" Tara had laughed.

Eric picked Tara up at noon and they went to the Cock and Bull for lunch. The place was jammed as always with studio people and Tara was not able to speak privately to Eric from the moment they sat down. Several people stopped by to offer their congratulations on the up-coming wedding, as well as on Eric's film. *The Savage Desert* was getting a lot of play in the press, and the November fourteenth premiere was being touted as the event of the year.

"Hello, you two! Still holding hands and necking in public, I see!" Doe Kingston swooped down upon them, muffled in dark mink from neck to knees, her enormous diamonds flashing. She kissed Tara's cheek and stuck her tongue out at Eric. "Mind if I join you for a cocktail?" She sank into an empty chair with a sigh. "God, what a lousy day. I hate rain." Flipping open a gold compact she checked her yellow, fluffy-duckling coiffure.

"Doe, it's good to see you." Tara smiled with genuine pleasure. "When did you get into town? We just saw you last night on the Tonight Show."

"Just flew in this morning." She twisted around in her chair and signaled the waiter, causing her diamonds to blink and flash in the candlelight. "Gin and tonic, please —make it a double." She shrugged out of her mink and reached for Tara's cigarettes, shook one out. "Christ, it's dark in here!"

"You were fantastic, baby," Eric said, as he held his lighter for her. "I thought Carson would crack up when you told that story about the tarantula who fell in love with you on location." They all laughed, remembering the big, hairy, rust-colored spider who had for some reason known only to him taken a shine to Doe and would have literally followed her around like a dog had the trainer allowed it. He had somehow managed to escape from his cage several times and could always be found in Doe's tent or in some of her belongings. She had named him Harry (after her first husband, she had said; they had the same smile) and swore that she was able to tell him apart from the fifty other tarantulas they were using in the picture.

"Yeah, good old Harry. I kinda miss him." Her drink arrived and she lifted it in a toast. "Well, kids, here's to us and a life of ease. When *The Savage Desert* opens we'll all be millionaires." Not as dumb as her image, Doe had taken a percentage of the film.

"I'll drink to that," Eric said and they clicked glasses.

"Hey, Doe, I really appreciate your going on this promotion tour. I know it's a pain in the ass hitting all those talk shows."

"Tell me about it," Doe groaned. "God, if I never see another hotel room again it'll be too soon!" She took a long pull of her cocktail, shuddering delicately when the strong gin jarred her stomach.

"Who are you meeting?" Tara asked, knowing that the blonde star never dined alone.

"Billy-baby—or William Benson to you." She gave them a wicked grin. "God, what a hunk! He has the most gorgeous blue eyes I've ever seen!"

"Oh, yeah, the writer," Eric said. "What are you trying to do, Doe, improve your mind?"

"My mind has nothing to do with it," Doe laughed.

"Oh, I've heard of him," Tara said. "I read his last novel and thought I'd die laughing. I really dig his style."

"I dig his style, too." Doe chuckled suggestively, then took another long sip of her drink. She glanced toward the door. "Oh, there he is—gotta run." She tossed off the rest of her drink and stood, gathering up her mink and handbag. "Call me in a couple of days, Tara, and we'll have lunch. I plan on sleeping for at least twenty-four hours." She bent and kissed the space near Tara's cheek, then leaned over for Eric's kiss. "I haven't decided what to wear to the premiere yet, have you? Maybe we'll go shopping together. And I want to hear *all* the wedding details, so don't forget to call . . ."

"Will do," Tara said to her departing back. She turned to Eric and laughed. "God, what a gas. I certainly never thought we'd become such good friends when I first met her, but I really do like her." She sipped her drink, watching him over the rim of the glass. "Do you remember the first time I met her?"

"How could I forget? It was also the first time we met." He reached across the table to squeeze her hand and his eyes were filled with love when he whispered, "That was the luckiest night of my life."

"Mine, too." She returned the pressure of his fingers, and they gazed into one another's eyes until they became aware of the waiter standing self-consciously to one side. "Would you care to order now?" he asked when they finally glanced up.

"Yes, please." Eric gave Tara's hand a final squeeze before releasing it. "Dover sole for the lady, no potato, oil and vinegar on the salad—and I'll have the New York, rare, baked potato and onion soup." He passed the menus over and turned his attention back to Tara. "What would you like to do after lunch? We have the rest of the day."

"How about going out to visit Mandy? It would be a nice surprise and maybe cheer her up a little. She's been down ever since Halloween because she couldn't go trick or treating."

"Sure, we can do that. In fact, why don't we just take her for the weekend? The school wouldn't object to letting her out an extra couple of days, would they?"

"No, of course not." Her heart swelled with love for him for understanding her feelings without her having to put them into words. "That's a wonderful idea, darling. It'll give me a chance to take her Christmas shopping. I'm sure she will want to buy gifts for some of the other kids—and we should get a little something for her teachers and doctors."

"Then it's settled. Why don't you go give Miss Pearson a call and tell her to have Mandy ready at, say"—he consulted his watch—"three-thirty. I'd like to beat that freeway traffic if possible."

Tara leaned over and kissed him hard upon the mouth. "Do you have any idea how much I love you, Mr. Marlowe?"

"I have a pretty fair idea, Miss Remington, but any time you'd like to further enlighten me, please don't hesitate . . ."

It was dark by the time they had loaded Mandy and her various bundles into the car. She always traveled with several stuffed animals as well as whatever else she was currently attached to (this week it was horse books), and Miss Pearson had added to the load the child's schoolwork and speech therapy records, reminding Tara of the importance of keeping up Mandy's lessons for the days she would be absent from class.

Eric eased his Cadillac out of the parking lot, flipping on his headlights as they turned onto the main road. "God, can you believe it's only four-thirty?" he said.

"It's already dark at four o'clock sometimes," Mandy said. "Then we have to come inside 'cause Miss Pearson won't let us play outside in the dark." She was snuggled between Tara and Eric, her legs sticking straight out in front of her as they were still too short to reach the floor.

"Miss Pearson's right," Tara said. "It's not a good idea to play outside after dark."

"Why not?" Mandy wanted to know. She leaned against Tara's shoulder, rubbing her face against the soft fur of her mink coat.

"Oh, because you might trip or step on a nail or something." Tara smiled down at her little sister, marveling as always at her beauty. She looked nothing like the Woodhausers with her inky black curls and vivid blue eyes. "Besides, it's scarey at night, with everything all dark and spookey."

"No, it's not. I like the night." Mandy set her mouth in a firm, stubborn line so like Tara's that Eric grinned to himself. "And I'm going to play at night whenever I want —when I'm bigger and we have our own house." This last was said softly and she peeked at Eric from beneath lowered lashes.

"Soon, Princess." He grinned down at her. "Your big sis has promised to find us a home with ample space for playing outside in the dark. In San Fernando Valley yet!" He wiggled his eyebrows comically in Tara's direction. "Are you still gung-ho on living amongst the horse stables, orange groves and peasants of questionable descent?"

"Yep. I've had enough of those cold city sidewalks to last me a lifetime."

"What?" Eric exclaimed in mock horror. "You're not hooked on Hooray for Hollywood, the glitter of Tinseltown, the roar of the crowd, the—"

"Let me break it to you gently, chum. All that glitters

in Hollywood is the sequins on the stripper's G-strings!" They both laughed and clasped hands in front of Mandy, glancing briefly into one another's eyes before Eric turned his attention back to the freeway. Mandy looked from one to the other, smiling, feeling the warmth of their love and she added her own small hand to theirs in her lap. Tara gave it a squeeze and said, "Look out there, Mandy, to your right. See all those trees and fences? That's where they have all the big horse ranches." She turned her face to the dark, cool window and watched the rolling hills speed by. To no one in particular, she whispered, "Just think—if we lived here, we'd be home now."

CHAPTER FOUR

TARA lay in the curve of Eric's arm, her body pressed as close to his as she could get. They were both silent, having spent a lazy evening watching television.

"Ready for a drink," he asked as he walked barefoot to the bar.

She watched him walk naked across the bedroom, her gaze going fondly over each familiar, beloved angle of his body. She loved the way he was built, lean as a cougar, his buttocks taut and narrow. She sometimes fell a couple of steps behind him when they were walking together to leer at his fanny. He got into bed and handed her a gin and tonic.

He took a swallow of his drink and pulled the blankets up around his waist. Slipping his arm around her, he drew her head down upon his shoulder and breathed in the sweet fragrance of her hair.

"You started to tell me about your father," Tara murmured. "What happened to him?"

"He was killed in a car wreck when I was thirteen. My mother, too." He reached for his cigarettes and lit two, passing one to her.

"Same with me. My foster parents were both killed in an automobile accident, but I was sixteen. It must have been tough, being so young. What did you do?"

"Hid out mostly, for the first couple of months. I was

terrified that the cops were going to come looking for me and lock me up in one of those awful places—you know, like Oliver Twist. So I split right after the funeral. Hid out in condemned buildings, abandoned cars, stole my food where I could." He laughed without humor. "Funny thing is, nobody ever came looking for me! Alice and Frank Marlowe had rated just about an inch of space in the obit column. There was no room to mention a surviving son."

"Poor baby," Tara crooned, hugging him close. "I wish I had known you then, you could have moved in with me." She kissed him softly, then with hungry urgency when she felt his arms tighten around her and his tongue seek hers. They slid down in bed, drawing the blankets around their shoulders, wrapping their arms and legs about one another. The angles and curves of their bodies fitted together with comfortable familiarity. "Tell me more," Tara murmured against his lips. She raised her head, propping herself on her elbows as she gazed down at him. "You've never talked about your childhood to me at all, do you realize that?" She traced the outline of his mouth with one finger and then leaned down and kissed his parted lips. She felt a little guilty that she had never questioned him about his childhood. All she really knew was that he had been on his own since a very early age and had held any number of odd jobs. When he told her that he had spent a few years in Seattle, Washington, she remembered asking him what school he had attended and he had laughed and said, "The school of hard knocks. You might call me a *road* scholar." She knew that he had cut timber in Washington and Oregon, sold Bibles in Nevada and picked fruit in California, but she knew nothing of the little boy before that.

"Sure I have," he grunted, trying to capture her finger between his teeth. "I've told you every last, deep, dark secret of my miserable past." He trapped the tickling finger and bit it gently, then moved his head forward to nibble at her nipples. His hands traced round patterns on her back as he kissed her breasts, throat and lips.

"Umm, Eric, stop—you're going to make me spill my

drink." Tara giggled and sat up a little higher. "Come on now, I want to know what you were like as a little boy. Surely you weren't chopping down trees until much later in life."

"Oh, yeah, much later." Eric sighed and pushed himself into a sitting position beside her. "I was an old man of fifteen when I signed on with my first logging outfit." He drained his glass and set it on the nightstand, reaching for her again.

She held him off, laughing. "Come on, talk, mister. I want to know if there's insanity in the genes or any old family curses I should know about before I marry you." She did not feel like making love. She wanted to talk and just be held quietly against him.

Eric sighed and threw the blankets off, swinging his legs out of bed as he sat up. It would do no good, he knew, to try and force Tara into anything she did not want to do. He just wished to hell she would get over her depression. It was not like her to be so melancholy. Especially with the wedding only two weeks away. "Family curses?" he said, picking up his empty glass and heading for the bar. "The only curse in the Marlowe family was the curse of poverty." He opened a fresh bottle of gin and sloshed some into his glass, looked at it, then added more. "But I laid that to rest the year I paid taxes on my first legitimate million bucks."

"Eric, you're not getting another drink, are you?" Tara's voice was slightly accusing. "I still have over half of mine."

"So you're a slow drinker." He added a splash of tonic and a couple of ice cubes, then raised his glass to her. "If I can't get laid, I might as well get drunk." He took a long swallow before walking back to her. He saw her gaze lower to his semi-erect penis and he reached down and fondled himself before getting into bed.

Tara turned her head away from the coarse gesture. She knew that he was getting drunk. There was an unfamiliar and frightening chill that had settled around her heart as if all the happiness was going to leave her. It was suddenly very important that she know every single detail of Eric's past. As if knowing the intimate secrets of his childhood would somehow bind him closer to her.

"Ain't cha gonna fuck me no more tonight, fair Tara?" Eric mumbled, falling heavily against her. He righted himself, holding his drink high and somehow managing not to spill it. He took a drink, closing his eyes and leaning his head back against the tufted headboard. "Thas' what Glasser calls you, isn't it?" He opened one eye and peered at her, his words more slurred than she had ever heard them. In fact, she had only seen him drunk a very few times, and then he had simply and quietly passed out.

"Yes, that's what Jim calls me," Tara said softly. She stroked his damp hair back from his forehead. His face was flushed and there was a fine mist of perspiration on his upper lip. She stretched across him and turned off the electric blanket, then gently wiped his face with the hem of the sheet.

"He's in love with you, you know." Eric took another drink, and this time it spilled down his chin and ran in tiny rivulets through his dark chest hair.

Tara dried him with the sheet. "Jim Glasser? Oh, don't be silly. He's old enough to be my father—"

"Grandfather—" Eric mumbled.

"—and if he does love me, it's purely platonic." She knew better, but didn't want to get into that discussion again. Her crusty Irish boss had let it be known from the beginning that he was against this marriage. It had broken his heart to think of his fair Tara going off with an ignorant pornographer. When she had told him, Jim had actually felt weak at the thought of them making love aboard a softly rocking yacht, and he had had to down two stiff scotches before the painful palpitations went away. The closer it drew to the wedding date, the more surly and petulant Jim became, grinding his teeth in agony at the thought of Eric doing all the things to Tara that he had dreamed so often of doing. He kept a bottle of scotch in his desk drawer and laced his numerous cups of black coffee from morning on. He tried to forgive Tara for not knowing what a mistake she was making. He told himself that she was young and inexperienced. She did not realize that he, Jim, was the perfect mate for her. He told himself that Eric Marlowe was simply a physical attraction and Tara would grow tired of him. Then he would telephone her early in the morning and grit his teeth in helpless rage when Eric would answer to say that Tara was in the shower or still asleep. He even tried to understand what Tara saw in Eric—besides his obvious good looks and sex appeal. He was certainly charming, and, under different circumstances, Jim would have admitted to liking him. Being a self-made man himself, he admired the trait in others. But in his aching Irish heart he still felt no man was good enough for his fair Tara. Not even himself.

"Platonic, my ass," Eric mumbled and drank again, wiping his arm across his mouth. He fixed Tara with a bleary, lopsided grin. "I've seen the way he looks at you."

"So I'm irresistible," she said lightly. She sipped her drink, giving him a fond look. "I'll bet you were an irresistible little boy with those big blue eyes and curly black hair."

"Yep, the ladies couldn't keep their hands off me. I was one cute little stud, let me tell you." He chuckled to himself. "I remember the first time an 'older lady' got the hots for me. I was about eleven or twelve, before my parents were killed, and we were still living in relative comfort in a lower-lower class neighborhood—ya know, a step up from poverty and a notch down from poor. I used to run errands for the gangster types that ran the neighborhood, the bookies, the dudes that kept the crap games floating, like that. And talk about gorgeous pussy —those guys always had at least one dame on their arm and another stashed in the back seat of a block-long Caddy.

"But in those days, I was more interested in making a fast buck than I was in making some broad—until this one night when I delivered sandwiches to a bunch of guys shooting craps across from the deli where I worked. This kid, Johnny, who was currently king of that section of the street, wasn't much out of his teens. Twenty-one or two, and he was there with his girl, Maizie. I remember the name because she later told me she had gotten it from an old Ann Sothern role. Anyway, I dropped off the sandwiches and Johnny slipped me a five and told Maizie to let me out the back way, through the alley. The minute the door was closed behind us, she grabbed my hand and jerked me down the alley. There was a beat up old couch there with springs sticking out all over the place and she threw her mink coat down on it—and me down on top of her!

" 'Quick, honey, stick it in me,' she said and flipped up her dress. She wasn't wearing any panties and I was so shocked I don't even remember her putting me inside her. It was so damn fast! One minute I was standing in the alley and the next minute I was lyin' on top of Maizie with my cock in 'er! She said something like, 'Just give me a couple of fast, hard ones, kid, I'm so hot I could pop right now.' "

In spite of herself, Tara felt a stirring in her loins and she moved a little closer to him. "I don't believe it," she said. "A stranger just grabbing you and telling you to fuck her?"

"Yep—like I said, I was an irresistible little stud." He drank, reached for a cigarette and Tara held the lighter for him. When he spoke again his voice was even more slurred. "It was over in a couple of minutes and she gets up and straightens her dress and tells me 'Thanks, kid' as casually as if I'd held the door for her."

"I still don't believe it! Women don't do things like that —except in Harold Robbins' novels."

"Then he must have known Maizie. Later I got to know her—"

"You mean you saw her again? Did you—?"

"Fuck her? Hell, yes. That's the only reason I ever saw her." His words became slower, running together like melted butter and she had to strain to hear. "See, she was on cocaine, snorted about a gram a day, and it always made her hornier 'n hell. Johnny took care of her most of the time, but when he was tied up, usually in the evenings, that's when the coke really started hittin' real good and that old itch started in her pussy."

Tara frowned at the vulgar expression. She loved it

when he whispered dirty words to her when they were making love, but to hear them slurred in a coarse, drunken voice about another woman upset her more than she cared to admit. "But how can that be possible? You were so young." She still couldn't fathom an eleven- or twelve-year-old-boy (God, that was Mandy's age!) having an affair with a gangster's moll.

"I was big for my age." He laughed and fondled his penis beneath the blankets, giving her a lewd wink. "In more places than one."

"Braggart," she said lightly, determined to listen impartially and impassively to his story. She had not exactly led a sheltered life herself, but she had been lucky enough to know people like Sergeant Calhoun and the warm, kind Davidsons. She had learned from them that her early life was not the norm, as she had believed as a child. Other people lived in clean, quiet homes and spoke kindly to one another and ate hot food and slept between crisp, fresh sheets. She learned that her mother had been just one of a large number of hopeless statistics that succumb to the disease of alcoholism. And that her brother, Charles, was just another hapless victim of circumstances. She had also learned (with deeper appreciation each year) that she had been one of the lucky ones. She and Mandy. They had escaped and they were the survivors.

Eric tried to focus his bleary eyes on her, failed and fell back against the headboard. "It's true," he mumbled, eyes closed. "Christ, at twelve I was already about five-six, had a cock that was the envy of the boy's can in good ole P.S. 147. And Maizie, she was only about seventeen or so—just a kid now that I look back on it." He was quiet for so long that Tara thought he had fallen asleep. She took his cigarette from his limp fingers and put it out in the ashtray.

"Wha?" Eric struggled against her shoulder and pushed himself into a half-sitting position. "Whew, am I ever zonked." He ran a shaky hand through his hair and gave her a feeble grin. "Sorry, honey, guess that old evil gin just sort of sneaked up on me." He gave her a wet kiss, righting himself with difficulty. "Starting tomorrow, we're getting ourselves back together. Starting tomorrow," he said, taking a long swallow. "I'll just finish this one and we'll go to sleep, okay, honey?"

"Okay, darling." Tara smiled at him, shaking her head at the innocent little boy look he suddenly wore.

"So how long did you actually see this Maizie person? And how did you get away with it if she was Johnny's girl?"

"Johnny had a lot of business to take care of in the streets, the kind of business where a dame would be in the way. So when Maizie knew he'd be gone for a couple of hours, she'd send a message and I'd make a house call. See, I was like the neighborhood errand boy. Guy'd send me out for cigarettes, beer or sandwiches. There was always a crap game or poker party goin' on somewhere on the street, or just a bunch of guys sitting around a radio, bettin' the races or football—somethin'—anything—"

"Yeah, it was like that on my block, too," Tara said. "I knew a lot of kids who were involved in the street rackets but I stayed away from them. I used to go straight to the public library after school and stay until they closed. Then I'd check out as many books as I could carry and go home and read until I fell asleep. It's a wonder I didn't go blind, reading too much."

"I used to think books were for sissies. My heroes were the dudes in the street who made money by being just a little smarter and a lot tougher than the dumb clods they stole from." He drained his glass and handed it to Tara. "Get me another one, will ya, hon?" She took the glass and set it on the nightstand. He didn't seem to notice but went on speaking in a slurred monotone. "I remember this old hooker—used to read poetry to me out loud before she took me to bed. An' sometimes she'd read me these real racy passages from her 'collection of erotica,' she called it. Hell, they were just dirty books . . ." He smiled to himself, remembering how he had flushed at the descriptive love scenes in such books as *Lady Chatterley's Lover* and *Tropic of Cancer*. Even Harold Robbins and Mickey Spillane had shocked him back then. He

was not quite sure when he had become interested in the
stories themselves instead of skipping through the pages
looking for the "good" parts, marveling at the acts of
heroism, secretly identifying with the likes of Tom
Sawyer, Robin Hood, young Abe Lincoln and the steel-
fisted detectives who had made chopped liver out of six
bad guys with a single punch. But the success stories were
the ones that had finally hooked him. The rags-to-riches
epics. He had been captivated by the larger-than-life
heroes who had effortlessly spanned the chasm from
grinding poverty to glittering fame and fortune.

"Was this before or after hot-pants Maizie?" Tara
teased.

"After—way after. I was holdin' down an honest-to-
God legitimate job, drawin' a paycheck once a week just
like the squares I used to laugh at. Mos' guys couldn't get
a job unless they were sixteen, so I was pretty damn proud
of myself—head delivery boy for old man Pallerino."

The name jolted Tara's memory and she frowned, seeing a fleeting scene from her past. A brown paper bag
with the letters Pallerino's Meat, Fish & Poultry Market
stamped on the side. A slight chill passed over her and
she rubbed the sudden goose flesh on her arms.

"Thas' where I met this old hooker," Eric went on.
"Used to call up and ask for me—" He thumped his chest
and giggled. "Liked my style of delivery service—God,
could she fuck! Taught me everythin' I know about
fuckin' and suckin'—used to make me dance with her
first—all over the shittin' place—" He flung his arm in a
wide arc, giggling again. "Used to drink rum like a fuckin'
sailor—hot toddies, she called 'em—'Hot toddies good for
the body, kid,' she used to say. 'What's cher name, kid?
Can't call you kid when you're layin' it in me so good . . .'
I used to steal the booze from old man Pallerino and
then sell it to her for half price, take the other half out
in trade. Used ta steal her kid's library books, too—
take 'em home, read 'em and have 'em back before
the kid missed 'em." He giggled at the long-ago triumph
of having put something over on someone and nudged
Tara, inviting her to laugh with him.

But Tara was not laughing. A cold, icy hand had just closed like a vise around her heart. Her brain pounded and her face felt completely numb. She was acutely aware of each nerve and muscle closing up, shutting off every vestige of feeling. The hand holding Eric's was suddenly ice cold and clammy, the sweat melding their palms together. "What was this old—hooker's—name?" She wasn't sure she had spoken the words aloud. Her lips seemed not to have moved at all. As if reluctant to hear the answer.

"Belle somethin'-or-other. And she was as fat as a bell —big, saggy tits the size of watermelons—Christ, I remember feelin' like I was layin' on a cloud when she buried me against those big tits. I used to think she was the most sensual woman I'd ever met." He gave another giggle that ended in a snort of disgust. "Now I know she was just a beat up old lush—too fuckin' pathetic to even make a good livin' at hookin'—place a fuckin' pig sty—filth everywhere—"

"What was her last name, Eric? Belle what?" Tara's voice seemed to come to her from the stereo speakers in the four corners of the room, interlarding with the melodious crooning of Dinah Washington and Brook Benton, until it repeated itself inside her brain like an endless refrain; "Belle what? Belle what? What? What?" It seemed an eternity before she heard his mumbled reply.

"Woodpecker—Woodchuck—Woodchuck-chuck—" He giggled. "Woodhouse—"

"Woodhauser," Tara whispered and Eric snapped his fingers, grinning foolishly. "Thas' it—Woodhauser—how'd you—?"

"She was my mother!" The words exploded from her tight throat, resounding in the quiet room like a rifle shot. Eric jumped, startled into momentary soberness.

"Jesus—what did you say?"

"She was my mother!" Tara screamed and her fists beat at him, knocking his hands off her, pushing him as far away from her as she could. "That drunken old whore was my mother, you bastard! You pervert! You—you vile, dirty creep!" She was sobbing wildly, scrambling out of

bed, her whole body shaking with violent spasms that
caught in her throat and choked her. Her eyes burned and
her heart was pounding so fast and hard it ached. She
gulped in air and ran at him, her hands curved into
claws, raking at his face.

"Tara! Tara, for God's sake, what the hell's the matter
with you?" Eric tried to grab her hands and failed. He
leapt out of bed, warding off her blows and scratches as
best he could. "Get a hold of yourself, for Chrissake!
Please, honey—" He succeeded in grabbing her wrists
and she kicked him in the shin as hard as she could,
barely aware of the pain that jolted up her bare toes.

"You sonofabitch, you got my mother drunk and stole
my books—!" She rammed her head forward and bit his
arm as hard as she could, and he released her with a yelp
of pain. A sudden picture flashed before her eyes as clear
as a scene on television. She saw her mother waltzing
dreamily by herself in the shabby living room, humming
tunelessly as Tara searched the apartment for her library
books. If they became overdue she would have to pay
the fine out of her own miserable piggybank. "Where are
they, Mama?" she had cried, exasperated. "I put them
right here last night before I went to sleep." "A gentleman
friend asked to borrow them," Belle had answered
vaguely, taking a low dip in the arms of her imaginary
dance partner. Tara had gone off to school, returning that
afternoon to find that same boy from the grocery store
running down the stairs—and her books were on the
kitchen table. And her mother was passed out on the old,
sagging sofa, legs spread, smelling of sex and booze.

"Oh, God, Eric, it was you! It was you!" Her eyes grew
enormous with the stunned realization. "It was you! Oh,
God, no—I can't believe it!" Her eyes turned black with
shocked horror and rage. She backed away from him,
holding her arms straight out in front of her, the fingers
splayed wide apart. "Don't—don't—" she whispered in a
low, savage voice as he started to go after her. "Don't
touch me—don't come near me." She backed toward the
door, shaking her head. "Have to get out of here—" She
looked down at herself, ran her hands lightly over her

breasts and belly. "Must get dressed—don't come near me—" She stumbled about the bedroom, picking up her dress, shoes and coat like a blind person. Her movements were as jerky as a broken marionette as she pulled her dress over her head and stepped into her shoes. She stuffed her panties, bra and hose into her coat pocket before slipping it on.

"Tara, baby, don't go like this," Eric pleaded. He took a slow, cautious step toward her, keeping his voice low and soft. "Please, let's talk about it. We've always been able to talk to each other. Please, baby, I love you." He took another tentative step toward her, and when she didn't stop him he went quickly to her side and took her arm. "Tara—"

"Keep your filthy hands off me, you fucking degenerate!" she screamed shrilly and her eyes blazed with hatred. She drew herself up to her full height and backhanded him across the mouth with all her strength. Her face was contorted with ugly rage.

"Jeez, Tara, don't—" Eric was knocked back by the force of the blow and he felt his lip split and start to bleed. When he raised his eyes to hers, he saw it. That day long ago in that dreary Seattle slum when Belle's kid had come home unexpectedly and stood staring down at him with her dark, accusing eyes. He saw her as she had been then, standing in the doorway in her frayed coat and dingy-white socks that had worked down and buried themselves in the backs of her shoes, her white, clenched fists and the fury in her brown eyes. Mostly he remembered the fury in those huge, shocked, accusing dark eyes. Just like now. He felt a swift hollow pain in the pit of his stomach and had to swallow back the sudden bile that rose in his throat. Oh my God, his brain cried, it's her—Belle's kid . . .

"If you ever come near me again, I'll kill you!" Tara spun and ran through the living room, grabbing up her purse as she went. At the door she turned. "God, I can't believe it! You Eric! Oh, God, and I loved you so much!" She sobbed hard into her hands, the violence of her grief cutting through her like a sickle. Then she whirled away, shoving through the door, and it slammed behind her with a solid finality.

"Tara," Eric whispered. "Please forgive me—I didn't know." He stumbled to the door, leaned heavily against it and felt hot tears stinging behind his eyelids. "Please forgive me, Tara—my love." Tears overflowed and he pressed his face against the cool wood of the door, sobbing hard. In the quiet night he heard her car start up and tear out of the driveway with a squeal of tires that marked the ending.

Rain lashed against the windows and a jagged streak of lightning flashed across the sky, lighting up the living-room of Tara's apartment. The only other light in the room was the dull glow from the television set. Tara lay crumpled on the sofa, a quilted robe buttoned to her chin, legs curled up to her chest and covered with a heavy blanket. She held a cup of hot buttered rum in her hand and an almost empty bottle stood on the cabinet in the kitchen. It was the ninth or tenth bottle she had emptied in the last two weeks. Or was it an even dozen? She was not sure because Jim Glasser had just been there this morning (or was it yesterday morning?) and emptied her garbage, swearing at the number of empty bottles. He had said he was coming back with some food, but she could not remember when he had left. She could not remember anything but Eric's blue eyes and Mandy's blue eyes.

She swallowed the remainder of her drink and set the cup on the table. It fell to the floor but she did not even glance in the direction of the breaking glass. She stared straight ahead at the television screen where merry, brightly colored cartoon figures of Frosty the Snowman danced and sang, but she saw instead her mother's obscenely sprawled body and Eric's naked buttocks between her thighs. She heard the heavy pounding of the rain against the windows and cold air blew in around the partly open kitchen door, but she could not raise herself to turn on the thermostat. The pounding went on and on and she covered her ears with her hands and heard Eric's heart beating against hers—the way it had sounded when they had just made love. She thought she heard someone call her name, and the loud pounding went on like separate heavy blows to her heart. She started to rise, fell over on her face and lay still.

"Tara? We knocked—had to get the manager—my God—Tara!" Barry Wilde rushed across the room just as Tara toppled over and fell to the floor. He lifted her by the shoulders, shook her gently. "Tara? It's me—the Bear. Come on, babe." He looked at her puffy face, tear-stained and haggard. Her eyes were deep hollows, ringed in black, looking ridiculously like a sad raccoon. Her lips were colorless, trembling with cold and her hair had not been combed for days.

"Jeez, Bear, I didn't know it was going to be this bad." Charlotte stood beside him, staring down at Tara with a mixture of love and pity.

"I think she's passed out. Help me get her into bed." Barry picked her up and carried her into the bedroom, Charley running ahead of him to turn down the covers

"Let me get a clean nightgown first, Bear," she said. They stripped off the soiled robe, wrinkling their noses at the sour smell, and Barry held her upright while Charley pulled a fresh gown over her head. They lay her back against the pillow and Charley turned on the electric blanket. "It's cold in here. Go turn on the heat while I get her cleaned up. It looks like she threw up in her hair." She hurried into the bathroom for a washcloth while Barry turned on the thermostat and closed the kitchen door. Daisy was perched on the edge of the table, looking cold and miserable. When she saw Barry she leaped to the floor and rushed to her food dish, meowing pitifully.

"What's the matter, girl, your mama forget to feed you?" He opened a can of Kitty Queen and filled another dish with dry Friskies. She had water but it didn't look very fresh so he filled that as well. Christ, Tara must be in worse shape than he thought if she forgot to feed Daisy. The big, shaggy calico was like her own child. He looked around the messy, cluttered kitchen; never had he seen it so dirty. Every glass and cup in the place had been used and not washed. They stood everywhere, some partly filled with old drinks, most of them empty, crusted with hard butter and nutmeg. A half-loaf of bread lay spilled across the counter, green with mold. There were a couple of empty cans of Campbell soup next to a stack of dirty dishes and a saucer holding a hardened wedge of half-eaten cheese. He saw the cartons of Chinese food that Jim Glasser had left for Tara earlier that day. They had not been touched.

He went into the living room and built a fire in the fireplace, turned on the lights and closed the drapes. Immediately the room lost the cold, cheerless feel it had had when he entered, and took on the warmth he had always associated with Tara's apartment. He found a pack of cigarettes on the coffee table and lit one, then carried the overflowing ashtray into the kitchen and dumped it. He checked the thermostat again, then squatted and scratched Daisy's back when she rubbed against his leg. He wished he knew what the hell was going on. Jim had called an hour ago and told Barry to get his ass over to Tara's and stay put until he got there. He had cursed and shouted so much that Barry still was not sure what had happened. He only knew that the wedding was off and Tara was out of her mind with grief. Had been drunk for over a week and would not tell Jim anything but that she wanted to kill Eric.

Barry lifted Daisy in his arms and carried her into the bedroom. She leaped onto the bed and went to Tara's face, sniffing curiously.

"How is she?" he asked.

"A little cleaner," Charley said. "I don't know if she's asleep or not. She keeps mumbling. I can't make out what she's saying, though." Daisy sniffed all around Tara's head, purring softly, then curled herself on one edge of the pillow and began cleaning her paws. "What happened, anyway?"

"Just what I told you on the phone." Barry had called Charlotte to meet him at Tara's as soon as he had spoken to Jim and they had not had a chance to speak again until now. "I gather the wedding's off. I don't know why.

91

Glasser kept yelling that he was going to kill the prick—meaning Eric, I assume." He turned off the lamp by Tara's bed and took Charley's hand, leading her out of the room. "Let's have a drink while we're waiting—if there's anything left."

"Yuk, what a mess," Charley said as they entered the kitchen. She began clearing dishes off the cabinet and stacking them into the dishwasher. Barry found the bottle of rum and put on the kettle for hot water, then began helping Charley bring some order to the cluttered kitchen.

"Glasser said he called her for a week but couldn't get an answer, so he figured she and Eric were out shopping for their honeymoon or something. Then when she didn't turn in her column this week he got worried and called Eric's house. The answering service picked up and said Mr. Marlowe wasn't taking any calls and they didn't know where Miss Remington could be reached." He washed two cups and splashed some rum into them. "Then he called Mandy's school and spoke to Miss Pearson, but she didn't know anything. Mandy was fine and looking forward to the wedding and Christmas vacation." The kettle whistled and he poured hot water into the cups, added a pat of butter and a dash of nutmeg to each one. "So he came over here this morning, had to get the manager to let him in and found Tara passed out on the sofa. He brought her around with black coffee and tried to get her to tell him what had happened, but she just kept mumbling something about Eric and Mandy and crying so hard he couldn't understand a word she said."

Charley turned on the dishwasher, picked up her drink and tasted it. "Umm, that's good, Bear. Let's go sit down. I don't know about you but I'm beat. Been on my feet all day."

They went into the living room and sat down together on the sofa. The Bing Crosby Christmas Special was making cheery noises via the television set and they watched in silence for a moment.

Charley had had a long day at the beauty salon and she and her current lover were having problems, so was in no mood for men and broken promises. Her voice

was savage when she said, "If that prick has done anything to hurt Tara or Mandy, I'll kill him myself!"

"Easy, Bronco, down big fellow," Barry laughed. "What
are you getting so excited about? You don't know whose
fault it is. Maybe Tara broke it off."

"Oh, come on, Bear, she's crazy in love with him, for
God's sake. Why would she want to call it off?"

"Who knows?" Barry sipped his hot drink, then placed
the mug on the coffee table. He found Tara's cigarettes,
lit one and offered the pack to Charley. "Why do you
broads always blame the guy? Christ, Eric's okay. I got
to know him pretty well these last couple of years and I
know he's as much in love with Tara as she is with him."

"Then what could have gone wrong? They were supposed to be married on—what's the date?"

"The eighth," Barry supplied.

"Jeez, they were getting married on the twentieth! I
wonder if they've told the guests and everybody?"

"Don't know. Guess we'll have to wait until Tara
wakes up for the grisly details." He seemed calm, un-
disturbed and Charley turned on him in anger.

"Oh, you—men! You're all alike! Do something, for
chrissake! Call Doe Kingston. She must know." She found
the telephone buried under a pile of pillows and brought
it to Barry. "Go on—call her. Ask her if she's heard
from either Tara or Eric and if she knows what's going
on."

Grumbling, but anxious to hear Doe's sultry voice, he
made the call, spoke briefly. "She doesn't know what
happened. In fact, she said she'd just gotten a new dress
for the wedding and asked me if I wanted to take her."
He drew in on his cigarette, smiling a little. He liked the
idea of the blonde movie star asking him out. In all the
time he had known her, he had never asked her for a
date. When she wanted to see him, she simply called
and told him what time her chauffeur would pick him up.

In the bedroom Tara came awake with a start. She
sat up quickly, upsetting Daisy who meowed with injured
dignity and leaped off the pillow, tail twitching. For a moment Tara did not know where she was. The room was

93

dark, but she heard the sound from the television and saw that the hall light had been left on. She looked down at her clean nightgown, wondering if she had somehow managed to get into it herself. The last thing she remembered was Jim Glasser forcing black coffee down her and promising to come back with food. Maybe he had helped her change gowns. The clock's illuminated numbers read nine-fifteen. Jim had been there sometime that morning, so she knew she had lost another entire day. A day of blackness and despair and pain so deep it hurt her even while she slept.

She got out of bed, staggering, still drunk from the enormous amounts of booze she had consumed over the last two weeks. Her hands felt icy when she put them to her feverish forehead and she had to grab the nightstand or she would have toppled over. Carefully, like someone taking their first step after major surgery, she made her way down the hall toward the living room, one hand moving along the wall for support.

"Tara!" Charley cried and ran to her, putting an arm quickly about her shoulders. "Are you all right? Maybe you shouldn't be out of bed."

"No—no—I'm fine—fine—" She leaned against Charley and let her guide her to the sofa where Barry immediately jumped up and helped her to sit down. The blanket she had dropped earlier lay on the floor, and he took it and tucked it around her.

"What happened, babe?" he said softly. "Come on, you can tell the Bear." He put his arm around her, drew her against him, looked down at her with loving kindness.

"She doesn't have to tell us if she doesn't want to," Charley said quickly. She sat down on the other side of Tara, taking her icy hand in her own. Her big baby blue eyes were wide with concern, more serious than Tara had ever seen them. "How do you feel, honey? Do you want anything? Some tea or soup or something?"

"No—no, nothing, just—" Tara's voice broke and tears welled in her eyes and spilled down her cheeks.

"Hey, babe, don't. It's okay." Barry found a Kleenex on the coffee table and handed it to her but she just wadded it into a ball in her fist and let the tears flow unchecked. "Tell us what happened, babe—if we can do anything—anything at all to help."

"Nobody can help!" Tara cried and fell into his arms, sobbing so hard her whole body shook.

"Jeez, Bear, leave her alone," Charley snapped. "She doesn't have to tell us until she's ready." She took a fresh Kleenex and wiped Tara's face, but the tears came faster than she could dry them.

"I want a drink. Get me something to drink—rum." Tara made an effort to stop crying, gulped and covered her mouth with her hand. "Rum—my mother drank rum —mother and Eric drank rum."

"You certainly don't need any more booze," Charley said crisply and started toward the kitchen. "I'll make you a nice cup of tea and warm up some of that won ton soup Jim left."

"No! I want a drink! Rum!" Tara screamed. She flung off the blanket, jumped to her feet, staggered and fell back with a moan. "Just get me a drink—please."

"Get it, Charley," Barry said. "She'll have something to eat in a while, after we've talked." He covered her with the blanket again and drew her back into his arms. "Just relax, babe, I'm here. I'll stay with you until you feel better. We'll have a drink together and maybe later you'll feel like eating something, okay?" He hugged her and smiled down at her.

"Okay, Bear," she said in a tiny, weary voice. She let her head fall against his shoulder. "Oh, God, Bear, I'm so unhappy I could die!" Again heavy wracking sobs shook her body and he held her close, making comforting sounds until Charley returned with a drink. Her expression clearly said she did not agree with Barry that Tara should have anything alcoholic, but she handed her the warm mug and sat down next to her. Tara grabbed the mug, gulping hungrily, closing her eyes when the strong rum warmed her stomach. She opened her eyes and looked from Charley to Barry, her lips trembling. "Eric—" she said. "Eric and Mandy. They're—they're—" She drank again, closed her eyes. "Eric is Mandy's father."

"What?" Barry gasped. "What did you say?" Charley cried. Their eyes met over Tara's huddled form, shocked, disbelieving.

"He—he—my mother—" Tara stammered, eyes streaming tears. She gulped the rest of her drink, seemingly unmindful of how hot it was. "He was my mother's lover, or maybe I should say customer—john—her trick —oh, God, Bear, he's Mandy's father!" She poured it all out then, every sordid detail of the relationship between Belle and the young delivery boy, Eric Marlowe.

"And—and all those times he was with Mandy and me —playing with her, hugging her—laughing—he said—he said he wished I could have his child." She laughed shrilly, her face contorted and ugly. "But I did have his child, don't you see? I've had his child all along. I've cared for and raised and loved his child for eleven years! His child! Mandy—oh God, how will I ever tell her?"

"You won't tell her," Charley said firmly. "Not for a while. Not until we can decide what's best for—for—" She broke off, shaking her curly blonde head. Nothing in her past had prepared her for something like this. She was at a loss as to what to suggest. She picked up their cups and went into the kitchen for fresh drinks. Anything to keep busy. Anything to keep from facing the dark pain in Tara's eyes.

"Does Eric know?" Barry asked gently. "I mean— about Mandy?"

"No. I couldn't tell him. I was so—so shocked to find out about him and my mother, it wasn't until I got home that I—I realized that he—he was Mandy's—Mandy's—"

"Shh, babe, don't talk anymore. Just lean your head against me and rest. We'll figure something out."

Charley returned with the drinks and sat down next to them. She met Barry's eyes and they both shook their heads, sadly, not knowing what to say in this painful situation. Tara held her mug with both hands, drinking steadily, not lowering it until it was half empty.

"Do you really think Mandy should be told, honey?" Charley finally asked. "I mean, doesn't she think that her father was, well, your father?"

"Hell, no, she shouldn't be told. Why fuck up the kid's head with all that crap from the past?" Barry's voice was harsh, angry. "Really, Tara, there's no good reason to tell her. It'll just hurt her, make her hate Eric—"

"I want her to hate him!" Tara cried viciously. "I want her to know what a degenerate bastard he is!"

"You don't really, babe. You know you don't." Barry tried to pull her back against him, but she flung his hands away and sat up straight on the sofa, eyes blazing with hatred.

"I know who I'll tell! I'll tell Jim Glasser! He'll kill him!" She sounded almost glad. "I know he will. He told me—warned me not to marry Eric. He said he was no good, he'd break my heart." She sobbed again, doubled over as if a sudden pain had grabbed her stomach. She clasped her arms around her drawn-up knees, hugging them to her chest. "I want to see him dead—dead like my mother—his fault—doctor said no more booze—her liver. She couldn't afford to buy any. He brought it. Eric —he always brought her more booze—rum. He killed her." Her head lolled to one side, eyes rolling up until only the whites showed.

"She's passed out again!" Charley cried accusingly. "I told you not to let her drink anymore!"

"I'm okay," Tara mumbled weakly. She tried to raise her head but it flopped like a broken toy, and she gave up and let it rest against Barry's shoulder. "Why don't you guys go home and leave me alone. I just want to be alone for a while and—and think."

A knock sounded, then the door was pushed open and Jim Glasser strode briskly into the room. He went to them and looked down at Tara. "How is she? I got here as soon as I could. Family dinner—couldn't get out of it." He shucked off his raincoat and tossed his hat on the coffee table. "Is there anything to drink in this joint?"

"Yeah, come on in the kitchen. We're drinking hot buttered rum." Barry took Jim's arm and guided him quickly out of the room.

"When the hell did she get on this rum kick? I thought she drank gin."

"I'll tell you all about it—come on." Barry pulled Jim into the kitchen and closed the door behind them. "How much do you know?" he asked as he turned on the gas under the kettle.

"Just that her fancy pornographer broke it up, called off the wedding." He opened the cupboard where Tara usually kept her liquor and found it empty. "Shit, all she's got is that rum? Well, make it strong." He sat down at the table while Barry told him what had happened.

"Shit," he snorted. "What difference does that make? Her old lady was a hooker, right? She must have had more johns than Eric."

"Yeah, but for some reason Tara blames her mother's death on Eric. And there's his kid—Mandy." He handed Jim his drink and sat down next to him. "Got a cigarette? I'm—"

"You still bumming smokes, you cheap bastard." Jim laughed. He took out his Marlboros and tossed them to Barry. "Keep the pack." He tasted his drink, nodded and took another swallow. "I'll straighten her out. You kids go on home." He stood and laid a hand on Barry's shoulder. "Thanks for coming over and staying with her. I'll be in touch."

If Tara was aware that Barry and Charley had left she gave no sign. She lay like a rag doll on the sofa, eyes closed. She did not see Jim standing above her, his pale blue eyes misty with tears. "My little Tara," he whispered. "My own fair Tara. I'll take care of you from now on, sweetheart." He sat next to her, pulled her into his arms, felt the soft curves pressed against him. This was the way it should be. He and Tara together. His hands traced the outline of her breasts beneath the flannel nightgown and he kissed her forehead gently. "You're mine now," he whispered against her hair. "All mine."

Tara stirred in his arms, cuddled closer and sighed, "Hold me, Eric."

CHAPTER
FIVE

TARA SAT in front of the roaring fire, sipping her drink and staring through the enormous picture window. Snow fell softly outside, clinging to the red of Mandy's new ski outfit, covering her dark curls with a layer of white. She and three other children were building a snowman, and she turned and waved a mittened hand at her sister. Behind the children, in the far distance, Tara saw bright streaks of color as skiers hurtled down the slopes. Jim had insisted that she and Mandy get out of town for the holidays and had arranged this Aspen, Colorado, vacation, flying up with them and helping them get settled. He had stayed a couple of days but had had to return to spend Christmas with his family. He would be joining them later this afternoon and they would all fly back to Los Angeles.

During the two weeks that they had been at the ski resort, Tara had made a determined effort to act normal for Mandy's sake. When the child had questioned her about Eric, Tara had put her off with vague answers and quickly turned her attention to the sports the lodge offered. They had taken all their meals in the huge dining room, sharing a table with other holiday-spirited guests so that Tara would not be alone with her thoughts. Several unattached males, as well as a few attached ones, had tried to interest Tara but she had rejected all offers of intimacy. She spent most of her time with Mandy, shopping, sledding or just taking long walks in the snow-covered woods.

But at night, while Mandy slept in the twin bed next to hers, Tara had lain awake, her mind tortured with thoughts of Eric. She knew she was being silly and naive to blame him for her mother's deterioration but she couldn't help it. She knew that her mother had been an alcoholic and a loser long before Eric had come into the picture, but the vivid memories of her mother passed out, sated with booze and sex, would flash before her eyes and hate would fill her like bile. She felt as if her affair with Eric had somehow been incestuous, dirty, perverted. She would remember the feel of him inside her, hear the murmured words of love—then she would clench her fists in shame. He had also been inside her mother. Many, many times. Had he whispered those same soft words to her?

Tara sipped her drink, wishing she were already home. Jim had been a doll to fly them to Aspen, but she wanted the quiet of her own apartment. She had found it increasingly difficult to answer Mandy's questions. Why had they not gotten married as planned? She loved Eric and demanded to know why Tara had snatched this happiness away. "Now I suppose I won't get my pony or even a little ole dog," the child had cried, anger making her insensitive to her sister's pain. "Now I suppose we won't even get to buy the house and all live together like you promised!" When Tara had tried to explain that she would buy a house, just for the two of them, Mandy had demanded to know when. "When I can afford it, honey," Tara had answered wearily. "That'll probably be never! You don't want me to live with you! You've always kept me in that dumb hospital! I know it's a hospital—not a 'school' like you tell all your friends!"

Tara left her drink unfinished on the table and went upstairs to pack. Jim was not due for another four hours but she had nothing better to do. She finished packing Mandy's things, then sat on the bed and lit a cigarette. She would have to get herself organized when she got home. Start working on her novel again. Being productive.

Jim had assured her that the column was still waiting whenever she was ready to tackle it again. But that would not fill enough hours. She kicked off her shoes and stretched out on the bed. She had not known exactly where she was going with her novel before. But now she knew. She would write it just as it had happened. Maybe then she could purge herself of her mother's shame. And of Eric.

Tara stood by the window looking out on the kidney-shaped pool and the group of people drinking and laughing. It was only seven-thirty, but already they wore paper hats and blew noisemakers into one another's faces. New Year's Eve, Tara thought. I should be Mrs. Eric Marlowe. I should be sitting on deck and watching the stars come alive in a velvet black sky. The ship would be softly rocking with the gentle slap slap of waves against the hull. There should be dusky silhouettes of islands in the distance and palm trees swaying and the sound of native music floating across the water. Tara wondered if she should change before Thorton arrived but then decided against it. She was not looking forward to this party and wondered why she had let Thorton talk her into it. She was not ready to face the world and make merry. The wounds Eric's confession had inflicted still felt raw, and she wondered if they would ever heal entirely. He had called many times since she and Mandy had returned from Aspen, but the second Tara heard his voice she slammed down the receiver. She knew he had called her friends, begging them to tell Tara how sorry he was and how much he still loved her. She knew that he had called Mandy, had, in fact, gone out to the school and taken her out for the day. When Mandy had told her, Tara had gone into a rage and called Miss Pearson, fairly blistering that good woman's ear with curses and threats should she ever let Mandy go off with Eric Marlowe again. Nor was the child allowed to receive his calls or even be informed that he had called.

She closed the drapes and wandered aimlessly through the apartment, wishing Thorton would hurry and get there so they could get on with it. She knew he was right about going out and circulating again, moving among the living even though she still felt dead inside. Eric had killed everything. Even her relationship with Mandy, for now the child blamed Tara for spoiling her chance at happiness.

Thorton arrived and whistled appreciatively at her revealing black dress and they drove through the crowded streets to Benedict Canyon. When they turned into a narrow drive and climbed a steep hill, Tara roused herself and looked around. A majestic white mansion stood at the top, the rolling lawn decorated like Santa's Village. She gasped. "Thorton! I've been here before. I know this house—but I thought you said we were going to Zock McBain's."

"So I did," Thorton replied. A red-jacketed parking boy opened her door and helped her out, while his twin took the wheel from Thorton. They went up the red-carpeted walk that was lined with giant candy canes. "Zock lives here now. He just closed the deal a couple of months ago, as a matter of fact."

"But wasn't this the house that—?"

"Dick Wilson used to have? Yep. Remember I told you that he wouldn't be on top for more than a couple of seasons. He blew it last year with all those no-talent broads he signed to recording contracts. Not one of them could carry a tune in a bucket. Gossip has it that he was balling all of them and—" But Tara wasn't listening. She had begun to tremble violently. This was the same house in which she had met Eric three years ago. God, was it really three years? She stepped through the massive double doors and looked around. Everything was exactly the same. Same white carpet and furniture. Same gilt mirrors and chandeliers. Even the guests looked the same, and Tara supposed they were. But there was only one guest she remembered from the first party. She pulled Thorton close and whispered tightly, "Eric won't be here, will he?"

"How should I know?" Thorton shrugged. "I didn't ask to see the guest list before I accepted the invitation. Besides, you'll have to run into him sometime, Tara, you can't—"

"Thorton, sweetheart!" Zock McBain had seen them and pushed his way through the crowd to hug and kiss Thorton. Then his pale blue eyes settled on Tara and his too-handsome face split into a wide grin. "Well, hello there. Thorton, you bastard, where have you been hiding this tasty little dish?" His eyes swept her bare legs and he took her hand and leaned forward as if to kiss her.

"Don't do that, please," she said coolly and removed her hand from his.

"Well!" Zock said, stepping back and bowing low from the waist. "Allow me to introduce myself. I'm Zock Mc-Bain. Perhaps you've heard of me?" He said it facetiously, giving Thorton a raised-eyebrow glance over his shoulder.

"Yes, I've heard of you," Tara replied in that same cool voice. "I've also heard of the swine flu, but I wouldn't want to get too close to that, either."

There was a moment of stunned disbelief on the rock star's face and then he laughed. "Well, well, a girl who is not crazy about me. Will wonders never cease!"

"I haven't been a 'girl' since I started my period eight years ago," Tara said coldly, feeling mean. She wanted to put this preening peacock in his place. "And I hate men who continue to call grown women 'girls.'"

Zock threw up his hands in mock terror as if warding off her verbal blows. "Help, Thorton, she's got me. Call her off, please." He was laughing at her and it made her even angrier. She was on the verge of telling him what intimate act he could perform on himself when a gorgeous brunette slithered up and pressed herself against him. In a moment they had disappeared into the crowd.

"Well, you're certainly in fine form tonight," Thorton said, not without humor. "I'm sure that's the first time a girl—excuse me, a *woman* has ever refused Zock." He laughed. "It might do him some good."

"Nothing will do him any good. I know the type. Conceited baboon."

"If you can control your hatred for the male race, I'll buy you a drink," Thorton laughed. "As I recall the bar's

103

on the other side of the dance floor." He took her arm and began leading her through the crowd. They passed the huge white Christmas tree laden with gold ornaments and found places at the bar.

"God, even the tree's the same," Tara said when they had settled themselves on stools and ordered a drink. "Everything is exactly the same as it was when Dick Wilson lived here." She sipped her drink and remembered sitting in this very same spot three years before, watching Dick Wilson's face flushed with his new success. He had probably thought it was going to last forever. Just as she had thought her love for Eric was going to last forever. She had met him at this very bar. Had fallen in love with him on that same dance floor, now crowded with clinging couples in silly paper hats. She tossed off her drink and signaled the bartender for another. Might as well get high and lay the ghosts to rest. This was, after all, a brand new year. A year in which she hoped to finish her novel and accept the accolades Jim Glasser knew she deserved.

"Tara, excuse me, Miss Remington, may I have a moment?" Zock McBain stood next to her, looking rather abashed. "Forgive me for being such a fool. I didn't recognize you a moment ago. You're the Tara from *Hoots 'n Toots,* aren't you?" She nodded curtly, her eyes cool. "I met you here two or three years ago, don't you remember? At Dick Wilson's Christmas party." Again she nodded. "Well, I just wanted to say, that is, to tell you that I'm sorry if I offended you earlier." The power of the press, Tara thought with malicious glee. It brought even conceited baboons to their knees.

"That's perfectly all right, Mr. McBain. I'm accustomed to stars making fools of themselves." She reached for her cigarettes, and he was holding a gold lighter before she had even brought it to her lips.

"Yes, well." He grinned self-consciously. "It *is* the holiday season. Time to be jolly and all that." The grin grew more animated. He extended his hand. "Truce? Can we start over?"

She let his hand dangle there a moment before taking it briefly in her own. "Truce," she said.

"You know, you're the first girl that ever—excuse me, I mean you're the first *lady* who ever gave me the brush." He laughed as if he still could not quite believe it and ran a bejeweled hand through his sun-streaked hair.

"Before or after you became a star?" Tara asked innocently and he had the grace to flush slightly.

"Touché," he said. Again that wide, charming grin and Tara felt herself warming to him. Maybe he was not as bad as she had thought. She supposed it must be quite an ego trip to be panted after by millions of screaming fans. Most of them "girls."

"Would you like to dance?" he asked, and she nodded her assent and slid off the bar stool and into his arms. He drew her close and she was surprised to find that he was not as tall as she had thought. Even with the ludicrous high-heeled boots. Or perhaps it was because Eric was over six feet and she hadn't been in anyone else's arms in three years.

"This is really a lovely home," she said as he whirled her around the white marble dance floor. The huge revolving ball of lights above cast everything in a pastel glow and he looked suddenly youthful. The hard glitter in his pale eyes was softened, and she saw that the color was closer to gray than blue.

"Yes, isn't it. But it's a little too small, really. I've got a bid in on a really groovy place in Bel Air. Used to belong to Tony Curtis. Twenty-one rooms, tennis court, acres of land—a real gas."

"You're kidding—Thorton said you just bought this place."

"Yeah, but only as an investment and temporary quarters until I close the deal on the Curtis place." He danced her across the floor and out through the sliding glass doors. Several couples were dancing on the patio near the pool, and others were sitting on chaises, drinking and talking.

"Then will you sell it?"

"No, rent it. Thorton says with property values going up like they are in California, land is the safest thing to invest in." The music ended and he took her hand and led her to a swinging bamboo chair built for two. "Care to sit out here for a while and get some air? It's groovy out now that the rain has cleared the smog away." He was doing his best to charm her and she let him lift her into the chair, thinking, why not? She gazed out across a vast span of twinkling city lights. It seemed all of Beverly Hills was spread out below them like sparkling gems on a jeweler's black velvet cloth. She thought of her tiny one-bedroom apartment and how she had looked forward to moving into a house like this with Eric and Mandy. Now here was this young rock star telling her this spacious mansion was really a bit too small. My God! A white-coated waiter approached with a silver tray of champagne glasses and Zock took two of the chilled glasses, handing one to Tara.

"Oh, I don't think I should," she protested. "I've had a couple of gin and tonics and I don't think they mix too well with champagne."

"Don't sweat it, pretty lady," he said with his charming smile. "I won't let anything happen to you. Besides, old Thorton's driving, isn't he?"

"Yes, but I don't think he'd appreciate being called 'old' Thorton. He's very vain about his age, you know, now that he's turned forty." She took the icy glass and sipped. The champagne was heavenly and she decided then and there that she would drink nothing else in the future. Hard liquor showed too much on a person's face. "Not that forty's exactly ready for the Motion Picture Retirement Home."

"Forty years old," Zock said, shaking his head. "Wow, man, that seems light-years away when you're young, doesn't it?"

"How old are you?"

"Twenty-four next month—February tenth. You'll have to come to my birthday party." He turned to face her squarely, looking her up and down as if she were a prize poodle on display. "Hey, why don't you be my date that night? I sort of thought of asking Sandy Sinclair but you're a hell of a lot classier." As if he had just thought of it, he snapped his fingers and grinned. "Wow, you can write it up in your column, okay? That'll be a real gas."

Tara smiled to herself. Anything for publicity. She wondered if he would have invited her if she had looked like Louella Parsons. She was forming a refusal in her mind when she suddenly thought, why not? He was not so bad once she had put him in his place, and he was right about the party being a good item for her column. She would make it the first column of the new year. (Jim had already decided that Tara needed to take off the month of January to get her novel blocked out and head back into working.) Zock McBain was hot. Right up there with the Beatles and Presley. It wouldn't hurt to be seen around town with him. And maybe it would get back to Eric. "Why, thank you, Zock, I'd love to come."

"Hey, wow, I don't believe it!" He laughed like a small boy and hugged her against his necklace-strewn chest. "I didn't think you'd say yes."

"Is that why you asked me?" she teased.

"Hell, no I asked you because you're the most beautiful girl—uh, lady, I've ever met!"

"Uh-huh, that's why you didn't recognize me when I came in tonight."

"Wow, you're really tough on a guy, ya know that?" He gave her his special smile, the expensive caps dazzling in the moonlight. "Why don't you lighten up a little and give me a chance. I'm really a very nice guy when you get to know me." His fingers played up her bare arm.

"I'll be the judge of that," she laughed and suddenly she felt young and happy. She could not deny the warm feeling that swept through her when he looked adoringly into her face. He was, after all, one of the most famous rock stars in the world. Millions of females would have killed to change places with her. And she knew that several of the ladies inside wished Zock had asked them out into the moonlight for a glass of chilled Dom Perignon.

They sat talking and drinking champagne in the cool light and not once did Zock leave her side. He had called a waiter over and instructed him to bring a fresh bottle of champagne and leave it with them. It now set at their feet, empty in a silver bucket of melting ice. Even when the guests began drifting off to find their coats and spouses, Zock had stayed by Tara's side, forcing them to come out to the patio to say their thank yous and goodbyes. When Thorton appeared, Tara had been surprised to find it was after two in the morning. She had spent the entire evening sitting alone with Zock McBain, and the hours had flown.

"We'd better hit the road, Tara," Thorton said. He adjusted his glasses and peered at them curiously, surprised to find them so cozily together. He was not sure if he liked the idea or not. He was glad that Tara seemed to have forgotten Eric, at least for the moment, but he was not too happy that Zock McBain was the man who had made her forget. Everyone in the business knew that Zock was a doper, as were most musicians, and Thorton did not want Tara mixed up in that crowd.

"Please stay," Zock urged, his fingers gently squeezing, his pale eyes pleading.

She hesitated, then firmly shook her head. "I can't, really, Zock, but thank you for a lovely evening." She returned the pressure of his fingers. "I really enjoyed talking with you and it was a great party. I'm glad I came." She stood and placed her glass in the silver ice bucket.

"Give me your number," he said quickly, following them through the almost-empty living room. "I'll call you and we'll have dinner tomorrow night."

"Not tomorrow, Zock, I'm picking up my little sister for the weekend." They stopped at the front door while a butler in an elegant evening uniform brought their coats.

"Your number," Zock prompted, snapping his fingers at the butler who immediately withdrew a card and gold pen from his inside pocket, handing them to his young master. Tara gave him the number and he quickly scribbled it down. "You're sure you can't make it tomorrow night? I'll only be in town a couple of days, then I have to fly to Las Vegas to do a show. I'm opening the fourth at The Sands."

"I'm sorry," Tara said. "But I haven't seen Mandy,

that's my kid sister, for a few days and I promised she could come this weekend."

"Then why don't you come to Vegas with me? We'd have a ball. We're leaving the third and I open the next night. We'd have a whole day and night together . . ." He was holding her hand again, his ringed fingers squeezing. "We're taking my private jet up, so you wouldn't have to hassle the crowds at International. And I have a fabulous suite of rooms at the Sands. All the comforts of home and then some." He smiled winningly but she still shook her head.

"No, really, Zock, I can't. I have to work for a living, remember?" She smiled and withdrew her hand. "Maybe some other time—when you get back in town."

Zock's attention was taken by another departing couple, and Thorton and Tara slipped quickly out the door. Thorton's black Cadillac stood purring softly at the bottom of the steps, the doors held open by the parking boys. As they pulled away from the blinking mechanical Christmas figures on the lawn. Thorton said, "Tara, I hope you're not falling for that punk. He's definitely not your type."

"Why?" She leaned her head back against the soft white leather upholstery and closed her eyes.

"He's not interested in anything but a good time—"

"What's wrong with that?" Tara interrupted with a chuckle. "God, I'd love to have a good time again."

"That's not what I mean. Zock's idea of a good time is snorting a gram of cocaine, smoking a lid of grass, popping some Amies and balling three girls at once."

Tara laughed. "God, that I'd like to see! All at the same time, huh?" She was teasing him and he knew it.

"Okay, maybe this isn't the right time to be serious, but if he calls you be sure and remember what I said before you agree to go out with him." His voice was father-stern.

Ordinarily Tara would have been angry at anyone telling her who she could or could not date, but tonight she felt too relaxed to be upset at anything. The bottle of expensive champagne had mellowed her considerably. She remembered with a tiny shiver of delight the feel of

Zock's lips against hers. At midnight he had turned to her and placed his hands gently on her shoulders, not pulling her to him but merely holding her. Then he had kissed her. A tender, sweet kiss without the probing tongue of passion. And her response had startled her. She had leaned into him, her mouth answering his, lips parted and trembling. She was aware of the deep rumbling of Thorton's voice but was too tired to answer. She leaned her head against the cool window and promptly fell asleep, the memory of Zock's kiss still warm.

Tara awoke to the loud, insistent ringing of her door bell. She quickly slipped into a robe and went to answer it. "Miss Tara Remington?" The voice came from behind an enormous bouquet of white and red roses.

"Yes?" Tara answered and the delivery man pushed the roses into her arms, tipped his cap and left. She carried them inside, breathing in the sweet fragrance. A card was nestled in a cluster of baby's breath and green foliage, and she took it out and read: "For a beautiful lady— Love, Zock." She felt a warm flush of pleasure, remembering the almost chaste kiss he had given her at midnight.

The roses were magnificent. She counted quickly. Two dozen red and two dozen white. She wondered if the rock star was always this flamboyant or if he was still trying to impress her. She fed Daisy and was putting on the kettle for water when the telephone rang. Thinking it must surely be Zock McBain, she let it ring a few more times before picking it up.

"Happy New Year, honey!" Doe Kingston cried boisterously. "Christ, where the fuck have you been? I've been trying to reach you for weeks!"

"Hi, Doe, Happy New Year. Oh, Mandy and I spent Christmas in Aspen." She spooned instant coffee into her cup and waited for the kettle to whistle. "Mandy had never seen snow up close and besides, I wanted to get out of L.A. for a while."

"Umm," Doe murmured, taking a noisy drag, then holding her breath as she said, "Good grass." She let out

110

her breath with a loud whoosh. "Well, I'm glad you're back. Let's get together later on today. Do you have any plans?"

"Nope. I had planned on sleeping most of the day, but a delivery boy just woke me with four dozen gorgeous roses." The kettle whistled and she poured water into her cup and stirred. "What did you have in mind?"

"Oh, hell, I don't know. Let's get high and be somebody." She giggled and dragged again on her joint. "Christ, I haven't been to bed yet—I mean, I haven't been to *sleep* yet. Friend Bear just left a couple of hours ago."

"Barry? Gee, you're seeing a lot of him, aren't you?"

"Uh-huh. He's my good luck charm. I figured if he brought me luck on my movies, why not a good fuck on New Year's Eve to start the year right." She sucked in noisily, exhaling with a sigh. "So, how about it? When shall I pick you up?"

"Give me an hour to shower and put on my face and then let's go someplace fancy for breakfast. Okay with you?"

"Sure. I think Chasen's is having a special brunch. That fancy enough for you?"

"Perfect. See you in an hour."

They had breakfasted elegantly on eggs Benedict and icy Ramos fizzes, which Doe swore had added ten pounds to her curvy frame even as she sat there. Dave Chasen had stopped to chat with them a moment before moving on to greet other illustrious guests, and several tourists had approached their table asking for Doe's autograph. When one stout lady had leaned over to peer into Tara's face and ask, "Are you anybody?" Doe had answered dryly, "Yes, she's my mother. Doesn't she look wonderful for fifty-three?" The woman had gasped, then turned to her companion and commented, "What did I tell you, Gladys. Everyone in Beverly Hills has a face lift!" And even though Doe and Tara were openly laughing at the joke, the woman persisted, demanding to know the name of the plastic surgeon who had turned a fifty-three-year-old woman into a stunning beauty who looked nineteen. Trying to keep a straight face, Doe had given the woman Barry Wilde's telephone number.

"The Bear will get you for that, Doe," Tara laughed as the two women rushed to the nearest telephone booth. She took a cigarette from her pack and instantly a waiter appeared holding a light for her.

"Will there be anything else, ladies?" he asked.

"I'd love a gooey French dessert," Doe sighed, eyeing the pastry cart laden with tarts, eclairs and other forbidden goodies. "How about you, Tara?"

"Good God, no," Tara groaned. "I couldn't eat another bite. But you go ahead if you want to."

"No, if you can resist I guess I can." She gave the waiter her famous smile. "Just the check, please." When he had gone she said, "It's that damn grass. Makes me ravenous as a bear." The waiter appeared with the check, which Doe signed with a flourish, adding a generous tip and dazzling him with another smile. "Let's get out of here before I weaken," she laughed.

Outside six parking boys fought over who would deliver Doe's silver Rolls Royce and they were finally on their way. "Where to now?" Doe asked, expertly steering the big automobile through the holiday traffic.

"I don't know. What do you want to do?" Tara leaned back in the comfortably cushioned seat, gazing out of the window. She thought briefly of picking Mandy up earlier than planned, but decided against it. Lately the child had been petulant and sulky and not very much fun to be with. She should just wait until tomorrow to pick her up, but even as the thought formed in her mind she knew she would not do it. She still felt guilty about spoiling Mandy's plans to finally leave the school and have the family she had never had.

"Let's go back to my place and smoke a little grass and then decide what to do, okay?" Doe turned on Rodeo Drive, honking and giving the finger to a slow-moving car of tourists who gawked at her in surprise.

"I've never smoked marijuana before." Tara was a

little embarrassed admitting it. Everyone she knew, with the exception of Jim Glasser, smoked the illegal weed and sang its praises.

"Hey, a virgin!" Doe cried, turning to stare at Tara in amazement. "I don't believe it. You mean you've *never* even tried it?"

"Never."

"Well, well, I finally get to turn somebody out." The big blonde laughed huskily and gave Tara a mischievous wink.

An hour later they were sprawled comfortably on Doe's pink velvet sofa listening to Frank Sinatra albums and passing a joint between them. A warm gust of air blew through the open doors leading to the pool area, and the day was white-bright with sunlight. "God, you'd never know it was January, would you? It must be eighty degrees outside."

"Want to take a swim?" Doe murmured. Her voice was slightly slurred, her eyes heavy-lidded and glassy.

"Good God, no," Tara laughed. "I'd probably drown." She watched with interest as Doe clipped the half-smoked joint onto a narrow gold prong. "What's that?"

"Roach clip. Don't tell me you've never seen one before." Tara shook her head and Doe passed the clip to her. It was about three inches long, elegantly slim and bore Doe's initials in mother of pearl on the handle.

"It's beautiful. Where did you get it?"

"That new little head shop in West Hollywood." Doe took the clip, dragged in deep and held the smoke in her lungs as long as possible before exhaling with a loud sigh. Tara watched her closely. She had had as much to smoke as Doe had but she did not feel that much different. Just a little more relaxed and her mouth felt dry, but she was still alert and aware of her surroundings. Doe seemed to be floating in and out of reality and her conversation was becoming disjointed. She would start a sentence, then abruptly stop speaking and gaze off into space for several minutes before continuing. Her eyes were bloodshot nar-

113

row slits and Tara wondered if her own eyes looked that strange and unfocused.

"Do I look any different?" she asked suddenly.

"Yeah—you have two heads," Doe giggled. "Why?"

"I was just wondering if my eyes looked as, well, weird, as yours do." She waved away the short roach and Doe dropped it into the ashtray after removing the clip.

"Yeah, that's the only thing about grass I don't like. It fucks up your eyes and everybody knows you've been smoking. But I just wear shades when I'm high in public." She pushed to her feet and stretched her arms above her head, letting out a long sigh. "I'd better move around a little before I grow to the sofa. How about a drink? I can have Lupe fix us something."

"I don't know—what time is it?"

"It's early, why? I thought you didn't have any plans for today." She went to the bar and pressed a button on the intercom. "Lupe, whip up a batch of strawberry daiquiris, please." There was a murmured response and Doe sauntered over to the door and gazed out at the bright day for a moment, then turned back to Tara. "Got a hot date tonight?"

"Not exactly. I'm picking Mandy up for dinner and the weekend and I don't want to be too stoned to drive."

Doe came back to the sofa and sank down, resting her bare feet on the coffee table. "How is Mandy? I haven't seen her since—" She broke off, glancing quickly at Tara. She had almost said, "since you and Eric broke up."

"She's fine," Tara answered, pretending not to notice Doe's blunder. "Growing up so fast she's almost as tall as I am. And getting prettier every day." She lit a cigarette, trying to ignore the vision of Mandy with Eric's inky black curls and vivid blue eyes.

"She always was a pretty little thing," Doe said carefully. She knew the facts behind the breakup, as she had pestered Barry Wilde until he had told her. She reached across the stretch of pink velvet and squeezed Tara's hand. "Hey, honey, don't let it get you down. Worse things have happened and people go on living and sometimes they're even happy. If it would help to talk about it . . ."

"Nothing will help," Tara said stonily. She set her mouth in a stubborn line and looked away. The effect of the marijuana made her feel suddenly very sorry for herself and she was afraid she was going to cry. Her lips trembled when she whispered, "I just feel all used up, empty, you know? Like I'll never be happy again."

"Bullshit! Nobody can make you unhappy unless you allow it," Doe said roughly. She lifted the lid of a gold filigreed cigarette box and took out a fresh joint, lit it and passed it to Tara. "Besides, no man on earth is worth it. You should start getting out again, dating other guys. Eric sure as hell isn't sitting home pining away. I saw him twice this week with that little tramp Sandra Sinclair."

Tara's heart missed a beat and she turned wide, shocked eyes upon Doe. "Sandy Sinclair? You actually saw them? Where?"

"Oh, once at Ciro's and again at a sneak preview for Zanuck's new film at Fox."

"Oh." Tara drew shakily on the joint, holding in the smoke a long time before exhaling. Eric and Sandy Sinclair? But she was just a child. Surely Doe was mistaken. "Are you sure it was—Eric? I mean, gosh, Sandy Sinclair is only about fifteen, isn't she?"

"Closer to eighteen. It's just those roles she plays. With that baby face of hers, she can pass for thirteen or fourteen years old, but believe you me, honey, that's where all similarity to childhood ends. That little bitch is a real barracuda." Lupe entered with a silver tray holding a pitcher of strawberry daiquiris and two frosted glasses which she placed on the coffee table. She served them before silently withdrawing.

Doe smiled brightly, holding her glass toward Tara. "Well, here's to a super new year—may we both get everything we want out of life."

I just want Eric, Tara thought, but aloud she said, "I'll drink to that" and took a sip of the frothy pink mixture. I could have him, she thought, any time I want. But I'd never be able to forget how he's hurt me. I couldn't bear to see him and Mandy together without remembering every ugly detail of her birth.

"Well, keed, what'cha wanna do? Hugh O'Brien is having a little do later on. We could stop by for a few minutes, have some laughs—"

"No thanks," Tara said shortly, interrupting her. "I don't really feel up to a bunch of merry-makers. Last night was enough to last me for a while."

"Oh, that reminds me. I meant to ask you. Where did all those gorgeous roses come from? Some exciting new man in your life you're trying to hide from your old pal?" She grinned, slapped Tara playfully on the arm. "Come on, 'fess up, honey, who is it?"

"Oh, really, Doe he's not a 'new man in my life'—he just sent me roses, that's all." She sipped her daiquiri, watching the curiosity build in Doe's eyes. "It's Zock McBain."

"Not Zock the Cock, the scourge of young maidens everywhere! Quick, tell me more!"

"There's nothing to tell, really. I went to a party at his house with Thorton Kennedy. Thorton is doing some publicity work for him, as well as advising him on investments—things like that."

"And?" Doe prompted.

"And, well, Zock and I spent some time together talking and, well, just talking, really." She shrugged.

"Honey, you must be one hell of a conversationalist if Zock McBain sends you four dozen long-stemmed roses! Do you realize he's the hottest thing in bed since the invention of the electric blanket?"

"So I've heard. In fact, I think I heard it from Zock." She laughed and then told Doe about the rock star's invitation to join him in Las Vegas.

"Go, for chrissakes!" Doe cried. "He's just what you need right now."

"Really? And just why do I 'need' him?"

"Because he's young, he's gorgeous, he's a super stud, he's as rich as Howard Hughes and better known than Jesus Christ!"

"All that, huh?" Tara teased. She sipped her daiquiri, waving away the offered joint.

"Okay, if that doesn't grab you, how about this? You go to Vegas on the arm of Zock McBain and every newspaper and magazine in the country will have your picture on the front page." She paused dramatically. "And Eric Marlowe is bound to see it."

CHAPTER SIX

ERIC MARLOWE lay on his back, legs spread, his head lolled against the headboard of his bed. One hand absently stroked the tangled mass of Sandra Sinclair's hair that was spread upon his stomach. Her lips devoured him, long-nailed fingers raked his hips as she tried to suck him even deeper into her open mouth. She made little animal sounds in her throat and writhed passionately between his legs. He tangled both his hands in her hair, holding her head tight to his crotch. "Suck it off, baby," he whispered and bucked against her greedy mouth, grunting with the suddenness of the rush, the quick release.

Squirming up his body like a snake stretching in the sun, Sandy wrapped clinging arms about his neck and tried to kiss him. He turned his head and her wet mouth sucked at his ear. She murmured soft obscenities and he took both her hands and disentangled her arms. "Christ, it's hot in here," he said. "Cool it a minute, okay?" He swung off the bed, swaying slightly as he stood. His head pounded with the enormous amount of booze he had consumed that evening and his one clear thought was to get away from Sandra Sinclair. If even for a moment. "I'm going for a swim." Not looking at her, he stumbled to the sliding glass doors and out into the night air. It was still and warm, a faint haze of steam rising from the heated pool. He fell forward in a bellyflop, gasping at the shock of water. He swam to the diving board and grasped it with shaking hands, dangling there until he got his breath back. "God, I'm out of shape," he said aloud. He ducked his head under water, swam to the other end of the pool and sat on the bottom step, the water gently lapping about his heaving chest. Unbidden, a picture of Tara came to him. Tara sitting on these same steps, leaning her head against his shoulder and giggling as they had just made love in the pool and she had wondered if the neighbors had heard their cries of passion. He could almost hear them now. Then he realized that he was indeed hearing passionate moans and sharp little gasps.

He looked toward the bedroom and saw Sandy, legs raised and spread wide as she plunged a vibrator in and out. He saw her fumble to the nightstand with one hand, then bring it back to her face and he knew that she was popping another Amie, breathing in the pear-scented fumes that would take her soaring even higher than the tab of LSD she had swallowed earlier. He turned away with disgust. Disgust for her—and with himself for being with her. He kicked off the step, plunging underwater for half the pool length, then surfaced and swam slowly to the far end, turned and swam back.

The small effort had winded him and he sat back on the steps. He would have to stop dissipating and get his act together. He had a start date of March third for his next picture and the male lead still had not been cast. This would be his first time out as a director and he knew he should be paying more attention to business and less to his personal problems, but he couldn't get Tara out of his mind. Or heart. His every attempt to contact her had been met with failure, which only made him more determined to see her. He still could not understand why she was so angry. Okay, so he had boffed her old lady, but Christ, that had been years ago. And Tara admitted to knowing that her mother had been a whore. Why then did she continue to blame him as if he had been personally responsible for the old hooker's demise? As he remembered it, Belle Woodhauser had already been well on her way down the tubes before he had met her. He tried to believe that it must have been the shock of Tara actually seeing him naked with her mother that had somehow made him despicable to her. But that really did not make any sense either. She must have seen her old lady with other "clients" over the years. Belle was not exactly what one would call discreet.

Sighing, he slipped back into the water and swam slowly about the pool, shaking the images from his mind. Clearing it to think about the picture. He should have been thrilled. After the success of *The Savage Desert* (and at Tara's urging), he had decided to try his hand at directing, something he had long dreamed of. But now, with Tara gone, he could not concentrate. He had thought often of backing out of the deal, sticking to the producing and letting his good friend, Bill Goldfeld, direct this one as he had *The Savage Desert*. But Bill was better as an "action" director, and *Love in the Morning* would be a tender love story. Something Eric had long wanted to make. He had obtained the rights to it three years before when he had read the slim paperback novella that had hardly made a stir in the publishing world. It was a bittersweet love story of a couple, married to other people, who could not, for intricate and tragic reasons of their own, divorce their respective spouses and so had to arrange their rendezvous in the morning hours.

Doe Kingston would play the female lead. She and Eric had become close friends and found that they worked exceptionally well together—now that the physical aspect of their relationship was no more. Eric knew that Doe was capable of becoming a hell of an actress, given a chance. Unfortunately she had been labeled as just another big-titted, empty-headed broad. Doe had proven her talent in *The Savage Desert*, and Eric was convinced that he could get an even better performance from her in *Love in the Morning*. His problem was the male lead. He thought of the currently reigning stars. Paul Newman, perhaps. But Eric needed a more sensitive type, an Oskar Werner that looked like Newman or Burt Lancaster but was still gentle enough to weep. Gregory Peck would be good, but Eric somehow could not see him paired with

Doe Kingston. For all the toning down he planned, Doe was still a volatile blonde bombshell and needed a strong, macho type to play against. Brando would be perfect. He had the toughness and tenderness the role called for, but his price was too staggering for Eric to even contemplate.

His thoughts were suddenly interrupted by a loud blast of rock music, and he turned to see Sandy dancing toward him. She was still nude and carried a drink in one hand, a joint in the other. She stumbled down beside him, tripped and would have toppled into the pool had he not caught her. She giggled, falling against him, thrusting the glass into his hand. "Thought you might be thirsty," she slurred, gazing blankly up into his face. Her pupils were contracted to pinpoints and her eyes were glassy, unblinking vast depths of nothingness. Eric shuddered and involuntarily drew back from her. It was like seeing a corpse —the brain dead but the body unchanged. He drank quickly, not looking at her. Eighteen years old and already burned out. He felt an annoying tug of guilt, realizing suddenly that he was contributing to her dissipation as much as anyone else in Hollywood. Had he not always had booze, grass and cocaine handy? Just tonight he had furnished the champagne to wash down the tab of LSD—which she had brought herself. Eric drew the line at taking any sort of psychedelic drugs. But he did insist on popping amyl nitrate when they were balling, because he could not get it up without that added stimulant. Not since Tara had walked out on him.

Another record dropped into place and the husky, sultry voice of Zock McBain singing *Lady Love* filled the air. Eric jumped as if someone had doused him with cold water. How the hell had that fucking album gotten into his house? Then he remembered that Sandy had brought a stack of LP's over last weekend when they had had a few friends over. He gritted his teeth against the sexy love words, the lyrics that the entire world knew had been written especially by Zock for his real-life lady love— Tara Remington. Eric had been appalled when he had first seen their names linked in one of the notorious scandal sheets. He had read, with growing astonishment, items in the trades and other Hollywood gossip columns that the hottest new twosome in town was "none other than rock genius Zock McBain and that sexy young writer Tara Remington." And *The Late Beat*'s Twosomes Around Town had this to report: "Zock McBain and Tara Remington—again!"

Eric stalked into the bedroom and switched off the stereo. He stood breathing heavily for a moment, rage causing his hands to tremble. With a terrible cry he snatched the record off the turntable and flung it through the door. But instead of smashing into a thousand pieces on the flagstones as he had hoped, it sailed gently into the pool and floated there. Sandy stared up at him with blank curiosity. She laughed and clapped her hands together.

"Hey, man, that was super! Can I try?" She giggled. Looked at the record floating in the pool, at Eric standing with clenched fists by the door. "What are we playing, anyways? Huh, baby?"

Eric walked the length of his office, glancing absently at the book-lined walls, the teak desk the size of a pool table flanked on both sides by gold crushed-velvet easy chairs. A chocolate brown leather sofa that could easily seat a dozen people stood in front of the desk and the carpet was a warm honey, rich and luxurious. Eric stopped pacing and stood staring down at the letter in his hands. *The Savage Desert* had been nominated for Best Picture of the Year; Doe Kingston for Best Actress. He read it again, elation building as the message finally penetrated. My God! He was up for an Oscar! He reached for the onyx-ivory telephone and pushed a mother-of-pearl button on the intercom, ready to instruct his secretary to get Tara on the phone when he remembered. And silently replaced the receiver. It rang almost immediately and he heard Doe's excited voice squealing and congratulating both Eric and herself on the nominations.

The rest of the day was a madhouse of congratulatory calls and telegrams. But the one call that Eric waited for never came. He knew he was a fool to even hope she would call. But he had hoped just the same.

The next two months, Eric devoted every moment to getting his act together. He was the first one at the studio and worked through the day, leaving long after the last secretary and writer had departed. Once home, he worked out in his gym, spending an hour in the sauna sweating out the poisons his body had absorbed the past few months. He stopped drinking, lost ten pounds and went to bed alone. He hired Thorton Kennedy and together they mapped out a publicity campaign for *The Savage Desert,* taking out ads in the *Hollywood Reporter, Variety* and the *Los Angeles Times.* Doe cooperated beautifully, making the rounds of the talk shows, and at least twice a week one network or another ran a film clip of Eric's movie. And still Tara had not called. At first he had been hurt. It was as much her success as his. She had been involved from the first, sharing his problems, listening to his ideas, contributing her own. Then he became angry. Cunt, he thought, doesn't even have the common courtesy to drop a guy a fucking telegram, to even acknowledge that he's up for the highest award in show business. So he doubled his efforts, spent enormous sums of money on advertising, literally deluging the media with publicity for *The Savage Desert.*

So engrossed was Eric in proving himself to Tara that it was not until a couple of weeks before the Awards that he discovered that Zock McBain had also been nominated for an Oscar. Zock had written the lyrics and sang the title song of an independent European entry, *Ashes,* a hauntingly lovely, slick little thriller that scored with the critics but bombed at the box office. Zock's recording of *Ashes,* however, had zoomed to the top of the charts and remained there for weeks. Ironically, Thorton Kennedy was also handling Zock's publicity for his try at the devoutly coveted gold statuette. But if Eric had been oblivious of that fact, the press had not. Gleefully they rehashed the entire love affair of Eric and Tara, the Golden Couple of '72 and '73; Tara, the young beauty who had snagged Tinseltown's most eligible bachelor away from the reigning sex symbol, Doe Kingston; enter rock star, Zock McBain who steals sexy writer away from genius producer, who eases his broken heart with precocious teeny-bopper Sandra Sinclair, but who is once again paired with sultry Miss Kingston—both on the set and off! With three of these talented, highly volatile stars in the race for Oscars, it was simply too juicy to pass up.

It was true that Eric and Doe had been together often since the start of *Love in the Morning,* but as friend and partner—not lovers as the press would have it. They both worked long hours and would often meet for a late supper at Stefanino's or one of the other "in" eateries on the Strip. When, on the eve of the Academy Awards, they both found themselves without dates they had decided to go together.

Oscar night. Eric gripped Doe's elbow as he guided her through the tight throng of reporters and photographers. They both smiled bravely as flashbulbs exploded in their faces and screaming, waving fans lunged against the restraining velvet ropes, chorusing Doe's name. Impassive guards stood at the ready lest they become too anxious to touch their idols and trample them to death instead. Army Archerd stopped them as they reached the door and asked Doe what she thought her chances were of winning. Doe dropped the red fox stole off her creamy shoulders, revealing a pearl-pink strapless gown that plunged to a deep V between her famous breasts and the crowd went wild. She threw them a kiss, leaning slightly forward so one and all could feast their eyes upon her gorgeous cleavage.

"Really, darling," she chastised Army in her most seductive tones. "You *know* it's bad luck to speculate on Oscar night." She dazzled him and the crowd with her famous smile, the lips wet and inviting. "But I will say that I'm simply thrilled at being nominated." She giggled prettily. "Oh, I'm just so excited I've forgotten who else is up!" She kissed his cheek. Waved to the crowd. "Wish me luck, sweetie!" Another kiss blown to the screaming fans and she turned and swept inside, Eric on her arm.

An enormous roar went up behind them and Eric turned to see Zock McBain stepping out of a gleaming white Bentley. The crowd became hysterical, grabbing the air even before he straightened up, reaching out for him, straining the velvet ropes to their limit, greedy to touch a part of him. Any part. Anything to have that one moment's contact with Greatness. Zock paused a moment and the lights and flashbulbs reflected off his sequin-studded white tuxedo, turning him into a gloriously, dazzlingly brilliant god. He held out his hand, and a slim bejeweled hand from within the Bentley took it and Tara stepped out into the limelight. She too was dressed in white, a diamond tiara glittering in her auburn hair. She was every bit as dazzling as Zock McBain. Every inch the Queen befitting the King of Rock. She raised her head, shrugged back the floor-length white mink cape and stepped majestically onto the red carpet.

Eric turned away as they started toward the entrance and the roar of the fans doubled, if that was possible, growing to a deafening roar that threatened to lift the roof off. Spotlights and flashbulbs arced off them, seeming to set them gloriously aflame. Clenching his teeth to keep his smile in place, Eric nodded hellos and thank yous to other nominees, friends and associates.

Later Eric would remember the Academy Awards as passing in a sort of hazy montage of color and sound. *The Savage Desert* had been wiped out in spite of his extravagant advertising. But Eric's worst moment came when Zock's name was announced for Best Song and he had scooped Tara up for a lusty kiss before running up the aisle to claim his prize.

Eric and Doe had moved with the rest of the crowd to the Beverly Hills Hotel for a party in one of the exclusive banquet rooms, their Rolls-Royces, Masaratis, Bentleys, Ferraris and Mercedes queuing through the streets like a funeral procession. And for some occupants of these luxurious automobiles, it was a sort of funeral if they had been a loser and had bet their next picture on the success of this year's picture. Eric had gone immediately to the bar, where he had downed several Jack Daniels before rejoining Doe at their table. By the time the familiar roast beef au jus had arrived, he was finally feeling numb —a condition he had longed for since losing the Oscar.

Doe was drowning her rejection in a bottle of Mumms champagne and an assortment of dance partners. She was out there now, pressed close against the broad chest of some cowboy television star. Eric didn't bother to notice which one. They all looked alike to him. Just as the detectives, doctors and cops all looked alike in television-land.

It was well after midnight before he spotted Tara. He was dancing methodically with a twittering starlet who was practically dry-humping him on the floor when he glanced up and saw the glittering sequins of Zock's tuxedo. Tara's head rested on his resplendent shoulder, her diamond tiara sending out a phosphorescence of its own. Her eyes were closed, the long lashes resting on cheeks that seemed brushed with gold dust. A tightness gripped Eric's heart and he maneuvered the starlet through an opening in the crowd until he was a yard away from Tara. He was not sure if he had spoken her name aloud or if she had heard the wild pounding of his heart, but she slowly opened her eyes and looked directly into his.

"Hello, Eric," she said softly, calmly. "I'm sorry about the Oscar." Zock turned, saw Eric and grinned triumphantly, waving his gold statuette.

"Yeah—how about that?" Eric mumbled. "Congratulations." He sought Tara's eyes again but Zock had turned her and was moving away through the crowd, accepting handshakes, backslaps, hugs—the accolades that Eric had seen himself receiving. He left the starlet standing in the middle of the dance floor and went looking for the bar.

An hour later Eric was still at the bar, slumped on a stool watching the thinning crowd posing one last time for the insatiable photographers. Doe had long since departed with a young actor a dozen years her junior, and Eric was deciding where to go next. He had been invited to several intimate "house" parties, but none had appealed to him. There would be the "A" crowd, mobbed with winners proudly flourishing their Oscars, a lesser "A" group of losers valiantly cheering up one another, and the younger stars, the pot-smoking, coke-snorting crowd who jeered at the meaning of an Oscar even as they clutched tightly the ones they had just won.

"Hey, Marlowe, you trying to drink the place dry?" Jerry Schaffer, a young director whom Eric knew only casually, slid onto the stool next to him and stuck out his hand. "Sorry as hell about the Oscar, man, you deserved it. *The Savage Desert* was one hell of a picture."

"My sentiments exactly," Eric said, although he really had no idea what Schaffer was talking about. He had reached that numb stage where people and sound seemed to be coming at him from another dimension. However, he was aware of the bright, happy chatter flowing from this young man, the lavish praise for Eric's talent and wisely concluded that this meant Schaffer was a friend to be trusted. Therefore he threw his arm about the young director's shoulder and thanked him profusely for having the exquisite taste to recognize a truly magnificent film when he saw one.

He turned to order a drink for his new best friend and found that the bar was closed. Dismayed, he asked, "Whadda we do now?"

Schaffer replied, "Never fear—I know of a groovy private party just up the hill—come on."

Shaking his head with wry amusement, the parking boy stood patiently holding the door of Eric's Caddie while he and Jerry argued who was sober enough to drive. Jerry won and they tumbled giggling into the car and were off with a squeal of tires, winding up the sharp curves of Benedict Canyon.

The house was a mansion. Tudor style and intimidatingly large, it spread over the entire hilltop, its myriad of lights spilling in beneficence upon everything below. Eric and Jerry were drawn into the room by a throbbing,

pulsating mob of merry makers who greeted them as if
they had actually been invited. A joint was pressed into
Eric's hand before he had taken three steps and a
pretty young man wearing mascara and lip gloss brushed
suggestively against his crotch in passing. A stoned actress whom Eric had seen at other such parties ground
her pelvis against his and whispered that she gave the
best head in town. Another actress, equally stoned, pulled
him away and offered to take him to the powder room for
a snort of some real high-grade cocaine. In this fashion
they stumbled through the crowd and found leaning space
at the bar in the billiard room.

Eric ordered a whiskey and stood people-watching for
a while. The room was so dark it was difficult to make
anyone out unless they passed within a short distance of
him. He became aware of shadowy forms moving languidly in the darkened corners, occasionally emitting small
passionate moans. He felt a rush of heat in his groin
and realized, with something of a start, that he hadn't
been laid in weeks. He had poured all his energies into
the Oscar race and hadn't even thought about sex until
now. He thought he should have asked Doe to stay the
rest of the evening with him, but even as he formed the
thought, he rejected it. Doe wasn't who he wanted and
sex wasn't what he needed. He tossed off the rest of his
drink and pushed his glass across the bar for a refill. As
he turned back toward the pool table, illuminated in a circle of light from the Tiffany lamp above, he saw a bright
flash of sequins as Zock McBain leaned over to take his
shot.

Eric's breath caught in his throat and he would have
gagged on the whiskey had he not hurriedly spat it back
into his glass. He wiped a shaking hand across his mouth
as he peered into the dimness and his heart began beating
like a triphammer. He saw a glimmer of white silk, a
subtle flash of her diamond tiara as she turned her head
and smiled at someone standing next to her. A candle sitting on the table next to her highlighted her face, bringing
into detail every familiar, beloved curve and angle. He sat
stone still, staring at her as she moved and spoke and

laughed and sipped her champagne. A million thoughts raced through his mind. Should he approach her? What should he say? How would she react? He gulped down his whiskey and ordered another, still not making a move toward her. He shrank back in the darkness of the corner bar stool and watched, feeling like a peeping tom when Zock bent over Tara and whispered something in her ear. He kissed her briefly and disappeared into the darkness of the living room. Eric saw Tara's expression tighten and she pushed through the crowd and out through the door leading onto the patio. Eric looked after her for a moment, then tossed off his drink and followed.

She was already well down the path, walking fast, and Eric hurried to catch up with her. The path wound enticingly through clumps of lush foliage and sweet-smelling flowers toward a magnificently landscaped lawn that stretched for at least an acre and was bordered on all sides by towering eucalyptus trees. A white latticed gazebo set far out in the center of the lawn and a man-made waterfall tinkled delicately as it cascaded over exotic shells and splashed into a miniature tropical pool. Tara paused a moment, listening to the waterfall, then moved into the gazebo and sat down upon a chaise longue. She stretched out her legs and leaned back, closing her eyes.

Silently Eric moved closer until he was standing only a few feet from her. He gazed down at her face, in repose now and looking more lovely than he remembered. Her lips were slightly parted and her long lashes lay like spread fans upon her cheeks. He remembered the hundreds of times he had seen her like this; sleeping next to him in the mornings, falling asleep on Sunday afternoons while he watched a football game on television. God, how he loved her! He took a step forward and she opened her eyes and half-sat up on the chaise, calling, "Who's there?"

"It's me—Eric." He stepped into view, cautiously, lest she bolt like the frightened fawn she now resembled. "Don't go, Tara, please. I have to talk to you!"

She sat up fully and tucked her legs under her, pulling her skirt primly down around them. "There's nothing to talk about, Eric. I'm finally over it now and I don't want to be reminded of it all over again."

"Reminded of what?" Eric cried. "Reminded of how much in love we were? Reminded of the fantastic times we had together? The beautiful things we did together?" He rushed to her and sank to his knees by the chaise, taking her hands in his. Losing all restraint, he bent his head and began kissing her hands wildly. He had to get her back. Had to make her understand how much he loved her. Needed her. He pressed his head to her breasts and sobbed hoarsely, "Tara, please forgive me, I love you— god, how I love you! Please—please—" She took his head gently between her hands and stroked his hair back from his forehead. Tears stung his eyes and he buried his face against her softness, giving himself up to the rhythmical caressing.

"Don't, Eric, please don't say anything more." She dropped her arms to her sides and sat perfectly still while he wept against her breasts. He hugged her close in that bone-crushing embrace that she remembered so well and she almost weakened and raised her arms to hold him.

Instead, roughly, she said, "No, it's too late, Eric."

He raised his eyes and looked up into her face. "No," he said firmly, shaking his head. "No, it's not too late. It's not. We still love each other. You must still love me, Tara, you couldn't have stopped—just like that! We were too good together, too perfect not to always be together. You know how it used to be with us, darling—remember? Tell me you still love me!" He was talking wildly, not willing to believe that she would not even give him a hearing.

"Stop it, Eric!" she cried and tried to pull away, but he tightened his grip on her hands, pulling her closer.

"Then tell me you don't love me! Say it!" He took both her wrists in one hand and slipped his other hand around her, holding her tight to his chest. "Remember how you used to beg me to fuck you, Tara? Remember?" His face was very close to hers, her struggling body pressed hard against his crotch and he felt himself getting an erection. He pressed it against her, his heart pounding with excite-

131

ment. "God, see what you do to me, baby? Remember all the times we made love? How can you forget something that beautiful?" He leaned forward and kissed her, forcing her mouth open with his tongue. She jerked back, turning her head away.

"Stop it, Eric, God damn it, I mean it!" She struggled furiously, futilely beneath him, his weight holding her securely down. "Damn it, I'm getting mad, Eric, you'd better let me up!" He laughed at her anger and she tried to knee him in the groin. He flattened her with a leg, moving it roughly down to spread her thighs. "You bastard, I said let me up this minute!" she screamed and he kissed her again, cutting off her words. She managed to free one hand and took a swing at him, but he effortlessly captured it again and this time held a wrist in each hand so that she was spread eagled on the chaise. He lowered his full weight upon her, shoving his erection hard into her stomach.

"All I want you to do is admit how good it was between us," he said softly, the wild edge gone from his voice. He gazed down at her with such love that he felt tears coming again to his eyes. She turned her face away. "Tara, it can't be over between us. Give it another try. Please, darling, just try it for a while. For me. For us. We'll go away someplace and talk everything out." He kissed her softly, and she jerked her mouth away with a sob.

"Don't, God damn you! How dare you kiss me, you—you—" She jerked against his hands but he held her fast, slamming her back against the chaise.

Sudden anger flared in Eric's eyes, turning them icy cold, and he growled, "Why, you little cunt! Don't try to pull that virgin act on me again. I fell for it once, remember?" His hands gripped her wrists so hard she thought she would faint from the pain and his knee pressed sharply into her soft belly. "Hell, everybody in the industry knows that you're Zock McBain's whore!" He snatched the diamond tiara from her head and she cried out as a handful of hair went with it. "Don't tell me Glasser is paying you enough to buy trinkets like this!"

He flung it into the bushes and took a handful of her white silk gown and ripped it to the waist, exposing her naked breasts. He began kissing them hard, wanting to hurt her. He sucked at her nipples until she moaned in pain, and he raised himself and tore her gown all the way off. He tangled his fist in the elastic band of her pantyhose and ripped them from her body. "I'm gonna fuck you, Tara. Might as well lay back and enjoy it." He held her down with his knees on her arms as he unzipped his pants and shoved them down. He removed his tuxedo jacket and unbuttoned the ruffle-fronted white shirt.

Tara lay staring at him in fascination. She couldn't believe that he actually meant to rape her! "Eric, that's enough now," she said as calmly as she could. "Let me up, please."

"Nope." He took off his shirt and let it drop to the floor.

"Eric, this is crazy, come on now, let me up." She struggled a little against him, but he did not give an inch. She was totally helpless beneath him and her arms were beginning to ache and throb. "Eric, please, you're hurting my arms." Her voice rose on a faint note of fear. What if he was not kidding? What if he really meant to rape her? No, of course he would not dare!

"Darling, I wouldn't hurt you for the world," he said softly and removed his knees from her arms. He held her hands tightly in his, still not releasing her.

"Then let me go, please. This isn't going to prove anything. Just that you're physically stronger than me." She tried to raise herself but he pushed her back down and kissed her, pulling her arms above her head. He moved his knee down and nudged her thighs apart, forcing them when she tried to resist him.

He removed his mouth from hers and murmured, "God, you're so beautiful, Tara—just the touch of you drives me crazy—such incredibly soft skin . . ."

He held both her wrists in one hand and traced the outline of her nipples with the other, bending to kiss each one. His lips moved down, licking and nibbling at her

133

navel, and she twisted her body away and cried, "No! Don't!"

"Yes, by God, I will!" Eric gritted savagely. "If you can let that fucking asshole junkie stick it in your precious little pussy, then by God I can too!" He ran his hand roughly down her flat belly, between her resisting thighs. She tried to squeeze them together, then gasped aloud when he shoved one finger deep inside her. He began moving it back and forth, and she moaned and tried to pull away from the steady pressure. "I know what you like, baby," he whispered huskily. His hand moved with deep, hard thrusts and he felt her body began to arch up to meet it, to move with the erotic sensation. "Does he do it for you this way, baby, huh? The way you like it—a long, long time before I give you my cock—playing with your pretty pussy—" His warm breath tingled in her ear, sending shivers through her body, and she quivered helplessly against his hand, responding in spite of herself.

Eric stared down at her writhing body. Never had a woman been more beautiful to him. Even in her anger and indignation she was so sensual, so tempting and inviting. "God, Tara," he groaned and jerked forward, releasing her wrists and fumbling in his eagerness to be inside her. Then quickly, urgently, he was filling her and whispering her name, striving to become a part of her.

"Eric—" She pushed against his chest, then collapsed with a sigh, wrapping her arms about him. She raised her legs and crossed them around his waist, urging him closer still. The waterfall in the background rose to a deafening roar in her brain and she clung to him, whispering his name, hearing him whisper hers, their bodies greeting one another with an old familiar intimacy that was somehow sweetest of all.

Eric felt as if his chest would explode when she opened herself up to him and pulled him closer. His mind soared with wonder of how much more fantastic sex was when you were in love. He would love Tara always. Just as she would always love him. They were meant to be together always. His mind vacillated with the rhythmic movements of their bodies and he floated breathlessly for what seemed a long time. Then his urgent physical need blocked out all thoughts and he yelled aloud in painful joy as he climaxed.

They lay quietly for several moments until their breathing became normal, then Eric rolled off her and pulled her into the curve of his body, her back against his chest. He cupped her breasts in his hands, held them gently, kissed the nape of her neck. She sighed and moved more comfortably against him, and he was amazed anew at how perfectly they fitted. He wanted to tell her that. Wanted to pour out his love to her. Tell her how much he adored her and always would. How he would do anything in the world for her. They were a matched set. You could not break up a perfectly matched set like that. He smiled to himself, not wanting to break the spell of contentment. She lay so peacefully in his arms, when a moment before she had exploded with wild abandon, her passion more than matching his own. He wanted to tell her so many things but he was so damn tired from all the booze he had drunk. That, and the pressure of the Oscar. His eyelids were so heavy he could barely keep them open. He let them close briefly, just for a moment, thinking, I'll tell her everything in a minute—just have to rest for a second . . .

When he awoke, sometime in the early morning hours with the sun blazing into his face, she was gone.

CHAPTER SEVEN

STRONG FINGERS kneaded her back, palms pressing in hard as Tara lay face down on the table. The masseur was Danish, male, efficient, with talented hands and the torso of a Mr. Universe. This, coupled with his undeniable sex appeal and charming discretion, had quickly made him a much sought after young Dane—as well as an expensive one. He appeared at the mansion in Holmby Hills each morning exactly at ten o'clock to give the young and beautiful Mrs. McBain her massage—and the young and beautiful Mrs. McBain would sigh blissfully, wondering how she had ever lived without him. His big, strong hands slid expertly over her body, spreading creamy lotion into her skin as he loosened and toned her muscles.

"Umm, that's fantastic, Palle," Tara murmured. She grunted as he pressed in hard on the small of her back, released, pressed again.

"The pleasure is mine, Mrs. McBain," Palle replied in his soft accent, with just the proper inflection of intimacy in his voice. His many years as private masseur to the rich and famous had taught him one very valuable lesson: always let the lady make the first move. And they usually did, sooner or later, these deliciously horny lovely rich ladies who were bored to distraction. They soon found that Palle could be a rather exciting and stimulating distraction on an otherwise mundane afternoon.

Mrs. McBain, Tara repeated to herself. She still was not sure how it had happened so quickly. Not that she minded all that much. It was a gas to be so fabulously rich that she could buy anything she wanted, go any-place she chose, do anything that turned her on. Her head still spun with the suddenness of it all, Zock's happiness when she had finally said "Yes," her dizziness when he had swung her around and around until she thought she was going to throw up. It had been the morning after that dreadful Academy Awards party and she had been hung over and feeling miserable about her encounter with Eric.

Tara squirmed on the table, pressing her mound briefly against the hard plastic and experienced a swift thrill of pleasure. Palle's hands squeezed knowingly and slipped down to stroke her inner thighs, the tips of his fingers barely brushing her pubic hair. Just the slightest pressure but enough to further heighten the thought of Eric. It would never have happened if she had not had so much champagne to drink and grass to smoke, and if she had not been so angry with Zock. She had been dead tired and more upset than she cared to admit that Eric had not won the Oscar. She had wanted to go home but Zock had insisted on stopping by "just one more party," and when they had arrived he had met an old acquaintance who just happened to have the best coke in town. Which just happened to be for sale. When the two of them had left together, leaving Tara in the billiard room while they went to make the score, she had been furious. Her first impulse had been to get out of that godawful, loud party and she had fled to the sanctuary of the gazebo to decide what she should do. She knew that Zock had ex-pected her to wait patiently like a good little girl but she felt like walking out then and there. She had been lying quietly on the chaise in the gazebo, listening to the musical splashing of the little waterfall when she had looked up to see Eric standing over her. Her first thought had been: *God, he's still as gorgeous as ever!* and her heart had beat quickly with excitement. But when he had fallen drunk-enly at her feet, sobbing apologies, she had coldly held

herself back from him. It was not until he had gotten
angry and started caressing her with such violent lust
that she had finally surrendered, no longer able to deny
how much she still desired him. How much she still loved
him.

The next morning Tara had met Zock at the Beverly
Hills Hotel for a press party given in honor of the Oscar
winners. After being questioned and photographed steadily for twenty minutes, Zock and Tara managed to escape
into the Polo Lounge for brunch and Zock had laughingly said, "Are you sure you won't change your mind
and marry me now that I'm a big-time Oscar winner?"
And Tara had surprised herself almost as much as Zock
when she had answered flippantly, "Sure, why not? It's
been a rather slow week." He had let out a whoop of joy
and picked her up, swinging her around in front of the
entire room of diners, laughing, "I knew I'd finally wear
you down!" It was true that he had asked her to marry
him numerous times almost from the first date, swearing that he would eventually convince her what a charming fellow and great catch he was. Of course, she had not
really taken him seriously and therefore had been stunned
when he had welcomed her acceptance with such en-
thusiasm. He had agreed so quickly, in fact, that Tara
had not fully realized she was engaged until three hours
later when they went aboard his Lear jet heading for Las
Vegas.

Zock's social secretary cajoled (and overpaid) a local
printer into getting out, overnight, three hundred engraved
invitations. Every one of them were acknowledged with
the swiftness of a summons to the White House. Every one
of them accepted with pleasure. Zock took over the entire top floor of The Sands Hotel and instructed his staff
of secretaries, managers and go-fers to arrange for an
orchestra, caterers and florists. A doctor was hastily admitted to administer blood tests and a small squad of
dressmakers swiftly measured, nipped, tucked and pinned
Tara into an elegant white satin wedding gown. Zock's
road manager (glorified pimp and go-fer, Tara called him)
Stanley Mann, had been instructed to hire a fleet of

limousines to meet the guests at the airport and drive them to the various hotels where rooms awaited them, reserved with the compliments of their host, Zock McBain. Stan had also arranged for police barricades to keep back the fans that were sure to swamp the hotel once they discovered that the King of Rock was getting married.

It had taken a mere three days to arrange everything, and then Tara had found herself standing in front of a minister saying "I do." They had spent a week in the bridal suite of The Sands, partying all night (with the aid of the little cocaine-filled vial that Zock kept with him at all times) and slept until late afternoon, when it would begin all over again. It seemed to Tara that every second of every day was filled with a constant buzz of noise, shouting voices, roulette wheels spinning, lights flashing and blinking, the shrill clang of a slot machine paying off. They stood in long rows, one after another, greedily gulping down any coin from a nickel to a silver dollar. And they were fed regularly. Young kids just turned twenty-one and wanting to try their luck against the machines; housewives and grandmothers in broken-in slippers clutching paper cups in their hands; tired-looking hookers mechanically pulling the handle of a dime machine while their gaze sweeps the room for a likely john. In the main room one could actually feel the electric charge in the air, the thrill of being close to the Big Spenders who lost and won fortunes on the black-jack and crap tables in a matter of minutes—the turn of a card, the roll of the dice.

Their wedding had been as garish, boisterous and flamboyant as Las Vegas itself. It had been held in the main show room, where Zock had just recently wowed record-breaking crowds night after night. Three hundred "intimate friends" packed the room, while almost that number of waiters, bartenders, caterers, busboys, cigarette girls, photographers, reporters and party-crashers shoved for their own bit of space.

The reception was outrageous. Numerous tables were laden with every delicacy known to man: live lobsters

flown in from Maine; escargots from Paris; a whole suckling pig complete with apple and grapes in the proper ori-
fices; cases of Dom Perignon; tubs of caviar; massive silver
trays piled high with silver-dollar-size breads, pumper-
nickel, rye, sourdough, wheat, french; an assortment of
cold cuts that would be the envy of any New York deli;
and in the center of this ambrosia a towering wedding
cake topped with sugar images of Zock and Tara.

Tara had drifted through it all as if it were happening
to someone else. She feared that she had been perma-
nently blinded by the hundreds of flashbulbs that had exploded in her face and thereafter had witnessed the rest
of the festivities through polka-dot vision. She had not
been aware of actually leaving the reception because
most of the guests had left with them. At least fifty of
Zock's "best buddies" and their ladies had laughingly
followed them to the bridal suite, where more champagne
was waiting and the party continued for another couple of
hours.

Then, suddenly, they were gone and she and Zock were
alone. Her head cleared at once and every nerve ending
came instantly alive. She was married. She looked at
Zock sprawled on the sofa, eyes bloodshot and glazed,
sensual mouth lax with drugs and alcohol, and she wondered what had ever possessed her. To get back at Eric?
Or to be safe from him? Was she frightened that a repeat performance of that night in the gazebo could easily
happen again? But not if she was a safely married woman?
She found cigarettes and a lighter on the littered buffet
table and lit one as she walked toward her husband. She
was nervous and a little excited too. That all too brief
encounter with Eric in the gazebo had aroused desires
she had thought were long dead. Even though she had
been dating Zock for three months, they had yet to be
intimate. Not that the rock star had not tried—and tried
again. But Tara had not felt sexually attracted to him and
therefore would not go to bed with him. Now, after that
night with Eric, she had been tortured with the most
erotic dreams and fantasies, her young, healthy body
remembering all the good loving she had gotten on a

steady basis for the past three years—and longed for again.

"Zock," she whispered, leaning over to kiss his ear. "Are you asleep?"

"On my wedding night? No way, baby!" He struggled into a sitting position, reached into his pocket and withdrew the vial and spoon. "Just let me get straight here," he grinned as he snorted in the white powder. He offered it to Tara but she shook her head. "Aw, come on, baby," he urged, scooping up a generous portion into the silver spoon and holding it toward her. "Get high with me." Dutifully, she sniffed in and immediately felt the rush, the sensation of heat flooding her veins—the subtle snap of brain cells that would never again function as they once had—but for this split second they fired Tara with their dying energy. Zock rubbed some cocaine on Tara's gums and instantly she felt the freeze, the sudden numbness that tingled through her mouth like an overdose of Novocain. He kissed her hard, opening her mouth with his tongue, and hers felt thick and numb when he sucked at it. Sighing, she opened her mouth wider, drew him close and rubbed her nipples back and forth against his chest. She liked kissing him. Liked the lazy feeling she got when he worked over every inch of her body with hands and lips. Even though she had never been turned on enough to actually have intercourse with him, she did enjoy thoroughly necking with him. She had never allowed him more than a few titillating caresses, an almost innocent suckling at her breasts and an occasional lingering stroking of her downy pubic mound— and she had allowed him to talk her into watching him masturbate on rare, stoned nights. Now all the juices were flowing again, set free by Eric's wild lovemaking on the night of the Oscars.

"Umm, darling," she murmured huskily against his mouth. "Let's go to bed."

Zock pulled back, surprised, not quite believing he had heard her correctly. He had waited so long to hear those words from her. To see that dreamy, sensual expression on her face. "I thought you'd never ask," he said lightly, but his voice cracked with emotion when he whispered, "Oh, baby, God how I love you!" And he gathered her close, kissing her deeply.

They stood together; mouths still locked, and swayed drunkenly across the room. Bumping into a coffee table they broke apart, giggling, and he scooped her up into his arms and carried her into the bedroom. He pressed a button on the intercom and soft romantic music filled the room. Reaching for another button, he said, "Close your eyes" and set her feet upon the floor. He pressed a button and peach-colored lights on either side of the king-size bed came on and the tiny bulbs in the overhead chandelier dimmed accordingly. Taking her by the shoulders, he turned her toward the bed. "Okay, you can open them now."

"Oh, Zock," she breathed, genuinely moved by the scene before her. The bedspread was a rich, luxurious chinchilla, the same one she had admired a couple of weeks ago when she and Zock had been out shopping together, and spread on top of it was a lovely white Gorringe nightgown. A white velvet jeweler's box, oblong in shape, lay next to the gown and a silver ice bucket holding a chilled bottle of Dom Perignon stood on a handsome bed tray with two rose-shaped crystal wine goblets. He handed her the velvet box, opening it for her, and she gasped in awe at the magnificent diamond pendant.

"To match your ring," he said blithely, but she could hear the pleased note in his voice and went into his arms and hugged him tight.

"Thank you, darling, it's beautiful. Put it on for me." She turned, holding up her hair in the back as he clasped it about her slim throat. The large marquise diamond hung down between her breasts and she raised her left hand, comparing the size of the gems.

"Both twelve carats," he said with a grin. "That makes exactly twenty-four carats in all."

Matching his bantering tone, she said, "Or twelve of one, two dozen of the other?" She kissed him tenderly. "I love it, Zock, and I love the ring and the gown and the bedspread and—and everything. Thank you, darling.

Now why don't you pour the champagne while I slip into this gorgeous Gorringe."

He watched her disappear into the bathroom, then took the Dom Perignon and expertly popped the cork. The cocaine was swirling through his bloodstream, flooding him with waves of excitement, wild anticipation. God, he had waited so long for this night! He would finally see her naked, finally sink his cock into her soft cunt. And just knowing it had kept him in a state of semi-erection all day and evening. He reached down to rub his crotch, readjusting his swollen penis in the tight pants. Quickly he took a couple hits of coke, then shucked off his tuxedo and got into bed. He set the glasses of champagne carefully on the bed tray and put out a box of joints, a lighter. He sipped nervously at the wine, glancing about the bed to make sure he had not forgotten anything. He uncorked the vial of coke and set it on the bedside table next to a tin of amyl nitrate. He leaned over, checking to make sure the vibrator was plugged in and still under his pillow where he had placed it earlier. He finished the champagne in one swallow and refilled his glass, looking toward the bathroom. Any moment now she would walk through that door and into his arms. As she had done a thousand times in his fantasies. He reached beneath the silken sheet to grip and stroke his penis, feeling a fleeting stab of pain.

As much as he loved her, there had been times when Zock had hated Tara passionately for the agony she had put him through, the degradation. Three months of mental and physical torture. No matter how much he had pleaded and swore undying love for her, their evenings together inevitably ended the same way; she would neck with him until he was dizzy with desire, his cock throbbing painfully against his zippered trousers; let him suck and kiss her wonderful breasts; and sometimes even let him sink the tip of one finger into her moist, furry box— and when he thought he would go mad unless he fucked her, she would push him away. Firmly. Positively. No half-ways. No deals. ("Please, just let me put the head

144

in." "I promise I won't come inside you . . ." "Just let me eat you a little bit . . .")

Zock had developed prostate trouble and had had to undergo humiliating trips to his doctor for those little massages that were guaranteed to cure the problem. Christ, Zock had felt like he should have kissed the bastard when it was over instead of paying him. The doc gave good hand.

The bathroom door opened and Tara stood framed in the doorway, her body sharply outlined in the transparent gown. Soft white folds floated dreamily behind her as she walked toward him. High, firm breasts jiggled delightfully beneath the gown, nipples jutting, the light dusky-rose aureole muted by the sheer fabric. The huge diamond flashed and winked between her breasts as she leaned over to kiss him.

"Hi, Mrs. McBain," he said huskily and pulled her into bed and against his pounding heart.

"Hello, Mr. McBain," she murmured, snuggling against him. She took the glass of champagne and they clicked rims. "To us," they said as one.

They drained their glasses and let them fall to the floor, reaching simultaneously for one another. Tara drew him close to her breasts and wrapped a leg about his waist, squirming closer until their crotches were interlocked. Her mouth sought his in a lingering kiss that grew hotter and harder as she writhed against him. Thoughts of Eric flashed through her brain, tantalizing her, increasing her passion until she was actually panting against Zock's mouth. But it was Eric's name that repeated itself inside her head and Eric's body she felt pressed to hers. She rolled over onto her back, pulling Zock on top of her, scissoring her legs about him, murmuring, "Umm, love me, darling—love me—" She arched her body, trembling, ready. She wanted to feel him hard and impatient against her as Eric had been. Wanted to feel his kisses bruising her mouth. His fingers tangled painfully in her hair.

"Tara—Tara," Zock groaned, crushing her to him and burying her face against his chest. He felt her violent quivering, the heat from her body, and he gritted his teeth in agonizing shame. He drew his lower body a little away from her, not wanting her to feel his limp penis. What the hell was the matter with him? He had thought of nothing else for three months. Had gone through the entire wedding and reception with a hard-on just anticipating this moment. Now that it was here he could not even get it up! He was so damn hot he felt he would explode from sheer frustration. Just touching her skin sent shivers burning down his spine. God, he wanted her more than anything in the world. But he could not consummate his love for her.

He drew away, propped himself up on an elbow and gazed down at her. She lay on her back, long dark hair spread upon the pillow in wild disarray. The sheer white gown was tangled about her hips, the straps falling enticingly off her shoulders, exposing her heaving breasts. Her eyes were stormy-green with passion. Softly, she asked, "What is it?"

"I don't know." He stared as if hypnotized at the huge diamond trapped between her cleavage, sending off sparks of brilliance. She was so beautiful and sexy. So sensual. And she was his. More than anything in the world he wanted to prove that to her—and to himself. He fumbled to the nightstand and scooped up a couple of hits of cocaine, keeping his back to her. Shaking a little of the white powder into the palm of his hand, he applied it to the head of his penis.

"Let me help, darling," she whispered huskily, leaning forward to take the vial from his hand. She pressed him back to the pillows. "Just relax, sweetie, lie back and close your eyes." Her voice was a throaty purr, caressing his senses, and he obeyed. He felt her strong fingers manipulate him for long minutes, then she took him into her mouth, hands still moving about the base. Sliding firmly up and down. Lips nibbling. He felt himself begin to respond, tremble just a little inside her hot, wet mouth. He pressed closer. Held his breath. Her lips and fingers devoured him. It was growing harder, the blood coursing so swiftly it made him light-headed. He expelled his held breath with a cry and crushed her to him, plunging deep, hard—coming immediately. Violent spasms racked his body and he slipped out of her, already limp, drained.

She held him on top of her, not letting him move off even when he tried. "Shh," she whispered, holding him tenderly. "It's all right. Just relax, okay? Lay your head on my shoulder. There." She held him, murmuring softly, and he buried his face in her throat, burning with shame. "There's always tomorrow, darling, please don't feel badly. It's been a hectic week for both of us—everything happening so fast. Just relax, sweetie."

"I love you," he mumbled. Too humiliated to look at her, he kept his face hidden in her hair. The one woman he had wanted more than any other and he had blown it. Zock the Cock couldn't get it up on his wedding night. He was mortified, expecting her to break out laughing at any moment. Or worse, sneer at him for his immature ejaculation. "I love you so much," he said again, arms creeping up to hold her tight. "Please don't ever leave me, baby, promise!" He kissed her throat, breasts and lips, clinging to her. "Forgive me, please forgive me, my beautiful baby—my wife. I love you! I love you!" He fell to kissing her again, keeping his eyes closed so that he would not have to meet hers. Trying to tell her with the intensity of his caresses how much he desired her. He moved upon her, pressing impotently against her—and cursed his disloyal body for the traitor that it was. "I'll always love you, Tara, always. You're so fucking beautiful. Tell me you love me, please tell me!"

But Tara had not heard him. Her mind churned with images of Eric and she had to force herself to stop trembling, stop remembering. She slid further down in the bed, unaware that she had drawn away from Zock's clinging arms. Unaware of Zock. She turned on her side, burrowed her head deeper into the pillow and closed her eyes, giving herself up to the poignant memories. In a moment she felt his arms circle her from behind and the length of his body press against her. She sighed and allowed herself to be held, wishing it were Eric.

Strong hands half-lifted her, urging her to turn over and she looked up into Palle's carefully polite face. He dropped a small hand towel over her body, covering breasts, belly, crotch, and set to work massaging the bottoms of her feet. She closed her eyes again. It was kind of amusing, now that she looked back on it. Her unconsummated wedding night. Like something out of a Gothic romance. And it had remained unconsummated for the next four days.

"Light me a cigarette, will you, Palle?" she said and the handsome masseur quickly complied, placing an ashtray within easy reach. He poured more cream into his hands and began working it up her legs from ankle to thigh. Every second or third trip up her leg, his fingertips came a little closer to her vagina, questioningly, knocking politely for entry. She tried to discourage his gentle questing thrusts with a subtle drawing back of her body, but instead of deterring him it seemed to have the opposite effect. When his strokes became bolder and his hands moved higher, Tara said, dryly, "Okay, Palle, that's far enough. I don't need to lose any weight in my pussy." And instantly she was appalled at saying such a thing. Six months ago she would never have used such language.

"Terribly sorry, Mrs. McBain," Palle murmured quickly and dropped his hands a respectable six inches from her crotch.

She had learned more than just bad language since entering Zock's world, she thought wearily. She had learned the name of every upper and downer on the market, as well as how to test cocaine for purity and how to recognize superior marijuana. She knew precisely what combination of drugs worked to bring her out of depression, put her in a sexy mood or simply make her appear "normal" and happy. She had learned how to bring herself to swift, sweet climax with a vibrator when Zock was too coked out to make love, and she had learned to close her eyes and make her mind go blank when urged to join in the group sexual play—an activity of which her husband was quite fond.

She had also learned how to spend money. She

thought nothing of flying to New York to drop by her favorite Seventh Avenue designers, Bill Blass and Donald Brooks, for an entire new wardrobe. She had her jewelry designed especially for her by Jean Schlumberger of Tiffany's or Fulco di Verdura, the Fifth Avenue Sicilian duke. Her hair was done in the new look, the wild, restless savage style, by Kenneth, of course. Her closets in the Holmby Hills mansion were stuffed with creations from the leading couturiers, Christian Dior of Paris, Sybil Connolly of Dublin, Marguery Bolhagen of Bergdorf Goodman in New York; silk Pucci blouses and velvet pants, Gucci morocco handbags with bamboo handles; two-hundred-dollar alligator bags to go with her hundred-dollar alligator shoes—the new chunky ones created by Roger Viver.

She had grown accustomed to traveling by limousine or Rolls-Royce (her own), relaxing in the back seat while the silent chauffeur delivered her to this elegant dinner party or that leisurely luncheon. She could smoke a joint or have a cocktail, protected from prying eyes by the shades on the windows and supplied by the well-stocked bar in the back of the Rolls. She now expected to be seated first in a packed restaurant, to be escorted directly to the plane from the VIP room, past the line of waiting passengers and made comfortable in the first class section before anyone else was allowed to board.

Yes, she had learned many things since becoming Mrs. Zock McBain. Many of them pleasant and fun. Why then was she so miserable? Why did she pop black beauties every morning like they were life savers? Because in a way they were. They got her through the day, and if she was too wired to sleep at night there was always a bottle of reds or tuies in the bathroom. She sighed and crushed out her cigarette, half-sitting on the table.

"That will be all today, Palle," she said. "I have a luncheon engagement in less than an hour." She reached for her robe and he immediately held it for her, averting his eyes respectfully as she stood and slipped into it.

"Very well, Mrs. McBain," Palle said and began

gathering up his various lotions and implements. "Same time tomorrow?" He subconsciously held his breath while awaiting her answer. She was by far his favorite client, and he was afraid he had lost her by the subtle pass he had made earlier. He would have to be more careful with this one, he told himself. She obviously could not be rushed or flattered like many of the others. But he meant to get her into bed no matter how long it took. And in the meantime it was a pure physical pleasure to stroke and massage her perfect body.

"Of course," she said lightly, "I'm addicted to your Danish hands." She waved her fingertips at him and disappeared through the bathroom door, closing it firmly behind her. Palle had no further reason for hanging around and turned reluctantly to let himself out. Mrs. McBain did not pay for her massages after each visit, as did most of his clients. All her expenses were handled by her personal secretary, and Palle received a check each month for the full amount.

Tara waited until she heard the bedroom door close, then went back and sat down on the burgundy brocade chaise and picked up the telephone. Doe answered on the first ring.

"Hi," Tara said. "Are we still on for lunch?"

"Hi, honey, I was just picking up the phone to call you. How about meeting at The Hungry Tiger in the valley? I've heard it's great." She made a sucking noise, and Tara knew that she was smoking a joint. "You ever been there?"

"Yeah, Zock and I put in an appearance on opening night. It's not bad. Good steaks." Tara reached to the filigreed gold cigarette case on the table and took out a joint. Each morning the box was refilled by Stanley Mann, whom Zock claimed rolled the best joints in Beverly Hills. She lit it, sucked in deep, waited for the rush.

"Good, I'm on a diet and a steak and salad is about all I want," Doe said. "Let's see, it's almost one—can you make it in forty-five minutes?"

Tara said she could and they rang off.

They had finished lunch and were relaxing over coffee and a liqueur, anisette for Tara, cherry heering for Doe. They had gossiped nonstop all through lunch, catching up on all the happenings on both coasts as well as most of Europe. Doe had never looked more lovely, Tara thought. Her expressive topaz eyes were bright and sparkling, her complexion clear and rosy, and she seemed on the verge of breaking into laughter at any moment. "Okay, what's going on, Doe," Tara finally asked with a grin. "You've been dying to tell me something all through lunch so let's have it."

"I'm in love," Doe giggled and hugged herself as if she still could not believe it.

"You're kidding? With whom? I thought you'd been seeing a lot of Barry Wilde lately." She gasped. "Doe, it's not the Bear, is it?"

"No, no," Doe laughed. "The Bear is just my fucking buddy—this is the real thing! I'm really in love!" She actually shivered in delight. "And he loves me . . ."

"Who?" Tara asked.

"Wesley Cunningham," Doe sighed. "Can you believe it? Isn't he just the sexiest hunk you've ever seen? And he's so talented and intelligent and rich and—and—"

"And married," Tara said dryly. She finished her liqueur and signaled the waiter for another round.

"He's getting a divorce," Doe said quickly. "Just as soon as he talks to his wife. We're leaving for London in a couple of weeks on *Love in the Morning* and he plans to tell her then."

"How is the picture coming?" Tara asked casually, even though she already knew. She searched the trades every morning for any item concerning Eric and knew that they had just completed interior shooting in the studio and would be going to London on location for the exteriors. She had also read that Wesley Cunningham had taken Hollywood by storm and that Beverly Hills hostesses were fighting for the privilege of throwing a party in his honor.

An English actor who had spent his formative years studying at the Old Vic with such illustrious thespians as Richard Burton and Sir Laurence Olivier, Wesley Cunningham was one of those "theater" actors who preferred the stage to motion pictures—even while he demanded (and got) the staggering sum of one million dollars per film. He had visited Hollywood on occasion but this was the first time he had consented to working here, preferring to force American producers to come to him in Europe. He had been married for twenty years to the long-suffering Sybil Cantford Cunningham; long-suffering because during those twenty years Wesley had had as many much-publicized love affairs with his leading ladies. However, at picture's end he always returned to London and Sybil's understanding arms. He was as handsome as a Greek god, powerfully built, rugged and explosive. His drunken brawls were common knowledge in the media, as was his mesmerizing talent as a Shakespearean actor. He was a bit of a dandy, elegant and suave, spouting soliloquies from Hamlet or King Lear at the slightest urging, and considered it barbaric to drink scotch or champagne that was less than twenty-five years old. He had six children, ranging in ages from the lanky seventeen-year-old to the just-toddling fifteen-months-old. He had won two Tonys and had been nominated twice for an Academy Award.

"Oh, the picture's a gas," Doe said. She finished her cherry heering, surrendering the pony glass to the waiter when he placed a fresh one in front of her. "I really can't wait to get on the set each morning for all those delicious love scenes with Wesley." She laughed huskily. "Even though he's usually just left my bed a couple of hours before. He keeps a room at the Beverly Hills Hotel and has the chauffeur pick him up there and drive him to the studio. I understand, of course. He has to be careful. He doesn't want any gossip about us before he talks to his wife." She sipped her liqueur thoughtfully, then abruptly asked, "You don't think he's bullshitting me, do you, Tara?" Her topaz eyes darkened to a deep golden brown, shadowed with doubt. There was a troubled look in them that Tara had never seen before. Always Doe was so confident, so sure of herself and her power over men. For her to be so concerned, it must indeed be the real thing. Tara knew about Doe's earlier marriages, as did anyone who picked up a fan magazine.

She had married her first husband when she was sixteen and dancing in the chorus line at the old Macombo nightclub on Sunset Boulevard. He had been a hard-drinking newspaper reporter, a two-fisted barroom brawler, fifteen years her senior, who had killed himself one night by plunging his car over the side of Mulholland Drive while drunkenly trying to maneuver the sharp curves. Her second try at the marital golden ring had been with young Jeffrey Mitchell, son of the famous Western star Rod (Mitch) Mitchell. That one had lasted two years, ending in a messy but sensational divorce when a photographer discovered Mrs. Jeffrey Mitchell in the arms of her father-in-law at a notorious hotel in Zuma Beach. The resulting photographs appeared in every magazine from *Time* to *Confidential*, and the divorce was given more space than the preparations for man's first walk on the moon.

Husband number three had been a muscle man, a former Mr. America who preferred the company of his handsome valet to that of his sultry blonde wife. They had remained friends, however, even though Doe was aware that he had used her to further his career. "At least he was honest about it," she had shrugged.

But Wesley Cunningham, debonair, continental, capricious—and married? Tara did not know what to answer, so she reached for a cigarette and took her time lighting it.

"Well, do you?" Doe prompted. She took the pack from Tara and shook one out for herself. "I know he's been involved with other women—Christ, who doesn't? You can't pick up a magazine without seeing some shit about the Wesley Cunningham's marital problems." She dragged deep on her cigarette, wishing it were a joint. "But I believe him when he says those were just affairs, one-nighters as it were." She laughed in the suggestive, slightly lewd manner that her fans had come to know and love. "Hell, honey, I've been through enough one-night stands myself to understand what he means. It's lonely as hell on location, boring and uptight and just plain hard work. You need something to help you unwind after a long day on the set. And it's more bearable if that 'something' is a warm, agreeable lover."

"Well, Wesley Cunningham has certainly done his share of unwinding," Tara said lightly. She wished Doe had not confided in her and asked her opinion. She hated getting involved in other people's love lives. No matter what advice you gave, invariably it would be the wrong advice.

"I know," Doe said miserably. "That's what kills me. I don't know if he's just putting me on and this is the same line he fed all the others, or if he is really in love with me. He says he is—and if he doesn't mean it, baby, let me tell you he's a better actor than I give him credit for!"

"Well, I guess you'll find out when you get to England," Tara said carefully. "You said he was going to tell his wife then, didn't you?"

"So he says." She frowned and shook her head. "Jesus, Tara, I just don't know! I'd hate like hell to think he's just making a fool of me, but damn it, I love him! I'm head over heels in love for the first time in my life and I feel like such a jerk!"

Tara laughed and reached across the table to squeeze Doe's hand. "That's part of it, I guess, feeling stupid and jerky. I remember how it was with Eric. I couldn't say a single intelligent sentence to him for the first three months. I just sort of followed him around like a little puppy dog—" Her voice trailed off and she suddenly looked as if she would cry.

Doe gripped Tara's hand tighter and asked gently, "You still love him, don't you?" When Tara nodded miserably, Doe sighed and asked, "How is it between you and Zock? Do you get along okay?"

"Oh, sure, we get along just great," Tara said bitterly. "He's usually so damn stoned he doesn't know where he is or who he's with, and when he's straight he's on the road doing concerts. Oh, it's a great life, let me tell you! I rattle around in that enormous mausoleum all by myself —just me and forty servants!"

Doe laughed. "God, that place is gigantic, isn't it? How many rooms does it have anyway? I've never been able to get through them all when I've been over."

"Well, I don't want to say it's big, but when it's five o'clock in the living room it's three hours later in the kitchen!" They both laughed, then Tara sobered and shrugged her shoulders. "It really isn't all that bad, I guess. I have everything I've ever wanted, I can go any-place I please, buy anything I want—"

"Cut the crap, honey. This is me, remember? You can tell old Aunt Doe what's troubling you."

Her voice was so warm and soothing that Tara could not hold back any longer. "Oh, God, Doe, I'm just so un-happy I could die! I can't stand for him to touch me un-less I'm bombed out of my mind on something. Then I pretend it's Eric. I get high every day just to get through that day. And—and I drink everyday, too. I feel so lost and afraid and trapped. I hate my life with Zock. His world is killing me and I seem powerless to do anything about it. I'm confused all the time. I know it's probably due to the drugs, but I can't seem to get by without them. I'm always so tired, just bone-weary and—and so damn tired of everything!"

Tears gathered in her eyes and Doe quickly blotted them away with her napkin. "Come on, honey, let's get out of here. We'll go to your place and have a nice long talk, okay? Just like old times, remember?" She smiled and shook Tara gently. "We used to get together at least once a week and catch up on all the gossip—then start some of our own, remember?" She left a couple of twen-ties on the table and hurried Tara outside.

Tara held herself in check until they were in Doe's Rolls and pulling out into the midday traffic, and then she let the tears come. She sobbed with relief at having finally put into words what had been troubling her these past months. She could now admit that she hated her husband, had almost since the first week of their marriage. Since the first time Zock had made love to her. She remembered how shocked she had been, then terribly embarrassed, when Zock had brought in the tall, sexy redhead and or-

dered her to give him head while he made love to Tara.
She had been stunned silent and had lain like a statue in
his arms, trying not to stare at the leggy showgirl going
down on her husband even as his hands and lips caressed
Tara. She had been fascinated by the scene, had even
been turned on in spite of herself as she watched Zock
grow hard and ready with the showgirl's expert adminis-
trations, and when he had pushed the redhead away and
entered Tara with savage urgency she had gasped aloud
with passion.

That had been four days after the wedding. Four days
in which Zock had been unable to get an erection. Four
days in which Tara had masturbated behind the locked
bathroom door, consumed with memories of Eric. Four
days of staying constantly high, partying until dawn and
exhaustion drove them to bed, each on their own side.

The three-way with the Las Vegas showgirl had broken
the spell, however, and thereafter Zock had been able to
perform his husbandly duties with vigor.

Tara lay against several pillows in the enormous round
bed that she sometimes shared with Zock. The chinchilla
bedspread was rumpled carelessly at the foot of the bed
and the sheets were a matching pearl gray satin. She was
staring at the television set, half-watching a Frank Sinatra
special as she thought about her conversation with Doe.
For the first time in six months, she had been entirely
truthful and it felt good. Ever since her marriage to Zock
she had been living in a sort of X-rated Disneyland, soaring to thrilling heights, made dizzy by the opulence, then
plunged to terrifying depths of despair when the drugs
wore off. She had not had a moment to herself. A moment
when someone was not bugging her for something. A de-
signer wanting to show her his new line. Reporters wanting interviews. Photographers wanting picture sessions of
Mrs. Zock McBain at home and at play. Strangers wanting anything they could get. Forgotten acquaintances
wanting a loan or a job in show business. Always someone
wanting something of her, until she felt there was nothing
left.

She lit a cigarette and sighed wearily. She was always

weary these days unless she was flying on black beauties. Bone tired, she had admitted to Doe. She did nothing she really enjoyed anymore. She was no longer her own person but an extension of super star Zock McBain. Her life was regulated by secretaries, managers and her husband's concert dates. She was expected to dutifully follow him all over the world and stand for hours smiling as though she enjoyed it while rude photographers shoved and pushed for a closer shot of the newlyweds. She was expected to hold her ground bravely when ten thousand hysterical fans almost trampled her to death trying to reach Zock. And when she was ready to drop from sheer exhaustion, she was expected instead to drop her pants and take the shot of "vitamins" from whichever "doctor" was currently administering them. At first, she had believed Zock when he had told her they were vitamin B-12 injections for fatigue, but when she had gone without them for a couple of days and felt the nervous twitching in her hands and eyelids, in all her pulse points, and it did not go away until she had gotten an injection, she knew it was speed. She had been only mildly surprised. This was, after all, the Age of Aquarius, when anything and everything went. The open drug permissiveness and sexual promiscuity had shattered the remaining barriers of exclusiveness for movie stars. The glamor was fading, like a bad color shot that bled at the edges. Being married to the King of Rock seemed to mean that Tara now belonged to the public as well. There were constant demands made upon her time, until she had no time to herself. It had been two months since she had seen Mandy or Jim or the Bear, and twice that long since she had even spoken to Charley.

Tara felt a twinge of guilt every time she thought about Charley. Zock had insisted that now that Tara was his wife she should have the best of everything. Naturally Vidal Sassoon was a hell of a lot better than Charlotte Holmes from Burbank! He had told Charley himself, calling her one morning when she was expecting Tara for their regular appointment and telling her quite bluntly that his wife would no longer be needing her services as a hairdresser. Tara had slunk from the room like a coward unable to explain to Charley when her old friend asked to speak to her. She had meant to call Charley back as soon as Zock left for his recording session, but by then she was high and too embarrassed. As the days turned into weeks and the silence built between them, it became too late.

Barry Wilde and Jim Glasser seemed the only ones of Tara's old friends who understood her new position and all it required of her. Surprisingly, neither of them thought it anything too special that their Tara had snagged the most popular singer in the world and was living a fantasy life in a glorious palace in elite Holmby Hills. Even though she was too busy to see them often, she spoke to them regularly by phone. At times they seemed her only link with reality and she missed them more than she admitted. Sometimes alone at night she would remember the times she and Jim and Charley and the Bear had sat around her tiny apartment, bullshitting each other, laughing a lot. She could not remember the last time she had really laughed with pleasure.

In the past six months she had traveled to Paris, Rome, London, Tokyo and Madrid—and she showed it in her tired face and thin body. She had lost twelve pounds and Doe had told her at lunch that she looked like hell.

"Get out while you can, honey," she had said when they had returned to Tara's house. She made Tara get into bed, then pulled a chair up beside her and lit a joint.

Tara had felt like a fool, breaking down in front of Doe, but she couldn't hold it back any longer. The sadness and pain of the last six months had come rushing over her like a tidal wave and she had sobbed out the whole story.

"My God, Tara, can't you see what that prick has done to you? You're strung out on drugs. You're a nervous wreck—look at your hands."

Tara had glanced down to see her hands trembling on the chinchilla bedspread, opening and closing, clutching the soft fur almost desperately. "I know," she had whispered. "I know—but it just seems such a hassle—so much trouble—" Her head fell back against the headboard and she closed her eyes. "Everything is such a hassle lately."

"Then I'll get the ball rolling for you," Doe had said firmly and had done just that. She had dialed her attorney and set up an appointment for Tara the following morning. "And I will be here at nine sharp to pick you up," she had told Tara. "So don't think you're going to put it off. You know you have to get out of this sick relationship, and the sooner the better."

Tara sighed and crushed her cigarette out in the bedside ashtray. Of course Doe was right. She wanted a divorce. She hated her life and she hated her husband. A soft knock sounded on the door and Penny, the stout English maid, entered with Tara's dinner.

"Evening, ma'am," Penny said, bobbing a curtsy before placing the bedtray over Tara's lap and removing the silver domes that covered the dishes. The light delicate aroma of baked chicken breast and wild rice drifted to her and Tara realized that she was hungry. She had not been truly hungry in months due to the pep pills and injections, but Doe had gone through her medicine cabinet and removed every upper she found. She had left one bottle of tranquilizers, realizing that she would most assuredly need them to help her through the next couple of days. Penny removed the crystal stopper from a half liter of white wine and poured a glass for her young mistress. "Will there be anything else, ma'am?"

"No, thank you, Penny. This is fine." She smiled at the woman, really seeing her for the first time. She was a plain but pleasant-looking woman in her late thirties, plump and pink-clean. Tara knew that she was one of the serving maids, not to be confused with the cleaning maids, and that she was one of four others who worked in the kitchen. She watched her back respectfully from the room, closing the door softly behind her, and wondered what she did when she was not bringing dinner trays to her employers or serving their guests. She had no idea what any of the servants did in the huge mansion. She hardly saw them at all. Once a week, the head cook would meet with her to go over the menu and enquire if the McBains were planning a party of any sort so that she might shop accordingly. She knew that many of the servants lived in because the house was always spotless, day or night, and there was always someone to answer her ring should she want something. She knew that their gourmet cook made a flawless soufflé and that their twin Rolls-Royces were always polished to a high sheen and ready to take them anywhere they wished to go. She had seen the suave butler on several occasions but did not know his first name or anything else about him, referring to him as "Williams," as Zock had instructed her. The house seemed to run itself, but Tara was aware of the executive housekeeper who issued orders like an admiral—but so smoothly and unobtrusively that the help seemed to materialize from the walls, do the job, then disappear again in the same silent fashion.

She forked a piece of tender chicken into her mouth and chewed thoughtfully. If someone asked her what it was like to be so fabulously rich, she could not have told them. Many answers came to mind, like lonely and bored, but it was more than that. She could not honestly expect anyone to believe that being able to have anything in the world you wanted was boring and lonely. She knew that it would have been exciting and wonderful if she were sharing it with someone she loved, but seeing the world by Zock's side was killing her. She found herself playacting almost all the time. Pretending to be happy when she was not, enthusiastic when she was dead tired, sexy when she felt cold and hollow inside.

She remembered her trip to Paris and how she had looked forward to it. The huge suite at the George V that had been filled with roses. She had rushed out to the enclosed balcony, leaning over the balustrade to gaze at the magnificent chestnut trees that lined the Avenue George V, shrouded in the evening mist. She had wanted to go out for a walk, to stroll down the Champs-Elysées and perhaps stop for a Cinzano at one of the quaint little sidewalk cafes. But Zock had had other plans. A phone call later and they were in bed with two of Paris' top prostitutes who performed their hearts out for the American rock star and his bride.

Tara had finally done the tourists' rounds by herself. Zock slept until late afternoon, as his concerts kept him up until two each morning—and the cocaine kept him wired until almost dawn, when he would pop a handful of seconals and fall into bed beside Tara. She had spent a fortune at Cardin's in the Faubourg Saint-Honoré and at Boucheron's on the Place Vendôme, getting a little satisfied thrill of pleasure when she had had the bills sent to Zock.

They had stayed at the Savoy in London, their room overlooking the Thames, which rolled silently between dark trees, slick and black. They had attended a press luncheon at Les Ambassadeurs; posed patiently for photographers on such street corners as Fleet, Bond and Regent and had topped the long session off with dinner at the Dorchester Hotel. The next two nights Zock gave a concert at the Pigalle, and then they were off to Japan for two weeks.

Tara had hated Tokyo. Zock was appearing at The Latin Quarter, next door to their hotel, the New Japan, and after the first night Tara did not bother to accompany him. The people irritated her and the language grated on her nerves like a fingernail drawn across a blackboard. She discovered the native high, opium, and thereafter had passed many semi-unconscious hours in the darkness of her room with the odor of the little red ball smoking in the bowl of her pipe. From there they had flown to Hong Kong for a couple of days and, finally, back to the States.

They had been home only a week, and just this morning Zock had told Tara that they would be leaving soon for an engagement in New York. Well, he could just leave without her this time, Tara told herself firmly. She had not even seen Mandy yet, as she had been suffering from jet lag (as well as her run-down condition due to drugs and alcohol) and had not wanted to call her little sister until she was "straight." She took a sip of icy wine and smiled to herself. This was the first decision she had made in months and it felt good. She would keep her appointment with Doe's attorney and file for divorce first thing tomorrow morning.

She finished her dinner and telephoned Barry Wilde. "Hi, Bear, it's me," she said when he answered. They exchanged a few words and then she quickly told him what she planned.

"Well, it's about time," Barry said with obvious relief. "We all thought we'd lost you for good."

"What do you mean?"

"Christ, Tara, you haven't exactly been yourself lately —not since you married that creep and started sampling his 'goodies,' if you know what I mean." He paused and she heard him light a cigarette, and wondered if he had broken down and bought a pack or if he had bummed one for later as he often had from her in the past. She found that she missed supplying him with smokes and tears came to her eyes at the thought. "I was talking to Glasser the other day," Barry was saying, "and he's worried as hell about you. I guess we all are."

"Thanks, Bear," Tara said in a tiny voice. "I didn't know it showed so much."

"Yeah, well, it sure as hell does, babe. Christ, you looked like death warmed over the last time I saw you, and Thorton said you haven't written a damn thing on your novel for months." He dragged in on his cigarette and continued in a stern voice. "You should get the hell out of there tonight. You can sleep at my place, and Doe can pick you up here in the morning."

"I can't do that, Bear. I have to tell Zock first. I can't just run away—disappear." But that was exactly what she wanted to do. She looked around the huge, luxurious bedroom, silent and empty, darkness outside and inside the numerous rooms that were never used. She wondered briefly what the servants were doing. Did they actually stay here in this house night after night when there was no one to serve, nothing to do? She fumbled to the nightstand for a joint, lit it and waited with trembling hands for the calming rush. Doe had not taken her supply of pot, as she did not consider it a dangerous drug like the uppers and other pills she had removed from the bathroom.

"Why the hell can't you? Where is the big man, anyway? Out picking up a new batch of teeny-boppers to bring home to his old lady? Maybe you're getting used to that kind of life, huh, babe? Maybe you'd miss the excitement if you left him." He deliberately made his voice harsh and cruel. "By the way, how does it feel to have so many cocks stuck in you that you lose track of who they belong to? Or so many tongues sucking at you that you don't know if they're men or women—"

"Stop it, Barry, stop it!" Tara cried. "You know I hate it—I told you what happened—I told you that Zock makes me do it—I hate it—" She began to cry then, great racking sobs that choked her and tears that spilled down her face and splashed on the telephone receiver in her hand. "Oh, God, Bear, come and get me, please! I can't drive—I—I took a couple of tranquilizers and I've been drinking and—please come and take me out of here!"

"All *right!*" Barry's voice was suddenly animated with delight. "I'll be there in half an hour, babe, get dressed and bring what you'll need for a couple of days." He waited until she agreed, then added, "Now don't back out on me, Tara. I'll be there in thirty minutes and if you're not ready I'll take you just the way you are. Got it? I'm not going to fuck around with you. I love you and I'm going to help you, but you have to help a little too, okay?"

"Okay, Bear, I promise I'll be ready." She gulped back her sobs and took a trembling drag of the joint. "But hurry, please, Bear. I just want to get out of this awful house and never see it again!"

She got shakily out of bed and almost fell on her face. She had taken a mini bomb, or tuie as they were called on the street, those double-dose sleeping pills that thickened her speech and turned her legs and arms to rubber. But she struggled against the effects as she stumbled about the bedroom, throwing clothes, makeup and shoes into a bag. "This is the last time I ever pack a suitcase in

163

this goddamn house," she said aloud as she closed the lid and snapped the latches. She did not have the strength to dress herself so merely slipped on her full-length sable coat over her nightgown and shoved her bare feet into a pair of beach thongs. Catching her reflection in one of the many mirrors, she laughed out loud.

The doorbell rang and Tara rushed to answer it, but saw that Williams had already opened the door and was standing politely aside for Barry to enter. Tara went to him, almost falling, and he caught her in a hug. "Oh, Bear, you really came!"

"Of course I came," he grinned, hugging her and then keeping a supporting arm about her when she almost sagged to the floor again. "Come on, let's get out of here. Where's your bag?" She told him and he gently placed her in one of the lushly upholstered foyer chairs that, to Tara's knowledge, had never been sat in before.

Williams had discreetly withdrawn into the woodwork, and there was absolutely no sound in the enormous mansion save for the brisk footsteps of Barry as he hurried toward her with her suitcase. "Let's go," he said, taking her hand and pulling her into the protective support of his free arm. And Tara stumbled quickly after him, out the wide front doors, down the marble steps without once looking back.

CHAPTER
EIGHT

FAVEL PERLS was having the time of her life. This was the first party she had attended in six months and Favel loved parties. Especially those given by Hollywood people. She loved the sounds and smells, the undercurrent of drama that was always present at one of Doe Kingston's parties. And it was deliciously exciting to speculate on the relationship between Doe and that sexy Wesley Cunningham. Of course, Favel had read the newspaper accounts of the "affair" but knew from personal experience that one could not always believe what one read in the newspaper. She lunched often with Sybil Cunningham and felt that she would have confided in Favel if there was any truth to the rumors. Actually, it didn't matter one way or the other to Favel. She was just glad of the opportunity to get out socially once more, having been reluctantly forced into mourning due to the death of her husband, Thompson. She had been furious that he had had the bad taste to die during the height of the season—but not entirely surprised. Thompson had always delighted in thwarting her one way or another.

Favel lifted a fresh glass of champagne off a waiter's tray and sipped delicately, her gaze wandering about the room. The women were elegantly gowned in the very latest fashion and Favel glanced irritably down at her skimpy black Dior, wishing it were the new mauve creation she had just picked up in Paris last week. Favel did not look well in dark colors. What a Victorian custom, mourning! Then she smiled, remembering Doe's comment when she had greeted her; "Love your widow's weeds, darling!" She heard Doe's husky laughter and looked up to see her hugging an incredibly good-looking man who had just arrived. His dark hair clung to his well-shaped head in crisp, damp curls and there was a sheen of wetness on the shoulders of his tan raincoat. He shrugged out of the coat, handing it to a butler, and Favel's gaze traveled slowly over his body, taking in the broad shoulders and narrow hips. He was wearing a red turtleneck sweater and tight charcoal-gray trousers that hugged his lean buttocks and just barely hinted at the bulge of his crotch.

Favel licked her lips and moved toward the group, wondering where in the world Doe had found this yummy hunk. He looked like a ski instructor or American playboy with his casual grace and easy smile. "Darling, the party is simply marvelous," she gushed as she stepped between Doe and Wesley and took the blonde's arm in an intimate embrace. Her round, powder-blue eyes crinkled at the corners and her mouth pouted girlishly. "I'm *sooo* delighted you asked me, chérie. I was bored to distraction." She giggled prettily in the direction of the red-sweatered stranger, a question in her frank stare.

"Oh, Favel, sweetie, I'd like you to meet Eric Marlowe," Doe said, grinning at the obvious interest in the older woman's eyes. "Eric, darling, say hello to Favel Perls."

"Hi, nice to meet you." Eric's voice was neither warm nor cool, and the smile he offered did not quite reach his eyes. He looked haunted, Favel thought, as if he had suffered a great tragedy. Favel liked tragedies almost as much as she liked parties. She extended her hand and he took it briefly in his own.

"Oh, an American, how perfectly charming," Favel cooed in her little-girl voice. "I simply adore an American accent. But where have I heard that name before?"

"Eric has just finished directing Wesley and me in *Love in the Morning,*" Doe said, smiling up at the handsome English actor. He returned her look of love and tightened his arm about her waist.

"Of course, that is where I heard it!" Favel clapped her hands together and turned a brilliant smile upon Eric. "But you are so young, no?"

"No," Eric said. He turned toward the bar that had been set up in the corner of Doe's suite and ordered a Jack Daniels, completely unaware of the small French woman staring hungrily at his back. He drank slowly as he leaned against a marble pillar near the window, his moody gaze on the Thames far below. It looked so sinister and deep, rolling silently between the dark trees. The cold drizzle of rain capped the night in a thick foggy mist and he wished he were back in sunny California. He couldn't wait to get into the cutting room and start to work on *Love in the Morning*. Just thinking of the picture brought a satisfied feeling. He took out a cigarette and was looking for a match when a gold lighter was suddenly held for him.

"Allow me, Monsieur," Favel murmured. Eric ducked his head to the flame and lit his cigarette.

"Thanks," he said, looking her over closely for the first time. She was a tiny thing, not over five feet and lushly curved—like a Jayne Mansfield hot water bottle, he thought. Her hair was platinum blonde and clustered in babyish ringlets about her heart-shaped face. Her eyes were a clear powder blue, framed in thick lashes, and her red bow of mouth was pouting and full-lipped. She looked vaguely familiar but he could not place her, so he shrugged and turned back to the window, sipping his bourbon.

"Doe simply raved about what a genius you are, Monsieur Marlowe," Favel gushed. She moved closer to him, forcing him to turn from the window and look down at her. "You also were responsible for that marvelously brutal film, *The Savage Desert,* were you not?"

"Guilty," Eric replied, wondering how he was going to get rid of this flirtatious little pest. She had pressed herself against him, one round breast coyly brushing his arm.

"Ah, you Americans, such strong, silent types—like John Wayne, no?" She giggled and batted her long false eyelashes at him. Eric shrugged and turned back to his view of the Thames. "You must tell me all about your new film, Monsieur," Favel persisted. "I have read much speculation in the press, now I must hear from the genius director himself. Come, we will sit over here and have a cozy little chat, no?"

Eric wanted to refuse but did not know how he could do so gracefully. He supposed she was harmless enough and her obvious interest in his work was flattering. "Sure, why not?" He grinned and took her arm, steering her to the sofa and they both sat down. Favel was chattering at once about the marvelous party and how thrilled she had been to receive Doe's invitation.

"This is the first time I have been to a, how do you call it, 'wrap up' party? Is this an American ritual? I did not have such a thing when I was an actress in France." She sipped her champagne, looking at him from beneath lowered lashes. He had said nothing about recognizing her, as most people did when introduced, and the slight rebuff made her momentarily piqued.

"Oh? You were an actress?" Eric asked without much interest.

"Oui, and a very good one, if one can believe one's own press reviews." Her girlish laughter tinkled gratingly on his nerves and he wondered how he had allowed himself to get trapped by this aging starlet. "You probably would recognize my screen name—Favel Frederick, oui?"

"Oh, yes, of course," Eric said. "The French sex kitten of the sixties." He looked at her then, remembering the many times he had sneaked into the racy French movies and watched the sexy Favel Frederick strip naked and make wild love to whoever was currently appearing with her. Her movies had been banned in most movie theaters, but the art houses had somehow managed to get hold of them and a legend was born. Favel Frederick had taken the movie audience behind the bedroom doors and had thus begun a sexual revolution in the movie industry. He was aware of her prattling on and on but did

168

not bother to listen. His thoughts were thousands of miles away, across the ocean and in sunny California. He had intended to fly back the same night after the final shooting on *Love in the Morning*, but Doe had talked him into staying for her party.

The month and a half that they had been in London seemed more like a year to Eric. As much as he had enjoyed directing the film, he had not been able to relax when the day's shooting was finished. He was still consumed with thoughts of Tara. He had been spitefully glad when Doe had told him that Tara was filing for divorce, and when the stories began hitting the papers, he had read each one with added glee. He had been furious, however, when he had read about the abuse Zock had heaped upon Tara in the brief months of their marriage and had almost telephoned her when he read that she had committed herself to a private sanitarium to kick the drug and alcohol habit. The thought that he was the cause of her impulsive marriage plagued him with guilt, and he promised himself that he would make it up to her if she would only let him.

He felt someone tugging at his sweater sleeve and glanced down to see Favel staring at him curiously. "Sorry, did you say something?"

"Oui, I asked if you would please get me another glass of champagne," she pouted. "But I am afraid you have not heard one word of what I say, Monsieur. You are preoccupied with your movie, no?"

"Uh, yeah, that's it," Eric said. He signaled to the waiter to bring his tray of champagne.

"Ah, do not worry, chérie. Doe tells me that this movie is the best she has done and she is convinced that she will win the Oscar this year." She accepted the glass from the waiter and raised it to her lips, flirting with Eric over the rim. "But you have not told me anything about yourself, chérie. Did you find England to your liking? Where do you make your home in the States?" She tittered coyly. "And, I must ask, is there a Mrs. Marlowe at home waiting for you?"

Eric groaned inwardly. Favel Perls was everything he

disliked in a woman. Obviously pushing forty, she still dressed in a youthful fashion and wore her hair like a sixteen-year-old. Her pale skin was crinkled faintly with lines around the eyes and mouth, and there was the beginning of a double chin shadowing her string of pearls. Her nails were much too long to be useful at anything other than spearing an olive from a martini glass and the tiny broken blood vessels on her pert, turned-up nose spoke of many martini lunches and dinners.

"No Mrs. Marlowe," Eric said shortly. He lit another cigarette, forcing himself to remain pleasant to this fool of a woman. "What about you? Is there a Mr. Perls and/or Frederick back in France keeping the home fires burning?"

"Ah, alas, no." Favel shook her head and the blonde curls bounced. "My husband passed away these six months ago and I am left all alone." She smoothed her black skirt over her slightly plump thighs. "As you see, I still wear mourning for poor Thompson."

"Thompson," Eric said. "You mean *the* Thompson Perls of the hotels?"

"Oui." Favel sighed deeply, careful to keep a certain sadness in her voice, but her blue eyes danced with mischief. "I am but a poor widow, all alone with nothing to warm me save for a chain of Perls Hotels . . ."

Eric laughed, suddenly liking her better now that he had seen a show of humor. "Yeah, that must be tough, just a poor widow lady and all those millions."

Favel laughed and tapped him playfully on the arm. "You make a joke with me, no? But it is true. I do not even have the estate yet because it is, how do you say in English, in probate?" Eric nodded and she frowned and sighed heavily. "In fact, I have been having such trouble over the estate I almost wish poor Thompson hadn't died!"

Eric worked around the clock to edit *Love in the Morning* and get it into the theaters in time for the Oscar race. He had returned to California at the end of September and had gotten the movie out by the holidays. He had called Jim Glasser upon his return to ask if he knew where he might find Tara, but the crusty Irishman had been curt to the point of rudeness, telling him nothing. Eric had then called Barry Wilde. "Tara doesn't want anyone to know where she is right now," the Bear had said. Then, softening under Eric's pleading, he had agreed to tell Tara that Eric had asked after her. "But I know she won't see you, Eric," he had said. "She went through hell with that prick McBain, and all she wants to do is get back on her feet and finish her novel. I drove up to see her last weekend and she was feeling good and raring to get back to work."

Eric had grasped that one phrase "drove up to see her" like a drowning man clings to a buoy. That meant Tara would have to be somewhere in the Los Angeles area, within driving distance. He could think of only one rehabilitation center, Camarillo, and had placed a call there to ask if Tara was a patient. The receptionist had been firm in not giving out any information on the patients, and Eric had reluctantly put aside trying to find her until the editing was completed on his film. He went to the premiere alone, then spent the rest of the evening at the bar in Stefaninos getting plastered. He had picked up a young starlet who reminded him a little of Tara and had fucked her until dawn, seeing Tara's face on the sweat-stained pillow.

Christmas Eve, and Eric was sitting alone in his Benedict Canyon house, a drink in his hand, listening to Christmas carols and remembering other holidays shared with Tara and Mandy. On impulse he picked up the telephone and dialed the number of Mandy's school. When he identified himself he heard Miss Pearson's shocked little gasp and rushed quickly on before she could hang up.

"Miss Pearson, just give me a minute of your time, please," he pleaded. "I just want to find out how Mandy's doing. Is she all right? She *is* still there, isn't she?"

"As a matter of fact, Mr. Marlowe, Mandy is no longer with us," Miss Pearson sniffed. "Her sister took her home with her only last week and I haven't had a moment's peace since." She sniffed again and her voice was coldly righteous as she muttered, "That poor child, how in the world she will manage, I don't know. I pleaded with Miss Remington to leave the child with us until she got her— uh—personal problems straightened out, but, no, she would have none of it. It's an outrage, Mr. Marlowe, taking that young innocent child into a notorious situation like the one Miss Remington is currently involved in. Show people, Mr. Marlowe, should not be allowed to have children if they insist on carrying on their nasty affairs in public. Why, have you been reading about the McBains' divorce? Shocking, that's what I say! Shocking!" She sniffed indignantly and her voice grew stronger with her puritanical outrage. "I read that they were both drug addicts and carried on shamelessly with members of both sexes at those wild Hollywood parties. What is this town coming to, I ask you, when married people no longer have respect for one another and engage in orgies and dope parties and I don't know what all!"

Miss Pearson continued to rage about the trash she had read concerning the McBains, practically smacking her lips over the more depraved details until Eric finally hung up in disgust. He had read the same stories these past weeks. In fact, he could not pick up a magazine without seeing some mention of Tara and Zock. But it was the photographs that really dug in deep under his skin and burned like an old wound. Tara dressed all in white, the diamond tiara nestled in her dark curls, the full-length white mink setting off her face like a Madonna. The same outfit she had been wearing the last time he saw her. The same outfit he had ripped from her body before he had raped her in a stranger's gazebo. Photographs of her at other functions, her hand resting lightly on Zock's arm, her marvelous dark eyes looking haunted and unhappy. Photographs of her leaving the Beverly Hills Municipal Court Building, trying to hide behind the enormous dark glasses as crowds engulfed her and reporters shoved microphones into her face.

Eric had asked Doe to try and find her, to see if she was okay or needed anything, but the blonde star had her

172

own sensational headlines to worry about. Wesley Cunningham had shocked everyone by accompanying Doe back to Hollywood and promptly moving into her Bel Air mansion, where he started divorce proceedings. They appeared everywhere together to plug *Love in the Morning;* went on talk shows together where Merv or Johnny or Mike would make some wisecrack about Love in the Morning, Noon and Nighttime too. Doe and Wesley laughed along with the best of them, never once denying their love for one another, but always being carefully gracious about Sybil and the six children in England. Eric was delighted for Doe as well as himself. He could not have bought better publicity for *Love in the Morning.*

Eric went to the bar for a fresh drink and felt loneliness descending upon him like a cold, black cloud. He had been invited to numerous parties but had declined them all. Sandra Sinclair had called several times trying to renew the relationship they had had before Eric had gone to England, but Eric had coldly brushed her off. He carried his drink to the sofa and sat down, staring at the telephone as if willing it to ring.

"Fuck this," he said aloud and reached for the instrument and dialed quickly. "Hey, friend Bear, how's your ass?" This was Barry Wilde's favorite form of greeting and he returned it, a little surprised to be hearing from Eric on Christmas Eve. "Hey, if you're not doing anything, why don't you drop by for a drink. I'd love to see you again and catch up on all the gossip." He knew it sounded feeble but he was desperate. And terribly lonely. Barry was the closest he could get to Tara and if anyone knew where she was, the Bear would.

"Well, no, I'm not doing anything until later," Barry said, wondering what Eric was up to. He had promised Tara he would stop by around ten o'clock, after Mandy was asleep, to help assemble the bike and toys that Santa had left. "I suppose I could stop by for a minute. What was that address again?"

Eric and Barry sat on the sofa with their stockinged feet propped up on the coffee table, holding warm mugs of Tom and Jerry. They had passed the evening in this manner, taking time out for a hastily prepared dinner of broiled steak and baked potatoes, the only meal either of them knew how to prepare. Eric had carefully skirted the issue of Tara until he was sure that Barry was considerably mellow from the hot brandy drinks, then had asked him point blank where she was and what was going on.

"Well, she seems to be getting it together," Barry said. "She was one sick little gal when I took her to Camarillo." He told Eric about his late-night visit to the Holmby Hills mansion and their escape just minutes before Zock had arrived. "She was so fucking skinny you couldn't see her if she stood sideways—and shook like a leaf from the time she got up in the morning until she went to bed at night. Doe said she had to feed her tranquilizers the entire time they were talking with her attorney, and then she got sick and barfed all over Doe's Rolls-Royce on the way home. Glasser and I got a cop friend of his and went to Zock's to pick up Tara's clothes and things, but we didn't really need the dude. Zock was as docile as a kitten, following us from room to room and actually helping us pack Tara's things. He kept saying he knew that she was sick and that he would make it up to her when she came home. 'Just tell her I love her,' he kept repeating. 'Tell her I'll always be here, waiting for her to come home.' Jesus, Eric, it was all I could do to keep from punching the prick. Thank God that cop was there or I probably would have mopped the floor with Zock the Cock! He was sloppy-stoned, mumbling about Tara and how much she meant to him. Shit, man, he's the one who turned her out. Tara had never even seen drugs up close until she met that bastard. And she probably thought a three-way was a light bulb!"

Eric cringed at the word "three-way," hating to think of his Tara involved in sexual games with strange men and women. Had he done this to her? Made her so unhappy that she no longer cared what happened to her? "Did she, well, you know, did she ever mention me?" he asked, not sure he wanted to hear the answer.

174

"No, not in so many words," Barry said truthfully. "She did talk about the plans you had made about taking Mandy to live with you. She said ever since you broke up, things have gone from bad to worse. She's had to cope with Mandy's moods as well as the wild speculations in the press. That kid can be a real little ball buster when she wants to, and I guess she gave Tara all kinds of hell about breaking up with you, accused her of wanting to keep her locked away in a hospital because she was ashamed of her. She said Tara was jealous of the interest you showed her, Mandy, and that's why Tara had called off the wedding. They got into battle royals every time they were together, and Mandy hated Zock with a passion. So, finally, Tara simply stopped picking Mandy up on weekends and the breach between them widened. Tara wrote her a few times from Camarillo, but Mandy never answered. I understand now that Miss Pearson and most of the kids at school were giving Mandy a pretty rough time about all those 'shocking' headlines.

"Mandy suddenly found herself the main topic of conversation, the step-relative of the most famous singer in the world and the sister of the most talked about woman on both continents. When Mandy wasn't reading about Tara's scandalous private life, she was seeing her on magazine covers modeling the latest fashions or appearing at the newest disco, attending some fabulous rock concert where the King of Rock sang all his songs just to her. Mandy told me that just about every teenage girl in her school had the record *Lady Love* and constantly bugged her to get Zock and Tara to autograph them."

"Poor kid," Eric said. "She used to be such a shy little thing. I remember when I first met her. She kept her chin tucked to her chest for the first three months and wouldn't look at me no matter how hard I tried to win her over." He laughed softly. "Then one day she raised her eyes and looked at me full in the face and smiled, and I thought I was seeing an angel. She used to slip her little hand in mine and hold on for dear life when we went out together. As if she were frightened of being kidnapped or somehow separated from me. And when I realized that she had finally accepted me, finally loved me, it was—well, it was just about the greatest feeling in the world. Almost as great as the feeling I got when Tara said she would marry me." He took a long swallow of his drink and stared into the fireplace for so long that Barry thought he had forgotten he was there. He wanted to tell him that Mandy was his daughter but he knew that Tara would kill him if he did, so he remained silent, waiting for Eric to speak.

"You know, they both wanted to live in the San Fernando Valley, if you can believe that." Eric laughed hollowly. "Mandy wanted a pony and a dog and Tara was going to have a vegetable garden. God, how I was looking forward to seeing that!" He turned toward Barry, grinning. "Can't you just see it now, Bear? Tara Remington, the most beautiful woman in the world, in a pair of overalls with a hoe in one hand and a bunch of radishes in the other? Now wouldn't that stun the fashion world?" He turned back to stare into the flames of the fireplace, remembering the current issue of *Vogue* that carried a six-page spread of Tara modeling the new holiday fashions.

"They *are* living in the Valley now," Barry said. He patted his shirt pocket absently, then reached for Eric's cigarettes and shook one out.

"You're kidding? Where?" Eric clutched Barry's arm and shook him a little. "Where are they, Barry? You've got to tell me."

"Hey, you're bending the threads, man," Barry laughed and removed Eric's hand from his sleeve. "They live in Thousand Oaks in a great old barn of a house with a couple of acres out back and a real stream running through the property. Tara has every book she could find on gardening and has already had the gardener plow up a section of the back yard in preparation of spring planting. Mandy has a cute little Shetland pony named Macaroni and takes riding lessons three times a week. Of course, Daisy is with them, and quite indignant at having to share quarters with

Mandy's new puppy. Otherwise, everything seems serene on the farm, and they're both so busy and happy they simply haven't time to dwell on the past."

"That's great," Eric said. "I'm really happy for them." He tossed off the rest of his drink and sat staring into the empty mug.

"So am I," the Bear agreed. "This move was just what they both needed; to get away from the spotlight and spend some time getting to know one another again. The slow pace of country living gives them that time and they both seem to be thriving. Tara's working on her novel again and the parts she has let me read are fucking brilliant. It'll be published by Griffin Publishing, and, get this, Eric—they're putting out a million copies of the first printing. That's unheard of for an unknown writer." He laughed and added, "But I guess she isn't exactly unknown anymore, is she?"

"That's for damn sure. By the way, how is she handling all the crap in the fan magazines and tabloids?"

"Ignores it for the most part," Barry shrugged. "And Charley is living there with them as Tara's secretary and sort of buffer against the outside world. She takes care of all the mail and telephone calls, so I doubt that Tara even sees any of the garbage written about her. I usually go out a couple of times a month to see how they're getting along and often run into Thorton Kennedy or Glasser or some other old friend from the past. So she's not exactly hiding from everyone—just Zock's crowd and the reporters."

And me, Eric thought. "Why the hell can't they leave her alone?" he said harshly. "Fucking parasites, making a living off someone else's pain. Can't the pricks see that she's been ill?" He gripped Barry's arm. "She's better, isn't she, Bear? She's cured, isn't she?"

"Completely. She won't even take an aspirin, she's so down on drugs. She will have a little champagne now and then, but that's it. And it doesn't seem to bother her to be around other people who are drinking. She's always got the bar well stocked and the joints rolled and ready in case someone drops in. She's cooking her annual Christmas dinner for her Hollywood orphans tomorrow and plans on serving eggnog as usual. But she won't touch anything stronger than wine." He took a couple of walnuts from the bowl on the coffee table and cracked one against the other in his palm. "Which reminds me, I have to get out there and help put some of Mandy's toys together." He finished the walnut and brushed the bits of shell into the ashtray. "Tara bought her a pony cart, thinking it would be delivered all set up and ready to hitch to the pony, but it just arrived today in a big carton labeled 'assembly required' and she's in a panic." He stood, stretched, then sat back down and put his shoes on. He finished his drink and bummed another cigarette for the drive to Tara's.

Eric walked with him to the door and helped him on with his coat. He stalled a moment, not wanting to be alone just yet. "Thanks for stopping by, dear friend Bear. I really enjoyed it." They shook hands and Eric gave him a hug, keeping his arm about his shoulders.

"Same here, and thanks for dinner." Barry buttoned his coat and opened the door. "Well, see you around, Eric. Merry Christmas." He stepped outside, a little surprised that Eric followed, his arm still draped around Barry's shoulders.

"Sure thing, pal, same to you. Make it a good one." He gripped Barry's shoulder again, reluctant to release him. He did not want him to go. He did not want to turn and walk back into that empty house. But he could not think of any reason for asking him to stay.

He closed the door behind him and went directly to the bar and poured a large tumbler full of Jack Daniels. He paced aimlessly through the silent rooms, pausing a moment to look out at the brightly decorated streets. His neighbors' homes and lawns were vivid splashes of color and he thought he could hear the faint sound of laughter coming from within. He went to the sofa and sank down with a weary sigh. He aimed the remote control at the television set and clicked it on. Gay holiday noises leapt out and he changed channels until he found an old John

Wayne movie, not trusting himself to watch families celebrating Christmas together. The booz had made him melancholy and he felt a sudden wave of self-pity at being all alone on the holidays.

Tara would have her new home completely decorated, he knew, and there would be delicious odors coming from the kitchen. She would have her tree ablaze with twinkling lights and the scent of cloves would fill the air from the little sachets she made each year and hung about the room. There would be bowls of freshly popped corn and homemade fudge and divinity—which she would hide from the Bear (but not very carefully so that he would be sure to find it) and cookies shaped like Santa Claus. Eric wondered if Mandy had helped to make the cookies this year, and the thought brought a swift sudden pain. He had not realized until now how much he missed her. Almost as much as he missed Tara. He had gotten so close to her during the three years he and Tara had been together. And he had grown to love her almost as much as he loved her sister.

He sipped his drink, leaned back against the llama skin throw on the sofa, wondering what Tara would do if he just showed up there tomorrow. Would she kick him out in front of everyone? Or worse, allow him to stay but refuse to speak to him? He knew Tara was too gracious to turn anyone away on Christmas Day, but he was not sure he wanted to see her under those conditions. Perhaps he would call first and simply invite himself. It was possible that she had gotten over her anger and hurt since undergoing analysis at Camarillo. Surely she had had to admit the part Eric had played in her fucked-up life. That was part of getting well. Letting out all the old hurts and hostilities. Impulsively, before he could chicken out, he reached for the telephone to call her. It rang the second his fingers touched it.

"Monsieur Marlowe?" a voice purred huskily. "This is Favel Perls. We met in London at Doe Kingston's party, remember?"

"Uh, yes, of course, how are you?" Eric stammered,

trying to place the name. Then he remembered the wrap up party in Doe's suite at the Savoy Hotel and the short, curvy little French dame who had made such a blatant play for him. How in hell had she gotten his number?

"I am so very happy to catch you at home," Favel said in her soft accent. "Doe thought perhaps you had gone out of town for the holidays but suggested that I give you a ring just to be sure." When Eric did not reply she rushed on breathlessly, "And I am glad that you did not go out of town, Monsieur—Eric." She gave a throaty, sexy chuckle, her tone more intimate than was warranted by the words she spoke. "I may call you Eric, oui? And you simply must accept my invitation, chérie. We will have a most fabulous Christmas feast, oui?"

"Uh, Mrs. Perls—or Miss Frederick, I don't quite understand what you're asking." Was she inviting herself over for dinner or was she asking him to take her out someplace?

"Oh, I am so very sorry—I did not explain myself clearly, no? I am in town for a couple of months and Doe has so graciously invited me as her house guest over the holidays. We thought it would be a marvelous time to have a little dinner party, just a few close friends. You will say yes, won't you? I would not have a moment's pleasure if you refused."

Now how the hell do I get out of this? Eric thought. He knew he could not very well refuse, as the dinner would be held at Doe's house and she and Wesley had been so supportive of Eric during his personal problems. And if Eric knew Doe, she had probably been the one to suggest that Favel invite him as she suspected that he meant to spend Christmas alone with a bottle of Jack Daniels. She would not have been wrong, as that was just what he had planned. He took a swallow of his drink, stalling an answer. He knew he would have to at least put in an appearance. He owed Doe and Wesley that much. But to be paired with that hungry little French tart—he sighed in resignation. "I would be delighted, Miss Frederick."

"Please, chérie, call me Favel. Always you are so for-

mal and stuffy." She giggled in that irritating way he
remembered. "Perhaps I can help you unwind and relax
a little, no? You must come early so that we may have
some time together before the others arrive to—to get
better acquainted, oui?"

Eric mumbled some reply and she breathlessly told him
what time she would be expecting him before ringing off
with a deliberately sexy, throaty, *"Au 'voir, mon amour."*

Well, at least I won't be alone, he told himself as he
replaced the receiver. He stared moodily at the television
screen, wishing he had the nerve to call Tara. John
Wayne was mopping up the saloon floor with six bad
guys—three in each hand—while Dean Martin kept the
rest of the crowd covered with a sawed-off shotgun. Eric
had seen the movie so many times he knew the plot by
heart. In a moment the doors would swing open and
Ricky Nelson (as the Tennessee Kid) would back into
the saloon with his pearl-handled pistols drawn, ready to
take his place alongside the Duke in cleaning up the town.

Eric sighed and stretched out on the sofa, pulling the
llama skin throw over his shoulders. He propped his head
up on a couple of pillows and watched the Tennessee Kid
discharge both pistols into the face of a nasty outlaw who
was preparing to shoot John Wayne in the back. He wondered what Tara was doing at this very moment. She and
the Bear were probably trying to assemble the pony cart,
laughing, kidding around like they always did when they
got together. Like he and Tara had always done. They
had had such fun together. Had shared so many simple
pleasures and were always able to find humor in any
situation. Theirs had been a happy love, Tara had once
said.

Eric closed his eyes, giving himself up to the memories,
recalling each lovely expression, the sound of her laughter, the feel of her lips against his, the way their bodies
fitted so perfectly together . . . He gritted his teeth and
groaned at the sudden wave of desire that swept over him.
He could almost feel her silken skin, her breasts crushed
flat to his chest, her long legs gripping his waist as he
plunged into her. "Damn it," he cursed aloud and flung

the llama skin throw off as he got quickly to his feet. He clicked off the television set and weaved unsteadily into his bedroom and undressed. Without turning on the light he got into bed and reached quickly for his penis, bringing himself to a swift, bitter-sweet climax, Tara's name on his lips.

CHAPTER
NINE

TARA WAS IN THE LIVING ROOM, waiting for Charley and Mandy to come downstairs. She sat at one end of a long burgundy sofa, sipping a cup of coffee and filling her eyes with the elegance and luxury that surrounded her. The living room was the size of a football field (or so the Bear insisted), with an enormous natural stone fireplace reaching up to the second floor and dominating the entire wall at the far end. A magnificent portrait of Tara and Mandy hung above the fireplace. They were both dressed in white and the background was a deep royal wine, bordered in an intricately handcarved gilt frame. The angle of their heads, the slightly haughty lift to the chin, the squared shoulders spoke louder than words of their blood ties. Tara smiled as she looked at the portrait, remembering how impatient Mandy had been at the numerous sittings that had been required by the artist. It had just been delivered yesterday morning and no one had seen it except Hazel, the housekeeper, as Tara wanted it to be a surprise for Christmas morning. She glanced at her watch, wondering what was keeping Mandy and Charley.

She wandered about the large room, straightening a bowl of poinsettias, smoothing the lace cloth on a table, checking the Christmas tree lights to see if any needed replacing before the guests arrived. She straightened a chair, moving it a little closer to the intimate grouping near the fireplace. Most of the furnishings were European antiques (purchased on Robertson Boulevard without having to leave the country) and the warm cherrywood walls were hung with dozens of canvases, each a masterpiece: Renoir, Vermeer, Rembrandt, a charcoal sketch by Picasso and a couple of smaller sketches by da Vinci, all part of the more than generous divorce settlement from Zock. A smallish alcove was warmly inviting with crushed velvet love seats, the walls hung with *toile de jouy,* an exquisite printed fabric depicting a rural scene.

She wandered into the dining room, which was more than twenty yards long and held an enormous banquet table which had already been set for twenty-four. Tara paused to look at the delicate white Noritake china edged in hammered gold, the *vermeil* goldware properly arranged on either side and the holiday napkins of white linen folded in the shape of crisp roses. One whole wall was an art gallery, attractively arranged around a huge oblong gilt-frame mirror. Light and airy white sheers covered the ceiling-to-floor windows, bordered on either side by rich, café au lait drapes held back with thick braids of deep gold. The dining set was quietly opulent, an antique white Louis XV table with twenty-four chairs upholstered in satin brocade with *boiserie* arm rests and gently curved legs. Three large crystal vases held clusters of poinsettias, and there were six sets of tapering red candles ranging down the long stretch of snowy lace tablecloth. She picked up one of the name cards, smiling at the childish scrawl: Uncle Bear. Tara had asked Mandy to write out the cards and arrange the seating and the child had been at it for hours, changing the places so often that Tara had been afraid that the ink would be rubbed off.

There was a sliding panel and serving counter in the center of the opposite wall and she opened it a crack and peeked into the kitchen. Immediately her nostrils were filled with the delectable aroma of baking bread and brown sugar glaze and other succulent odors mingling together. "How's everything going?" she asked Hazel, and the plump cook turned and gave her a wide smile.

"Just fine, honey." She replaced the foil cap over a casserole of candied yams and slid it back into the oven. "How about another cup of coffee before the girls come down to breakfast?"

"No thanks, Hazel, two is my limit." She glanced around the immense, orderly kitchen. The floor was made of large, bold blocks of white and yellow tiles, and the ruffled curtains were sprigged with spring greens and yellows. There were two stoves, four ovens, a refrigerator and freezer that held enough frozen goods to feed an army and one very large antique chopping block that was Hazel's pride and joy. It was a cheerful kitchen, and Hazel filled it with strong, vigorous song as she went about her daily chores.

Tara closed the sliding panel and went back into the living room, glancing about to make sure that everything was perfect. Of course, she knew it would be; she had had excellent help from Mandy and Charley with the decorations. She wondered what was keeping them. She was anxious to show Mandy her new pony cart. She had instructed Teddy, the stableman, to have Macaroni hitched up and brought around to the front of the house by nine o'clock. She glanced at her watch. Just eight-thirty. Well, perhaps she was a little too anxious. This would be her first party since her divorce and her rehabilitation. And her first party with Mandy. She loved this house because it was all hers. No one could tell her what to do in this house. No one had ever slept in the king size bed before it had been installed in her upstairs bedroom. Always before she had been second, seeing things through the eyes of someone else. First, as a wide-eyed young girl working for Jim Glasser then as a love-blinded innocent following adoringly after Eric Marlowe, and finally as the wife and possession of Zock McBain.

Now all that was changed. She had her own ideas and was no longer afraid to act upon them. She had finally become comfortable within her own skin and knew, at last, who she was. No longer would wealth or worldliness intimidate her or make her feel self-conscious. She was her own woman now and her self-esteem had been heightened enormously since walking away from Zock and taking on her own life. Like purchasing and furnishing this sprawling, elegant mansion all on her own. She felt strong, invincible.

She stood at the glass doors and looked at the pool area with its shaded patio and man-made waterfall tinkling musically as it tumbled over rocks and splashed into the pool. A white wrought iron fence circled the patio that perched precariously on the edge of a cliff high above the San Fernando Valley. Great redwood buckets of lacey ferns and lush plants stood next to the iron railings, and several large palm trees cast a cool shade over most of the patio. To the right was an endless stretch of beautifully manicured lawn, dotted throughout with eucalyptus and walnut trees. The stable area began where the lawn ended, a solid red building trimmed in white at door and windows, with four stalls inside and a large holding corral outside. Half of the barn was used for storing hay, the other half a tack room complete with saddles, bridles, hackamores, blankets, exercise pads and all the equestrian implements that were needed. Five acres afforded Mandy ample riding space and held a small stream that ran down from a high mountain river. Large ancient oak trees dropped their acorns to the pine needle covered floor of the pasture, sharing the space with towering "Christmas" trees, as Mandy delighted in calling them.

Tara folded her arms across her breasts as she gazed at the beauty of *her* estate. She sometimes still could not believe it was really hers. But it was and she hugged herself, wanting to laugh out loud. She had fallen in love with the house the first time she had seen it. She had just been released from Camarillo and was staying with Barry Wilde, as she certainly would not think of going back to Zock's, and had taken a ride toward the beach one day. She had felt a need to get away from everyone for a while, to just drive and not have to talk to anyone. She had not taken the beach turn off but had continued on the Ventura Freeway until she was surrounded by rolling green hills and wooded valleys. The marvelous old oak trees seemed to beckon to her, and she had turned off to find herself in a little community called Thousand Oaks. She had never heard of the place before but had instantly loved the name. It sounded so regal and grand, like an old southern plantation.

She had driven slowly through the suburbs and then farther still until she had come upon the house. It set back a half mile from the road, a majestic two-story mansion with towering pillars in front and four honest to God turrets protruding elegantly from the roof. It was shrouded in enormous trees, pine, fir, oak, palm, eucalyptus, pepper, a fascinating pot pourri of trees as if someone had simply tossed a handful of mixed seeds into the wind and let them grow wherever they fell. The effect was wildly unique.

Tara had pulled her car into the circular driveway and saw that the house was empty and there was a for sale sign drooping on the dry lawn. She found an open window and crawled through without quite realizing what she was doing. Once inside she had caught her breath in wonder. Even totally empty and dusty, the house had captivated her, charmed her in a way nothing ever had. She went from room to room, marveling at the size, the extraordinary beauty of the leaded windows and stained glass skylights. She stood in the center of the massive living room and closed her eyes, seeing it as it should be. As it would be as soon as she bought it and called in a decorator. She had no idea how much this fantastic rustic castle would cost her but she did not care. She had to have it. And, thanks to Zock the Cock, she could have it. He had been more than generous in the divorce settlement, two and a half million dollars generous to be exact —not to mention the priceless paintings the lawyers had divided between them. And there would be royalties from *Lady Love*, as Zock had insisted that she had been wholly responsible for its being recorded. At first, she had turned down every settlement offer that her attorney had suggested, wanting nothing to remind her of the months she had spent as Mrs. Zock McBain, but after she had recovered she began to see the wisdom of his words. She had let her own career take a back seat to Zock's during the marriage, had followed him all over the world and seriously endangered her relationship with Mandy, had, in fact, gambled her health and almost lost it.

"You deserve everything you can get from that prick," Jim Glasser had said and Charley, Thorton and the Bear had emphatically agreed.

"Quite frankly, he won't even miss a couple of million," Thorton had said. "I've seen his income tax statements and he doesn't know himself how much money he has."

"He owes you, the bastard," Charley had said savagely, still smarting from the treatment she had received from Zock. "I'd make him pay through the nose."

"If you don't want to think of yourself," the Bear had said, "think of Mandy. You'll be able to buy the kind of house you've always wanted and get her that pony you promised her."

That had been the clincher. Tara still felt guilty about the months of anguish she had put Mandy through and wanted desperately to make it up to her. She knew that they would never get back their warm, close relationship as long as Mandy remained at the school, and Tara desperately needed someone close to her at this time in her life. She told her attorney to ask for whatever he thought fair, never dreaming that it would be so much— but delighted that Zock had agreed to such a sum without a whimper. She knew that he felt guilty about "turning her out" and getting her hooked on drugs. He had sent several letters of apology, as well as pleas to come back to him. She had answered none of them. That chapter of her life was over.

She had bought the house and had had it completely decorated before she had told Mandy anything about it. She and Charley had stayed in the house while it was being refurbished, and that was when Tara had asked her if she would consider working for her on a full-time basis.

"Just give me enough space to write my novel," she had said. "You'd be answering the phone and mail and keeping my appointments straight, handling the monthly bills, that sort of thing." She had grinned and added,

"Of course, I'd expect you to be reinstated as my personal hairdresser—that is, if Vidal-baby doesn't mind!"

Charley had accepted at once, saying, "Well, well, Tara's back and Charley's got 'er!"

Charley had chosen the upper corner suite that overlooked the pool area and had its own sitting room and private bath. Tara had had an outside stairway built that led up to the balcony on the second floor so that Charley could come and go privately if she so desired.

They had all been together for just a little over a week and so far it was working out beautifully. Mandy had been sulky and silent the first couple of days, stalking about the house like a prisoner unjustly jailed, barely speaking to Tara and treating Charley as if she were hired help, ordering her to fetch and carry as if Mandy were royalty. Tara had been amused at first, wondering where the child learned such high-handed manners; then she realized they were not manners at all but a lack of them, and had gone to her room to have a talk with her. She had not spared herself when she explained about her breakup with Eric (without telling the child that he was her father; she still could not bring herself to speak about that part of it) and her subsequent marriage to Zock. She tried to explain that newspapers were not always truthful and that the brief, stormy marriage had not been quite as outrageous as the press had depicted it. She told Mandy about her six weeks at Camarillo and how tough it had been to kick the drug and alcohol habit, and how much she needed Mandy now to help her stay well.

Mandy's lips had curled as she sneered, "Yeah, you *need* me all right—about as much as Elvis Presley needs another hit record!"

"Mandy, that's not true," Tara had protested, leaning forward to take her little sister's hands in her own. "I do need you. Very much—and I love you and want us to be together—"

"Since when?" the child had interrupted, jerking her hands from Tara's. "You've never wanted me. And you've

189

never loved me! Only Eric loved me and you sent him away!"

Tara had been stunned silent, staring at the look of pure hatred that twisted Mandy's pretty face into something quite ugly. She was almost thirteen years old and her tee-shirt showed small bumps of just-budding breasts. Her lanky frame was beginning to take on curves where scraped elbows and knees had been last year. Her vivid blue eyes were cold as ice, and her lower lip seemed in danger of falling off if she stuck it out any further. Tara had reached for her hands again, but Mandy jerked them back and folded her arms across her chest. "I *do* love you, Mandy, more than you will ever know. My God, everything I've done has been with you in mind—to—to get you home with me and—"

"Oh, sure," Mandy had sneered. "What for? So your stinky ole husband can turn me out like he did you? I know all about you and him and those awful girls in Europe!"

Tara's mouth had fallen open with surprise and she had been stunned for a full minute. Then she grabbed Mandy's arm and jerked her across her lap and slapped her on the buttocks as hard as she could. Sharp pain stung her palm and she grabbed a book lying on the table and proceeded to spank Mandy until she could not lift her arm. "Why, you little ingrate," she panted, smacking the book down hard and gritting her teeth against Mandy's loud wails. "How dare you speak to me that way! You are going to straighten up your act, young lady, and I mean now!" A couple of more well-placed smacks with the book and Mandy screamed bloody murder, struggling futilely against Tara's hold on her. "I've gone through hell these past six months and I'll be damned if I'm going to take any shit from a snot-nosed little brat who doesn't know the first thing about life!" She tossed the book to the floor and jerked Mandy upright, still holding her by the shoulders half on and half off her lap. She was a long-legged child, tall for her age, and her eyes were on the same level as Tara's as they glared at one another. "Okay, that's just for openers," Tara panted, trembling with the emotion and violence that had swept through her. "Every time I even so much as *see* a surly expression on your face, you're going to get more of the same. And if I ever hear of you speaking to Charley or any of the servants as you have these past couple of days, you'll get it again!" She shook her, snapping the child's head back and forth as if she were a rag doll. "Do I make myself clear? Do you understand exactly what I mean, Mandy? You are a part of this family and you are going to behave like it. I refuse to make excuses for you or explain your abominable behavior to anyone! Do you understand me, Mandy?"

Mandy gulped back tears and stood before Tara with eyes round and wide with shock. She reached both hands around behind her and gingerly rubbed her buttocks, staring at Tara. "You spanked me," she whispered.

"Yes, I spanked you and I'll do it every time I catch you being a brat. I love you and I will not allow you to grow into a spoiled monster whom no one wants to be around! We're starting a new life together, just you and me, Mandy, and I want it to be so perfect for us. So beautiful. But I can't do it without your help. You have to want to make it work too."

"You spanked me," Mandy repeated. "Nobody ever spanked me before."

"That's certainly obvious," Tara said dryly. She closed her eyes briefly, sorry that she had given in to her fit of anger but realizing that she had to set the precedent for the future then and there or Mandy would walk all over her.

"You spanked me because you love me," Mandy whispered and threw herself into Tara's arms, fresh tears streaming down her cheeks. "Oh, Tara, you *do* love me! You do! I thought you didn't. I thought you didn't even care what happened to me. You never scolded me or told me to stop being a brat when I knew I was being one. And—and Mindy Harmon at school said that parents only spank their kids because they love them and want them to grow up right—and you never ever spanked me, so I thought you didn't love me or want me! And the only time anybody ever told me 'no' was when Eric swatted me on the butt at the zoo, remember? You know that time when I almost fell into the seal's pond because I climbed up on the fence and Eric grabbed me right off and swatted me and told me never to do that again, remember? I knew then that he loved me and was worried about me hurting myself." She sniffed and wiped her nose on the back of her hand. "But you never did hit me and tell me 'no' or anything. You just let me do whatever I wanted to and I thought you didn't even care if I got hurt or anything."

"Oh, Mandy, Mandy," Tara cried, shaking her head, torn between laughing and crying. Dear God, where did kids get such ideas? Here she thought she had been showing her love for Mandy by allowing her to do things she enjoyed, and all the time Mandy wanted someone to tell her what *not* to do. She hugged the child close and Mandy clung to her, her tears wetting Tara's cheek and neck. She petted her for a moment, then wiped the tears from her eyes and kissed first one then the other.

"I've always loved you, baby, always, and if I didn't tell you 'no' it's because I wanted you to have a chance to do all the things I didn't get to do as a child. I guess I wanted too much for you—just as I wanted too much for myself." She held Mandy's face between two hands, gazing with tenderness at the tearful smile and trembling mouth. "So we've both been wrong—now we start over and make everything right, okay?"

Mandy nodded her head, gulping back a hiccough, and they had hugged one another for a long, long time. When Charley had joined them a few minutes later, Mandy had proudly showed her still-red and smarting buttocks and declared, "I got a spanking today, see? Tara really loves me! Just like she was my own mother."

Tara smiled at the memory as she went to the window and looked toward the stable to see if Teddy was on his way. She had taken Mandy out that same afternoon of the spanking and bought her a chubby little pony named Macaroni, and the child's behavior had been perfect from that moment on. Tara had not enrolled her in school yet, feeling it would be best to wait until the semester break in January, so that Mandy had plenty of time to become acquainted with her new pony. The first thing after breakfast she was out in the stable, hanging onto Teddy's every word and learning all she could about caring for Macaroni.

"Merry Christmas, Tara, Merry Christmas!" Mandy's high childish voice came to her and Tara turned to see her dashing madly down the stairs, Charley a couple of steps behind. Mandy ran directly to the tree, skidded to a stop on her knees and reached for the first present she saw.

"Hold up there, keed-o," Tara laughed. She went to her and gave her a big hug. "Merry Christmas, sleepy head—I've been up for hours." She smiled at Charley and the two women embraced warmly. "Merry Christmas, good friend," Tara murmured and then sank down next to Mandy amid the jumble of presents. "Do you want to dig them out on your own or shall I play Santa Claus?" she asked.

"You play Santa," Mandy cried, excitement keen in her voice. She settled herself next to the tree and waited expectantly. Tara handed her the first gift, a paint by number set that Thorton had dropped off earlier that week. Mandy tore the paper off, made oh-ah sounds, tossed it aside and reached for the next gift.

Charley excused herself to get a cup of coffee and when she returned Tara handed her a large box. "This one says 'open me first,' " she said with a chuckle. "Wonder how Santa knew where to find you?"

"For me?" Charley said broadly, feigning surprise. She opened the gift and caught her breath in surprised amazement. "Oh my God, Tara!" Both hands dug into the tissue paper and withdrew a luxurious morning dawn mink jacket trimmed in darker leather at the collar and pockets. She immediately slipped it on and snuggled the soft fur up about her chin and face. "My God, I can't believe it! Is this really for me?" She stroked the front of the jacket as she turned to look at herself in the mirror. "This *is* real mink, isn't it? I mean, you didn't trap a muskrat and have it dyed, did you?"

"Well, as a matter of fact—" Tara began and then was almost knocked off balance as Charley flung herself upon her and hugged her tight.

"Oh, Tara, thank you, I can't believe it! I don't even know if I should take it, it's so expensive and Mother always said to be wary of expensive gifts unless they were from your husband. Is this a proposal, lady?" Tears sparkled in her eyes and her smile wavered a little. "Mandy, get that red and gold package back there, will you, honey?" When the child gave it to her she handed it to Tara, saying, "I hope you understand."

Tara opened it to find a daily record book of appointments (she was notoriously forgetful) with her name in gold leaf on the leather cover. She flipped through the pages and saw that Charley had had each page printed with a poem or saying by one of the masters, Shakespeare, Ben Franklin, Thoreau, Khayyam, Hess, Wilde—and on each page, just beneath the date, were these words: Today is the first day of the rest of your life.

"Oh, Charley, it's beautiful." She glanced down at a page and read aloud, "To thine own self be true. Boy, did you ever hit it right on the ole head—what can I say? Thank you so much. I love it."

Hazel stuck her head around the door and called, "Breakfast in fifteen minutes, Miss Remington." She smiled at the warm family scene by the Christmas tree, then added in a stage whisper, "I think Teddy is coming up to the front door right about now in case you're interested."

"Oh, good. Thanks, Hazel." Tara held out both hands to Mandy, helping her to her feet. "Come on, pumpkin, I think Santa left a little something for you outside."

"What?" Mandy cried, scrambling to her feet. "What is it? Why couldn't you bring it into the house? Is it a pet? It's an animal, isn't it? What is it, Tara?" She practically danced out of her slippers in her eagerness to get to the door first, but Tara held her back and told her to close her eyes. Charley held the door open and Tara

led the child down the stairs to the driveway. Teddy
stood holding the bridle of Macaroni's new harness. The
cart was bright red and white, the brass buckles polished
to a high sheen and shining in the morning sun. Macaroni's hooves had been polished a glossy ebony and his
coat had been brushed until it shone. There were several
bells on the harness that jiggled merrily as the pony
stamped his feet and snorted impatiently.

"Oh, wow, a pony cart!" Mandy cried and ran and
climbed into it, hitching up her nightgown and robe as
she clambered onto the seat. "Just what I wanted!" She
gathered up the reins and clicked her tongue at the pony.
"Giddup, Macaroni, let's go!" She flicked the reins across
his back and he snorted and shook her head as if saying
"no way" and she flicked him again. He braced his
front feet in the driveway like a stubborn donkey, refusing
to budge. Everyone laughed as Teddy took the bridle
and tugged the pony forward. He urged him into a trot,
taking him down the driveway and back again.

"He'll have to get used to pulling a cart, ma'am," he
told Tara. "But we shouldn't have any trouble breaking
him to it, right, Mandy?" He tousled the child's hair
and she smiled shyly up at him, a look of pure adoration
in her eyes. She had announced to Tara that Teddy knew
everything in the world there was to know about horses
and he was going to teach it all to her. She would have
liked to take Macaroni around the driveway once more
but climbed down when Tara told her to with only a min-
imal amount of fuss.

They breakfasted elegantly on Hazel's famous eggs
le Goldenrod (Mandy complaining good naturedly that
the sauce was "guckie" and she would rather have corn
flakes), then went back into the living room to finish
opening their presents. Tara sat on the floor next to the
fireplace and looked around at the jumble of wrapping
paper, ribbons, cards and boxes, smiling softly. This is
the way it should be, she thought. This is the way I've
always dreamed of spending Christmas, surrounded by
loved ones. She thought suddenly of Eric and a deep
loneliness fluttered in the pit of her stomach. He had

always been in her dream of the perfect family gathering, and his absence took some of the joy out of the morning. She raised her eyes to look at the portrait of Mandy and herself and could almost see Eric standing between them.

Tara lay in her bed watching the last flickering flames in the fireplace turning into glowing white embers. The antique cuckoo clock in the downstairs hall struck midnight and she sighed and snuggled into a more comfortable position. She loved having a fireplace in her bedroom. Loved to lie in bed at the end of a long day and watch the flames dancing and swaying, performing for her eyes alone. It had been a long day, but a beautiful one. Hazel's ham dinner had affected everyone like an exotic drug, lulling them into a languid mood that lasted throughout the afternoon and early evening. To ensure that they stayed mellow, a huge cut crystal punchbowl was kept constantly filled with creamy eggnog, also a large pot of hot mulled cider or buttered rum for a change of taste, and an occasional joint had been passed around the group. Mandy had been perfectly delightful, helping Tara see to it that their guests were kept satisfied, taking charge of the stereo and selection of Christmas carols and even emptying ashtrays when the cleaning girls were busy elsewhere.

Thorton came with his usual sexy starlet clinging to his arm. Tara had met so many of Thorton's "pinkies" (as she called them) that she no longer bothered trying to keep them straight. They all looked the same to her: cute, dumb, ambitious, under twenty, blonde, brunette or redhead, it made no difference, they were all big-busted and slightly bewildered-looking. They all had names like Debbie, Mitz, Bunny or Sandy and they all (curiously) seemed to need something when they met Thorton. Teeth straightened or capped, dancing or singing lessons, a mysterious operation, and all were consistently behind in their rent and/or car payments and phone bill.

Charley and the Bear teamed up as dinner partners and later spent so much time under the mistletoe that

Jim Glasser told them they should charge admission. Glasser had arrived after dinner, apologizing for having had to spend the day with his family, and Tara wondered for the hundredth time how his wife put up with it. He was rarely home, even on holidays, and then only for the sake of his three children. Tara had met them once when Frances had brought them to the office to show them where Daddy spent all his time. (She had said it facetiously, but Tara had seen the look of pure hatred in her eyes before she had turned away.) There were two boys, fourteen and six, and a girl of ten who was so like Jim she could have been a miniature clone. Tara knew that Jim loved his kids but just barely tolerated Frances, who was a devout Catholic. Therefore divorce was out of the question. Tara felt sorry for Jim's being trapped in a loveless marriage and knew that it contributed to his drinking. He had behaved himself impeccably today and seemed as smitten with Mandy as she was with him. After he had fortified himself against the nip in the air (with several nips of bourbon), he had gone out to the stable with her and spent over an hour leading Macaroni around the pasture with Mandy perched in her new cart.

Doe had telephoned to wish everyone a Merry Christmas and then had said, "Wait a second, honey, there's someone here who wants to say hello."

Thinking she meant Wesley, Tara waited. She heard the deep familiar voice and her heart seemed to stop beating for a full minute. She took a deep breath and said as calmly as she could, "Hello, Eric, Merry Christmas." He had asked her how she was and she had answered politely that she was well. They exchanged a few more stilted words, speaking like proper strangers. Then Eric had whispered huskily, "I love you, Tara, I'm still so much in love with you I ache all over just hearing your voice. God, baby, come back to me! Please!"

And Tara had gently replaced the receiver and stood trembling for several moments, his words repeating themselves inside her brain. And heart. She had been so shocked to hear his voice that she had been totally unprepared to respond. Damn Doe! She had no right putting Eric on the phone without warning her!

Tara sighed and squirmed deeper into the soft fur of the chinchilla bedspread. (Zock had insisted that she keep it. It was, after all, her wedding present.) She had managed to get through the rest of the day without thinking about Eric, but now that she was alone the bitter-sweet words came back to her: "I love you—please come back to me." Damn it, would his memory forever haunt her? Would she never forget the beauty of her first love and find someone else to be happy with? Was there anyone else in the world as wonderful as Eric had been those days long ago when love was all that mattered? Why had the ugliness had to come into their perfect love? She sighed again and turned over on her stomach, burying her face in the pillow, deliberately forcing thoughts of Eric from her mind. She did not want to think about love. She had her life neatly organized now, all the corners carefully tucked into place, and she did not want anything disrupting it.

Tara lay on her stomach on a chaise longue by the pool, reading the current issue of *Time* magazine. There before her, in living color and an all but topless gown, was Doe Kingston grinning broadly as she clutched the Oscar to her bared breasts. Lee Marvin stood next to her, one arm about her waist, the other raised high and clutching his Oscar.

Tara did not bother to read the article, as she had been present when Doe and Lee won for Best Actress and Actor. Tara had gone to the Awards with Barry, and both of them had been surprised that Doe had won. The current publicity about the blonde sex symbol and England's finest, Wesley Cunningham, had not been too flattering. The press had accused Doe of husband-stealing and home-wrecking, printing photographs of her half-nude from some old movie or modeling session she had done as a brazen starlet struggling to be recognized—and next to it a photograph of Sybil Cantford Cunningham, demurely dressed and surrounded by her six children. Photos of

Wesley also appeared, looking bloated and fuzzy sitting at a table littered with cocktail glasses and booze bottles, the inference being that Doe had bewitched him and driven him to drink out of guilt for his wife and poor fatherless children. It was enough to make you want to barf, Tara thought, but she knew that bad publicity could seriously affect Doe's chances of winning the Oscar. Ironically, as bad as it could be for Doe, it could only be good for Eric's movie, as everyone wanted to see Doe and Wesley actually falling in love on the screen.

Therefore it had come as quite a surprise to Tara that Doe had won and Eric and Wesley had lost. But Tara had also lost.

Tara had seen Eric at the Awards with a stunning redhead on his arm and had felt a swift pang of jealousy. Later at the party at the Beverly Hills Hotel, she had casually asked a few friends who the girl was but no one seemed to know. She had hoped that Eric would show up at the party so she could get another look at the redhead, but when they hadn't arrived by midnight she asked the Bear to take her home.

Tara let the magazine fall to the ground and laid her head on her crossed arms, closing her eyes against the glaring sun. It was unusually warm for April and she had turned a shade darker just since this morning. The soft murmur of the waterfall splashing into the pool lulled her and she felt drowsy for the first time since finishing her novel. She had mailed it off two days ago and had been so wired she had not been able to come down yet. She could not seem to turn her brain off. It whirled with questions, fears, excitement, apprehension, a thrill in her belly that was almost sexual as she awaited news from Griffin Publishing Company.

Writing her story had been the hardest thing she had ever done. It had been like therapy, as painful as childbirth. She had actually wept all alone in her office when she had written about her mother's death in that cold, dispirited apartment with a three-month-old infant half-dead from malnutrition sleeping a few feet away from her mother's stiffening corpse; and a frightened ten-year-

old now completely alone in the world. The words had
flowed, tumbling over themselves in their eagerness to be
written, to have the story told and the author purged. She
called it *Seattle Slum*.

She had moments of anxiety wondering what Mandy
would think if she should ever read it. Would she recognize that it was Tara's childhood, and therefore her own?
Tara rather doubted it, as most of the story took place
when Mandy was too young to remember. And she had
been very careful about using real names, not quite brave
enough to admit that *Seattle Slum* was her own life story.

Thinking of Mandy, she suddenly remembered that she
had promised to meet her at the White Oak Stables that
afternoon to watch her compete in a gymkhana show.
With a sigh she got to her feet and went inside the house
to her bedroom to shower and dress. She would have
liked to just loaf around all day in the sun, not bothering
with clothes or makeup, but Mandy had pleaded so
prettily that Tara had been unable to refuse. This would
be her fourth show and she was getting awfully good,
bringing home a stack of ribbons every weekend. She had
yet to win a First Place blue ribbon but had solemnly
promised Tara that today was the day—if Tara would
come out and root for her to bring her luck.

Tara sat on a bale of hay next to the arena, watching
Mandy and Macaroni tear around a series of barrels, the
pony's hooves kicking up a thick cloud of dust. They
turned on a dime at the end barrel and raced back to the
starting line, sliding to a halt in front of the judge's stand.

"Mandy Remington," the judge bawled through a loudspeaker. "Time, twelve point four seconds."

Tara started slightly at the name, still unaccustomed to
hearing it spoken. At midnight on New Year's Eve when
she and Mandy had been toasting in 1975, Mandy had
asked if she could have her last name legally changed to
Remington. "It would just make things a lot easier when
I start my new school," she had said, looking anxiously
at Tara as if she were frightened that she might refuse. "I
mean, when the teachers send home papers and stuff for

you to sign, you know. It feels funny to have two different names."

Tara had been so touched she had almost cried and had taken Mandy into her arms and hugged her a long time. She knew this was Mandy's way of saying that she had forgiven Tara, that she was once more proud of her big sister and anxious to show her off to her new friends. She looked up at her as she wheeled Macaroni through the gate and came cantering toward her. She rode with ease, her lithe young body moving with a sensuous grace as if she were a part of the pony. She leaned slightly forward in the saddle, her hands holding the reins loosely and comfortably as she guided the pony with her knees.

"Darn it, we blew it on that last barrel," Mandy said as she reined Macaroni to a stop in front of Tara. She dismounted and went to sit on the bale of hay.

"Twelve seconds isn't too shabby," Tara grinned.

"Yeah, except Tommy Wheatly got ten seconds," she said with a grimace. "Gosh, I'm thirsty. Do you have anything to drink?"

Tara handed her the can of Coke she had been drinking, shaking her head at the child's sweaty, dirt-streaked face. She was dirty all over, her tight Levis were sweat-stained in the crotch and down the inner thighs where she had ridden Macaroni bareback, her Western boots were covered in a layer of dust and her baggy tee-shirt was grass-stained and covered in horse hair. Tara shook her head again, grinning. Kids today dressed as if they were on welfare, the more raggedy and faded the better. Mandy would spend hours in Saks or I. Magnin, searching for just the right pair of blue jeans, then would dunk them in bleach, cut off the hems and fray the cuffs, then sit in a tub of cold water until they shrank to her every contour. Until then they were not considered fit to wear in public.

"You'll probably get a second, won't you?" Tara asked. "I don't remember anyone else getting a twelve point four."

"I think Val Nelson beat me. I was getting ready for

my ride and didn't hear what her time was." She looked down at the ribbons she had already won that day; three second places, one third and four fifths. She hated getting fifth place because there were usually only five contestants in a class. It was like coming in dead last in a horse race. "I have to win a first place today! I just *have* to!"

Tara glanced at her watch. "The show's almost over, isn't it? How many more events have you entered?"

"Just the boot race and single pole," Mandy replied. She finished the Coke and tossed the can into a trash basket. "Mac's really good at sharp turns, so we might have a chance in single pole." She stood, tucked her tee-shirt into the waist of her jeans and bent to give Tara a kiss. "Wish me luck, sis."

"You've got it, honey," Tara smiled. "Get out there and knock 'em dead." She waved her off, marveling anew at how well she rode. She had a natural grace that could not be learned but was born into a good horsewoman. Or so Teddy had said. After a few weeks of working with her, Teddy had told Tara that there was nothing else he could teach her.

"She takes to horses like she's been around them all her life," the seasoned stableman had said. "All she needs now is a little polish if she wants to get into competitive riding like English or Western pleasure or gymkhana." So Tara had found an instructor for her, and soon after she was entering shows every weekend.

Tara squirmed on the scratchy hay, wishing the show was already over. As much as she admired Mandy's riding ability and liked to see her involved in a sport she loved, Tara often found the shows overlong and boring. The arena was dusty and smelled of horse manure, and her fanny inevitably fell asleep from so many hours spent just sitting. She lit a cigarette, careful of where the ashes fell, as there was dry hay everywhere, her thoughts turning once more to her novel. God, they had to like it, she thought for the hundredth time since mailing it off. She had submitted only a sketchy outline of *Seattle Slum* to Griffin Publishing and had been amazed when they had responded immediately with an offer of a contract. Thorton had handled the negotiations and had told her that a million copies for the first printing was unthinkable for a new author, as was the advance of twenty thousand dollars. She was aware that the publishers were capitalizing on her name and the notorious publicity she had gotten the past year, but if it would help sell *Seattle Slum* then she didn't mind.

She heard Mandy's name over the loudspeaker and looked up just in time to see her little sister pull her lathered pony to a stop in front of the judge's stand. She had won first place in single pole and Tara had been so preoccupied with her own thoughts that she had not even seen the ride. Well, at least the show was over and she could get out of this choking dust and back to the quiet of her beautiful home. She gathered up Mandy's ribbons and put them in the car and then waited until she trotted over to show her the prized blue ribbon. Gloria Smith, Mandy's instructor, would trailer Macaroni home and Mandy wanted to know if she could ride with her.

"Sure, honey, go ahead," Tara said, giving her a hug. She held her at arm's length and their eyes were almost on the same level. "Hey, keed-o, I'm really proud of you. It was a terrific ride." She could not admit that she had not seen it, as Mandy was practically bursting with pride at how well Macaroni had run the poles. "See you at home. Maybe we'll have dinner out tonight to celebrate. Would you like that?"

Mandy agreed enthusiastically and asked Tara to invite Uncle Bear and Charley so "the whole family can be together." And Tara felt the familiar wrench of missing Eric every time the word "family" was mentioned. God damn it, would his memory always be there to ruin everything she had dreamed of? She slid behind the wheel of her red Mercedes and revved up the motor, as if the sound of the powerful engine would drown out the sound of Eric's name repeating itself inside her brain.

CHAPTER
TEN

TARA SAT waiting in the Green Room for her call. She was watching the Tonight Show on the monitor and laugh-aloud at the crazy antics of Don Rickles as he cavorted about the stage. He was sweating profusely and Ed Mc-Mahon gave him a large white handkerchief, which Rickles immediately draped over his head and the audience screamed with delight. Carson, still chuckling, said for the ninety-sixth time that evening, "We'll pause for this and be right back. Don't go away." And a dancing fe-line pushing cat food pranced across the screen. Tara glanced at her watch. God, the show would be over in fifteen minutes and she still had not been called. Just as she was debating if she should haughtily stalk out, the producer stuck his head around the door and said, "Two minutes, Miss Remington, okay?"

It's about frigging time, Tara thought, but said aloud, "Fine, thanks." She stood and straightened her pencil-slim skirt over her hips and adjusted the low V of her silk Pucci blouse. Catching her reflection in the glass panel she thought: Not bad, no one would ever guess I've been in twenty different states in the last two weeks and haven't slept a whole night through in twice that time.

The sky-rocketing success of *Seattle Slum* had plunged her into a kind of crazy fantasy over which she had no control. She felt like Alice following the white rabbit beyond the looking glass.

She remembered the exact day that her carefully made serene world had been shattered. She had been doing research for her next novel and had, for the moment, forgotten *Seattle Slum* and her anxiety about its acceptance. When she had mailed it off last spring Griffin Publishers had been delighted and had gone to press at once upon receipt of the manuscript, sending her endless galleys and art work for the cover, as well as requesting a photograph of Tara for the dust jacket and a brief biography, any amusing anecdote she may remember, her travels, education, past successes, etc. *and* etc., until Tara's head had spun with it all. She had no idea publishing a book could be so involved and had slightly resented the invasion of her privacy. After a month of steady demands she had taken Mandy and gone to Palm Springs for a week, leaving Charley to make her excuses.

That summer she had decided on the subject of her next novel. She had been exhausted when she had completed *Seattle Slum* and had taken a couple of months to simply lie around the pool, working on her tan and reading Gothic romances. She loved those sprawling epics of love and adventure, and the more she read the more she began to think that she could write one just as well as Victoria Holt, Mary Stewart or Phyllis Whitney. She went to the public library and browsed for hours, finally deciding on New Orleans as the setting for her novel for no other reason than that she loved the era of dusky Creoles and leisure plantation life in the old South. Almost all the historical romances she had read dealt with the Civil War and the racial upheaval, the buying and selling of slaves, the beautiful daughter of a wealthy plantation owner forced to submit to the damn Yankees and/or stand off the entire Northern army singlehandedly to protect the old homestead. Tara was weary of such tales and decided to write her novel about the gentle days before the blood bath of the war. The days when elegance was the order of the day and genteel ladies and gentlemen made languid love beneath the sweet-scented boughs of a magnolia tree.

She had checked out several books on Louisiana dealing with the late 1700's and early 1800's and was now sprawled on the floor of her bedroom going through them when the phone rang. It was her private line (Charley or Hazel answered the house phone), so she picked it up and heard Thorton's excited voice on the other end.

"What did I tell you?" he shouted. "Didn't I say *Seattle Slum* would be the biggest book of the year? They've sold out, Tara! Already! Before the damn thing's even on the stands!"

"Wait a minute, slow down," Tara laughed. "What happened?" She sat up and lit a cigarette, tossing the match into the fireplace.

"I just spoke with Hy Griffin and he says they've already gotten a million orders for *Seattle Slum.* They're ready to go into a second printing and want you to start making the rounds of the talk shows. I'll get on the horn tomorrow and line up Carson, Douglas, Griffin, Kup and, let's see, who else? We've got to make all the little local shows too. Can't afford to offend anyone."

"You're kidding," was all Tara could manage. She leaned back against a chair and sat staring into the flames of the fireplace as Thorton's excited voice went on about the publicity campaign. She had dreamed of this moment, had both dreaded it and expected it, but now that it was actually here, she found she really could not believe it. *Her* book a smashing success? Would she be listed in *Time* magazine under Best Sellers, Remington, Tara? She was barely aware of what Thorton was saying and finally interrupted him. "Listen, can we get together tonight and talk about this? I have to sort out my head. This is too much all at once."

That had been the beginning and Tara still could not believe it was happening to her. She had been on the talk show circuit for three months now and there wasn't a television or radio show between California and New York that she hadn't visited. Her keen wit and slightly racey manner of speaking had garnered her a following, and she had found herself becoming something of a minor celebrity. As she had suspected, most talk show hosts eventually got around to the subject of Zock McBain and how it felt to be married to the most famous singer in the world. Tara kept her answers light and playful, refusing to be tricked into making an ass of herself on national television. She discussed her former drug addiction in the same bantering tone, slightly self-deprecating and with a lot of humor. One of her comments had appeared in every gossip column and magazine in the industry the following day. The host had leaned in close, fixing her with his stern-father expression, and asked, "But what about LSD, Tara? What did it do for you? We've heard so much about psychedelics, I'm sure we'd all like to know what happens on an LSD trip or whatever you young people call it."

And Tara had replied, dryly, "It isn't all it's cracked up to be. The last acid trip I took was hardly worth the brain damage."

There was a soft rap on the door and the producer opened it and motioned to her. "Ready?" he asked and Tara nodded, took a deep breath and stepped through the door with her heart in her throat. No matter how many shows she had appeared on, there was always the initial fear that she would make a fool of herself, forget the name of her book or some such stupid thing. Several members of the crew looked her up and down appreciatively as she went to the curtain and stood waiting for Carson to introduce her. She was used to it. In every town she had appeared in she was inevitably told, "Gee, you don't *look* like a writer," to which Tara would counter, "Really? What does a writer look like?" Thorton had warned her that her looks would go both for and against her. There would be those men who refused to believe that anyone as sexy and beautiful as Tara could have a thought in her head, and others who would believe that she was some sort of freak, a smart female.

"We're back," Tara heard Johnny Carson saying. "And we've got a real treat for you tonight. Tara Remington is here." The audience whistled and cheered and Johnny waited for quiet before continuing. "That's right, the sexy author of *Seattle Slum* is with us." He turned to Ed Mc-

Mahon and asked, "Is that author or authoress?" and Ed replied, "Try writer," to which the audience laughed louder than the joke merited. "All right buffalo breath," Johnny grinned. "Here she is, ladies and gentlemen, the sexy *writer*, Tara Remington. Let's give her a big welcome."

The curtain was swept aside by an invisible stagehand and Tara took a deep breath and stepped onto the stage, nodding slightly to acknowledge the applause and whistles. There were several wolf whistles thrown in and she unconsciously straightened her shoulders and sucked in her stomach. Well, here I go again, she said to herself, and headed for the small platform.

By Christmas the sales of *Seattle Slum* had doubled and Thorton was in a paroxysm of ecstasy as he busily negotiated paperback rights, movie rights and serialization. Every top producer in Hollywood was vying for the rights to *Seattle Slum*, and Thorton was gleefully playing one against the other to get the price even higher. When he had called to tell Tara that Eric had offered seventy-five thousand for the screen rights, she had said without hesitation, "Turn it down. No way is that bastard going to have anything to do with my book." And deep inside she pushed away the fact that Eric *was* her book in more ways than one. Thorton had argued that seventy-five thousand was fantastic, unheard of for a new writer and that they should accept it and personal feelings be damned. But Tara had remained firm. "Anyone but him," she had insisted stubbornly.

The screen rights had finally gone to Jonathan Monash, a veteran film maker who was considered a top specialist in the field, a genius, acutely aware of every nuance of the picture making business and one who had consistently made movies that won Academy Awards.

By the spring of 1976 Tara had exhausted the talk shows and had settled down to begin writing her new novel. She was now a celebrity, and Thorton was deluged with offers for her to write magazine articles, to go on the lecture circuit, to be interviewed, etc. *Seattle Slum* had been on the best seller list for months and had sold over four and a half million copies. Tara received so much fan mail and just plain mail of all kinds that she had had to hire someone to help Charley in the office. After interviewing several females for the job, she had hired a rather flamboyant homosexual, Izzy Strait, for no other reason than that he amused her and she liked his style. Charley always traveled with Tara, leaving the office work to pile up until they returned home, so Izzy was a godsend.

He was in his late forties, an aging dandy who leaned toward bright silk ascots to hide the age wrinkles about his throat and specially made corsets that nipped in his waist and held back his tired stomach. He always dressed elegantly, loved to cook—did so divinely—and was just catty enough to be interesting. He and Tara spent hours giggling together over the latest Hollywood gossip, as Izzy knew everyone's darkest secret. How he managed to find out such intimate details of the stars' lives Tara never knew, but delighted in hearing just the same. He was a witty dinner companion and a staunch friend who made no bones about the fact that he clearly adored Tara. He often would sigh, "If only I were into women . . ." He wore his hair curled to his shoulders, and Tara suspected that he tinted it the rich auburn shade that set off his hazel eyes to such advantage.

Tara sat on the leather sofa in her office, listening to Izzy reading her a letter from a Sicilian duke who had read an article about her and was inviting her to spend a week on his yacht. He sat perched on the edge of the swivel chair, one ankle tucked behind the other, his long pale fingers playing with the loose knot in his paisley ascot. "I think you should go, sweetie," he said when he had finished reading the letter. "Santino Crocetti is a fox. And richer than sin if all I hear about him is true." He fitted a cigarette into a long, thin holder and clenched it between his perfect white teeth, lighting up and blowing a perfect smoke ring. "Let's go, Tara. It'll be a gas!"

"Where do you get this 'we' stuff," Tara said, raising

an eyebrow. "I didn't hear the duke inviting you to join us."

"But, sweetie, someone has to go along as your traveling companion. It simply wouldn't do to visit royalty without an entourage."

"Charley travels with me, remember? That's why you were hired. To hold down the fort while we're away." Tara stifled a laugh at the sudden crushed expression on Izzy's face.

"Merde," he sulked. "Why do women always get the cushy jobs?"

"Don't worry about it, Izzy," Tara laughed. "I'm not going to meet the duke this weekend or any other weekend. I have to get to work on my book so the press can tell the world how prolific I am." She lit a cigarette and added, "Besides, I thought you had your hands full with your new crop of pinkies."

Izzy grinned mischievously, his pale gray eyes twinkling at the thought. "Indeed I do," he murmured. "Indeed I do. You met Bobby, didn't you? That sweet young thing I took to Big Sur last weekend?" Tara nodded and he went on. "He's madly in love with me, the dear boy, and *begs* me to let him move in with me. What do you think? I'm not sure I'm ready to set up housekeeping with anyone just now—but he's awfully tempting!"

"You just got rid of a roomie, didn't you?" Tara got to her feet and went to the bar and opened a bottle of champagne. "Want some?" she asked, already knowing the answer. Izzy never turned down an invitation for a free drink—or anything else for that matter.

"Please." He went to stand next to her as she filled the glasses. "As if I could ever forget that two-timing little bitch," he said savagely. "Not only did he ball my other lovers behind my back, he walked away with all my jewelry and left me with a three-hundred-and-fifteen-dollar phone bill!" He accepted the glass and took a swallow. "Chin chin, sweetie."

"That's what you get for shacking up with a Hungarian," Tara laughed. "Especially a Hungarian addicted to calling home two or three times a week."

"Well, thank goodness Bobby's family lives in Redondo Beach," Izzy chuckled. "That's a point in his favor." He sipped his champagne and moved to sit down on the sofa. "What about you, Tara? I'm beginning to think you're a neuter. Don't you like men? I don't think I've ever seen you date anyone seriously. I mean, besides you're numerous pals who escort you here and there."

"Sure, I like men fine. Show me where to find one and I'll do the rest." She sat next to him on the sofa. It was a hot summer day and she wore only shorts and halter, while Izzy was impeccably dressed in his usual colorful shirt and ascot with matching tailored trousers. He crossed his legs tucking one slim silk-stockinged ankle behind the other.

"What you're saying is, the men you meet aren't really your idea of a man, is that it?"

"That's it exactly." She glanced at her watch and saw that it was almost dinner time, time for the first joint of the day. She had put herself on a rigorous schedule while working; an hour in the sauna and gym every morning, no wine or grass until after five o'clock in the afternoon and usually to bed by eleven. "Want to get high before dinner? You're staying, aren't you? Hazel especially asked that you stay and try her poached turbot with sautéed cucumbers—"

"Starting with her marvelous vichyssoise, of course," Izzy interrupted with a grin. "And artichoke hearts and truffles, ending with soufflé au chocolat." His grin was triumphant. "I peeked when Hazel was at the market, but don't you dare tell her."

"I wouldn't dream of it," Tara laughed. From the first day Izzy had come to work for her, he and Hazel had had a friendly battle over who was the best cook. Hazel had stubbornly refused to allow Izzy into her kitchen until Tara had intervened, saying that it would put an end to the silliness and put Izzy in his place once and for all if Hazel allowed him to cook them a dinner—and thereafter Hazel would have her kitchen all to herself. Both women had been amazed when a couple of days later Izzy had prepared a fabulous dinner of vol-au-vent of fillets of sole la Vallière and the following night a flawless fillet of beef Wellington—just to prove that he was equally talented with both meat and fish, he had said smugly. Hazel had grudgingly admitted that Izzy knew his way around a piece of meat, and the slender homosexual had rolled his eyes at Tara and giggled naughtily behind his hand. "Do I ever," he had retorted wickedly, "and I know how to cook, too!"

Tara lit a joint and took a deep drag before passing it to Izzy. "I must admit, ever since you came to work for me, Hazel has been turning out the most outrageous meals I've ever tasted." She leaned back and put her bare feet up on the coffee table, watching Izzy. He held the joint between his middle and ring finger, elegantly, the pinkie curved at an angle.

"Umm, my, you always have the best weed in town, sweetie," he sighed appreciatively as he passed the joint to her. "Yes, I certainly did show Hazel a thing or two, didn't I? I must say, she reacted just like a woman when I told her I could cook circles around her. Why is it that all women think they are the only ones who can cook? Why, the best chefs in the world are men!"

They sat quietly for a moment, each unwinding from the day of work, sharing the joint comradely, then Tara stood and stretched. "Guess I'd better go shower before dinner. Be an angel, Izzy, and go call Mandy in, will you?"

"Sure, luv, where is she—in the stable?"

"Where else?" Tara laughed and Izzy shuddered delicately.

"Ugh, how she can stand to be around those huge, fearsome beasts, I'll never know. They absolutely terrify me!" He got to his feet, adjusted his ascot and tucked a tiny wrinkle of his shirt into the smooth waistband of his white trousers.

"Be careful you don't step in any horse manure," Tara chuckled, glancing at his immaculate white shoes, and he stuck out his tongue before stepping daintily through the sliding glass doors.

Izzy walked slowly down the brick path that led to the stable, pausing now and then to admire the profusion of roses and other flowers that edged the walk. As he neared the barn he wrinkled his nose at the pungent smell of horses, even though he apparently was the only one who could smell them. Teddy kept the stables immaculate and claimed you had to get up damn early in the morning to find even one horse turd in Midnight's or Macaroni's stall. Izzy saw the gnarled old man now, leaning on his rake as he watched Mandy racing toward the stable. She was riding bareback as usual and Izzy was amazed anew at how she was able to accomplish such a feat. Mandy rode with the easy grace of an Indian, her long bare legs gripping the sleek sides of her new horse.

He stopped at the clean white corral and said hello to Teddy and drew back a little as Mandy's horse galloped closer. He had been appalled when Tara had bought the child such a large and terrifying animal, as he was still half afraid of the short, chunky little pony and had just recently become acquainted with him. "She's getting too long-legged for a pony," Tara had explained. "Besides, now that she's really getting into horse shows, she needs one that can get out there and win for her." There was never any mention of selling Macaroni. Mandy loved him with a passion usually reserved for human creatures, or so Izzy thought, and swore that she would give the pony a home for the rest of his life. After all, he had been her first, and little girls never forgot their first pony, just as big girls never forgot their first lover.

"Hi, sugar," Izzy called, stepping even further away from the corral as Mandy pulled the big black gelding to a halt in a swirl of dust. He coughed delicately and brushed imaginary specks from his silk shirt. "Tara sent me to fetch you in for dinner."

"Hi, Izzy," Mandy called and threw her leg over the gelding's arched neck, sliding gracefully to the ground in one smooth motion. "Say hello to Midnight." She took his reins and led the beast to the fence and Izzy managed to hold out his hand without fainting as the black nuzzled him and made a low whinny. "He thinks you've got a treat for him," Mandy laughed. "Don't be such a baby, Izzy. He isn't going to bite you." At that moment Midnight's soft muzzle curled questioningly around Izzy's trembling fingers and he jumped back with a yelp of sheer panic. "Oh, Izzy," Mandy said with exaggerated weariness. "I guess you'll never be a cowboy!"

"I'm afraid you're right, sugar," Izzy laughed nervously. "Now will you please give that—that beast to Teddy and come along like a good girl?" Mandy laughed and tossed the reins to Teddy, climbed over the fence and held out her arms for Izzy to catch her. He caught her and immediately released her, his fine, long nose quivering at the acrid odor of little girl and horse sweat mixed with a generous portion of trail dust.

Slipping her grubby, sun-warmed hand into Izzy's pink, beringed one, Mandy laughed up at him mischievously, knowing full well how he hated to touch anything dirtier than a once-used cocktail napkin. However, Izzy's genuine affection for Mandy enabled him to withstand the hand-holding until they had reached the house.

Mandy burst through the door and ran into the kitchen, yelling, "Hi, Hazel, I'm home! What's for dinner? I'm starving!" She went to the plump cook and hugged her, leaving dirt smudges on her clean apron. Hazel laughed and hugged her back, unmindful of the stains.

"Fish," she said and swatted Mandy on the butt. "You get yourself into a shower or you'll be dining alone in the stable if your sister sees you looking like that." She peered at her over her Ben Franklin glasses and clucked, "Tsk tsk, how in the world do you manage to get so dirty in just one day? I'd like to know. I just washed and ironed those jeans yesterday." She gave Mandy a mockstern look, shaking her head at the grubby Levis stained in the crotch with horse hair and sweat, the pink teeshirt with a dainty butterfly in bright yellow now so dirty the colors were almost indistinguishable.

"Aw, Tara won't mind," Mandy said and lifted the lid of a skillet to peek in at the bubbling sauce. "What can I eat before dinner? I'm starved." She opened a drawer and took out a bag of potato chips, running quickly from the kitchen before Hazel could take them away from her.

Izzy had gone directly to the guest powder room, where he washed and creamed his hands thoroughly and then lavishly applied a spray cologne he always carried for just such emergencies. He was relaxing in the den, watching the evening news when Tara came downstairs and joined him. He was sipping a fresh glass of champagne and waved a languid hand at her, indicating the bar. "Like a glass of the bubbly, sweetie?" he asked as if he were host, she the guest.

"Sounds lovely." Tara went to sit in one of the large chairs facing the television. "Anything interesting on the news tonight?"

Izzy unwrapped his legs and stood smoothly, tucking a nonexistent wrinkle into his waistband, and went to the bar to pour a glass of champagne for his boss. "Not really." He brought her the wine and a joint. "Where's Charley tonight? Isn't she joining us?" As usual, he wanted to add. His thin aristocratic lips curled slightly, exposing his jealousy. He worshipped Tara and hated it that it was Charley, and not he, whom Tara liked best. It made him feel petty and mean and he often told himself Charley was probably a dyke, out to get Tara's fortune by making her fall in love with her. Of course, he knew this was not really true and only thought it when he felt particularly nasty.

"She's out with the Bear," Tara answered. "They went to a sneak preview of that new musical at Fox." She crossed her legs, smoothing the pale blue silk skirt of her sundress where it caressed her thighs.

"That reminds me, what's this I hear about Doe Kingston doing Shakespeare?" He raised his eyebrows in exaggerated surprise, leaning forward expectantly.

"Oh," Tara chuckled. "You know how Wesley loves to dress up in pantyhose and brandish a sword about, well he's been trying to talk Doe into doing *The Taming of the Shrew* with him."

Izzy rolled his eyes heavenward and clucked, "May the saints preserve us! Tell me it isn't true!"

Tara laughed and took a sip of icy champagne. "Of course it isn't. No way will Doe do it. She knows her limitations and knows the kind of vehicles that made her a star. Doe doing Shakespeare would be like John Wayne playing a child molester. The public just wouldn't buy it."

"Dinner in ten minutes, Miss Remington," Lupe called softly from the doorway. She was a small, slim Mexican girl who helped Hazel in the kitchen.

"Thank you, Lupe, we'll be right in." Tara finished her wine and handed the glass to Izzy, who had risen quickly to take it from her, making the gesture seem casual rather than subservient, a charming trait of which Izzy was master.

Mandy bounded down the stairs dressed in a bright yellow sundress that set off her inky curls, her suntanned bare feet in brief sandals. She slipped her hand into Tara's and grinned up at her. "Hi. How was your day? Get a lot of writing done?"

"Uh-huh." Tara returned the pressure of Mandy's fingers. They had not seen one another since breakfast, as was often the case when Tara was working on her novel. She closed herself in her office at nine-thirty each morning and worked through the day, stopping for a light lunch which Lupe would serve to her in the study, and not quitting until five o'clock. She had put herself on a strict schedule since beginning her historical romance, and everyone in the house knew not to disturb her unless it was pretty damn important. "Don't you look pretty and fresh," she said, glancing down at her little sister. Mandy carried herself proudly, standing tall and keeping her shoulders back like an athlete. Gone were the days of downcast eyes and keeping her chin tucked to her chest. Her young breasts seemed even more prominent than Tara remembered, and she made a mental note to go shopping for bras with her soon. That is, if Mandy wanted to wear them. Were girls still wearing bras these days? "My God, honey," Doe had gasped once, "can't you just see *me* without a bra? My tits would be down around my knees, for Christ's sake!"

"How's Midnight coming along?" she asked as Izzy held her chair, then Mandy's.

"Oh, just super," Mandy said and proceeded to rave excitedly about how well the gelding was doing at barrels and jumps until Tara was almost sorry she had asked. She had just gotten the new horse for Mandy a couple of months ago, and they had become as inseparable as she and Macaroni had once been. Not that she ignored the pony; she still spent a great deal of time with him, but she was simply too tall to ride him any longer. She was just an inch shorter than Tara's five-four and still growing. She would be tall like Eric. The familiar name caused the familiar swift pain in her heart, and she glanced quickly down at her plate lest it show on her face. Damn him to hell for haunting her still!

Izzy and Mandy did most of the talking, but if either of them noticed Tara's sudden quietness they gave no sign. Both were used to her sudden changing moods and knew better than to mention it.

Hazel entered and began picking up the dessert dishes and Izzy caught her hand and sighed expansively, "Simply divine turbot, Hazel, dear." He stood and bowed over her plump hand, brought it to his lips and kissed it.

"Thank you, sir." Hazel's manner was demure, but her smile was purely triumphant as she looked over his head and winked at Tara. "Will you have your coffee in the billiard room tonight, miss?" Izzy's third passion, after boys and gossip, was pool and he always insisted on a game with Tara when he stayed over for dinner.

"Yes, please," Tara said and Izzy was immediately at her side to take her arm and escort her into the billiard room.

They had just begun their first game when the door bell rang and Tara muttered, "Who the hell could that be?" She wasn't expecting anyone and, as a rule, did not answer the door if anyone had the bad manners simply to show up without calling first. She leaned over the table to take her shot, deciding to ignore the ringing bell, but it persisted and Mandy asked, "Aren't you going to answer it, Tara? Maybe it's important."

She too had come to fear the ringing of the door bell

218

late at night since all the bad press due to Tara's divorce. Reporters and curiosity seekers had somehow managed to discover where Tara lived and would actually climb the eight-foot fence surrounding the property to try and have a word with her. And if that failed, they would sneak up to any open window and blatantly shoot pictures of whomever they saw inside. She had put a stop to the fence climbing when she had had an electric wire installed that circled the top of the fence and gave anyone a nasty jolt if they so much as touched it.

"Shall I see who it is, miss?" Hazel stood at the doorway drying her hands on her apron, a worried crease between her brows. The first few months she had worked for Tara she had been followed and accosted everywhere she went, to the bank, to the market; she was even cornered by one determined reporter who had disguised himself as a pool man and caught her at the kitchen door demanding to know what her famous boss was really like. She had become as wary as everyone else who lived with Tara.

The door bell persisted and Tara sighed, "Oh shit, I guess so. Izzy, go with her in case it's a reporter. They usually don't insist if they see a man on the premises."

Izzy raised an amused eyebrow at the reference and left the room with Hazel. A moment later Tara heard his high squeal of pleasure and then the billiard room felt as if a whirlwind had struck it. Doe Kingston flung herself into Tara's arms, all pale blonde curls, pale ivory skin, pale pink silk dress and long, pale bare legs in very high-heeled mules. Doe abhorred the sun and had never, to Tara's knowledge, ever had a suntan in her life. "I'm pink and blonde all over, honey," she liked to coo to reporters and interviewers when asked if the pinkish-platinum of her hair was real. "Fucking idiots," she would snort later. "As if anyone ever had hair this color naturally. Shit, it costs me a bloody fortune to keep up!" She was followed by Wesley Cunningham who was loaded down with so many packages and bags Tara could just barely see his head over the bundles.

"Doe, my God, what are you up to, you crazy broad?"

She returned the blonde's hug and kiss and smelled liquor.

"Guess what? Guess what?" Doe cried, hugging Tara again and forcing her around the room in a crazy little dance step. "We're getting married!" She released Tara and scooped Mandy up in her arms, swinging her around and kissing her soundly upon the mouth.

"Terribly sorry not to have telephoned first," Wesley said from behind the bundles. "But Doe insisted that you wouldn't mind."

"Not that it would do me any good if I did," Tara smiled. "Here, Wesley, let me help you—what is all this stuff, anyway?" He dropped the packages and shopping bags on the billiard table with a sigh.

"My trousseau," Doe cried and danced Mandy about the room. "Or my underwear trousseau, I guess I should say." She winked and hiccoughed charmingly behind a fluttering, long-nailed hand.

"Aunt Doe's drunk," Mandy giggled, wrinkling her nose when the blonde kissed her again.

"Yep, Doe's drunk." She held out her hand to Wesley and he took it, pulling her into the curve of his arm. "Drunk on a lot of love and a little bit of champagne. Right, darling?"

"Right, luv." Wesley bent his dark head to her pale one and their lips met in a lingering kiss.

"Married? Did I hear married?" Izzy's eyes were bright with interest and he glanced quickly at Tara. "Shall I break out the champagne, boss?"

"By all means—break out the bubbly, Izzy!" Doe spun away from Wesley and caught Izzy's slight frame against her ample bosom, almost obscuring him in a big hug. "Make it Moët et Chandon, if you have it, darling. It's Wesley's favorite."

"I'm afraid you'll have to settle for Louis Roederer," Tara laughed and was immediately engulfed in Doe's hugging arms again. "Sit down, for heaven's sake, Doe, you're smothering me! Now, tell me all about it. When did you decide to make an honest man of Wesley?"

"The moment he decided to get rid of his tight-assed

British albatross," Doe said with an arched eyebrow in Wesley's direction. "Sybil has finally consented to living the rest of her life in luxury and ease, thanks to the outrageous settlement. But I still think I got the best of the bargain—I got Wesley." They kissed again, snuggling close on the sofa, hands clasped

Izzy arrived with the champagne and Mandy asked, "Can I have a glass, too, Tara? Please? It isn't every day that my Aunt Doe gets married."

"No, it just seems like it," Tara laughed, reminding them of Doe's previous marital record and the blonde stuck out her tongue, pulling a face. "Oh, all right, but just one—a very small one," she warned as Izzy poured half a glass and passed it to Mandy.

"Well, my gracious, what exciting news," Izzy bubbled, his mind racing as to whom he could call with the news and perhaps pick up a few extra dollars for scooping the major papers. His hazel eyes sparkled with excitement as they lingered overlong on Wesley's tight-fitting trousers. "To the lovebirds," he tittered, raising his glass and the others followed suit.

Doe and Wesley swallowed theirs in one swallow, laughing and kissing again. Doe's cheeks were flushed and her topaz eyes seemed to glow like new gold as they gazed adoringly into Wesley's. "To us," she whispered when Izzy had refilled their glasses. "Forever and ever . . ." They looped arms, each holding their glass for the other to sip from.

"For God's sake, will you guys knock it off? You're making me a little sick," Tara laughed. "And poor Izzy is in an absolute tizzy!" He had moved a little closer to the couple on the sofa, his bright gaze riveted to Wesley's crotch as the English actor seemed on the verge of erection from Doe's caresses. His breath came in tiny sighs and he squirmed in his seat, wishing he could reach into his trousers and adjust his tingling penis. God, but Wesley Cunningham was a fox! A real man's man, Izzy thought, with a wicked grin.

Mandy was wide-eyed, her gaze going from the clinging couple on the sofa to Izzy and Tara and then back again.

She had never seen Doe so excited. Usually the blonde feigned boredom, or at the very best, disinterest about most things. Mandy had grown up knowing that Doe was her sister's very best friend and therefore had not been in awe of her as she supposed she would have been otherwise. Doe Kingston, was after all, the biggest star in Hollywood.

"When are you getting married, Aunt Doe? Can I come?" Mandy asked. She wrinkled her nose at the bubbles in the Louis Roederer and swallowed quickly lest she cough and embarrass herself. She wanted to be one of the adults tonight, and adults seemed to consume enormous quantities of champagne without so much as a tiny burp.

"The tenth of September, my sweet," Doe bubbled. "And I want you to be my flower girl, and Tara my special bridesmaid—and, Izzy, gee, I wish you could be a bridesmaid too!"

"I'd rather be Wesley's best man." He said it with a straight face but the implication was clear and everyone laughed.

Another bottle of champagne was opened and when everyone had a full glass, Doe told them how it had happened. As Tara already knew, Sybil had fought the divorce bitterly since Wesley had moved out two years ago, stubbornly refusing to even discuss it with him. As if in ignoring it, the problem would go away. But Sybil had not counted on Doe's power over men. Wesley had not come home when the fling was over, as he had always done in the past—because obviously this fling was far from over. "When I love 'em, they *stay* loved!" Doe had once told Tara. Wesley had stayed in Hollywood with Doe, communicating with Sybil through his attorney until he had simply outwaited her and worn her down. Until public favor had turned from Sybil to Wesley and Doe. At first, the public had crucified the lovers, sympathizing with poor Sybil and those six children, but after two years had passed and Doe and Wesley were still together, handholding in public, telling everyone they could not get married because Sybil refused him a divorce, public favor swung the other way. Their fans blamed Sybil for standing in the way of true love, and unflattering articles began appearing about the cold English woman who still clung to a man who no longer wanted her. It was the age-old but still popular love triangle that Americans so adore— and now it seemed it would have a happy ending after all.

"Of course, it cost Wesley a bloody fortune. But I'm worth it, aren't I, darling?" Doe leaned in closer, if that was possible, and Wesley bent to kiss her.

"That you are, pet," he murmured in a deep, faintly accented voice that had thrilled millions of females of all ages. She was worth it in more ways than one, he thought, with a secret smile. Since moving in with Doe and carrying on a public love affair, his price per picture had jumped from a paltry quarter of a million to one million dollars. Unheard of for a Shakespearean actor. Unheard of for any actor, save for a small select handful of such super stars as Elizabeth Taylor, Richard Burton, Brando or giants of that ilk. After *Love in the Morning,* they had teamed again for *The Robin,* a light love farce which bombed with the critics but was box office gold. Together, the two movies had earned over thirty-five million dollars for their respective studios, and Doe and Wesley were now in a position to name their own price. The trades had been full of little else but speculations about the pair teaming again in *The Taming of the Shrew,* and the prices suggested were staggering: a million each for Doe and Wesley, plus a percentage of the picture, and twenty thousand dollars a day for every day that it went over schedule.

Tara asked Doe about the speculations and she laughed. "That's just Hollywood hype, honey. I have no intention of making an ass of myself in something like that. I'm basically a comedienne."

"But Aunt Doe, you won an Oscar for *Love in the Morning* and that was dramatic," Mandy said. "And so was *The Savage Desert.* I'll bet you could do anything you wanted to do."

"Precisely," Wesley said. "Perhaps you can help me

talk some sense into this stubborn yankee female, my dear." He favored Mandy with his famous smile, and she blushed and moved a little closer to Tara. She still was not used to the type of people who dropped by the house to visit her big sister—movie stars, famous producers and directors, politicians—all those glittering illustrious names that daily graced the pages of magazines and newspapers, their lives spread out for all to read and gossip about.

"Now, Wesley, don't start that again," Doe warned, her eyes narrowing to yellow slits. "I am not going to do it, and that, my dove, is that!" She tweaked his nose and forced a laugh, but not before Tara had seen real anger flash in those magnificent eyes. Uh-oh, she thought, wonder how long it will be before Wesley-baby realizes the pussycat he fell in love with is really a full-grown tiger used to ruling the jungle and all those in it?

They talked far into the night, emptying another bottle of champagne, and when Mandy had gone to bed, Doe opened the packages Wesley had brought in and showed Tara her "underwear trousseau." There were several short, fabulous babydoll gowns cut low and high to show off a lot of flesh, crotchless panties in a rainbow of colors, Karma Sutra oil, his and hers vibrators (pink for Doe, chocolate brown for Wesley) and jars of Joy Jell in various fruit flavors, as well as fruit-flavored douche and even a slim volume of erotic positions of intercourse.

"Where on earth did you get all this stuff?" Tara asked as Doe held up an enormous black dildo with an apparatus that squirted warm milk at the crucial moment.

"At a new little shop on Santa Monica Boulevard," Doe said. "It's called Paraphernalia From Eden and, honey, if they don't have it there, it isn't being manufactured anywhere! The guy that owns it, Charles, is something else, too. He's a raving faggot—oops, no offense Izzy—and dresses like Dame Whitney in yards of flowing chiffon and skin-tight silk pants that look sprayed on, boots with heels so high I was constantly afraid he was going to topple over on me. He reeks of Joy and his hair is almost waist length, styled by Gene Shacove, he assured me several times. What a mad character! Couldn't take his eyes off poor Wesley—right, love?"

"Yes, he actually propositioned me right in front of Doe, if you can imagine that."

"Not just you, sweetums," Doe chuckled. "Don't you remember he said I could come along and watch if I wanted to? Sweet boy, that Charles."

"Ah, yes, he did make that concession, didn't he?" Wesley sipped his champagne and looked about the erotic display of sexual costumes and toys. "I must say he does run a rather quaint little shop. I was vastly impressed."

"Oh, I must go there at once!" Izzy gushed. His long fingers played with the lace edging of a pair of crotchless panties as if it were all he could do to keep from trying them on.

"If you hurry, maybe you can catch him before he closes shop," Tara said, stifling a yawn. She stood and stretched. "Well, kids, I'm for bed. Sorry to be rude but I have a lot of work tomorrow."

Doe and Wesley immediately got to their feet and began gathering up their paraphernalia from Eden, murmuring apologies for intruding on Tara's evening. Doe slipped a jar of strawberry Joy Jell in Tara's hand and whispered, "Try this—it's wild." They walked to the door and she hugged Tara and kissed her briefly on the cheek. "I'll give you a ring tomorrow, honey. When's a good time?"

"I break for lunch around one. Give me a call then, okay?" She returned Wesley's chaste kiss and waved them down the wide marble steps and into their Rolls. "Goodnight, you two. Drive carefully. And I'm delighted about the engagement!"

"Well, sugar, it's off to the fleshpots of Santa Monica Boylevard," Izzy giggled, kissing Tara's cheek. "Wish me luck!"

"Get out of here," she retorted good naturedly, giving him a playful slap on the fanny. "And don't be late tomorrow. There's a stack of mail to be answered." Izzy pulled a face as he slid behind the wheel of his white Thunderbird and Tara blew him a kiss before closing the door. She wandered into the billiard room for her cigarettes and lighter, not bothering to gather up the glasses and empty bottles. One of the servants would tidy up before turning out the lights and putting the house to sleep. She walked slowly upstairs, thinking of Doe and Wesley and their plans to be married. She hoped it worked for them, but doubted that it would. Doe was too volatile for the average man, and for all of Wesley's talent (which was awesome) he still struck Tara as a rather average man offscreen.

She removed her makeup, patted on a little night cream and slid between the cool satin sheets. Doe and Wesley getting married. It made her sad, somehow. As the word marriage always seemed to make her sad these days. Turning over to bury her face in the pillow, she realized that for the first time in years, she felt lonely. And utterly alone.

CHAPTER
ELEVEN

ERIC SAT behind the wheel of his white Cadillac, glancing impatiently at the thick stream of Rolls-Royces, the cluster of shining Cadillacs and Lincolns, the softly purring Bentleys, Ferraris and Maseratis that all stood gently vibrating in line awaiting the parking boys. A gleaming Excalibur S.S. crept an inch closer to the red-carpeted sidewalk and two parking boys leapt at the doors. A sleekly coiffed, scantily clad starlet slithered out on the arm of an aging producer whom Eric recognized as Jonathan Monash. He ground his teeth and reached for a cigarette. The man's name always left a bad taste in his mouth, ever since he had outbid Eric for the screen rights to Tara's novel. He did not dislike Monash personally, had in fact admired him until the producer had obtained rights to *Seattle Slum*. The movie would be out in a couple of weeks, and even though Eric had yet to see a sneak preview, he stubbornly maintained that he could have done a better job.

Someone honked impatiently behind him, and Eric glanced up to see that he could now move forward another six inches. The crowd of star-gazers on the sidewalk craned their necks and pointed excited fingers at the occupants of the luxurious automobiles as they recognized their favorite stars. A crimson Porsche, covered with so much chrome it looked like a hall of mirrors, braked to a halt at the red carpet and Eric saw the parking boy's eyes widen as he leaned in to help Sandra Sinclair from the white leather seat. She was wearing skin-tight gold lamé stretch pants with two wide straps attached at the waist by large diamond buckles, looking like elegant overall suspenders, and knee-high boots in the same shade of deep gold. She wore nothing else and her large breasts spilled dangerously from between and from both sides of the wide suspenders.

A roar went up from the crowd and Eric groaned aloud when he saw Zock McBain step out to take Sandy's arm. He raised a hand to the crowd, and jewels sparkled and flashed on fingers and wrist. "Jesus, it looks like he borrowed Sammy Davis Jr.'s entire jewelry collection," he said with a snort that he hoped passed as laughter. He savagely ground out his cigarette and reached into his shirt pocket for a joint.

"Eric, do you think you should? I mean, we're almost there." Pamela Howard glanced nervously out of her window at the squad of armed cops who tried in vain to hold back the screaming, lunging fans. It was August and most of the automobiles in the long queue had their windows rolled down and there was the unmistakable odor of marijuana drifting lazily on the summer breeze.

"No one will know the difference in this crowd," Eric said, dragging almost angrily on the joint before passing it to her. She shook her head and her short red curls bounced. "Suit yourself," he shrugged, returning the joint to his mouth and sucking like an infant feeding on mother's milk. "But I can see right now that I'm going to need a lot more of this to get through the evening."

"Then why did we come?" Pamela asked quietly, shyly. Her large brown eyes turned toward him and the pink lips, barely tinted with color, trembled slightly. He wanted to slug her. She was too timid, too trusting, too complacent. And always too worried about everything he did.

"I told you, I had to," he answered shortly, not looking at her and finished the joint and dropped the roach into the ashtray. I had to because I heard that Tara would be here, he thought and felt himself flush guiltily in the

228

semi-darkness of the Cadillac. "Newman and Lawford are both owners and, as I've told you, I'm trying to get them for my next picture. This opening seems like as good a place as any to talk to them about it."

"Yes, of course, Eric, it's just that you seem so—so—well, angry." She twisted her long pale hands in her lap, eyes cast down. Eric frightened her when he got into one of his unreasonable moods, and she did so want everything to go well tonight. She had something important to tell him after the party and wanted him to be in a good frame of mind.

"I'm not mad at you, Pam," he said quickly, reaching over to squeeze her shoulder. "It's just these fucking crowds. You know how I hate to wait in line for anything." He smiled, forcing one from her, and leaned over to kiss her briefly. "That's my girl," he said soothingly. "We'll just stay a couple of hours, I'll lay the script on Newman or Lawford and we'll get the hell out of here, okay?"

"Okay, honey." She smiled up into his eyes, feeling her heartbeat quicken as it always did when she looked directly into his handsome face. She too hated crowds, but not for the same reason that Eric did. She was so much in love with her "renegade lover," as she liked to call him, that she hated to share him with anyone for even a moment. She would remember for the rest of her life how she had met him. She had been just a weather girl then, working for the local news show at KTTV, and was leaving the studio one night after the eleven o'clock news, walking alone to the parking lot. She had just inserted her key into the car door when she had felt a strong arm clamp around her throat from behind and a low, guttural voice growled at her to be quiet or be killed. Of course she had screamed in sheer terror and her would-be assailant had jerked her back violently, cutting off her breath and began dragging her toward a darkened corner of the parking lot. Obviously he was bent on rape, for his rough hands tore at her breasts even as he dragged her into the darkness.

He had thrown her down behind several large garbage

bins and slapped her across the face before ripping off her blouse and skirt. When he had shoved his hand into her pantyhose and began jabbing at her vagina, she had screamed so loudly she could still hear it sometimes in her sleep. He smashed a fist into her face and ripped off the nylons, fumbling at her body with fierce fingers. Suddenly the rapist was jerked bodily away from her and a fist appeared out of nowhere, clipping him neatly on the chin and knocking him staggering into the garbage cans. Then Pamela had looked up to see an extraordinarily handsome man dive after her attacker and wrestle him to the ground. Pinning him there, he yelled at her to call the cops.

"But I don't have a telephone," she remembered foolishly stammering, and he had motioned impatiently toward the parking lot. "There's one in my car," he had panted. "That white Caddie over there. Hurry, for Christ's sake!"

The police had arrived in record time and hauled the guy away, after taking her statement, and then she was alone with Eric. She remembered how embarrassed she had been, standing trembling before him, practically naked, feeling one eye swelling rapidly shut, and he had taken off his jacket and wrapped it about her.

"What the hell were you doing out here alone at this hour?" he had chastized her. "Don't you know that's just asking for it in this neighborhood?" She had stammered out who she was and what she had been doing there, and Eric had smiled for the first time. "Of course, Lady Pamela's weather forecast. I thought you looked familiar." And he had insisted on driving her home. But he had not driven her to her home. He had taken her to his house in Benedict Canyon, tenderly washed the cut eye and lip, after seeing that she was demurely covered in his dressing gown, and had made her drink a large tumbler of brandy.

"This is what they always do in the movies," he had teased as he held the snifter to her swollen lips. "Apparently brandy has amazing healing powers—for everything from the vapors to being stranded in an Alaskan blizzard for six months!" And she had looked up into his incredibly handsome face and fallen madly in love for the first time in her twenty-three years.

Eric had taken her to bed that first night, saying that she had to get over her (possible) fear of sex—just like a rider thrown from a horse; she had to get right back in the saddle and conquer it before it became blown out of proportion. She did not dare tell him that she had no such fears. She had simply let him lead her into his bedroom and gently make love to her until almost dawn. That had been the beginning and they had started dating on a steady basis. When she realized who he was, she was naturally impressed. Eric Marlowe was the youngest and richest producer in Hollywood, as well as the most eligible bachelor on both coasts. She remembered with a tight pang of jealousy the night they had attended the Academy Awards and Eric had seen Tara Remington and had hardly spoken a word to Pamela for the rest of the evening. Of course she knew who Tara Remington was. Didn't everyone after her sensational divorce from the King of Rock? For almost a year the one couple grabbing most of the newspaper space all over the world had been Tara and Zock, the star-crossed lovers of the universe.

Pamela wanted to hate Tara, dismiss her as just another pretty face who had captured the sexual interest of Eric, but after her novel, *Seattle Slum,* had come out to such rave reviews and shot up the best selling charts faster than a speeding bullet, Pam had grudgingly admitted that the sad-eyed beauty obviously had a brain under all that wild chestnut hair. She had gone to the newspaper morgue and looked up every gossip column that had ever written a line about Eric and Tara and found, to her dismay, that they had been the Golden Couple of 'seventy-two and 'seventy-three, a sort of contemporary Hollywood Romeo and Juliet. And it had hurt like hell when she realized that Eric was still in love with Tara, probably always would be. Unless she could change it. She had asked discreet questions of Eric's friends and learned that it had been Tara who had called off the wedding and that Eric had taken it very hard. But no one seemed to know why she had broken it off. It remained one of the unsolved mysteries of the Hollywood grapevine. She had questioned Eric about it one night when they had just finished making love and she was snuggled against him in his kingsize bed, and he had turned on her in fury. "Don't *ever* mention her name to me—*ever!*" he had snarled, his handsome face dark with passion, and she had flinched as if he had struck her.

Pamela was forced back into the present by a cherub-faced parking attendant bending solicitously over her as he held the door of the Caddie. "Good evening, miss," he smiled as he drew her out and the crowd of on-lookers pressed closer.

"Who is it? Who is it?" she heard them shout. "Is she anybody?" And then the sweetest sound of all. "It's Pamela Howard! Hey, Pamela—over here!" Waving hands, sweaty, excited faces pressing in closer and cries of, "Can I have your autograph?"

"Christ, let's get inside, quick!" Eric said and took her arm, pulling her roughly after him under the black awning and into the ugly, nondescript two-story building. A modest sign with small letters stated "The Factory," and there was a drawing of a monkey wrench on a waving banner of faded red.

They entered the freight elevator with other elegantly outfitted members of the Hollywood elite and traveled up to the second story, where they were met by a semi-naked black girl who asked in a husky Arethra Franklin voice if she could take their wraps. No one had any wraps, it being August and one of the hottest that Pamela had seen since moving to California from Pennsylvania.

"Gosh, it's really something, isn't it?" Pamela heard a girl say in a hushed whisper to her companion. And it was that. Thirteen thousand square feet of private paradise, from the steel-beamed ceiling thirty feet above to the numerous red-covered tables on the lushly carpeted floor. Row upon row of crystal chandeliers sparkled and flashed from the steel beams, catching and sending back the radiance from the strobe-lit dance floor. A live band strummed madly on a raised platform, while near-naked

women and men in sprayed-on pants and see-through
body shirts danced and sweated on a postage-stamp-sized
dance floor. Every one in the huge crowd was Someone,
the chosen ones who had shelled out five hundred dollars
for membership in this newest, "in"-est and most fabulous
of all private discotheques. The founders (or directors as
they were billed on the menus) were as famous as their
guests: Paul Newman, Peter Lawford, Peter Bren, Sammy
Davis Jr., Ronald Buck, Jerry Orbach, Pierre Salinger
and Richard Donner—fabulously wealthy business scions
or movie stars all.

Eric took a tighter grip on Pamela's hand and they
were carried along with the surging crowd into the massive dining room. A denim-clad waiter with a red scarf
tied rakishly about his neck found them a table and took
their drink orders, and then, to their amazement, began
dancing wildly with one of the customers on the dance
floor.

"What the hell is this?" Eric grumbled, badly in need
of the whiskey he had ordered. He reached out a hand to
get the waiter's attention and the young man smilingly
danced off in the direction of the kitchen, never missing a
beat.

When their drinks arrived, Eric turned his chair so that
it was facing the entrance and gloomily set up watch for
Tara's entrance. The Bear had assured him that she
would definitely be there, even though she rarely made
the Hollywood scene these days. "Who does she think
she is," he remembered grumbling to Barry. "Greta
Garbo?"

"Oh, honey, look," Pamela said in an excited undertone, even though no one could have heard her in the
noisy room. "Isn't that Natalie Wood?" She pointed in
the direction of a lovely dark-haired woman who glim-
mered in a gold lamé dress, matching gold stockings and
gold dust aura, making her way through the crowd toward
the back of the room.

"Huh? Yeah, that's her. Beautiful, isn't she?" Eric's
glance traveled over Miss Wood's radiant figure as she
clung to her escort's arm and was soon swallowed up in

the moving mass of bodies. For an instant she had reminded him of Tara and the old familiar ache started in his heart. Jesus, would he never forget her? Never get her out of his blood? She was like a hauntingly subtle disease of the heart, causing little or no pain on a day-to-day basis, but always he was acutely aware of her *being* there. Deep inside where nothing could touch or tarnish her memory.

"Yes, she's gorgeous," Pamela sighed. "I wish I had her figure." She smoothed the demure neckline of her simple black gown and glanced down to make sure nothing unladylike was showing. Eric had tried, unsuccessfully, to change her wardrobe but she had pleaded shyness, insisting that her figure was not built for flesh-exposing outfits. Which was not true. She had a magnificent figure naked. Long and lean, with legs that seemed endless, she reminded Eric of a frolicking colt, graceful in her awkwardness. Her face was more interesting than beautiful—stunning, she had been called by several reporters—and her natural red hair seemed to move with a life of its own. It had been long when he had met her, but just recently while covering a brush fire in Topanga Canyon for her newscast, she had gotten a little too close and the lovely tresses had been singed beyond repair. That act of bravery had won her the spot of anchorperson on the six o'clock news, and she was fast becoming a local celebrity. She now wore her hair cropped close to her head, the natural curls framing her face and setting off her large brown eyes to perfection.

Looking at her now, Eric still could not reconcile the woman Pamela Howard from the newsperson Pamela Howard. The two just did not seem to jell. She was not the average hard-nosed, pushy, aggressive woman one usually associated with anchoring a news show. She came on soft and kittenish, her low, well-modulated voice sounding as if it belonged in a boudoir instead of a newsroom, and her wardrobe was strictly Eastern society. But none of this really mattered to Eric. He wanted her for one thing only. Someone to adore him and look after him. She caused him no grief, made no demands and clearly worshiped the ground he trod upon. She never chastized him for not calling every day and when she saw his name in the columns linked with this or that actress, she demurely accepted his explanation that it was a "business meeting," even though he suspected that she knew better.

"Can we order now, Eric?" she asked timidly, sensitive to his black mood. She knew he was upset about something, had been ever since he had seen Zock McBain arrive with Sandra Sinclair. She knew that he had dated the sexy teenager and wondered if he still carried a torch, then dismissed it as ludicrous. Sandy Sinclair was notoriously promiscuous, not at all the type that someone of Eric's class would seriously go for. She forced all jealousy from her mind and took his arm possessively. "I'm starving, aren't you? And the menu looks delightful. Shall we start with the spinach salad?"

"Sure, anything you say." Eric tossed off the last of his Jack Daniels, pushed the empty glass away and drew the full one to him. The waiter had set up three drinks each for them, as it took him so long to make his way through the crowd. He had also left a silver bucket holding a bottle of chilled champagne, compliments of their host, he had said. Eric studied the menu, keeping watch over the top lest Tara come in, and they decided on the beef fondue.

It was almost midnight by the time Eric saw Tara. He and Pamela had finished dinner and gone into the back room which held several pool tables, a long stretch of polished mahogany bar and six black leather booths intimately arranged about a blazing fireplace. Why the fireplace on a warm August night Eric could not guess. Tara was at the closest table shooting pool with Richard Dawson and when she straightened up from taking her shot, their eyes met like magnets. She was with what Eric could only describe as a flaming faggot: he was of medium height and elegantly slim with bright auburn hair to his shoulders and dressed all in pale lavender from his flowing ascot to his high-heeled boots. She stopped in mid-stroke, stared hard at Eric, then ducked her head to the table and sank the eight ball, ending the game. Tara left the table and drifted to the bar with the purple pansy, her back resolutely to Eric's table.

She wore a mauve silk dress with a plunging neckline and her shapely legs were enhanced by high-heeled strap sandals just a shade darker. She and the fag had obviously color coordinated their outfits for the evening, Eric thought sourly and downed his Jack Daniels so quickly that he gagged.

"Oh, honey, here." Pamela solicitously handed him her napkin and he wiped his mouth angrily, wanting to slug her. Thank God Tara's back was still turned and she had not seen his faux pas. Jesus, she could make him madder than any female he had ever known—and by doing nothing except just being there. He wanted to go over and jerk her away from the lavender fag and throw her into his car and take her home. With him. Where she belonged.

"Hey, give me another one," he said to the waiter who was bending over the next table. His skin-tight denim Levis tucked suggestively between the cheeks of his ass and there was a large red handkerchief in his back pocket, and his perfect body was as sensual as a dancer's. When he turned and let his gaze travel slowly, interestedly, over Eric's body, Eric wanted to slug him too. He wanted to slug *somebody*. Maybe he should go to the bar and pick a fight with the lavender fag. He glanced sourly at him, the auburn curls bouncing gaily on his shoulders as he leaned in close to Tara. Naw, he wouldn't do. He looked like a timid white rabbit in this sea of masculine movie stars and quietly powerful business men.

"Want to go home now, honey?" Pamela asked. She had to speak to him before he got too drunk to know what she was saying. A little drunk was okay. Then he would be loving and gay, but too drunk and he would just ball her and go to sleep.

"I'll let you know when I want to leave," he snapped, and immediately felt guilty for the hurt look that appeared in her eyes. "Sorry, Pam. I didn't mean to bite your head off." He favored her with one of his better smiles. "But I still haven't had a chance to speak to Lawford or Newman yet. I thought I saw Paul a little while ago but he seems to have disappeared somewhere." He accepted the drink from the smiling waiter who was obviously flirting with him, grunting a thanks of sorts. "Let's give it a little longer and if I can't corner either one of them, we'll leave. You still have the script, don't you?"

"Uh-huh, in my purse." Pamela smiled back at him, her good humor restored. Just one of his soft looks could melt her and they both knew it. She snuggled closer to him in the booth and Eric wished that he could move away without offending her. He did not want Tara to see him so cozily close to another woman. But Pamela had to have body contact with him when they were out together, as if staking claim to her property. "Then I guess I may as well have another drink if you can find a waiter. Gosh, isn't this a madhouse?"

"Yeah, it sure as hell is," Eric agreed. "I guess that'll make the owners happy." He saw their waiter and held up two fingers, motioning to their empty glasses. The young man gave him a jaunty wink and hurried to the bar. Returning a moment later, he served the drinks and said in a high-voiced stage whisper, sing-songing it, "I know who you are!"

"Terrific," said Eric. "That makes two of us."

"Oh, aren't you cute!" He made it sound like "cue-it" and put a familiar arm about Eric's shoulders. "I saw *The Savage Desert* five times and almost came every time!" He announced it so loudly that Eric glanced quickly around the surrounding booths to see if anyone had heard. Jesus, what kind of nut was this dude, anyway? He said something inconsequential and the waiter floated off to answer another thirsty call closer to the bar. This was not the first time Eric had heard that *The Savage Desert* had been violently attractive to some people. "It's kinda a sexy Sam Peckenpah, ya know what I mean?" Jim Glasser had once told him. "Jeez, what guy doesn't see himself ravishing a wild mountain maid in the midst of a holocaust. His pistol in one hand, his cock in the other, as it were." Eric hoped that his reputation had been somewhat salvaged by the tender *Love in the Morning*.

He drank his whiskey slowly, his eyes hardly leaving Tara. And she kept her back toward him as if unaware of his presence, but let him catch a fleeting glimpse of her profile now and then when she turned to say something to the lavender fag. Eric was getting quite drunk and knew it. And ordered another Jack Daniels. What the fuck had Tara done to him, anyway? What was the magic? How could one relatively small girl with huge green-gray-brown eyes have such an incredible impact upon his life? She was like an indelible dye under his skin. A tattoo he could never erase. And sitting there in the noisy, crowded room he found that he hated her for it. But knew that he was tied to her for life. For better or for worse. In an emotional bondage that had no key.

He drank gloomily, almost unaware that Pamela had excused herself to go to the ladies' room. He was remembering the easy camaraderie that he and Tara had once shared. The light bantering. The sexy teasing and horseplay that inevitably landed them in bed. And for all the women he had had after the breakup, he still felt incomplete. It was almost as if he had not had a climax since Tara had left him. He could fuck all night and never be fully satisfied as only Tara satisfied him. She had always had such an overwhelming, stunning impact upon him and their lovemaking had always left him totally drained—but still hungry for her a second after he had come. What was the magic, damn it? he asked himself again—and answered himself: love.

"Oh, Eric, you have to go to the men's room," Pamela cried as she slid into the booth next to him. "It's a gas!"

"The men's room?" What the fuck was she talking about? And what was she doing here with him and Tara? He shook his head to clear the whiskey away. And remembered and wanted to weep. Or slug somebody. "Yeah, the men's room," he mumbled and shoved out of the booth and started toward the bar. He had to pass Tara and mentally straightened himself out as his uncertain footsteps approached.

"Well, good evening, Miss Remington!" He said it

louder than he had meant to, grandly, actually bowing a little. And immediately felt like an asshole.

"Eric, hello! How are you?" God, she was so cool. Her voice so controlled. And she looked as unruffled as if she had just inquired of the saleslady where the yardage was kept. "I'd like you to meet my secretary, Izzy Strait." She smiled sweetly, her gaze somewhere above his left shoulder. "Izzy, of course you've heard of Eric Marlowe."

"Of course," Izzy gushed, slipping from the bar stool to shake Eric's hand. *"Sooo* pleased to meet you, Eric. I simply *adore* your films." His bright parrot's gaze zeroed in on Eric's crotch and stayed there until he felt Tara's elbow in his ribs. "I must have seen *The Savage Desert* a dozen times and, ohhh, it almost gives me *shivers* just thinking about it!"

Good God, another one, Eric thought and mumbled, "Thanks."

"Eric directed Doe and Wesley in *Love in the Morning,*" Tara was saying. She turned her cool gaze upon him and added, "Oh, by the way? Have you heard the good news?"

"Good news?" Eric repeated dumbly, feeling like a jerk and still wanting to slug the purple pansy.

"Yes, Doe and Wesley are getting married next month." The words hung there briefly, but to Eric's whiskey-laden brain they seemed to grow louder and louder, filling his very pores until he knew he had to say something or break into tears. Damn, she was so close he could reach out and touch her. Take her into his arms if he wanted to.

"Isn't it a scream?" Izzy said, his hand playfully light upon Eric's shoulder. "The blonde bombshell and the British Beefcake. My dears, it's simply toooo Hollywood for words!"

"Yeah—Hollywood," Eric mumbled, surprised to find his speech slurred. The countless whiskies had caught up with him. Why were they looking at him like that? Why was he swaying and having trouble hearing? "Well, I'm going to the men's room—heard it was a gas. You been to see it yet, Lizzy?" He squinted, frowned and found that his vision was as blurred as his speech was burred. "It's 'spose to be wild—all sorts of graffiti on it—stars and stuff—wrote it, ya know? 'Spose to be a real gas . . ."

"Lizzy—what a scream! Tara, did you hear what he called me?" Izzy threw back his head and the one gold earring danced in his earlobe, the rich auburn hair swishing gently about his silk ascot. "It's *Izzy*, dear fellow," he pouted, "And I'd love to see the men's room with you." He looped his arm through Eric's and turned to wink at Tara. "I'll just go along and make sure he gets there all right. Order me another gin fizz, will you, sugar?" And he hustled Eric away before Tara could answer.

She turned back to the bar, a feeling of disquiet settling over her like a borrowed mink stole. She was shocked by Eric's appearance. He did not seem like her Eric anymore. Eyes bloodshot and hair disheveled, his sexy mouth lax with drink and his once-marvelous body looking crumpled and sad.

She sipped her drink, feeling uncomfortably as if someone was watching her. Without seeming to, she turned slightly and glanced toward the booths near the fireplace. A stunning redheaded woman in a black Halston was staring hard at her, the large brown eyes unblinking in their appraisal. Tara recognized her at once as the woman she had seen with Eric at last year's Academy Awards. Oh God, she thought, don't tell me there's going to be a scene. The woman did not take her eyes off Tara even when Tara met her gaze fully. The hell with it, she thought. I'm not going to get involved in anything as trashy as a cat fight. She casually lit a cigarette, keeping her back to the woman in black. Besides, for a cat fight you had to have two women who wanted the same man and she most definitely did not want Eric Marlowe. He seemed to have shrunk in size in the three years since she had seen him, was heavier and puffy of face. Certainly not her golden lover who had swept her off her feet, causing her such joy. And such pain.

She could still feel the redhead's eyes boring into her back and thought, oh shit, where the hell is Izzy? I want

to get out of here right now. Before Eric comes back.
The redhead wore a mean, petulant expression and
did not even try to disguise it when Tara had caught
her eye.

She asked for the check, signed it and slid off the bar
stool. The Factory did not deal in cash—too gross, Tara
had thought when she had read the instructions on the
membership application. She gathered up her cigarettes
and handbag and walked briskly toward the hallway that
led to the restrooms. There was a pay telephone on the
wall and a long line of actors waiting to use it. Adam
West had temporary custody of the instrument and Tony
Curtis stood next in line. My God, Tara thought, even
at a party they had to stay in constant touch with their
agents.

"Tara, what are you doing out here?" Izzy minced
toward her, a Cheshire cat smile on his lips.

"I want to get out of here," she said shortly, already
walking toward the restaurant that led to the elevator.
"I've had it."

"But, sugar, what about my drink?" Izzy pouted, running a little to keep up with Tara's long strides. "And,
besides, I'm having a ball. Let's stay just a little while
longer, can't we?"

"You can. I'm going home." She pushed her way
through the crowd, not bothering to notice who she was
stepping on as she made her way toward the entrance.
Izzy ran breathlessly after her.

"Tara, slow down, for Pete's sake," he panted, catching
her arm as she reached the cloakroom. "What's got into
you? I thought you were having a good time?"

"I was. Now I'm not anymore." She pressed the button
and stood tapping one foot as the pulleys ground, bringing
the lift up to the second floor. She turned on him, exasperated. "Look, Izzy, you stay. I'm sure you can manage a ride home. Perhaps Eric and his date will give you
a lift."

"Ah, so that's it!" Izzy's bright parrot gaze swept over
her knowingly and she flushed and turned away.

"Miss Remington, surely you aren't leaving, are you?"

A deep, polite voice spoke next to them and Tara turned to see an enormous black man in an immaculate tuxedo, his broad chest strewn with numerous gold chains, smiling down at her. "We have a champagne breakfast planned for a little later. Eggs Benedict as only The Factory can make them." He smiled warmly, dazzling her with his white teeth and obvious charm. "I trust you were treated well? It's rather difficult to see that everything always runs as smoothly as one would wish, but I assure you that in the future, this will be a place where folks such as yourself can come and relax, away from the probing eyes of the public." He took her hand in his huge black one, squeezing gently. "Tell me you weren't insulted in any way or I shan't rest until I find the culprit." Again the wide, engaging smile.

"Oh, no, nothing like that." She smiled back at him, liking his style. "It's just that I have a very busy day tomorrow and it's already past two. Thank you for your concern, but we really do have to run."

"Well, then, let The Factory buy you one for the road while I call down for your car." He led them to the bar and helped her onto a stool. "The parking boys are swamped, as you can well imagine, and I understand there's a twenty-minute wait downstairs." He snapped his fingers to the bartender and said, "Give these nice folks whatever they're drinking." Then, turning to Tara once more, "May I have your parking check and I'll just run it downstairs and have the doorman give you a jingle when your car is brought round."

"Well, I guess so. Thank you very much. This is very kind of you." She handed over the check and smiled up at him. "If you treat all your guests so wonderfully, I predict The Factory will always be a smashing success."

"Not all, Miss Remington," he smiled, his fingers lightly brushing hers as he took the check. "Just special ones like yourself."

"I'll bet you say that to all gorgeous young writers," Izzy laughed, his eyes traveling hungrily over the big black's body. "By the way, I'm the gorgeous young writer's secretary, in case you need any letters written—or

242

anything . . ." He let just the tip of his tongue flick
around his lips and the black maître d' threw back his
head and laughed good naturedly.

"Marvelous," he chuckled. "I love show biz folks—
they're so amusing, don't you think?" He gave Izzy a
pat on the fanny and the slender homosexual almost
swooned. "Well, I'll just run this check downstairs and
you two enjoy your drinks, hear?"

"My God, I think I'm in love!" Izzy sang, rolling his
eyes. "Did you ever see so much of one man before in
your life?"

"No," Tara laughed, liking the black man's attitude a
lot. Most men would have felt threatened had a homosexual made such a blatant pass at them. Their drinks
arrived and she sipped hers, watching the dancers still
sweating and gyrating on the small floor, their undulating
bodies bathed in psychedelic colors.

"Oh, Tara, I almost forgot," Izzy shouted to be heard
above the loud din of rock music. "The men's room is a
gas! You must go see it. The graffiti were actually written
by the stars themselves, you know. Things like 'Paul Newman is a hustler' and 'Edith Head gives good wardrobe'
and, let's see, oh yes, 'Shakespeare eats Bacon'—just
nutty things like that. Simply wild!"

"Oh sure, I'm going to just casually stroll into the men's
room and start reading the walls." She chuckled and
shook her head. Izzy's normally bright eyes were glazed
and reduced to pinpoints and two bright spots of color
were high in his cheeks. She suddenly realized that she
had never seen him drunk before. Always he was the
epitome of decorum, taking his leave with elegant gracious-
ness when he knew he had had a little too much to drink.
But tonight he was animated and wickedly naughty,
making outrageous comments about the celebrities and
keeping Tara in a state of hilarity.

"Oh, you can go in if you like. There were three or
four ladies in there when I escorted Eric to the john. Chap-
eroned by a waiter, of course, lest they become carried
away and try to grab some star's dong." He squealed and
gripped Tara's arm. "And speaking of dongs, my dear,

you didn't tell me! Eric is hung like a bloody horse! What a *whang!* I mean, my dear, he *unreeled* it—like a length of garden hose! And it was *soft!* What in the world is it like when it's hard, I wonder?" Again the rolling eyes. "Ah, it must be sheer heaven to see him standing at attention . . ."

Jesus, this is all I need, Tara thought wearily. A discussion of the size of Eric's penis.

"I almost *died* when he flipped out that massive tool and stumbled against *me* for support!" He giggled merrily. "No wonder he almost fell over, all that weight pulling him down. And, sweetie, you would have been proud of me. I didn't even *try* to touch it. *Honestly!*" He sipped his drink, squirming on the bar stool as his fantasies built. "Ohhh, it was the hardest thing I've ever done, let me tell you. I mean, *there* he was, that fabulous flaccid pee-pee just *inches* from me and I stood there like a good little boy and didn't even *peek* at it. Well, maybe just a *little*. But, you know, sugar, that's the time to strike, when they're standing at the urinal. They're so vulnerable then, you know? Especially when they're bombed . . ."

"Izzy, shut up, please," Tara said wearily. "You're giving me a headache." Christ, where the hell was her car? She glanced at her watch and finished her drink, determined to go downstairs and wait, when she saw the tall maître d' walking toward them.

"Miss Remington, your car is ready." He helped her from the bar stool and led the way to the elevator, pressed the button and bowed them into it when it arrived. "Good evening. Come back real soon, hear?"

Tara thanked him, smiling a little at his "hear?"—but everyone was saying it these days.

She pulled Izzy in beside her just as the elevator door slid shut and heard someone calling her name. The door was not solid but grilled iron work, and she glanced up to see Eric's flushed face slowly disappearing as the lift carried them downward.

She hurried quickly outside, Izzy running along behind her. The crowd on the sidewalk seemed to have doubled since they had arrived hours earlier, and they set up a loud clamor as they recognized her.

"It's Tara Remington!" "Hey, Tara, where's Zock?" "Hey, Tara, over here!" "Tara, can I have your autograph?" "Tara! Tara!"

She glanced toward the entrance of The Factory and saw Eric lurching through the door, the redhead hanging grimly onto his arm. "Fuck him," she said aloud and quickly slid behind the wheel of her Mercedes, shoving it into gear and floor-boarding it.

"My God, sweetie, slow down or we'll scatter these people like pins in a bowling alley!" Izzy shrieked as she pressed the gas pedal to the floor and left a couple of yards of rubber on the street behind them.

"I guess she didn't see me," Eric mumbled to Pamela. He gave his parking ticket to one of the attendants and leaned heavily against the side of the building, his eyes on the red blur of Tara's Mercedes as it made a right turn on Santa Monica Boulevard and disappeared from sight.

"That's all right, honey," Pamela said soothingly. "I'll meet her some other time." Conceited bitch, she gritted to herself. Squealing away in her big expensive car and laying rubber like some idiot teenager. No wonder Eric had dropped her!

Eric lay panting on top of Pamela, her long black Halston tangled up around her waist as he tried to insert his fingers into the waistband of her pantyhose. "Christ, take those fucking things off, will ya?" He rolled off her and managed to push himself into a sitting position. He fumbled to the coffee table and found a joint, lit it, sucking in deep.

He was drunker than he had been in years. His stomach lurched sickly and his vision doubled. "How many times do I have to tell you I hate those fucking things. Get 'em off and come over here and suck my cock." He was in a mean, surly mood, wanting to hurt someone. And Pamela was always so eager to be hurt. Or so he thought.

"Oh, Eric, honey, please don't talk to me that way,"

she sighed. "Why are you being so mean to me tonight? What did I do?"

"You talk too fucking much." He aimed the remote control at the television set, clicking around the channels until he found an old Bette Davis and Zachary Scott movie. "Jesus, can't you ever just be quiet and do what you're told? Can't you see that I'm in no mood for conversation?" I just want to get blotto, he thought sadly. So damn blotto that all visions of Tara leave my mind. He turned on her angrily. "Why the hell can't you just relax and unwind a little? Shit, you never get drunk, you won't get high with me—what the fuck are you doing here, anyway?" He reached for his drink and saw that it was empty. "Get me another one," he demanded, sucking on the joint.

"Eric, do you think you should? You're already so drunk that you—"

"Oh, Eric," he mimicked sarcastically, shoving her off the sofa. "Just get me a drink or get the fuck out—I don't care which."

Pamela looked up at him from where she had fallen and tears ran silently down her cheeks. "All right, Eric, I'll get you a drink. Just please don't be mad at me anymore. I can't stand it when you're mad at me." She pulled herself upright, leaning over to place a trembling hand on his arm. "Please be nice tonight. I did so want everything to go well tonight, because I wanted to tell you something important and—and now—"

"Will you for Christ's sake get me a drink and shut your flapping face?" he snarled, shrugging her hand away so violently she almost fell again. "Jesus, what does a guy have to do to get it through your thick head? I don't want to talk tonight. Okay? You got that, cunt? Watch my lips. I . . . don't . . . want . . . to . . . talk . . . tonight. . . okay?" He finished the roach and flung it down, not bothering to see if it hit the ashtray or not. He pushed a button on the remote control, and the sound came on so loud that Pamela jumped and hurried to the bar.

With shaking hands she poured him a Jack Daniels and

made herself a vodka tonic. Maybe it would relax her.
She was determined to speak to him tonight about their
future. No matter what. Maybe if she drank with him, he
would be nice again. Take her into his arms and make
love to her and hold her close like he sometimes did.
Stroking her hair and telling her funny stories about Hollywood. She added a little more vodka to her drink and
carried them both back to the sofa.

"Come on and suck my cock," he mumbled, unzipping
his pants and kicking them off. "I wanna get my cock
sucked . . ." He reached up to take his drink, spilling it
half way to his mouth, pulling her down between his legs.
"Suck it, baby. Come on—" His head lolled back against
the sofa and he sighed mightily.

"Oh, Eric, please, not like this," Pamela cried, turning
her head away as he fondled himself.

"Oh, Eric—oh, Eric," he mimicked her, a sneer on his
face. "Shit, is that all you can say?" He sat up and shoved
her away, causing her to fall again. "Okay, then get the
fuck outta here. Who needs ya, anyway?"

"Okay, Eric, I will," she said quickly, crawling forward and taking his penis in her hands. "Just don't send
me away, honey, please don't close me out of your life.
I love you so much! You know I do, honey. I love you!"

"Shut up and suck," he mumbled, his interest turned
once again to the television set and Bette Davis.

Squeezing her eyes shut tight to keep back the flood of
tears, Pamela took him into her mouth and began to lick
and suck at his flaccid penis. He grunted and spread his
legs wider and she got upon her knees and bent her head
to her task. Why did Tara have to be there tonight? she
thought angrily. That's why Eric was acting so mean.
Tara made him so upset that he could not help himself
and just took his anger out on everyone around him. God,
how she hated that woman! And she would tell her so one
day, too. Just see if she didn't! She sucked faster, almost
gagging as she felt him grow larger inside her mouth, hating Tara with each tear that she could not shed. She was
aware of Eric raising the glass to his lips and calmly taking a drink as if nothing was happening to him. He leaned

to one side, placing his hand on the back of her head to keep her in place as he lit a cigarette. She wanted to scream at him, or better still, bite it off for the indifference he showed her. But she dutifully sucked on his semierect penis, knowing that for all her efforts he was much too drunk to ever get it up all the way. She felt like a public toilet and wished she had enough nerve to get to her feet and walk out of there. Out of Eric's life. Forever. But she knew she never would. Not as long as he would let her stay. So she sucked and licked and kissed him, making the appropriate sounds and digging her fingers passionately into his sides until he tangled his hand in her hair and jerked her mouth away.

"Ah, shit, it ain't doin' nothin'," he grumbled. "Get the vibrator." He did not look at her as she hurried into the bedroom. Tara, he thought painfully, Tara, Tara, see what you've done to me? Why don't you let me go? Why? He heard the soft hum of the vibrator and then the incredible thrill as Pamela applied it to the head of his cock. His eyes flew open and he stared down at her, still pressed in her perfect black Halston, the perfect string of pearls about her perfect white throat. And he wanted to kill her. Instead, he grabbed a handful of the black Halston and ripped it all the way down the front. "Get up here," he snarled, snatching the vibrator away from her and keeping it pressed hard against himself as she struggled onto the sofa. "Get those damn things off." She wriggled out of her pantyhose and he fell on top of her with a low grunt of pain, shoving into her so quickly that she cried out. She was dry and the insertion hurt them both, sending hot pains shooting through their genitals. Then he was moving deeper and deeper, wetting her and himself as he strove for release.

He pumped into her impotently, cursing his need to come. Wishing it were Tara lying beneath him. He felt himself harden slightly, then quickly subside, slipping out of her. With a curse he flung her away from him and buried his face in his hands.

"Darling, please don't," she said softly, crawling closer to him and stroking his hair. She took both his hands in hers and brought them to her lips, kissing them. "It's all right, honey, just lie back and relax, okay? I'll light you a joint and we'll just watch the movie, okay?" Her voice was a soft caress and he struggled into a sitting position and let her wipe the sweat and tears from his face.

"Oh, shit, Pam, I'm sorry," he mumbled, feeling like an asshole for his treatment of her. She was not a bad dame. Not really. And she loved him and would never leave him. Just flat-ass walk out on him as Tara had done. He tried a smile and made brief eye contact with her. "Forgive me, huh? I'm just so fucking drunk and—and—"

"Shhh, it's okay, really." She was all smiles now, secure in her sobriety. She ran lightly into the bedroom, returning a moment later with a blanket and tucked it around both of them. "Now, isn't this cozy?" She lit him a joint and took a swallow of her drink. "See? I'm having one too. Okay, honey? We'll just sit here and watch the movie until you want to talk or—whatever." She even giggled slightly, happy that his anger seemed to have spent itself. Bette Davis was throwing a fit on the television screen, screaming insults at Zachary Scott, and she thought, no wonder movie people are so volatile. They deal in such a passionate business. She would have to learn to be just as passionate. Stand up for herself. Trade insults with Eric like Bette Davis. Maybe then he would treat her with the respect she so craved from him.

"Hey, thanks, Pam," Eric said. His eyes had cleared somewhat and he managed to sit up straighter on the sofa. He reached for his drink and she quickly handed it to him, smiling softly into his eyes. "I guess I've been a bastard tonight." He drank deep. "I didn't mean to hurt you." He gave her the grin she so adored. "Am I forgiven?"

"Oh, Eric, of course you are, darling!" She kissed him and snuggled closer under the blanket. "I love you so much, honey. You know that. I think I would probably forgive you anything."

Eric did not answer. His mind was suddenly filled with thoughts of Tara. Why could she not forgive him anything? Obviously because she had not loved him enough.

249

Or was it because his sin was so much bigger than he had any right to be forgiven for? He felt beat. Bone weary. And his mind churned with bitter-sweet memories that he had tried years to forget. Years. It had been three years since he had held Tara in his arms. Well, not exactly. There was that one unforgettable night in the gazebo. Damn it, would she always be there, just under his skin like a cancer? Growing, always growing until he no longer felt in control of his own thoughts? He was able to function on a daily basis, get his work done, laugh with friends, even make love to other women. But all it took was seeing her one time and all the old scarred-over wounds broke apart again. Flooding him with such sweet sadness that he wanted to weep.

He tossed off the rest of his drink and lay back on the sofa, burying his face in the cushions. He felt Pamela tenderly tuck the blanket in around his neck and shoulders, then her lips gently kissed his. He thought he heard her say "sleep" but was too wrapped up in thoughts of Tara to respond. Fair Tara, he thought wryly, my fair Tara has murdered sleep . . . Then he remembered nothing.

CHAPTER
TWELVE

TARA made her way through the tight knot of customers waiting at the entrance of The Bistro. The luncheon crowd was thick, as always, the bar jammed and the waiting room filled. She saw Vince Hollander across the room and raised her hand in greeting, starting toward him. The crowd parted to let her pass, the men's eyes going over her appreciatively—the women's, appraising her outfit. Here and there she heard the pop of a champagne cork and at almost every table she saw silver buckets holding bottles of chilling wine.

"Hi, thought for a minute you were going to stand me up." Vince started to rise, but she waved him back into his seat and slid into the booth next to him.

"Hi, darling, now would I do a thing like that?" She offered her cheek for his kiss as she spread her napkin in her lap. "The traffic was incredible. Thought I'd never get here."

"It's the tail end of the Labor Day weekend traffic," Vince said, taking the bottle of Louis Roederer champagne from it's bucket of ice and pouring her a glass. "Everyone's on their way home—back to Des Moines, back to work, back to school, summer's over."

"Umm," she tasted the champagne and smiled at him. "I know. Mandy tried every excuse in the book to stay home from school today. She's starting high school, you

know, and is naturally a little apprehensive about it."
She sipped again, nodded. "Lovely, darling, thanks for
having it chilled and waiting for me."

"Your servant, madame. Always."

Tara glanced about the room, nodding or waving
hello to those diners she knew, acknowledging the recognition of the waiters. This was definitely the watering
hole of the rich and chic, she thought, taking in the beautiful women and dapper men. They were all a picture of
studied California casualness in their French-cut denims,
their necks hung with gold chains and medallions. The
new craze was for men to wear one gold or diamond earring, and she had to smile as she looked around at the
past-middle-aged gentlemen with flashing ear lobes. Their
carefully exercised bodies were encased in silk shirts
open to the navel, their slightly gray-haired chests strewn
with so much gold it looked like an explosion at Fort
Knox.

The women were equally turned out, their almost bare
bosoms peeking flirtatiously through see-through blouses,
the nipples hidden by a thin strip of cloth that passed as
a vest, the many gold chains and diamonds spilling in
resplendence over the expensive fabric. They looked as
if they had all shopped at the same boutique, had their
hair styled at the same salon and purchased their fash-
ionably thin bodies at the same cloning station.

Tara took a slim platinum watch from her handbag and
slid it across the table. "You forgot it again," she smiled
when Vince picked it up.

"So that's where I left it." He grinned as he slipped it
on his wrist, "Sorry, Tara. You're going to think I don't
like it if I keep forgetting it every time I come by your
place. Actually, it's an excuse to come back and see you
again." His dark eyes were soft and gentle with love as
they smiled into hers, and she had an urge to reach out
and tousle the boyish locks of his brown hair.

"Just see that you don't leave it lying around someone
else's bedroom. You might not get it back." She had
bought it for him at the end of shooting on *Seattle Slum*
some months ago, and since then he had left it at her

house at least a dozen times. Vince had been the still photographer on *Seattle Slum,* and she had met him on location in Seattle when Monash had asked if she would like to come up for a few days and watch the shooting. They had hit it off at once. She remembered how she had first become aware of him. She would be sitting off camera watching the action, when suddenly she would get the feeling that someone was looking at her. Turning, she could see no one except a tall, slim, slightly hippyish young man with tousled hair holding a camera to his face. Shrugging, turning back to the action, she would dismiss the feeling until once more she would feel eyes upon her. Monitoring her every move, it seemed. She had caught him one day when she had casually reached into her purse for her compact and had held it just right to see the young man adjusting his camera lenses as he pointed it in her direction. He had not been taking pictures of her, just merely watching her through the lens as she sat and watched her novel come alive under Arthur Spielman's expert direction.

"Busted," Vince had grinned boyishly when she had confronted him. "But I couldn't help myself. You're so damn beautiful that my camera just automatically turns in your direction whenever you walk on the set."

He had taken her to dinner that night and every night that she had remained in Seattle. When the location shooting was over, she had not been surprised to receive a telephone call from Vince asking if he might see her again. They had gone to dinner at La Scala and then to The Daisy, where they had danced until closing, laughing so much that Tara's stomach had hurt from muscles she had not used much in that activity lately. Since then they had met at least two or three times a week, either for dinner or a day with Mandy. Vince and Mandy had hit it off as famously as he and Tara had, and the fact that he loved horses had cemented the relationship.

"Little chance of that," Vince laughed, reaching across to squeeze her hand. "I haven't seen the inside of another lady's bedroom since meeting you."

"Then what do you do for sex?" Tara asked innocently.

"I take them to *my* bedroom," he retorted with an impudent grin.

It was true that for all their closeness, there had been no sexual relationship between them. Tara liked him as a buddy (Izzy insisted that she was most certainly turning into a neuter, asking if he could have Vince since she did not want him) and Vince had seemed to go along with her terms without complaint. Although she suspected that he was beginning to fall a little in love with her, he seemed content to just hang around the sprawling mansion/ranch, play with Mandy and her horses, get high with Tara, tease Hazel and Charley and more or less make himself a platonic member of the family. He had made a couple of half-hearted passes at her in Seattle, but she had gently warded them off.

"Ah-hah, I thought so," Tara said. "And you promised you were saving yourself for me."

"But I am, I am!" he protested. "I'm merely making sure that everything is in perfect working order when you finally decide you can't live without me."

"Don't hold your breath, sweetie. I find I can live quite well by myself, thank you." It was true. Her career was skyrocketing, and the money and acclaim that constantly poured in had made her feel confident and sure of herself in more ways than she would have imagined. She felt strong and on top of most situations, especially with men. She had discovered that she could have a brief affair and walk away feeling good about herself and the man. No guilt feelings about Eric. No self-doubts about her own sexuality. For the first time in her life she was finally beginning to understand the true meaning of being free. Free to make her own decisions. Whether they were good or bad, she was able to make them and learn from her mistakes. That she was no longer held back by inhibitions was perhaps the most exhilarating discovery of all. She was a success in her chosen field and had developed an awareness of herself as a powerful, together woman. She exuded a powerful self-confidence that showed in the way she moved, dressed, spoke and carried on her daily business of living and working.

She had grown most notably in the bedroom. She found that she could enter into a relationship with a man, go to bed with him and still feel free the next morning. She realized that sex did not have to shackle her to the hurts of love. It could be happy and free, with both partners giving as much or as little of themselves as they felt comfortable with. No more. And when desire wore thin, she was able to remain friends with her gentleman friends. Make them into buddies, as Izzy accused her. But she liked it that way and was not about to change. Izzy had also accused her of behaving like a man—picking a guy up, taking him home to bed, then showing him the door. She had had a few such one-nighters, but that was the beauty of her newfound freedom. She could have a satisfying sexual fling with a virtual stranger and not feel hung up about it the next day.

"Shall we order?" Tara asked, picking up the menu even though she knew it by heart. She often lunched at The Bistro, as she loved the noisy, nosey busy show business crowd as well as the excellent food.

"Okay with me." Vince scanned the menu briefly. "What's on your agenda for this afternoon? Doing anything special?"

"No, not really. I just have to stop by Doe's and pick up Mandy's flower girl gown. Since we can't seem to pry her away from the stables, Doe suggested I take it home and see if it fits."

They gave their order to the waiter and Vince filled their glasses again. "I don't think I've ever seen Mandy in anything but jeans and cowboy boots. Are you sure there's a girl under all that horse hair and dirt?"

"There's very definitely a girl under there. I happened to walk in on her the other night when she was in the tub, and, my God, she's getting a pair of boobs on her like Sandy Sinclair!" That was just one more step in her self-confidence; she could mention Sandy Sinclair's name without feeling the old stab of jealous pain it had once brought.

"You couldn't prove it by me," Vince laughed. "Every time I've seen her she looks like she's wearing Totie Fields' sweatshirt!"

"Trust me. Mandy the kid is growing up." She sipped her champagne, resting her elbows on the table and feeling the relaxation that comes with good friends and good wine. "Want to take a ride with me to Doe's?"

"No, I thought I'd go out to the house and do a little sketching, if it's all right with you."

"Sure, fine." Vince was a frustrated artist and spent all his spare time with a sketchbook under his arm, tramping the hills above Tara's house for something to draw. His paintings were excellent and she had been planning for some time to give him a one-man show on Rodeo Drive when he thought he was ready. Actually, she thought he was ready now, but he did not. He would actually blush and dig his big toe in the dirt like a tow-headed farm lad when she suggested that he could pull it off. "Not yet," he would plead. "Just let me get a few more paintings ready before I meet the glaring eye of the public."

She looked across at him now, sitting so casually slumped in his seat, his hair, as always, looking tousled and unruly, even though she knew that he had it styled regularly by Jay Sebring. He was extremely handsome, in a Dick Clark/Tom Sawyer sort of way. Dark curly hair, large expressive brown eyes, full-lipped sensual mouth and lithe frame that moved easily in dungarees or tuxedo. And she wondered again why she was not sexually attracted to him. She loved spending time with him and did so as often as possible. He was at the house several times a week and if the hour grew too late for him to make the long drive back to Hollywood he would stay over, sleeping in her bed as platonically as a brother. And he always left his watch on the nightstand, going blithely off the next morning without giving it a thought. Vince did not have much use for a wristwatch, he had often told her. Watches were for people who had to be somewhere on time and he never seemed to have to. A freelance photographer, he ambled casually from one assignment to the next, spending his offtime in some field or at the beach, sketching. He had told her once that watches were a waste of time.

Jim Glasser was convinced that Tara had a secret lover and had questioned her relentlessly whenever he happened to be in her bedroom and saw Vince's watch on the nightstand. (She often entertained close friends in her bedroom, as she loved the pretty, airy room overlooking the rolling green hills and reservoir that she liked to think of as a lake. There was ample room, with a sofa, two easy chairs and a small conversation table with straight-backed Queen Anne chairs.) Jim had been making himself something of a pest ever since Tara had shucked off her shell and stepped out as a grown-up lady ready to meet and take on men on their own level. She had had to ward off his advances more than once in the past couple of years, but still managed to maintain a close friendship with her former boss.

Tara had spent an hour with Doe, exclaiming over the decorations that had been arriving daily for the wedding party. She and Wesley had decided to get married at home, in the back yard, and all week workmen had milled about the pool area, erecting a huge tent and rolling out thousands of square feet of artificial grass to cover Doe's real grass, lest it be trampled and ruined by the wedding guests. Her swimming pool had been completely covered and converted into a dance floor, with a raised platform for the musicians near the diving board. The water slide was being filled with dozens of pink and white carnations, and in every corner of the vast lawn vases and urns were filled to overflowing with more carnations, as well as chrysanthemums, marigolds and gladioli. The bridal arch (especially built by Doe's Beverly Hills florist) would be covered with baby's breath and pink and white roses, and the fake grass would be strewn with rose petals leading to the alter.

"It's going to be just beautiful, Doe," Tara had said as Doe led her around the converted back yard. They had had a strawberry dacquiri and shared a joint, then Tara had taken Mandy's gown and started home. It was lovely in its simplicity. A pink so pale one had to look at the folds to catch the shimmering subtle rose tint. It had a sweetheart neckline, nipped in close at the waist and then flared out in soft gathers that moved in gradual tones of deep rose to palest pearl pink. A tiara of pink satin roses and a short train completed the outfit, with silk slippers dyed to match the gown. Mandy would look like a dream in it, Tara thought as she turned into her driveway and pressed a button on the dash of her Mercedes that opened the automatic wrought iron gates.

She turned off the motor and honked the horn for Hazel to come and give her a hand with her bundles. Shaunti, Mandy's german shepherd, reared up on the door of her car, tail wagging furiously, waiting for Tara to get out and pet her. She was taller than the top of the car as she stood with her front paws on the window. Remarkable, when only a year ago she had been a handful of fluff. Tara glanced toward the garage and saw a shiny black Mercedes parked beneath the shade of an oak tree. She did not recognize it and thought perhaps someone was visiting Charley.

"Here, Shaunti, get away now!" Hazel flapped her apron at the shepherd and the dog reluctantly lowered its paws and slunk a few paces away. "My goodness, what have you got here, miss Tara? Is this Mandy's flower girl outfit?" She took the cellophane bag from Tara and held the door while her mistress struggled with several more boxes and bags.

"Yes, isn't it pretty? Look at the color. It changes every time you turn it a different way." Tara bent to pet Shaunti, then gestured toward the Mercedes. "Who's here?"

"Oh, it's just Mr. Jim," Hazel said. "He's inside with Mandy playing a game of Scrabble."

"Good, he can bring in the case of champagne. Doe insisted I take one home she's gotten so many. In fact, she's gotten so much of everything her house looks like a department store."

They stepped inside the cool, immaculate foyer and Tara was struck anew at how good it always felt to walk into her own home. She loved the big old barn of a house even more now than she had when she had first moved in three years ago, if that was possible. It had such a welcoming air about it, yet retained its quiet dignity and calm elegance.

"Hi, Tara," Mandy called. She was lying on her stomach on the floor, elbows propped on either side of the Scrabble board, a Coke sitting next to her. "What 'cha got?"

Jim got quickly to his feet and went to Tara. "Thank God you're home," he growled good-naturedly. "The kid was beating me!" He kissed her cheek and gazed into her face with a mixture of love and embarrassment, as he always did when he was sober. Drunk, it was something else again. Then he tried to ravish her with arguments, pleas and more hands than Warren Beatty and Erroll Flynn put together. "Here, let me take those." He relieved her of the bundles and placed them on the sofa.

"Thanks, Jim. There's a case of champagne in the back of the car since you're in a helpful mood." She kicked off her shoes and went to sink into a chair near Mandy. "Hi, Toots, so you're beating the old pro, huh? Good for you." She leaned down to kiss the top of her head.

"Yeah, and I would've beat him the last game, too, but he kept looking my words up in the dictionary. That's not fair, is it?" She perched on the arm of Tara's chair and brought her Coke to her mouth, taking a swig.

"Mandy, I wish you wouldn't drink so much Coke, honey. You're going to have to start watching your complexion now that you're a teeny bopper. Oily skin makes yuky zits."

"Oh, Tara," Mandy wailed. "You always say that."

"Only because it's true." She took a cigarette from a silver tray on the table and lit it with a matching silver table lighter.

"Well, cigarettes cause cancer and you keep on smoking." Mandy gave her a righteously superior look.

"Oh, shut up," Tara grinned, smacking her on the fanny. "Go help Jim bring in the champagne and make yourself useful." As Mandy ran from the room, Tara turned to Hazel and sighed, "Smartass kids. I guess they're growing up in the cancer scare generation. Wish I had been. I would never have started this disgusting habit."

"Why don't you quit, then, if you dislike it so much? All it takes is a little willpower." Hazel considered herself a member of the family, not just a cook, and often chastized Tara and Mandy for their bad habits.

"You, too," Tara sighed, but she crushed out her cigarette just the same. Getting to her feet, she went into her office and took a joint from her supply in the desk drawer. Lighting it and puffing deeply, she went back into the living room. She flourished it at Hazel, her grin mischievous. "Maybe you're right, Hazel. I'll give up cigarettes and stick to pot. It's healthier, they say. After all, God grows his own grass!"

Hazel pursed her lips and tsk-tsked her way out of the room, her voice floating back, "All right, miss Tara, make fun of me, but you'll see I'm right one of these days."

Tara laughed and went to open the door for Mandy and Jim. They held the case of champagne between them and she said, "Just put it behind the bar in the billiard room, okay,"

"Christ, this is Moët et Chandon," Jim said as he eased the case to the floor and peeked under the flaps.

"Yeah, it's Wesley's favorite and I never seem to have any when they come to visit, so I guess Doe's making sure her new hubby doesn't have to go without even for one evening." She took a bottle out and held it up to the light. "Shall we pop a cork and have a prewedding drink,"

"Hell, yes, you never saw me turn down a glass of classy champagne, did you?"

"I've never seen you turn down a glass of anything," Tara chuckled as she handed him the bottle. "Careful now, it may have gotten warm on the drive home."

"No, it's still cold." He wrapped a bar towel around the neck of the bottle, opening it expertly and giving off the tiniest of "pops" without spilling a drop.

"Can I have some, too?" Mandy asked.

"No, you cannot," Tara said. "My God, Mandy, it's only five o'clock. You should be drinking milk and eating cookies."

"Cookies are bad for my complexion," Mandy grinned, edging closer to Jim who gave her a sip of his. "Besides, you drink champagne all the time and your skin is beautiful."

"Yes, and I have the bills from Elizabeth Arden to prove it," Tara answered dryly. "Oh, okay, just a tiny glass. But first, go tell Charley to come and join us."

"Gee, thanks, Tara!" Mandy ran to the door, yelling, "Charley! Charley, Tara's home and wants you to come and drink some champagne with us! Hurry!" She was back again without ever having left the doorway of the billiard room.

"I said go and tell her, not shout it clear across the house," Tara said. She turned to Jim, shaking her head. "I don't need an intercom with her around."

Charley entered the room, stretching the muscles in her back and squinting her eyes against the bright glare of sun that spilled in through the windows. "Hey, hi, boss— you letting me off early today? What's the occasion?" She accepted the glass from Jim and sipped. "Umm, good. Just what I needed."

"The occasion, children, is that you are all about to see something you've never seen before." She paused dramatically. "But first I want to have everyone here. Charley, did Vince come by this afternoon?"

"Yes, he's out back sketching, I think. I saw him down by the stables a little while ago."

"Mandy, go tell Hazel to ring the stable and see if Vince can join us." She added quickly, "Don't yell. Go into the kitchen and tell her. Jeez, what does she think we have phones for?"

Mandy ran from the room, returning a moment later. "Okay, he's coming. What 'cha gonna show us, Tara?"

"It concerns you, keed-o, so let's step into the other room and get you ready."

"Wait a minute," Jim said suspiciously. "Who the hell is Vince? I haven't met him, have I?"

"No, but you've met his watch," Tara laughed, giving Charley a wink as she led Mandy from the room. "Charley will make the introductions and we'll be right back. Come on, Mandy."

Vince was leaning casually against the pool table, a glass in his hand, when Tara came back a moment later and announced, "Okay, are you ready? I guarantee this is something you've never seen before." She ducked her head behind the door and said, "Okay, Mandy—you're on."

"I feel silly," Mandy grumbled as she stepped through the doorway and stood looking around at the group. She was wearing the pale pink gown, looking like an exquisite angel, her inky curls falling in glistening ringlets to her bare shoulders. Her adolescent figure was suddenly transformed into soft curves and rosy skin. The low neckline of the gown showed her new cleavage and her waist was as narrow as a wood nymph's. The dainty crown of satin roses glowed like pink pearls in her dark hair, and the slippers with their two-inch heels gave her height and an elegance not seen before.

"Jesus Christ, can this be the cowgirl I see covered in horse shit every day?" Jim gasped. He went to her and bowed over her hand, leading her the rest of the way into the room. "I think I'm in love. If I can't have the big sister, I'll take the little one and raise her to suit myself!"

"Heaven forbid," Charley cried, then, "Oh, Mandy, you look just beautiful. What a lovely gown." She turned the child this way and that, causing the skirt to swirl and float around her body.

"You look just like a fairy princess, honey," Hazel said from the doorway. "My, miss Tara, doesn't she look pretty in that color?"

"Yes, she certainly does," Tara agreed. "Now if I can just teach her to walk without tripping on the hem, we'll be all right."

"It's not the hem I'm worried about," Mandy grumbled. "These darn shoes feel like I'm walking on stilts." She pulled up her dress and stared down at the pink slippers, pretending to be staggering, and Vince caught her around the waist and swung her up on the edge of the pool table.

"I'd like to paint you just the way you look this minute," he said. "You're like a butterfly coming out of its cocoon and not quite knowing what to do with your new wings."

"I just feel dumb," Mandy complained, but she giggled at the attention everyone was lavishing upon her.

"Vince, get her down from there. She'll have the gown wrinkled before the wedding. And, Mandy, stop kicking your heels against the table. You'll scuff your shoes." Tara went to her and helped her off the pool table, her gaze going softly over her little sister. She was becoming a very beautiful young woman and did not even realize it. She was so wrapped up in horses and shows that she had not really gone through the silly stage most pubescent girls did. Her classmates often stopped by after school or spent the weekend, and their conversations were entirely of rock stars, dances, clothes and makeup. But not her little Mandy. She still scoffed at such nonsense and doggedly pursued her riding and showing.

"A toast," Tara said, raising her glass. "To Mandy and her first long gown."

There were cries of "Hear, hear" and Mandy blushed and moved to stand in the curve of Vince's arm.

"You do look very pretty, little one," Vince said softly, hugging her to him. "It wouldn't hurt to add a few dresses to your wardrobe, you know."

"Gosh, I don't know what the big deal is," Mandy protested. "I used to wear dresses all the time."

"Yeah, you wore dresses until you got your first horse," Tara laughed. "Then, goodbye little girl—hello bronc buster!"

Everyone kidded her good-naturedly as they finished the bottle, and then Tara told Hazel to help Mandy out of her new finery.

"Thanks for the champagne break," Vince said. "Now if you'll excuse me I'd like to get back to my drawing before I lose the sun." He set his glass on the bar and turned to Tara. "How about dinner tonight? There's a new restaurant on the beach I've been wanting to try. My roommate works there and says it's quite good."

263

"Not tonight, luv. But you can stay and have dinner here if you'd like."

"Thanks, but I can't. I promised Andy I'd drop by the beach tonight and look in on him. Jeez, I can't remember the name of the place."

"Is it the Tiki Tiki?" Charley asked. "I know it just opened a few weeks ago on Pacific Coast Highway."

"No, this place is in the Marina." He shrugged and started for the door. "That's okay, I've got the address at home someplace. See you all. Jim, nice meeting you." He paused to give Tara a light kiss on the cheek. "I'll give you a call tomorrow, so long."

"Where the hell did you find him?" Jim growled the minute the door had closed behind Vince.

"Actually, I found him behind a camera in Seattle," Tara said. "And you can stop scowling. He's just a good friend—no romance." She laughed and pinched his cheek. "What would I do without you to look after me and keep me straight, Jim? The way you act, I ball everything in pants."

"I just want to make sure you don't get hurt—" He didn't finish the sentence and they both knew that he had meant to add "again." "Ah, the hell with it," he grumbled, not unkindly. "You're a big girl now."

"You noticed." Tara arched an eyebrow at him and he had the grace to flush slightly.

"Well, if you two are going to fight again, I'm going back to work," Charley said. "I still haven't gotten a date for the Mike Douglas Show. I know he plans on having Roger Morrison on next Tuesday and they're running a film clip of *Seattle Slum,* so I'm trying to get you on the following day."

"Good," Tara said. "Gee, I hope it's the biggest picture this year. Roger was awfully good in it, wasn't he?"

"I thought so," Charley nodded. "But Joan Nathan stole it as the mother."

"Yes, she sure did." Tara remembered sitting in the theater, tears streaming down her face as she watched Joan Nathan dancing drunkenly to the music on the static-ridden old radio. A chipped and scarred cabinet

264

model like the one Tara remembered from her childhood. In fact, she had wept through most of the movie, the memories flooding back so poignantly that she had been left weak when the film had ended. Roger Morrison had played Calhoun, the cop (Tara had changed the name to Officer Francis Henaghan, as well as changing Bell Woodhauser's name to Franny Osenbaugh), and the actor had been so realistic that Tara had had to keep reminding herself that it was not happening all over again.

"I thought the direction was excellent," Jim said. "Speilman, wasn't it?" He reached for another bottle of champagne, held it up, a question in his eyes and Tara nodded her agreement.

"Uh-huh, Arthur Speilman. I thought so, too. Everything was so depressingly authentic, I couldn't help crying." She turned to Charley. "Want to take a glass of the bubbly in with you?"

"Love it—thanks." Jim poured all around and when Charley had exited, he and Tara went to sit on the sofa.

"Well, I sure hope everyone likes the movie as much as we do," she said.

"Hell, yes, they will. The book was a fucking smash, so the movie can't miss."

"Oh, I don't know. I've seen a lot of best sellers turned into box office bombs."

"That's true," Jim admitted. "But *Seattle Slum* has something going for it those other ones didn't."

"What's that?"

"You." Jim sipped and sighed, "Great champagne. That Englishman has better taste than I thought."

"What do I have to do with the movie?" Tara asked. "I mean, I can understand how appearing on talk shows to plug the book really helped to sell it, but I really have nothing to do with the movie."

"The hell you don't. Charley's in there right now getting you spots on talk shows to plug the movie as well. You've got a lot of loyal fans out there, Tara. If they read your book and liked it, they're going to go see the movie just because you wrote it. And the ones who were too fucking dumb to read it are probably going to go see the movie because they've heard it's dirty."

"Well, I sure hope so. Jonathan Monash had so much faith in my work that I want to see him make a bundle off the movie." She lit a cigarette and put her bare feet up on the table. "And if *Seattle Slum* hits for him, he'll be more likely to buy the screen rights of my new novel."

"Yeah, that's right. By the way, how's that tome coming along? You're almost finished, aren't you?"

"I finished a couple of weeks ago. It'll be out next spring, about April, I think."

"Great. Just keep grinding them out, kid, that's the only way to make a buck in the book business." He went to the bar and brought the bottle of champagne back to the sofa with him, refilling their glasses. "What the hell's the name of it again? *Passion Pits* or *Sweet Savage Strangeness* or something like that?"

Tara laughed. "It's *Passion's Rogue,* you dope."

"Oh, yeah, that's it." He grinned his Irish leprechaun's grin. "Shit, there's so many of those fucking novels around these days, I can't keep all the titles straight."

"But none like mine," Tara said smugly. She knew her new novel was good. Maybe even better than *Seattle Slum*. And she had had more fun writing it since it was pure fiction and not based on her tacky childhood.

"So you keep telling me." He looked toward the sliding glass doors where Daisy lay curled asleep in a shaft of sunlight. "Hey, fat cat, come over here and give your Uncle Jim a kiss," he demanded loudly, his normal way of greeting the shaggy calico. Daisy opened one round green eye and peered at him disinterestedly, closed it and went back to sleep. But Jim would not be put off. He got to his feet and went over and picked the cat up, carrying her back to the sofa. They had had a running battle almost from the first day that Tara had gotten Daisy as a kitten when she was working for Jim's *Beverly Hills Beat*. Jim would insist that Daisy come to him when he called her, and she had no intention of doing so. Instead, she would wait until Jim had exhausted every cat call and plea he could think of, finally giving up in disgust, cursing her for a fickle feline, then she would calmly amble over and brush against him.

"Oh, Jim, leave her alone," Tara said, grinning in spite of herself. "You know how she hates to be picked up when she's grabbing a suntan."

"The snotty bitch always wants to play with me when *I'm* not in the mood!" He tickled the cat's belly and she wrapped her front paws around his hand, digging the claws in just far enough to make him yelp and release her. Then she nimbly leaped onto Tara's lap and began cleaning herself, as if washing away Jim's touch.

"Fickle feline," Jim snorted. "See if I bring you any leftover lobster or prime rib next time I go to Lawery's!" But he was grinning as he reached over to tousle her thick fur, and she relented enough to rub her head against his hand.

"Hey, I saw the new Mercedes in the driveway," Tara said. "When did you get it?"

"Shit, I damn near forgot. That's what I came out to show you." He swallowed the rest of his champagne and reached for the bottle again, ignoring Tara's raised eyebrow. "Just picked it up this morning. It's a beauty, huh?"

"It's pretty cute." She shook her head when he offered to refill her glass. "I still have some." She hoped he would not get too bombed before dinner or she would have a hell of a time getting rid of him. "Jim, why do you drive those little things, anyway? I mean, you can certainly afford a real automobile instead of those little kiddie cars."

"Kiddie car!" Jim exclaimed. "I'll have you know, Miss Remington, that the Mercedes is *the* car of the future."

"Okay, okay," Tara laughed, giving up. Jim bought a new one every year, refusing to even think about something more prestigious, more befitting his position as publisher of a successful magazine. "Well, drink up, friend Jim. I have a hot date with a sunken tub." She drained her glass and set it on the table. "I stopped by Doe's for a few minutes and got trapped in all the wedding preparations. Workmen were spray-painting those lattice chairs and dividers and I think most of it blew on

267

me. God, that stuff really flies around. I told Doe she was going to wind up with a pink house if she wasn't careful."

"She'd probably like that," Jim said, reaching over to scratch Daisy's ears before Tara set her on the floor. The calico twitched her tail, indignant at having been dismissed, and went back to her spot of sun near the window. "Christ, every time I see that dame, she's wearing pink."

"I know. She says it makes her complexion look young and rosy." She stood, smiling down at him. "Well, I hate to kick you out, but I've been thinking about a hot bath all afternoon. Why don't you go bug Hazel while you finish your drink? You know how she loves company in her kitchen." She dropped a light kiss on his forehead and started for the door.

"Well, thanks a lot. Kicking me out, just like that, huh?"

"Yep, just like that." She waggled her fingers at him as she disappeared through the door, calling over her shoulder, "See you soon, luv. Thanks for stopping by."

Tara lay soaking in her sunken marble tub, two thin slices of cucumbers resting on her closed eyelids to ease the fatigue of the day. She had spent all morning shopping for a wedding gift for Doe and Wesley, but had not come up with anything suitable. She had been exhausted by the time she had met Vince for lunch at The Bistro, and then had had to stop by Doe's and pick up Mandy's gown. She was glad the dress fitted and there would not be any need for alterations. And Mandy had looked adorable in it. So grown up and lovely. Tara sighed. She would be fifteen on her next birthday. It did not seem possible. Especially since she stubbornly refused to act her age and insisted on dressing like Calamity Jane and hanging around with horses instead of boys.

Maybe horses were best, Tara thought. At least they could not break her heart, like a man could. "None of that," she said aloud, firmly. She had been thinking of Eric a lot since running into him at The Factory, and if the memories became too painful, she would get out of the house. Go for a walk or try to find Vince and watch him sketch for a while. Anything to keep from being alone with her thoughts. It was kind of a shock to find that she still loved him. But she knew that she did when she had looked up into his love-filled eyes. He had looked so unhappy and pathetic that her heart had gone out to him. Of course, she would have died before admitting it to anyone. Even Izzy, whom she suspected had guessed when, peeling away from The Factory so furiously, she had damn near killed a pedestrian. And Izzy had not let her forget it, either. Several times he had tried to bring up the subject, and each time Tara had told him she did not want to talk about it. Ever. But his natural curiosity, as well as his feeling for her welfare, had made him so persistent that she had finally exploded and told him to get the hell out of her house and not come back until she called him.

Perhaps that was why the house seemed quieter than usual the past few days. She knew Izzy had telephoned several times and talked to Charley and Mandy, but he had known better than to ask to speak to Tara. She seldom became angry, but when she did, everyone in the house ran for cover. She smiled, feeling a little guilty about jumping all over poor Izzy. She supposed she should call and tell him to come back to work. After all, he was just trying to be a friend. Trying to get her to talk about something that hurt her, telling her that maybe the hurt would go away if she said it aloud to another person. Maybe he was right.

She took the cucumber slices off her eyes and reached for the telephone next to the tub, dialing his number. He answered on the first ring. "Izzy? Where the hell have you been? I'm docking your pay for the whole week if you don't get your ass over here at nine o'clock tomorrow morning!" She tried to keep her voice mock-angry, but his high, shrill squeal of laughter flooded over her like healing balm. She had to admit that she had really missed him. He always made her feel so happy with his crazy antics and strange outlook on life.

"Tara! *Sugar!*" he cried. "You're not mad at me anymore!"

"Yes I am," she said sternly, "but I have a fitting tomorrow afternoon for my bridesmaid's gown and you know I don't trust anyone but you to tell me if it looks right."

"I *love* you, sugar," he gushed. "I knew you couldn't stay mad at poor little me for *too* long!"

"Don't press your luck," she chuckled. "Hey, Izzy, I'm sorry about the other day. Forgive me?"

"Do you even *have* to ask? You know I'd walk barefoot through brimstone for you—whatever *that* is!" Again the high, gay giggle. "Oh, sugar, I've been absolutely *miserable* since you booted me out. I'm the one who should apologize. You were right. It's certainly none of *my* business what you do about your love life." His voice dropped, becoming softly sincere. "But you *know* I only want to see you happy and if admitting that you still love that bum will—"

"Izzy," Tara warned, already regretting having telephoned him.

"All right, *all right,* sugar. Not *another* word." He made his voice bright and cheery. "Now, tell me about your gown. Is Doe still insisting that all her little girls wear pink?"

"Yes," Tara said, glad that he had given in so easily. He could be a real pain when he got on a subject, worrying it to pieces like a bulldog after a bone. "But at least mine will be a deeper pink, almost rose, really." She stretched her legs, wiggling her toes in the hot sudsy water. "Oh, you should see Mandy's new dress. She looks like a dream walking."

"What else, with that face and figure? How does she like it?"

"You know her, she says she feels 'dumb,' but Hazel told me she saw her preening in front of the mirror and practicing walking in her new high heels. Maybe she's finally coming around. I'd hate to think of her spending her entire teenage years in scruffy old Levis and cowboy boots."

"Oh, she'll come around—just as soon as some young stud tells her how beautiful she is!" Izzy chuckled wickedly. "I wish some young stud would tell *me* how beautiful *I* am! I'd be all over him like sap on a tree!"

They chatted a few more minutes and then Izzy asked, "What time is your fitting tomorrow, sugar?"

"Not until three, but I want you here by nine. Charley says there's a new batch of fan mail on *Seattle Slum* that needs answering. God, Izzy, can you believe I'm still getting letters on that thing?"

"But of course, sweetie. It's had more printings than *Valley of the Dolls,* if one can believe *Time* magazine."

"Well, anyway, I'm just grateful that people are still buying it."

"Oh, my, yes," he said broadly. "You need the money *sooo* desperately, poor thing."

Tara told him to go to hell and laughingly hung up the telephone. She felt a lot better for having apologized to him for her bad temper and finished her bath humming *Moon River.* Maybe someday she would tell him the whole story of Eric and Mandy so that he would understand why she was still pained by it. Mandy was a constant reminder, and each year she seemed to look more like Eric than ever. Lately Tara had also been troubled about telling Mandy who her real father was. Should she go on letting her believe that her father had been the long dead and forgotten Elmer Woodhauser or should she someday tell her the truth? When she was older and more likely to understand such things. Tara really did not know what would be best for the child and, for the time being, anyway, decided to keep things as they were.

CHAPTER
THIRTEEN

TARA SAT at a round pink table, glancing idly about the huge tented backyard. Everywhere she looked she saw pink. The centerpiece on her table was pink and white carnations, the napkins and tablecloth a matching pink. Even the crystal was tinted pink. And the late afternoon sun slanting through the tent openings cast everything in a rosy glow until the entire backyard seemed one color. Barry and Charley sat across from her, and Jim and Thorton, deep in conversation, stood nearby. The wedding had long since been over, and now the enormous crowd that had stayed for the reception was beginning to thin.

And what a crowd it had been. The women were dazzling in their Balenciagas and Givenchys as they draped possessive arms through the arm of some sexually powerful businessman, politician or scion of high society. They sparkled with each languid gesture, their diamonds and gold competing with the afternoon sun. Elsewhere, titled Europeans engaged movie stars in conversation, while bored jet setters from Palm Beach, New York and Scottsdale chatted with their neighbors from Beverly Hills, Palm Springs and San Francisco. At one point during the long afternoon, Tara and Charley had amused themselves by seeing how many Diors, Halstons and Saint Laurents they could spot. Then Jim and Barry had joined in the game, trying to guess the origin of accents, such as Grosse Pointe,

273

Boston or Washington. It had been a way to pass the slightly boring afternoon.

Mandy had been exquisite as Doe's flower girl and had stood patiently for the numerous photographs that were demanded of her, but as soon as the crowd had begun to mill about, eating and drinking, she had asked Tara if they could leave.

"I have to get home and feed my horses," she had protested when Tara had insisted that she eat a good lunch.

"Now, Mandy, you know that Teddy feeds the animals," Tara had sighed, feeling a little like leaving the party herself.

"I know, but I always help him." Mandy had wailed. "Please, couldn't we just run me home and then come back to the party? If I promise to eat a good lunch first?"

"Mandy, 'just running you home' would take over two hours," Tara had replied, wondering if she would be missed if she decided to leave early. Not that she was not enjoying herself. She was, in a way. It was good seeing old friends and being fawned over by new ones who had read her book and heard about the movie. But there was just something about this glittering collection of wealthy, famous people that turned her off. They seemed so shallow and involved in self, trying desperately to appear bored and/or amused by the wedding, that Tara found herself wondering why they had bothered to put in an appearance at all.

Vince had offered to drive Mandy home and then, a little sheepishly, he had added, "In fact, maybe I'll just stay there with her, if you don't mind. All day at one of these affairs is a little too much for me." He had looked as anxious as Mandy to get away from the grownups, and Tara could well imagine them ten minutes after they arrived back at the ranch. Mandy would be in her Levis and cowboy boots, down at the stable, and Vince would be in his faded jeans, sweatshirt and moccasins, his sketch pad under his arm.

"Oh, go ahead you two," she had finally said. "I don't really blame you. It *is* beginning to drag a little." She kissed them both, insisting that Mandy find Doe and thank her. "We probably won't stay much longer, either. I just want to wait until they leave for the airport."

She glanced at her watch now as she sat watching the thinning crowd. Just five o'clock, and their plane did not leave until eight something. Oh well, she supposed she could hold out another couple of hours. She reached into the silver bucket sitting on the plastic grass at her feet. Each round pink table had its own ice bucket and bottle of champagne, kept constantly replenished by one of the many waiters serving the crowd.

"How's your glass?" she asked Charley and the Bear as she poured hers full again.

"I'll have a little more," Charley said, sliding her glass across the table.

"Yeah, sure," the Bear said, quickly finishing off the last drop before holding it out toward Tara. "Great champagne."

Tara turned toward Jim and Thorton, standing a few feet away. "You guys need a refill?"

"Yes, please," Thorton said.

Jim grinned. "Hell, yes, I almost lost the habit, waiting for you to ask!"

"Fat chance of that, Glasser," the Bear laughed. "Hey, why don't you guys sit down and talk to us. I'm beginning to feel like a poor relative stuck out here on the sidelines."

"Then why don't you get off your ass and mingle," Tara said. "Nobody said you had to sit with us." She had chosen the table farthest from the festivities, as she wanted to keep an eye out for Eric.

"Testy, testy," the Bear said.

"Tipsy is more like it," she laughed. "God, I think I'd fall flat on my face if I tried to stand up now."

"Why don't you get something to eat, honey?" Thorton said solicitously, pulling up a chair next to her. "Would you like me to fix you a plate of something?"

"No, thanks, Thorton. I really couldn't eat a bite. I just wish Doe would wrap this up so we could get out of here. I mean, eight hours is a bit much, don't you think?

Even for a Doe Kingston-Wesley Cunningham production."

"Yeah, I'm ready to pack it in," the Bear said. He reached for Jim's cigarettes, a question is his eyes.

Glasser growled his assent. "Go ahead and have one, you fucking bum."

"Have any of you seen Izzy lately?" Charley asked. He had come with Tara, Vince and Mandy, while she had ridden with Barry in his car. Izzy had disappeared soon after the wedding vows were spoken and had not joined the group at Tara's table for lunch.

"Yeah, I saw him hanging around the orchestra earlier," Jim said, "making eyes at the trombone player. They're probably sucking each other's cocks in one of the bathrooms."

"Jim, really!" Tara gasped in mock shock. "Watch your language. You know it's improper to say 'bathroom' in mixed company!"

Everyone laughed and Jim, a little drunker than any of the others, said, "And speaking of cocksuckers, what in hell happened to our brilliant young producer, Eric Marlowe? I thought sure as hell he'd be here to suck whatever publicity he could out of the wedding."

"Yes, it is strange that he didn't show, isn't it?" Thorton said, peering near-sightedly at a young girl at the next table. She caught his gaze and crossed her legs, hiking the skirt up to give him a better view of her long, luscious legs. He turned quickly back to his group at the table. "He and Doe have been friends for so long it seems rather odd that he'd miss her wedding."

"Oh, well, maybe he'll catch her next one," Charley said flippantly and everyone laughed. Not that any of them wanted to see Doe's marriage to Wesley fail, but the blonde did have something of a record for short marriages.

Tara sat still, not joining in the good-natured teasing, thinking of Eric. She had been so certain that he would be here today. Had practiced over and over what she would say to him when she saw him. Had, in fact, watched discreetly for him all morning and afternoon, until she had finally accepted the fact that he was not going to show. It was then that she had begun to down the numerous glasses of champagne that now made her feel nauseous.

Eric stood to one side of the huge bay window so as not to be seen by the guests outside. He sipped his Jack Daniels, his gaze steady on the group at the pink table farthest from the festivities. Tara's table. He had watched her most of the afternoon from behind the heavy rose drapes in his hiding place in Doe's study. He had not arrived in time for the nuptials, but had sneaked quietly in the side door, bribing one of the maids with his charm to let him in. After an hour of sitting in the study, watching the crowd eating and drinking, he had managed to catch Doe's attention and gesture her inside.

"Eric, what the hell are you doing in here?" Doe had said when she had slipped into the study and closed the door behind her. "Why don't you come on out and join the party? Tara's around someplace—"

"That's why I'm in here," he had said. "I don't know what to say to her. God, every time I see her I think of the Academy Awards—I told you about it."

"Uh-huh," Doe had chuckled. "When you ravished her like some pirate rogue from a Rosemary Rogers novel. I'm sure she loved it. I know I would have."

"Well," he grinned, "I'm not so sure she did." He rubbed a hand over his handsome face, the brows furrowing in concern. "What should I say to her, Doe? Christ, you know I'm still crazy about her, but she hates me like the plague." He took a quick swallow of his drink.

"She doesn't hate you, honey," Doe said softly. "She's still in love with you—but, Jesus Christ, getting her to admit it!"

"That bad, huh?" Eric had chuckled, then, sobering, "Shit, what can I say to her to make her understand—to realize that I'm still in love with her and wish to hell I had never met her old lady. God, who would believe anything this fucking stupid could exist outside a Harold Robbins novel?" He smashed his fist against the soft brocade of Doe's rose-colored sofa. "Why the hell can't she realize that her old lady was just another hooker to me? Just a body to boff and get my rocks off with. Shit, the way she's been carrying on, you'd think I had a passionate love affair with the old whore!"

"When was the last time you saw Mandy?"

"Mandy? I don't know. About three or four years ago, I guess. Why?"

"Oh, nothing." Doe took his glass from him and took a tiny sip of the Jack Daniels. "She's really growing up. Almost fifteen years old and getting prettier every day." The dumb bastard, she thought. He would probably look right at Mandy and not recognize that she was the image of himself. But she had promised the Bear (when she had finally wormed the truth out of him) never to mention that she knew Eric was Mandy's father.

"Yeah, I guess that's a big part of it. With Mandy growing up and Tara so worried about her, anyway. Naturally she wouldn't want the kid to know about my relationship with her mother. I guess Mandy was just a baby when the mother died and Tara probably doesn't want her to know anything abut her occupation as a hooker. Right?"

"Yeah, that's right," Doe said, relieved that he had not picked up on what she had been hinting at and silently cursing him for being too stupid to know. She had been involved from the very beginning in his and Tara's torrid romance and all the bullshit that had followed. For years, it seemed now. And as much as she loved them both and wanted to see them get back together, she had her own marriage to worry about. As well as her own man to keep happy. She dropped a light kiss on Eric's forehead. "Well, I'd better get back to the party or poor Wesley will think I've left him already! By the way, you prick, why weren't you at the wedding?"

Eric grinned sheepishly. "Had a little trouble getting away from Pam. You remember her, Pamela Howard, the anchorperson?" He said it lightly but there was an undertone of bitterness in his voice. "She insisted on coming with me. I guess she knew that Tara would be here."

"Why didn't you bring her? Hell, you know I wouldn't have minded."

"Well, I didn't want to have anyone around in case I got up enough nerve to speak to Tara, you know."

"You big dumb bastard," Doe said affectionately, hugging him briefly to her ample bosom. "Well, I can't tell you what to do. You're welcome to hide in my study all day if you want to, and do a peeping tom number on Tara. But if you had any balls, not to mention class, you'd go out there and talk to her. My God, she's not going to slug you in front of all these people! And there're reporters and photographers from both coasts crawling all over the place. Tara's too classy to cause a scene." She nudged him a little with the toe of her elegant silk pump. "Come on, honey, why don't you come on out with me and mix a little. Work up talking to Tara if you have to. Hell, it'll take you at least an hour just to make it through the crowd!"

"Thanks, Doe, but not right now. If you don't mind, I think I'll just stay in here and drink a couple more shots of courage before I face the lions."

"Have it your way. I'll tell Juanita to make sure you're kept in Jack Daniels and she can bring you a plate when you get hungry. Men," she snorted, shaking her head until the yellow fluffy duckling hairdo bounced and jiggled against her perfectly made-up face. She would have looked angelic if not for the hard, glittering topaz eyes. Even when she was genuinely soft and caring, her eyes spoke volumes of the hard life she had known before fame had come her way.

Eric watched Doe through the window, smiling and posturing for the photographers, her arm possessively and securely looped through Wesley's. The dapper Englishman was as handsome as a god in his powder-blue tuxedo and ruffled-fronted shirt, the diamond studs and cufflinks competing with Doe's own flashing diamonds at ears, wrists and fingers. Together they could set the world on fire, he thought with a grin.

Not being able to force himself to go outside and "mix" as Doe had suggested, Eric had spent the entire afternoon in the cool, shaded study, quietly sipping whiskey and watching Tara's every move. He had gritted his teeth in agony whenever the tall, tousled-headed, young man (who was obviously her date) had bent in close to whisper in her ear. And he had sighed a great sigh of pure relief when the man had taken Mandy and disappeared around two o'clock, not to return again. That had made Eric happy. Mandy was too young to be exposed to such a chic, jaded crowd as Doe's wedding had gathered. But just who the young man was still bothered him. Oh God, he thought, please don't let him be someone Tara loves! Then sweet relief swept through him when he had seen the young man receive a chaste kiss from Tara before departing with Mandy. If there was anything Eric knew, it was how Tara kissed a man she was in love with, and the kiss she had given the young man was not that kind of kiss.

He picked up a piece of crab leg and nibbled as he watched Tara and the Bear laughing at some joke. Juanita had brought him a heaping plate filled with a little portion of everything on the buffet table, and he had already devoured most of it. He sat thinking how best to approach Tara. Should he simply walk up to her and say, "Tara, may I speak to you for a moment, please?" Surely she would not refuse him. Not in front of her friends. But something still held him back. He supposed it was the large quantities of champagne he had seen her consume all afternoon. In the back of his mind he realized that she would be far more susceptible to his charm if she were good and drunk. So he had waited. And watched. He had seen Thorton leaning over her, obviously offering assistance of some sort, because she had shook her head no, reaching for her glass again.

He finished the crab leg and ate a buttered roll, having to swallow several times to get the dough down his suddenly dry throat. He wanted to be cold sober when he finally confronted her. He would have the advantage this time, he told himself grimly. That last time, that awful beautiful night in the gazebo, he had been smashed and she had been straight. Tonight he would reverse the tables. Be in control of the situation. He leaned forward a little, parting the sheers with one finger as he watched Tara lean toward the Bear for a light. God, she was so fucking beautiful it almost pained him to look at her. He closed his eyes briefly, and when he opened them he was staring directly into a pair of startled, powder-blue ones with small crinkles around the corners. The eyes widened in recognition, then a big smile creased the powdered face, deepening the lines around the eyes. The pink lips parted, mouthing his name.

"Oh, shit," he said aloud, quickly dropping the drape and ducking out of sight. But he had not been fast enough. A moment later there was a brisk rap on the door and it was pushed open to reveal Favel Perls, blinking eyes animated with happiness at having found his hiding place.

"Eric! Darling! What a lovely surprise, no?" She minced across the room, swaying her hips suggestively, her hand wrapped around the stem of a champagne glass. "Ah chérie, you are hiding, no?"

"I was hiding, yes," Eric said wearily. "But apparently no longer." He arranged his face into what he hoped would pass as a smile. "Hello, Miss Perls. How are you?"

"'Miss Perls,' really, chérie, you are so proper always!" She giggled, the sound grating on his nerves, and kept coming toward him. Stopping close to him, she extended her hand for his kiss. He brushed his lips across the jeweled, slightly crepey flesh and quickly dropped it.

"What do you do in here, behind closed curtains?" she asked, her voice flirtatious. "You do not like our Doe's beautiful wedding party?"

"Yes, of course, it's just that I have a slight headache and wanted a little quiet and privacy for a moment." He quickly lit a cigarette, turning to glance toward Tara's table.

"Ah, poor chérie," Favel cooed. "Here, I will help to ease the pain." She set her glass on the table and reached for him. "Come, come, Eric, darling, do not be shy. Let Favel rub your poor head."

"No, really, it isn't necessary, Miss Perls." He tried to dodge the reaching hands but she grabbed him by the temples, drawing him to her, her short, chubby fingers prodding. He took her hands, forcing them away, jerking his head back before she could reach him again. "Please don't do that." His voice was hard; the eyes meeting hers directly left no room for argument.

Favel shrugged, pouted. "Oui, chérie, if you insist." She reached for her glass, drained it. "Oh, but it is such a lovely wedding, no? Just look how the people they enjoy themselves! Such lovely people too!" A big sigh, the light blue eyes fastening themselves on Eric's face. "Ah, but it does make one a little sad, yes? To see so many happy couples when one is alone." She gave him a smile that was more a leer. "As I am alone—and you are alone, no?"

"No," Eric said quickly. "Uh, no, I'm not alone. I'm with that table over there—near the pool." he got quickly to his feet. "So if you'll excuse me, I should be getting back to my date." He smoothed his tuxedo and straightened his bow tie. "Before she wonders what happened to me. Good day, Miss Perls—lovely seeing you again." He went quickly through the door without looking back.

"But, chérie, wait! Who are your friends? Perhaps we can all—" But her anxious words fell in the empty room and she shrugged, picking up his half-finished Jack Daniels and drained it. "Ah, well, perhaps next time I catch the elusive Eric Marlowe, no?"

Once outside, Eric walked directly to Tara's table. Having no idea what he would say but determined not to be caught in a room alone with the aging sex kitten, he strode purposefully toward Tara's group in case Favel was watching through the window.

"Hey, Thorton, how are you?" He went to him, shook his hand vigorously.

"Eric, old man," Thorton said, clapping him on the back. "Good to see you."

"Hey, Bear, how's your ass?" Eric leaned down to shake hands with Barry, avoiding Tara without appearing to.

"Hi, Eric, how the hell's yours?" The Bear glanced

quickly at Tara, relieved to see that she did not seem too surprised to see Eric. "You know Charley Holmes, don't you?"

"Of course, good to see you again." He shook Charley's hand, and then said quietly, "Hello, Tara. How are you?" He did not offer his hand but stood, almost at attention, by her chair. Unconsciously he held his breath.

"Why, Eric, hello!" Her voice was animated and she reached out to take his hand. "When did you get here? You missed the wedding and about half of the party, you know." She giggled and he knew that she was already pretty smashed.

"I couldn't get away any sooner. Had some business to take care of first."

"Does the business have red hair?" she giggled and Eric laughed in relief. Apparently she was not going to kick him in the balls or throw him into the pool, so he drew up a chair and sat next to her.

"Why, Miss Remington, how you talk! You know I've been practically celibate lo these many years." He leaned closer and whispered, "In respect for your memory . . ."

"Memory, shmemory," Tara said, sloshing more champagne into her glass. "Well, whatever. Let's drink to Doe's happiness." She looked at his hand. "What? No drink? That's a novelty. Thorton, pour the man a drink. We have to toast our ole pal, Doe. Right, Eric?" Her gorgeous eyes were deep pools of mystery as she stared at him, and Eric died a little wondering what she was thinking. The pouty red mouth was a little slack now, but still the most kissable mouth he had ever seen.

He could not read the message in her eyes but knew there was one there for him. "Thanks," he said, touching the rim of her glass with his own. "To Doe, and, of course, Wesley. May they be as happy as—"

"As happy as two clams in a pod," Tara giggled. "Or is that a pea pod. Hell, who cares." She suddenly felt so silly and gay. Eric was here and looking at her with those magnificent cobalt blue eyes that had always sent shivers of delight and desire dancing up her spine. She drank her champagne in one swallow and refilled her glass. "Gotta toast you, too, Eric, for—for—" She frowned. "What have you done lately that we can toast you for, anyway?"

"Well, let's see, I just signed a deal with NBC to produce four specials this year, made for television features—"

"Boring, smoring." Tara waved away his words with a flip gesture. "I mean, something personal. Like that redhead I keep seeing you with—you gonna marry her?" She surprised herself by asking such a personal question and wished like hell she could take the words back. She felt Charley kick her under the table, and she raised her eyes to meet those of the blonde. Charley gave a little shake of her head, a warning.

"Nope," Eric answered easily. "You've completely spoiled me for other women, stolen my heart . . ."

"Heart, shmart," Tara mumbled, feeling the drinks and hating herself for saying such stupid things. But the idiotic words kept tumbling from her mouth without any help from her at all, it seemed. "Well, here's to ya, anyway." She drank, watching him over the rim of her glass. God, he was gorgeous! He looked as young and handsome as he had when she had first met him. Not sloppy drunk and pathetic as he had been at The Factory that night. The bloat had left his face, his waist was narrow, the belly flat, his blue eyes clear and made even bluer by the incredible whiteness that surrounded them. He looked fit and healthy and sexier than she cared to remember. She wanted him—right this minute. Fortunately the others at the table began speaking, asking him about his television deal, and she was able to compose herself.

Eric spoke easily and with the sharp, throwaway wit that he had always had. But he kept a furtive eye on Tara. She was bombed out of her skull, he grinned to himself, and obviously not the least bit unhappy that he had joined her group. That old bitch, Favel Perls, had come along at exactly the right moment to chase him into Tara's arms. And that is where he wanted to be more than anyplace else in the world. He was barely aware of Jim and Thorton asking about his picture deal but he did manage to answer them intelligently, he hoped. Charley

284

leaned over and whispered in Tara's ear, and the two of them stood and excused themselves to go to the ladies' room. To straighten Tara out, Eric thought, hoping the nosy secretary did not screw up his chances with Tara. He watched them weave their way through the crowd, Charley's hand on Tara's arm, guiding her. With some difficulty, he pulled his attention back to the conversation.

Much later (as well as a couple of bottles of champagne later), Doe's voice called everyone to attention. She thanked them all for coming, gave them a rundown on her honeymoon plans, told them to stay and party as long as they wished, then threw her bridal bouquet. Straight at Tara. It sailed through the air and would have struck her squarely in the face had not Eric reached out to catch it. There was laughter and applause as he sat there foolishly, the dainty pink and white bouquet crushed in his large hands. "Here," he said gruffly, shoving it toward Tara.

Doe and Wesley joined them, hand and hand, Doe gushing, "What a marvelous surprise! My two favorite people —together again at last!" She gave Eric a sloppy, champagne-flavored kiss. "Darling, I'm so glad you were able to make it!" She gave him a conspirator's wink and he flushed and looked guiltily away. Only Doe and the maid, Juanita, knew that he had been there all day, watching Tara from behind the drapes.

"Of course," he said, as coolly as possible, returning her kiss. "You know I wouldn't miss one of your weddings for anything in the world!"

"You prick," she growled good-naturedly. "Well, it's just a damn good thing you caught this one, 'cause it's the very last time you, or anyone else, will see Doe-baby walk down the aisle!"

"One certainly hopes so, doesn't one?" Wesley murmured somberly and everyone laughed. "Well, my pet, shall we off?" He glanced at his elegant platinum watch. "Our plane leaves at eight forty-five."

Everyone spoke at once, offering congratulations, making the typical honeymoon jokes, and offering advice. Kisses were passed all around.

"Miss Kingston," a voice said demurely, and Tara glanced up to see Doe's chauffeur standing a few feet away, Doe's makeup bag in one hand, the leash of her Lhasa Apso in the other. "We really must leave if we are to make the airport on time." He smiled apologetically. "Heavy traffic, you know." The silky Lhasa Apso squirmed at the end of his leash, straining toward Doe and she stooped down and picked him up.

"You're not taking that long-haired rat with you to Spain, are you?" Jim said, peering at the little dog as if he were an insect under a microscope. "They'll lock him up in quarantine for at least six months."

"Of course not," Doe cooed, kissing the dog on the mouth. "Poopsie is just riding to the airport with us, aren't you, lover?"

More kisses and hugs and handshakes and they were off, Doe trailing her pale, pink-tinted mink stole after her on the plastic grass and Wesley with two bottles of Moët et Chandon stuck in the pockets of his off-white jacket.

"Well, that's that," the Bear said. "I sure hope to hell they make it, but frankly I don't think the marriage has a chance in hell."

"Why not, for goodness sake?" Charley asked. "They're so much in love they can't keep their eyes off each other."

"Yeah, but Doe forgot to ask me to give her a fuck for luck," the Bear chuckled mischievously and Charley hit him over the head with the wilted bridal bouquet.

"You bastard, I'll show you a fuck for luck! Come on, let's go!" She pulled him up and they went off into the crowd, giggling and wrestling like a couple of high-spirited kids.

"That's it for me too, kiddies," Jim said, finishing his champagne. "I'm going to the nearest bar for a good stout whiskey before I throw up." He also drained Charley's still full glass. "Fucking champagne'll make you sick if you don't watch out." He shook Eric's hand. "Nice seeing you again, Eric. Luck with the television shows." Kissing

Tara softly on the cheek, he whispered, "And you get home before you pass out! I love you, fair Tara."

"Night, Jim," Tara said, waving in the general direction of his retreating back. "Love you, too." She looked around her, blinking a little. "Hey, where'd everybody go?"

"Home, little one, where I'm about to take you," Thorton said sternly. He tugged on her arm but she sat where she was, not budging. "Come on, now, gather up your things and I'll drive you home."

"Can drive myself home," Tara said stubbornly. " 'Sides, don't wanna go home yet."

"Tara, Vince took your car, remember? Now come on. Don't make a scene."

"Why the hell not? Everybody else makes scenes all the time." She giggled and leered at Eric. "Let's make a scene, huh, Eric. We'll have to find Izzy first. Where the hell is he, anyway?"

"He left four hours ago with the trombone player," Thorton said. Again he tried to pull her to her feet, but she shook his hand off.

"Then how come the band is still playing without a trombone player, huh, Thorton? Just tell me that, huh?"

Eric tried not to laugh out loud. She was so damn cute when she was tipsy. "Look, Thorton, I'll drive her home—" He glanced at Tara. "That is, if you don't mind, Tara."

"No, no, tha's great—wunnerful. You go on home, Thorton. Eric'll take care of me, huh, Eric?" She swayed against him, hiccoughing delicately, then giggling at herself. "Oops, sorry."

"Well, I don't know." Thorton frowned down at them, adjusting his glasses as he always did when he was thinking. He wondered if Tara knew what she was saying. Would she wake up tomorrow morning hating him for leaving her alone with Eric? He gave Eric a hard look. He seemed sober, not threatening in any way. He shrugged. The hell with it. Tara was old enough to take care of herself, even though she did not look much older than Mandy at this moment.

"Sure, go on, Thorton, ole pal, ole buddy," Tara said, waving him away. "Eric'll take care of me, won't you, Eric? And, 'sides, I gotta help Doe change and get ready for her honeymoon and stuff . . ."

"Tara, Wesley and Doe left for the airport a half an hour ago," Thorton sighed. He really had little patience with drunks. Even someone he cared as much for as he cared for Tara. Eric could handle her, he decided.

"It's okay, Thorton. I'll see that she gets home in one piece. You go ahead if you want. And don't worry."

"Okay," Thorton said at length. He bent to kiss Tara's cheek. "Goodnight, then, and lay off the sauce, will you? You're going to have a monumental hangover tomorrow, do you realize that?"

"Well, if I'm already going to have one, why stop now? Right, Eric?" She fell back against him and he put his arms around her, righting her. His heartbeat quickened and he felt a warm flush spread through his groin. God, she could still turn him into jelly with a mere touch.

"Right, baby." He gave Thorton a broad grin. The one that inspired confidence. "It's all right, really. I'll look after her."

Thorton was still grumbling as he left them, and Tara giggled like a mischievous child pulling the wool over her parents' eyes. "Boy, we sure fooled him, huh, Eric? Now, let's drink some more champagne. Where's the bottle?" She leaned down to the ice bucket, now half-filled with water and almost toppled over. Eric pulled her back onto her chair. "Oops, all gone. Get us 'nother one, okay, Eric?"

"Okay, baby," Eric grinned, running his fingers lightly up and down her bare arm. How the hell was he going to get her out of here, he wondered. She clearly had no intention of leaving and was determined to get even drunker than she already was. It both amused and upset him. "But maybe we should go someplace else for a drink. I think the party's over. See?" He turned her toward the almost empty back yard where waiters were hurrying about, clearing tables.

"The party's over," Tara sang in a loud, vigorous voice and Eric shushed her.

"Cool it, baby," he hissed. "There's Joyce Haber and that newshawk from the East Coast over there. See them? I'm sure you don't want this plastered all over tomorrow's papers—'the intellectual and usually sedate authoress was swacked to the gills at Doe Kingston's wedding'—now do you?"

"Oops," Tara giggled, putting one finger to her lips, and ducked her head like a contrite child. "Shh, don't say a word, maybe they'll go away. Did they see me?"

"I don't think so, but if you keep doing your Barbra Streisand impression someone is sure to notice." He hugged her to him. "Hey, did anyone ever tell you that you should be in show business? You've got a hell of a voice there, lady."

"This is true," Tara said with what dignity she could muster, then collapsed against him in giggles. "Oh, Eric, I feel so silly. Why can't I stop giggling?" She hiccoughed. "And I've got the hiccups again—or still. What's the matter with me, anyway?"

"I think the term is 'drunker than a skunk,'" Eric laughed.

"That's dumb. Drunks don't skunk—I mean, skunks don't drink. Wonder why people say such dumb stuff like that? Drunker than a skunk," she mimicked, hardly noticing that Eric had lifted her to her feet and was guiding her across the plastic grass toward the exit. He had stuffed her purse into his pocket and thought about asking her if she had a wrap, but decided against it. She was following him so docilely that he was afraid any reference to leaving might cause her to balk again.

Eric helped her into his car and drove slowly down the steep drive that led away from Doe's house. The night was beautiful. A full moon hung so low in the sky, he felt he could reach out and pluck it from its dark nest and present it to Tara. Bright clusters of stars were dotted throughout the black velvet heavens, seeming to roll and tumble playfully on the softly drifting silver clouds. It was a night made for lovers, he thought as he turned onto

289

Sunset Boulevard and drove slowly through the early evening traffic. Of course, he had no intention of taking Tara home. He made a right turn on Benedict Canyon and climbed the twisting road toward his house, wondering how he would explain it if she roused herself to realize that he was not taking her home.

But Tara seemed oblivious to everything but her own silly high. She sang loud and happily, one song after another, urging Eric to join in. "Come on, sing with me, Eric. You know this one, don't you?" And broke into a racey verse of *Lay Me Down, Roll Me Over*.

He pulled into his driveway and shut off the ignition. "Here we are," he said, quickly getting out and pulling her after him.

"Hey, that was fast." She stopped, looked around. "Hey, this isn't my house." It dawned on her and she giggled. "Uh, oh, I know what you're doing. You're kidnapping me, aren't you?" She swayed against him "Good. I felt like being kidnapped tonight." She flung her arms out wide, almost tripping, and he caught her to his side, guiding her up the steps. "Just carried off somewhere— hey, where the fuck's your white steed? Some knight you are!"

"It's right there, baby," Eric laughed, pointing back at his white Cadillac.

"Boy, some knight—trying to pass off a mechanical white steed on me. I'm not that drunk, buster!" Giggling, she followed him into the house and kicked off her shoes. "Whew, those damn things were killing me. I told Doe they were too tight, but she had already had them dyed to match my dress and everything, ya know, so I wore the stupid things. Hey, wasn't it a pretty wedding? Didn't Doe look beautiful? I love Doe. Don't you just love Doe?"

"Sure, baby, I love Doe." He turned on the lights, helped her into the den and lowered her onto the sofa. I love you, my darling, he wanted to say, but instead went to the stereo and switched it on. "I'm not sure you can handle it, but would you like another drink?"

"Sure! Love it!" She made a face. "But not champagne. God, I'll never drink that stuff again as long as I live.

What 'cha got?" She started to rise and join him at the bar, but fell back, giggling. "Whew, I'm zonked. Did I do anything dumb or anything?"

"Nope, you were the epitome of decorum." He grinned at her as he poured himself a Jack Daniels and mixed her a very light screwdriver, just a dash of vodka and mostly orange juice. "Your manners were impeccable as always."

She smiled up at him as she took the drink. "Good. I must protect my reputation, you know." She said it formally, pursing her lips, then collapsing in giggles again. "Wow, why does everything seem so funny tonight?"

"It's probably because you haven't been drunk in so long, and it's kind of like the first time all over again." He took a joint from a dish on the end table and lit it.

"Tha's right—how'd you know? I mean, that I haven't been drinking?"

"Oh, I have my spies." He put his arm around her, drawing her close and held the joint to her lips. "Here, baby, take a hit. Maybe it'll mellow out all that expensive champagne you've been swilling down like water." She obeyed, sighed, let her head fall against his shoulder.

"Umm, fantastic. You know, I wanted to get stoned all day but I was afraid one of the photographers or reporters would bust me. I've got some in my purse in case you run out."

Eric laughed, loving the feel of her warm body so close to his. "Thanks, but I just scored a pound of Columbian, so I think that'll last us for one night."

"Am I going to spend the night?" She sat up, peering into his face curiously.

"Would you like to spend the night?" He held his breath, not daring to hope that she would say yes.

"Why the hell not? But ya gotta get me some other clothes. I'm sick of this dumb dress." She tugged at it, flipped the skirt in disgust. "Did you ever see anything so square and dumb-looking?" Suddenly she giggled again, putting her finger to her lips. "Oh, God, don't you dare tell Doe I said that. She thinks I love it."

"I wouldn't dream of it, love. Your secret is safe with me." He kissed her lightly. "Don't go away, I'll be right back." He returned a moment later with a short, brightly colored Happy Coat. "Here put this on. I'm sure it will fit."

Tara took the Oriental robe, held it up, looked it over critically, then nodded her head. "Okay, and you gotta feed me too, 'cause I'm getting starved to death." She stood and tried to unzip her dress but kept missing the zipper, so Eric slid it down for her. His fingers brushed her soft skin, and he had to force himself not to grab her and take her right there on the floor.

"Look, I'll see what's in the fridge while you change." He left quickly, already feeling the faint stirring of an erection. His hands trembled as he took out a couple of porterhouse steaks and bent to the crisper drawer to see if he had the makings for a salad. She was so drunk she obviously had no idea what she was doing to him. He leaned a little to the right, enabling him to look through the door and into the den. She was stark naked, trying to shove her arms into the silk Happy Coat, humming to herself. What an incredible body. No one had a body quite as gorgeous or perfectly proportioned as she did.

"Jesus, help me make it through dinner," he mumbled aloud, reaching down to grip his rapidly swelling penis. He placed the steaks on a platter, splashed some Worcestershire sauce over them, a sprinkle of salt and pepper, and left them to marinate while he went to change out of his tuxedo.

Entering the den a few minutes later, dressed in Levis and tee-shirt, barefoot, he smiled down at Tara sprawled on the sofa. She had one leg raised and resting on the back of the sofa, the other stretched out on the cushions, her sex plainly visible since she wore no panties. "For God's sake, Tara, do you want to get raped?" He jerked the Happy Coat down, laughing a little shakily. "Honey, if you want me to behave myself, you'd better sit up. I mean, I can only take so much."

"Who said ya have ta behave yourself?" But she sat

up and tugged the robe down as far as it would go. "There, is that better?"

He sat next to her and crushed her to him, his lips seeking hers. The kiss burned like fire, charging his blood and sending his senses reeling. "God, Tara," he groaned, "God!" Her arms were heavy around his neck and her breasts crushed flat against his chest as she squirmed closer to him, opening her mouth for his tongue.

"Umm, good," she sighed when her mouth was free. She gazed into his face, her dark eyes soft and dreamy, her lips parted and slightly pouting. "Kiss me some more, Eric—" And he groaned and pressed her back, falling heavily on top of her, his knee between her thighs. His penis jerked again at his Levis and he quickly unzipped them, pulling it free. Then he was inside her, not knowing exactly how it had happened so fast. She must have helped him, guided it and opened herself for him because never in his life had he been inside a woman so quickly and effortlessly. Then he blocked all thought and reason from his mind and just held her and fucked her. Drove into her deep, hungrily, feeling her envelope him with her incredible warmth. The perfume of her skin filled his nostrils and spun through his head like an exotic drug and he was drowning in her, filling her, crying out as he came with a shudder that rocked him to his toes.

"Jesus, I love you, Tara!" he cried and felt her arch up to meet his final thrust, then explode beneath him with the sweet familiar vibration that had always made him want to never let her go.

Minutes passed when the only sound in the room was their heavy breathing and the insistent spinning of the empty stereo. He did not want to move off her. Did not want to ever let her go. Did not want his cock to ever again be anywhere but inside her.

She spoke first, softly. "Darling, change the record. I want to hear music tonight."

He leaped off her, hurrying to do her bidding, hurrying back just as quickly lest she vanish. She was half-sitting, half-lying on the crumpled cushions, sipping her weak screwdriver. Her eyes were soft with what he prayed was love. Her features relaxed as only a passionate tumble with him could relax them. She looked cuddly and so fucking gorgeous, it hurt his eyes to look at her. He kissed her. Hard, deep, then soft, gentle, their mouths molding perfectly together like a matched set of book ends. "I love you so damn much," he whispered huskily. For an answer she closed her eyes, swaying against him for another long, deep kiss.

"Well, then feed me before I starve to death," she laughed. "Some host you are." She lit a cigarette with trembling fingers, not looking at him for a moment. "Wow, I'm ravenous, aren't you?"

"Yeah, I guess I am." He stood, zipped his Levis and pulled his tee-shirt down. Laughed a little shakily. Feeling foolish for having made love to her completely dressed, but it was almost as if his cock had sprung free of his fly without any help from him at all. And then he had been inside her before he could even shove his Levis down. Shit, what she must think! Next time, it would be better. Slower. "Damn it, I'd better get out of here before I make a complete ass of myself." He took her hand, lifting her to her feet. "Come on, woman, you can make the salad while I cook the steaks."

"No fair," she pouted, but followed him into the kitchen anyway. "You said you'd do all the work if I stayed."

"Now when did I say that?" He turned the steaks in the platter of sauce and switched on the broiler.

"Didn't you?" she said innocently. "Aw, come on, Eric. I'm too drunk to cook. I'll burn myself or something."

"How in hell can you burn yourself making a salad?" He placed the steaks on the grill and took the salad makings from the refrigerator.

"Please," she begged prettily, running light, teasing fingers up his arm and tickling him. "I don't want to do a thing tonight but sit here and watch you cook for me."

"Spoiled cunt," he said, trapping the tickling finger between his teeth and biting gently. "Okay, then get out of my way. Go over there and sit down and I'll feed you." He grumbled good-naturedly, his heart suddenly feeling too large for his chest. Damn, he loved this woman, this wonderful, silly, spoiled woman-child who sometimes seemed so old and wise and other times like an innocent, lost child. "Light me a joint, then, and bring me my drink if you're not going to help."

"Yes, master," she said, running lightly from the room, returning a moment later with their drinks and fresh joint which she placed between his lips. "Will that be all, master?"

"Not by a long shot," he laughed, grabbing her around the waist and pulling her to him. He kissed her, tasting the sweet orange juice on her breath, and playfully licked her lips. "Umm, you taste good enough to eat."

"Is that a promise?" she teased, playfully nipping at his tongue when he tried to insert it between her teeth.

"You'll find out in about two seconds if you don't get your ass over there and let me fix this salad." He swatted her on the fanny with a dish cloth. "Now get if you want to eat—I mean the steak and salad," he said when she reached for the front of his Levis.

"Okay, okay, I'm going." She went to sit at the kitchen table, taking the joint with her. She dragged deep, holding the smoke in as long as she could for the rush that she needed to feel. The suddenness of their lovemaking had surprised her. She still felt a little stunned by it, as well as embarrassed. How in the world had she allowed it to happen so fast? Not that she had not planned on going to bed with him. She had, ever since she had first seen him walking toward her table at Doe's house. She had thought, I'm going to take him home and fuck him and then tell him to go to hell. She was used to her new independence and accustomed to having her way with men and then discarding them rather casually. Now it was out of the question. She was on his turf. And loving it, surprisingly so. It felt wonderful to sit watching such a desirable, handsome man cooking for her, getting quietly stoned, coming down from the almost hysterical drunk she had been on all afternoon. She shifted on the cool plastic seat and felt a sticky moisture between her legs where he had filled her with his come. She squeezed her legs together, experiencing a shooting little thrill of pleasure and wanted him again. But in bed, slowly, languidly, and for hours and hours.

No man had ever made her climax as beautifully and as satisfyingly as Eric did. He filled her everywhere she needed filling. Body and soul, mind and heart. The old pain knocked questioningly at the rational part of her brain and she swiftly, furiously, shook it away. Drove it out. Not tonight, she told herself. Just for this one night she would enjoy herself totally with a man, love him and give up every vestige of herself to him. Not like with the lovers she had had since breaking up with Eric. With them she had taken the lead, commanded them what to do and let them know when it was over. Just this one night she wanted to be drained in a way that only Eric could drain her.

"Hey, cookie, want a drag?" she called. He looked up from tearing lettuce leaves into a wooden bowl. Ripe red tomatoes, crisp green onions and cucumbers, shiny black olives were lying on the cutting board, giving the scene a look of a still life painting. He tossed a handful of sunflower seeds into the salad and wiped his hands on the dish towel he had tied around his waist. She went to him and held the roach to his lips.

"Thanks, baby." He kissed her nose, turning back to his salad. "Do you think you can check the steaks or would that be asking too much?"

"It certainly would. I'm not going to lift a finger, remember?" She swayed her hips saucily as she went back to the table and sat down. "You're feeding me tonight, Marlowe, so quit trying to get out of it."

"Spoiled bitch," he grumbled, bending down to turn the steaks under the broiler. They sizzled and popped and Tara could smell them clear across the room.

"They smell heavenly," she sighed. "Gee, it's sure nice

to know a chef." He jerked the towel from around his waist and flicked it at her, popping her on the bare legs. Then took the short roach from her and dragged deep. "How long before we eat?"

"That depends on how you want your steak." He kissed her, exhaling the smoke into her mouth. He could not believe his good fortune. She had actually agreed to stay overnight and had already made love to him as swiftly and urgently as if she still loved him. Could he dare hope that she had forgiven him? He was glad he was sober. He would need a clear head to make sure he did not do or say anything to frighten her away. Or worse, remind her of any bitterness from the past. He said a swift, silent prayer that he would do everything exactly right and maybe this would be the beginning for them again. She must feel something for him. No one could respond so naturally and beautifully if they were not in love. He had found that out during the lonely years he had spent apart from her. Dating faceless bodies and calling Tara's name when he was finally able to climax. Even as fast as their coupling had been, it still had satisfied him as nothing else had in the past three years.

Pulling himself away from her with difficulty, he went back to the stove and checked the steaks. "Rare," he said. "Is that all right with you?"

"Leave mine in a couple of minutes longer." She gave him a smug look. "While you serve the salad and select the proper wine."

He flipped her the finger. "Wine, yet, the lady says. Okay, you're the boss." He was humming as he went to the liquor cabinet and searched through the bottles until he found a light rosé. "Is Mateus to your liking, madame?" He held the bottle for her like a wine steward in a fancy restaurant.

"I suppose so," she teased, "if you haven't anything better." She stood, stretched and padded barefoot into the den. "Let's eat in here, okay? I'll clear off the coffee table and we can watch Johnny Carson."

"Oh, darling, please don't go to any trouble," he said broadly.

"Oh, it's no trouble. I don't mind helping out—a little."
She blew him a kiss from the doorway and a moment
later he heard the television come on, Ed's voice pushing
his favorite beer, and he wanted to laugh out loud with
sheer pleasure. God, how he loved her! And, please God,
he prayed fervently, let the evening continue as beautiful
as it has been so far. Please!

CHAPTER
FOURTEEN

MOONLIGHT FILLED THE ROOM, highlighting Tara's bare legs in silver as she lay on the sofa against Eric. A cool September breeze ruffled the sheer curtains, gently caressing her and she shivered and snuggled closer to him.

"Cold?" he asked, drawing her nearer.

"A little." She kept her face turned toward the television set, not ready to meet the question she knew she would see in his eyes. Now that they had eaten and she had come down from her rather hysterical giggling fit, she felt embarrassed at finding herself so intimately comfortable with Eric. It was as if the past three and a half years had fallen away and she had always been in Eric's house and in Eric's arms. She knew she would go to bed with him, but wanted to postpone it a little longer. Just until she sorted out her thoughts. Being with him again had been easier than she would have thought possible. But there were still the old unhealed wounds to deal with. She sighed. Pressed her face into the soft hair at his neck. She would not think about it tonight. Just for tonight she would pretend nothing had ever come between them. They would be the golden young lovers they once had been, too smug in their love to ever believe that anything could touch them. Just for tonight she would let her heart guide her—and let Eric love her and fulfill her.

She snuggled more closely into the curve of his arm and

felt his heartbeat steady and strong against her side. He made her feel so protected and cherished. She closed her eyes and felt his mouth against her neck, moving around to kiss the pulse in her throat. Then he took her by the shoulders and turned her toward him, finding her lips.

She sighed and gave herself up to the kiss, parting her lips for his tongue, and gasped at the sudden wave of desire that swept through her. Every nerve ending seemed aflame, set gently vibrating, until she could hardly control the sudden explosion of breath that filled her lungs. She kissed him harder, gripped him tighter, hoping the uncontrollable shaking would stop. Every nerve and pulse in her body trembled and hummed and quivered with anticipation.

Eric pulled his mouth away, whispering, "I love you, Tara, I'll always love you no matter what."

"Oh, Eric, I—" Unable to say it, she crushed her lips to his again and filled her hands with his hair, tugging his head even closer as she kissed him. Her body squirmed closer too, her legs wrapping around his, their pelvises joined and grinding against one another. Gasping, she jerked her mouth away and groaned, "God, Eric, take me to bed! Now!"

He slipped his arms beneath her body and stood, lifting her as easily as if she were a child. "Yes, my darling, yes," he murmured, burying his face in the tangle of her hair. He kept her hugged close as he carried her into the bedroom and gently deposited her upon the bed. She lay looking up at him as he quickly shucked off his clothes, then he was next to her, pulling her arms from the Happy Coat and flinging it away. He ran his hands wonderingly, almost shyly, over her perfect body, lingering a moment on her breasts, then gently stroking down her flat stomach and cupping her sex.

"Oh, darling, you're driving me crazy," she panted, half-rising to grasp his hands and draw him to her. "Please hurry, Eric, I feel like I'll explode unless you fuck me right this second!" She let her head fall back when she felt his lips on her throat, burning her with his kisses. His lips grazed her everywhere—lips, eyes, throat, ears, breathing warm breath that made her tingle with desire. When his lips claimed hers he raised himself and covered her body, his penis hard and anxious against her pubis. She spread her legs, letting him fall naturally between her thighs, then gripped him there where his pulsations spread to her, making him tremble even more violently.

"Jesus, you're more beautiful than I remembered," he said huskily. "Your skin is so incredibly soft it's unreal . . ." His hands were everywhere at once, stroking her breasts, belly and buttocks, the fingers questing, opening her. He said her name as he entered her and then she heard nothing but the loud pounding of his heart as he thrust deep and true; the wild beating of her own heart as she clung to him and wrapped her legs high around his back, almost upon his shoulders in her eagerness to feel every beloved inch of him.

"Eric, Eric, Eric," she sighed over and over again, not even sure if she was saying the word aloud, but hearing it repeating itself inside her brain as orgasm after orgasm soared through her. She was acutely aware of the smallest details: the feel of his teeth clenched against her lips, the spasmodic tremors in his penis, the skin stretched so taut she feared it must pain him, his big, wonderful hands holding her so close and tenderly even as he fucked her like no one else ever had—as if he would drive her through the very mattress. They could not have gotten any closer had their bodies melted and melded together in a pool of liquid love. "Now, my darling," she cried, speeding up her movements when she knew he was ready. "Oh, yes, my love, my own Eric—I do love you—I do!"

He came with a loud whoop of joyous laughter that ended in sobs of passion as he gathered her closer still and filled her to her depths. His violent shuddering shook her as well when he pressed in as deep as he could get, then held there, slightly quivering, until he was spent. They dozed at the same moment, passion lulled, limbs heavy and unable to move, still joined together.

Sometime later, still in the limbo of half-sleep, half-wakefulness, they both shifted a little, rolled to the side, arms still holding one another, and they slept.

Tara awoke just as dawn was breaking, sending a dull pink light shining into her eyes. Her left leg was asleep where it still lay beneath his weight. She drew it out, careful not to wake him and massaged the circulation back. Tiptoeing quietly to the drapes, she closed out the early morning light, throwing the room into almost total darkness again. Eric sighed in his sleep, reaching for her and she went into his arms and hugged him lightly. He smiled in his sleep and one hand stroked her arm before curling itself around her breast. He looked so touchingly child-like that she felt tears blur her vision for a moment. His lashes were so long and silky, fanning out on his tanned cheeks; his soft lips slightly parted and looking so inviting that she had to suppress an urge to kiss him. He wore his hair much longer now than he had when she had met him, the sideburns thick and shaggy and a sexy mustache that gave him a rakish Rhett Butler look. He had taken her like Rhett had taken Scarlett in that unforgettable scene where he had swept her off her feet and stormed up the curved stairway to their bedroom—although Eric had not had to bother with stairs, thank God. Stairs would have slowed them down and she had been so hot she was ready to explode, she remembered with a wicked, satisfied smile. She squirmed a little, pressing her thighs together and feeling again the hot waves of desire that had consumed her when they had made love. Never had she been so ready, so incredibly hot for any man other than Eric. Not once (in her not-so-many affairs) since breaking up with him had she been so wet with lust and so violently anxious to couple with a man. Only Eric had ever made her feel this way.

Being careful not to wake him, she reached to the nightstand for a cigarette. The lighter illuminated his face, so handsome and relaxed in his slumber that she could not resist bending down to kiss him. He stirred and murmured her name, and his hand still on her breast squeezed gently.

Tara leaned her head back against the headboard, smoking silently, acutely aware of Eric's heavy arms across her chest. It was a good, warm, heavy feeling, a feeling she

302

had missed for a long time now. She remembered how he had always hugged her so tight that she had feared he would crack her ribs, how his big, heavy limbs completely enveloped her during their lovemaking, and how he had kept her pinned to the bed with an arm and leg thrown possessively over her even as he slept. As if even in his slumber he wanted it known that she was his woman. She smiled. God, it would be so easy to become his woman again. Too damn easy. His personality was too powerful, too dominating for her to ever hope to be able to refuse him if he asked her. But maybe he would not ask her. Just one night in bed did not mean it was time to move in and set up housekeeping. They were both older now. She had certainly grown a great deal since the days of being his naive fiancée. She had fought hard for her independence. She had her own home, her own career, her own way of doing things. She was no longer the starry-eyed innocent looking for roots, a home and family. She had them now —in a way. Where was it written that a home and family meant having a husband and child? It could also mean sisters and best friends and people that you love all living together and making a family.

She crushed out her cigarette, trying not to think of families. As much as she loved Mandy, Charley and Hazel, and all the rest of them, Izzy, the Bear, Thorton and Jim, she knew she still wanted the other kind of home. With a husband and baby. "Oh, my God," she said aloud, sitting up so suddenly that Eric's hand fell from her breast and he murmured, "Wha?" "Nothing," she whispered, "go back to sleep." She drew the sheet over him and let him pull her back into his arms. My pill, she thought wildly. I forgot to take my pill! Because she kept rather irregular hours when working on a novel, she often would rise any time between nine and noon and therefore had decided to take her birth control pill in the evening. Her doctor had said that it was important to take them at the same time each day, and she had gotten into the habit of taking them at seven each evening as she was usually home then. Either getting ready for an evening out or dressing for dinner with the family. Not expecting to stay at Doe's and Wesley's wedding too late, she hadn't bothered to take her pills with her.

Nothing will happen, she told herself, just missing once. She would take it the moment she got home. She slid down in the bed, snuggled close to Eric's warmth and closed her eyes, thinking she would catch a couple of more hours of sleep and then slip out before he awoke.

His hands moved against her bare flesh, sending little shivers skittering over her body and she half-hoped he would wake up and make love to her again. No matter how many times they had made love in the past, when they had been engaged, she had always wanted him again right away.

"Tara?" he murmured, his arms tightening around her. "Tara? Where are you?"

"I'm here, darling," she whispered. "Shh, go back to sleep." She covered his hands with hers, pressing them more firmly to her breasts.

"I thought I was dreaming." He opened his eyes, smiled at her sleepily. "I love you." He closed the short space between them and kissed her. "I dreamed I was holding you but when I woke up you were gone."

"I'm still here," she said softly, a little guiltily. She had been planning on doing just that, slipping away while he slept.

"Good, that's where I want you—always." He kissed her again. His hands moved from her breasts to her back, drawing her closer to his chest, turning her a little, pressing her as close as he could. She felt him growing hard as he kissed her again and pushed himself against her. He nudged her thighs apart and thrust his penis between them with a happy sigh, like a weary traveler coming home from a long journey. "God, I love you, Tara. You feel so good, so warm, so—wonderful."

"So do you, darling," she whispered huskily, feeling ridiculously like breaking into tears. She did not know why she felt suddenly so melancholy. So sad. His every word and touch made her feel more loved than she had in years, but a sense of gloom, or doom, prevailed that she could not shake. Could not understand. She closed her

304

eyes against his intimate look of love and kissed him back.

He rolled her over and lay on top of her, still kissing her until they both gasped for breath and drew apart laughing a little shakily. "Am I too heavy?" he asked, moving his legs between hers.

"No, no, never!" She reached up for him, drawing him down until their lips met once more, arching her back and bringing her legs up. He slipped inside her easily and naturally, his hands sliding beneath her to cup her buttocks and press her closer.

He pulled his mouth away for only a moment, just long enough to say, "I love you so fucking much, Tara!" Then he flung himself forward and crushed his mouth to hers once again, as he began moving rhythmically upon her. She circled his broad back with her arms and legs, matching his strokes with her own rhythm.

"Oh, Eric, darling," she sighed, murmured against his lips, nibbling them, tasting him.

"What?" he demanded huskily, thrusting deeper, harder, holding her so tight she could scarcely catch her breath. "What? Tell me . . ." He lowered his head to kiss her and suck at her nipples, his hands still holding her buttocks, moving her swiftly to meet his now frenzied thrusts.

"God, yes, fuck me!" Her head tossed from side to side upon the pillow, her mouth open and gasping for breath. Her legs thrashed wildly upon his back and hips, and her long nails dug into his shoulders as she held on. She was afraid her heart would explode, it pounded so fast and furiously. Her entire body was so hot, so hot and slippery with perspiration that she could hear the muffled slap-slap as they came together with aching, familiar regularity.

"Tell me, damn it! I want to hear you say it—just once!" He released her buttocks and moved his hands to her shoulders, flattening her against the bed, staring hard into her face. He held her there as he continued to fuck her, moving a little slower now, his dark, passion-filled eyes growing softer as they gazed into her face. "Say you love me," he whispered. "Please. Just tell me you love me—" He squeezed his eyes shut tight as he stopped in

305

mid-stroke and held himself still a moment, quivering as he forced back his orgasm.

Tara looked into his face and felt every vestige of strength and reason leave her. She locked her heels behind his back, tugged him forward, further inside her. "I love you, Eric—you know I do!"

"Oh, Christ, my darling!" He plunged in so deep she cried out with sudden pain, then lifted her hips and met him stroke for loving stroke. "I'm so much in love with you—so damn much!"

He murmured softly against her hair, whispered words she could not understand against her mouth, his warm breath now on her throat, now tickling in her ear, sending chills down her spine. "Oh, God, baby, I'm going to come!" He speeded up, his body enveloping hers with heat and muscle as he gathered her closer, his big hands hard on her soft flesh. "Come with me," he panted, "come on, baby—let's do it together!"

"Yes, Eric, now, my darling!" She hung onto him with all her strength, her mouth open and bruised beneath his, her arms and legs vise-like about his heaving body. She screamed when she came but the sound was lost against his mouth, mingled with his own cry of release.

They lay still joined for several long, exhausted minutes, their bodies wet with perspiration, limbs heavy and aching. Eric spoke first. "God, that was beautiful! You're beautiful! Love is beautiful! The whole fucking world is beautiful!" He tumbled her over, kicking the tangled sheet off their warm bodies and began blowing cool breath over her breasts and belly.

"Eric, you nut," she laughed, trying to grab the sheet and cover herself. "Stop that—it tickles." He crawled up to kiss her, his hands running lightly over her body.

"Don't move. Stay right there, okay?" He jumped out of bed and disappeared into the bathroom, returning a moment later with a warm washcloth and towel. He washed her tenderly, then patted her dry. "Never has there been a body like this." His dark eyes traveled slowly and appreciatively over her nakedness, savoring every beautiful curve, and she felt as if he were making

306

love to her again, this time with his eyes. She reached out
to him and he went eagerly into her arms and kissed her,
sighing against her lips, "I love you, lady."

"Umm," she murmured, thankful that his mouth made
it impossible to respond. Now that the wild, hysterical
burst of passion had subsided, she felt embarrassed once
again. She could not forget that she had made a concen-
trated effort to put him out of her mind and heart for the
past three and a half years—and now here she was in bed
with him. It made her feel uncomfortable, as if she should
apologize for her feelings. Shit, how did she get into this
compromising situation?

"I don't know about you," he said against her neck,
"but I'm beat. That's more exercise than I've had in
many a moon." He drew her closer, nibbling her neck.
"Wanton cunt, you still do it to me. Still drain me."

"That tickles," she giggled, squirming against him and
feeling his now flaccid member pushing intimately against
her. She turned her back and reached down to draw the
blankets over them, fitting herself into an S against him.
He circled her from behind, cupping her breasts in his
hands and sighed with contentment. "Goodnight, darling,
sleep well."

" 'Night, baby," he mumbled sleepily. "I love you."

Tara closed her eyes, aware of the faint throbbing of
her body. As exhausted as she was, she still felt wonderful. Felt alive and charged with energy, and serene at the
same time. Kind of like a mountain climber, she supposed,
who had used every ounce of energy to reach the summit
and once there had been renewed, refreshed. She did not
feel the least bit tired, just a little sleepy. But she must
not go to sleep, she told herself. She would just lie with
him until he had fallen asleep, then she would slip out
and call a taxi. She glanced at her watch, just able to
make out the time. Five-fifteen. Good God, they had
made love all night long. She smiled in the darkness, half-
wishing the evening was just beginning instead of ending.
Eric was by far the most fantastic lover she had ever
known. His endurance was not to be believed! She pressed
her fanny back against the curve of his crotch, rubbing

it gently against his penis, wondering if she could awaken it without waking him. It twitched, bucked lightly against her buttocks, grew a little even while he slept on. "I do love you, Eric," she whispered. "I do—but I can't!"

She covered his hands with hers, holding them tighter to her breasts and pushed herself closer still until their bodies were touching from neck to ankles. She would give it another five or ten minutes, to make sure he was sound asleep. She let her eyelids droop briefly, thinking how comfortable she was. How warm and secure in Eric's arms. I'd better get out of here before this becomes a habit, was the last thing she remembered.

Tara opened her eyes and sat up, looking around. Everything was so familiar and yet she knew she was not home. For a moment she thought she was in Doe's guest room, and then she glanced toward the dresser and saw a picture of herself and Eric taken on the night of the premiere of *The Savage Desert*. How young they both looked. She sat up straighter and stared hard at the framed photograph. His arm was possessively around her, his handsome face alight with the success of his movie; his dark eyes were filled with love for her. And she was gazing up at him, her expression clearly one of adoration and devotion. Her gloved hand rested on his arm just as possessively, and she was positively radiant. Whoever had captured them in that intimate moment? Either he had been one hell of a photographer or they had been so in love even an impersonal camera lens could see it.

She started to throw back the covers and get out of bed when she remembered she had nothing to put on. She remembered something about tossing her pink bridesmaid's gown into the swimming pool or fireplace. She could not remember which. But she did remember that she and Eric had gotten a big kick out of it and had laughed like a couple of crazies for longer than the act had merited. In fact, it seemed that they had laughed most of the evening—between hot and heavy bouts of lovemaking. A heady tremor passed swiftly through her and she wondered where he was. She stretched her arms over her head, her legs straight out, and wiggled her toes. Every inch of her body felt the aftermath of Eric's lovemaking. She was sore, but delightfully so. Her lips were puffy from his hard, bruising kisses, her vagina swollen and gently throbbing, but never in her life had she felt so totally and completely *alive*. She wanted to laugh out loud. Sing *Life is Just a Bowl of Cherries*. Ride the Matterhorn with Eric stark naked. Better still, make love on the Matterhorn. That was what last night reminded her of. A wildly hurtling rollercoaster ride, with all the high ecstatic peaks and thrilling, plunging depths.

The door opened silently and Eric poked his head inside. "Hey, you're finally awake. Good morning, darling." He walked toward her dressed in fresh, faded Levis, a red and white striped sweatshirt and tan desert boots. He bent and kissed her. "You look awfully damn good for a lady who drank two cases of champagne and a fifth of vodka last night."

"I didn't!" she protested, laughing when he kissed her again. "Eric, don't, I'm a mess." She tried to pull the covers over her but he grabbed them and jerked them off.

"Get your ass out of bed, woman, it's past noon and the help is beginning to talk about your slovenly habits." He bent to pull her from the bed, then stopped short, staring down at her. His gaze traveled slowly over her nude body, caressing her with love-filled eyes. He took one finger and gently traced the outline of her nipple before bending to kiss it. Then moved down to softly kiss and nuzzle her pubis. He straightened, his voice gruff when he said, "I'll go tell Maria that you're awake." He threw the sheet over her. "Jesus Christ, cover up, woman, before I—" He turned abruptly away, fumbling in his pocket for a cigarette.

"You're the one who took them off," she answered saucily, hugging the sheet to her breasts. Smiling a little at the effect she had over him. She toyed with the idea of teasing him back into bed. Just one more fuck and then she would call a taxi. Shocked by the thought, she blushed, hoping he could not read her mind. Almost sure that he could. She ducked her head and mumbled, "Okay,

I'll get up as soon as you leave. Would it be okay if I take a shower?"

"Of course, I'll tell Maria to hold breakfast for—how long? Half an hour?"

She nodded. "I guess I can pull myself together in that time. Boy, I feel like a Mac truck hit me." She laughed a little, embarrassed. "I guess I was pretty stinko last night, huh? Or what Glasser calls swacked to the gills."

He laughed. "Drunker than a skunk. But you seemed to be having a hell of a good time. Do you remember burning your clothes in the fireplace?"

"Oh, no, I didn't—did I?" She cringed beneath the sheets, covering her head. Peeking out, she giggled, "You know, when I woke up this morning, that's the first thing I remembered." She blushed. "Well, maybe not the very first thing, but anyway I couldn't remember if I had thrown them into the fireplace or the swimming pool. Thank you for clearing it up for me."

"Not at all." He paused, grinning down at her. "It was your shoes you threw into the pool—as well as my new Beatles album. You said they sounded too much like Zock McBain. Remember?"

She shook her head, laughing with him. "No, I don't. My God, what else did I do? No, don't tell me. I don't think I want to hear until I've had a shower and a cup of coffee."

"I don't blame you," he teased, rolling his eyes. "Boy, were you ever outrageous!"

She cried, "Oh, Eric! Don't tease me!"

Still laughing he bent and kissed her, then walked to the door. "Go ahead and have your shower and I'll try to find you something to wear."

Tara went into the bathroom and stepped into the shower, standing under the hot, stinging needles of water for a long time. As she soaped herself she found new evidence of her torrid evening with Eric. Sore, tender spots, light tan bruises, darker purple ones made by his lips and teeth. They all felt marvelous to her touch. Proof that she had been loved thoroughly and completely. She stepped out and toweled herself dry and was brushing her hair when Eric knocked on the door. He opened it a crack and tossed some clothes inside.

"See if these fit. Maria said she thought they would."

"Thanks. Be right out." She stood with the towel in front of her, staring at him and he stared back for a long moment.

"Well," he cleared his throat. "Well, come on in when you've dressed. I'll tell Maria to put breakfast on. Anything special you'd like? Eggs? Waffles?"

"Whatever you're having is fine. Thank you. I'll be right out."

The sudden awkwardness hung between them until Eric closed the door and she let out a deep breath. Why did he make her feel so strange? Happy one minute, shy and embarrassed the next? He had always made her feel just slightly off center. Never sure which course he emotions would take. "Damn him, anyway," she muttered aloud. She held the clothes up and looked at them. A pair of blue jeans, reasonably new, a blue tee-shirt with the slogan CHINO POWER in big yellow letters, no underwear, but a pair of rubber thongs that looked brand new.

Taking a deep breath, she opened the bathroom door and stood there a moment. It was facing-the-morning-after time and she was understandably nervous. What does one say to a man after hating him for three and a half years—then balling his brains out for ten straight hours? You're the writer, she told herself—think of something, for God's sake!

"Hi," she said brightly upon entering the dining room. "Good morning. Lovely morning, isn't it?" Brilliant dialogue, Tara, she thought as she smiled at Eric. He jumped to his feet and held a chair for her.

"Yes, it is. Here, sit down." He seemed as nervous as she, and that made her feel a little better. "Coffee?" He picked up the silver serving pot and poured her a cup.

"Thank you." She waved away the cream and sugar he offered. "Just black."

"Maria!" he called. "Our guest has arrived."

"Si, señor," a voice floated to them, and they looked at each other and smiled.

311

"Well," he said, his smile beginning to look a little strained around the edges. "Well, you look fine."

She opened her napkin and spread it in her lap. "Thank you." Why the hell was he staring at her like that, with that big dumb smile on his face?

"Jesus, let's stop the bullshit!" He shoved away from the table, went to her and bent and kissed her. A long, loving kiss. "There," he said, going back to take his chair. "That's the way to say good morning after such an incredible night of love." He punched her lightly on the nose. "Whether you want to admit it or not, young lady, it was an incredible night of love." His dark eyes held hers. "Wasn't it?"

"Yes," she said faintly, unable to look away. "Yes, it was."

"Ah, señorita Tara, buenos días!" Maria bustled into the room with two steaming plates and a wicker basket of toast. "How well you look." She served them, then extended her hand. "Cómo esta usted?"

"Hello, Maria, wonderful to see you again." She shook the small brown hand and the maid smiled shyly. "Thank you for letting me borrow your jeans and shirt." She laughed, glancing at Eric. "I, uh, seem to have misplaced mine."

"De nada," Maria said merrily. Her round face was wreathed in smiles as she looked down at Tara. "It is very good to see you here once more." She spoke slowly and carefully, but proud of her newly acquired English. She patted Tara's shoulder fondly. "You are well, si? The little muchacha too? She is well?"

"Yes, thank you, Maria. We are both very well. But the little girl is now a grown-up young lady. Taller than me, in fact."

"That's not saying a hell of a lot, shorty," Eric grinned. The exchange between Tara and Maria brought back so many happy memories. Memories of dinners served on this same table, with Mandy often joining them.

"Bueno, bueno," Maria nodded in satisfaction. "You eat now, Missy. I will find a small something for you to

312

take to the pequeña señorita, si? She like my sugar cookies, I think."

"How lovely—Mandy will be pleased. She's very fond of you, Maria."

"Then you must bring her again to see me." Maria beamed down at her, unaware of the glance that passed between her and Eric. "Si? You will bring her next time you come, Miss Tara?"

"Yes. The next time I come." She glanced at Eric and they both knew she had no intention of ever coming here again. "Well, these eggs look marvelous, don't they, Eric? Are you as ravenous as I am?" She began eating, not looking at him.

"Yes, starved." He wanted to say that making love all night always gave him an appetite but was afraid he would drive her away even sooner. He knew she would leave him as soon as breakfast was over and she could graciously make her getaway. She had the look of a trapped animal as she sat across from him, her great dark eyes shifting to the door every so often as if she were frightened she would be locked in. Held prisoner against her will. Damn her to hell anyway. What did she think he was? Some kind of sex fiend who would strap her to the bedposts and take advantage of her? She sure as hell had been willing enough last night. More than willing. And the higher she got, the more passionate and aggressive she had become. I should get her stoned again, he thought wickedly. Just keep her stoned and in bed all weekend. Damn it, she owed it to him.

They spoke politely, like formal strangers, of Doe's wedding and Tara's new book. "It will be out in the spring of 'seventy-eight, hopefully," she said.

Eric said, "No kidding? That's about the time my new movie will be released. We'll have to get together and celebrate."

"Yes, perhaps lunch sometime," she said vaguely, finishing her coffee and glancing toward the door. "Well, I really should be running." She gave a short, embarrassed chuckle. "Everyone at home will think I've been kidnapped."

He chuckled with her. "Don't tell me this is the first time you've stayed out all night, Miss Remington, a famous writer like yourself, sophisticated, worldly—"

"As a matter of fact, it is," she said coldly, sudden anger making her eyes flash directly at him. "If it's any of your business!"

"Whoa, easy, big fella," he laughed, holding his hands up in mock surrender. "No offense, I just thought—"

"Well, don't think," she snapped, pushing away from the table. "Now if you will excuse me."

"Hey, Tara, cool it." He stood and took her arm, swinging her around to face him. "I'm not going to let you go this way. Not after last night."

"I would advise you to forget last night. I'm certainly going to!" She jerked her arm from his grasp and walked quickly from the room.

He stood staring after her, wanting to slap her silly for being such a cold-hearted bitch. What the hell had gotten into her? What had he said? He clenched and unclenched his fists, took a deep breath and went after her.

She was in the den, looking for her purse, and he forced a smile when she glanced at him warily. He told himself to stay calm, to soothe her ruffled feathers with charm, not muscle. He could understand how she must feel, keeping as far away from him as possible for all this time, and then, in one evening, all the barriers had been broken down and she had given herself to him like a woman starved for love. Like a woman *in love*. She had aroused and awakened him again and again during the night, always so eager to have him take her again. The romantic part of him wanted to believe that she had had no other men since their breakup, but the reasonable part knew that would be asking far too much. He had seen her name linked often in the gossip columns with this movie star or that playwright or director. Always someone very wealthy or famous or both. And all of them handsome, virile, successful men who were sought after by countless beautiful women. But she loved him. Last night had convinced him beyond a doubt. No one could fake such emotional passion. Or derive such pure pleasure from the act of love unless they were truly *in love*. And she had been drunk and stoned on grass, all her inhibitions gone, her mental defenses down. She had responded to him honestly, with gut sincerity, almost innocently. He was damned if he would ever let her go again.

He crossed to the bar, saw her purse lying among some stacked newspapers and quickly pushed it out of sight. He took a joint from his stash beneath the bar, lit it and offered it to her.

"No, thank you. I really have to be going." She walked about the room, looking under cushions and tables. "Do you have any idea where I left my bag?" A tiny smile lifted the corners of her mouth. "Or did I throw it into the fireplace as well?"

It was the sign he had been waiting for. Moving quickly to her, he offered the joint again and this time she took it, rather automatically. "Beats me. I was as zonkered as you were, remember?"

She remembered nothing of the sort. In fact, something told her that he had not been drunk at all. Certainly not as drunk as she had been. She dragged again on the joint and passed it back to him. "Well, I have to find it. It must be around here someplace."

She glanced around the neat room. Not one sign remained of the disorder of the night before. Obviously Maria had been in earlier to clean. She wondered what maids thought when they cleaned up rooms littered with marijuana joints, panties turned inside out, stockings draped over lamps and tables, shorts and other intimate objects left where they had been hastily discarded. "Do you think Maria could have put it someplace?"

"I'll go ask her—here, keep this going, okay?" He handed her the joint and left the room. He did not go to the kitchen however. He stood just outside the door to the den, watching Tara.

She made another turn around the room, picking up cushions and peering under them, and then sat down with a sigh and proceeded to smoke the joint down to nothing. Dropping the bit of smoking paper into an ashtray, she leaned back and closed her eyes. She pressed her fingers to her temples as if her head hurt.

He waited a few seconds longer, walked in and said (he hoped not too cheerfully), "No, she says she hasn't seen it." He lit another joint, this time one of his "bombs." He had just scored some Purple Seedless, the headiest, most soul-satisfying grass known to heads, with the guarantee that "one toke'll do ya." It was true. One deep drag and you were soaring higher than the gods in a paradisiac lotus land. "Maybe you tossed it into the pool along with your shoes." He handed her the joint and she took it absently, frowning as she glanced around the room.

"I hope not. I had my credit cards and license and everything in it." She took another hit before passing the joint back to him—then did a double take. "My GOD, what kind of grass is that?"

"Purple Seedless," he said, grinning down at her when she tried to stand and fell back to the sofa. He lifted her up, pulling her against him. Where she belonged, he told himself. "How do you like it?"

"I'll tell you when my head stops spinning," she giggled, then straightened up quickly, pulling away from him and squaring her shoulders. "Well, look, I really do have to go. Do you think I could have tossed my purse into the pool?" Her expression said she hoped she had not been that stewed and stupid last night.

"Let's go take a look." He led her outside, both of them squinting their eyes against the white glare of the sun. The turquoise pool shimmered like broken glass, the tiny ripples on the surface catching and reflecting the blinding rays of sun. A man stood at one end of the pool, a long pole in his hands which he was raking slowly along the bottom.

" 'Morning, Benito," Eric called. He shaded his eyes and pulled Tara after him.

"Buenas tardes, señor Marlowe." The short, squat Mexican swept his hat off, bowing toward Tara. "Ah, señorita Tara! What a long time since you have been here. Since I see you. Buenas tardes—good afternoon. Cómo esta usted?"

316

"Hello, Benito. Muy bien, gracias. Y usted?" She offered her hand, and Benito quickly wiped his against his trousers before shaking it.

"Bien, bien, gracias." He beamed happily at her, his large teeth very white against his brown skin and drooping black mustache. He was almost on a level with her but built like a sturdy little bull, thick-necked, barrel-chested, legs as solid as tree stumps. He glanced toward the bottom of the pool, then toward Eric, winking broadly. "De la fiesta ultima noche, si, señor Marlowe?" He laughed indulgently, his sharp black eyes going from Eric to Tara, then to the pool's bottom.

They both stepped closer, following Benito's gaze and saw Tara's shoes at the bottom of the pool. They were bleached almost completely white, just the stitching and a narrow strip around the sole still pink. Eric's Beatle album lay next to them, strangely unbroken, but the label had come off and now floated on top of the shimmering turquoise water.

"Uh, you could say that," Eric grinned, putting his arm around Tara and pulling her close. He nodded in the direction of the shoes. "Think you can get those things out of there without diving for them?"

"Oh, si, si, no fue molestia—esta nada señor." He brought his long-handled net out of the water and plunged it in next to the shoes and deftly scooped them up. "Por usted, señorita." He presented them to Tara with a courtly bow, and raked the net into the pool again and scooped out the album.

"Thanks, Benito." Eric took the dripping album and tossed it into a trash barrel. "I didn't like it anyway," he said to Tara. "You're right—they do sound too much like Zock McBain." She was holding her wet, puckered silk slippers, and he took them from her and tossed them into the trash barrel as well. "And you weren't crazy about these, either, if I remember correctly."

"No, I wasn't." She laughed, embarrassed, conscious of Benito's knowing eyes traveling over her body dressed in his wife's clothes. She looked quickly away, peered into the pool. "Well, I don't see my purse down there. It has to be in the house someplace."

"It might be in the bedroom. Shall we have a look?" He started leading her toward the sliding glass doors and she followed him docilely enough, but her mind spun with thoughts about last night. How she had gotten into his bedroom. She remembered it vividly and felt a streak of pleasure in her loins. How he had swept her off her feet and carried her off like Rhett Butler in *Gone With the Wind*. The hot passion in his dark eyes when he had laid her upon the bed and stood looking down at her. She saw again his magnificent body, so hard and ready, his tenderness when he had undressed her . . .

She pulled away from him, grabbing the side of the door to steady herself. I've got to stop thinking about it, she told herself firmly, a little wildly. It probably just seemed so fantastic because she had been drunk and high and so turned on by the romantic setting. Doe's wedding. Her own private yearnings for *something*. It was not necessarily Eric who had caused her to feel that way.

"What's the matter, honey? Are you dizzy?" He took her hand and helped her inside, leading her to the sofa. "Can I get you something? A glass of water?"

"No, it's nothing. I just felt a little woozy for a minute." She laughed nervously. "It's probably that dynamite weed you laid on me. Plus my mammoth hangover."

"Do you have a hangover, darling?" He was all solicitous, worriedly pressing her back against the sofa and placing her feet upon the coffee table. He slipped off the rubber thongs, and massaged her feet. "Why didn't you tell me? I have the perfect remedy for a hangover."

"Oh, no, Eric, please. I really don't want a thing." She tried to rise but he gently pushed her back.

"Now just relax, baby," he soothed. He retrieved the roach of Purple Seedless and lit it, placing it between her lips. "Here, sweetie, take a toke and relax. Most hangovers are caused from tension, not enough oxygen getting to the brain. Marijuana relaxes the blood vessels and lets it flow freely. Allows you to open up and take in the fresh air you need to—"

"You don't say, Dr. Marlowe?" she laughed in spite of herself. She took a drag, holding the smoke in her lungs as she grinned up at him. "Like this?"

"By jove, I think she's got it!" He crowed in a perfect imitation of Rex Harrison in *My Fair Lady*. He kissed her before she could turn her head away, then went to the bar.

Tara heard the bottles and glasses clinking, the mixer whirring, but did not open her eyes or turn her head to see what he was doing. She was totally zonked. Stoned like a statue, she thought, for the first time really understanding what the term meant. She could not have raised a limb or moved a muscle if the Russians had landed in the back yard. From a moment before when she had felt so nervous and uptight, embarrassed and hostile, she now felt languid, flaccid, loose and very fragile. Like cool, lacey wisteria. Like Spanish moss. Like a soft tendril of hair curling on a sleeping baby's neck.

"Here you go, honey, drink this and I guarantee your hangover will vanish." He handed her a tall frosted glass of frothy white mixture.

"What is it?" She struggled into a sitting position, embarrassed again at having been caught with what she knew must have been a rapturous expression on her face. The conceited honcho would probably think that he had inspired it!

"Ramos fizz—my own recipe." He saluted her with his own glass. "Bottoms up!" He drank, watching her to make sure she did too. "I threw in a handful of vitamin C and B-12, a couple of raw eggs and a Dexie. It'll have your blood churning in no time. Trust me."

"If you say so," she answered a little doubtfully and took a tiny sip. "Hey, that's good. Tastes like a milk-shake." She drank again. "Doe used to drink these all the time, but swore off when she met Wesley because she said they made her gain weight like crazy."

"A couple now and then won't do any harm." He sat next to her. "Besides, you could stand to gain a few pounds. What do you weigh these days, anyway?"

"Oh, about a hundred and five, I think, something like

319

that." She leaned forward to get a cigarette and he quickly lit it for her.

"Too skinny." He lit a cigarette for himself, leaned back and rested his arm on the back of the sofa behind her, his fingers just brushing her shoulder. "You should gain five or ten pounds."

"No way. I work out every day just to stay at this weight. You know how much I love to eat—especially Italian food!"

"Yes, I remember." He turned to look at her and his eyes grew dark and soft with memories. "We used to go to Matteo's or Martoni's at least twice a week and you always had a side order of fettucini verde alfredo. No matter what else you ordered, you had to have your fettucini."

"Yeah, well, not anymore." She laughed and moved a little away from his arm. "God, I haven't had Italian food in ages."

"Then it's time you did. Let's go to Martoni's for dinner. I'll take you home to change and we can—"

"No, Eric, I can't." She said it firmly, looking directly into his eyes. "I'm leaving as soon as I finish my drink—and, well, I don't think we should see each other for—for—"

He turned quickly away so she would not see the stricken look on his face. Too fast, he warned himself, you're moving too damn fast, schmuck! He forced a light laugh and turned back to her. "Hey, cool it, baby. I'm not going to kidnap you and make you a prisoner of love, ya know. Hell, it's over between us. I know that. But can't we at least be friends, have dinner together once in a while—every three and half years or so." He laughed, forcing one from her. "We're both consenting adults, right? We can have any kind of relationship that we're comfortable with—and then walk away with no bruised egos or hurt feelings, right?"

"Yes, of course." She straightened her shoulders and faced him squarely. "After all, a woman has the same rights as a man about taking lovers, doesn't she? According to Gloria Steinem, anyway." She drank the rest of her

Ramos fizz and took a hit of the joint. " 'Sides, we should just forget about all the bad shit and play and have fun today—celebrate Doe's wedding. Let's see, they've been married exactly"—She peered at her watch—"twenty hours."

"And they said it wouldn't last," Eric quipped and they both laughed, leaning in toward one another.

Tara sobered a little. Jeez, that was some grass! "Well, I think I'll go home and play with Mandy. I don't feel like doing anything serious today." She started to rise, fell back and said, "Oops, Eric, what did you put in that drink? I'm not sure I can drive."

"You don't have your car here," he told her. "Some disreputable young man took Mandy home from the wedding in it, remember?"

"Oh, shit! Vince!" She clapped a hand to her mouth and giggled. "I wonder if he's still waiting for me?"

"Tara, you shock me," Eric laughed. "You mean you've had some poor sucker waiting in bed for you since yesterday afternoon?"

She did not tell him that she and Vince were not lovers. "Yep, that's where I like 'em—waiting in bed!" She made her voice Mae West bawdy and assumed a sexy pose. "Hard and happy, honey." She waved her hand as if dismissing a pesky fly. "I don't want 'em following me around or talking to me or bugging me about anything— just want 'em waiting in bed—hard and happy!"

Eric laughed out loud and hugged her to him, kissing her before she could pull away. He released her, still laughing, and went to the bar to refresh their drinks. "Tara, you really do shock me. How you've changed since last we met! Where, oh where, has the little girl gone?"

"Down the crapper," Tara sang. "Mired in the bullshit—" She took the fresh drink and sipped it, grinning up at him.

"Well, I can't say you look any the worse for it. In fact, you're more beautiful than I've ever seen you." His eyes teased her. "Maybe it's your maturity. You are getting on, you know. And still single, too."

"And loving every shimmering, pulsating moment of it,"

she retorted, tossing her head. "Happiness is not a warm puppy, as I've mistakenly believed all these years. Happiness is being single!"

"Hear, hear," Eric said, toasting her. "My sentiments exactly."

Tara gave him a startled look, surprised at the sudden, sinking feeling in her stomach. A dull thud. Surely he did not mean that. He loved her and wanted to marry her. Didn't he? How perfectly awful if he had finally decided to accept the fact that she wanted nothing to do with him. And a sly little voice whispered that she may say she did not love him, but she did not want him to ever stop loving her.

"Would you like to call home and tell your gentleman friend that you're alive and high in Benedict Canyon?" He placed the telephone next to her on the sofa.

"Yes, I guess I should."

"Excuse me while I check with Maria about dinner." He stood. "You *are* staying for dinner. I won't take no for an answer." He held up a hand when she started to protest. "I promise to take you home the minute you want to leave, okay?"

"Okay," she laughed, then took a quick sip of her drink before dialing. "Hello? Hazel? It's me—no, no, I'm fine. I just spent the night at a friend's house . . ."

He heard her asking to speak to Charley as he left the room and he grinned broadly, thinking, I've got her for another night! He knew he could talk her into staying over again because no matter how hard she fought it, she was still as crazy about him as he was about her. She could not resist one more fantastic evening of lovemaking. If he had to get her stoned *and* drunk, he would. There was no room for scruples when you were in love, he told himself.

He was whistling when he entered the kitchen and called for Maria. "She's staying for dinner!" he cried, as excited as a small boy. "We have to think of something fabulous for dinner. Something with wine or brandy—or both! What do you think, Maria? I want a meal, a feast for a goddess!"

"Is already four o'clock, señor Marlowe. Maria, she cannot cook a feast for a goddess in so little time—is better to cook feast all day—mebbe two, three days, even." She spoke so seriously, her round face solemn that she could not please him, and he laughed aloud and swung her around in his arms.

"Oh, Maria, Maria, I love you!" he cried happily. "God, I love *everything* when she's here! I don't care what you cook as long as it's magnificent! Superb! You can do it, Maria—I know you can." He kissed her cheek and she blushed and slapped him on the arm. "Just make sure you use a lot of wine or brandy, okay? I plan on getting her drunk and taking advantage of her."

"Oh, señor Marlowe, you are one bad hombre," Maria giggled, her dark eyes flashing. "But the señorita, she is muy hermosa, eh? You love her very much. This I know." She nodded her head approvingly and marched to the corner desk where she kept her cook books. "I cook you one plenty damn good dinner, señor Marlowe, you don't worry, eh?"

CHAPTER
FIFTEEN

TARA SAT at her desk in her office, scowling at Izzy. "You had no right to accept for me," she said angrily. "You, of all people, should know how I feel about openings. I loathe them!"

"Oh, sugar, I'm *so* sorry," Izzy wailed, twisting his long hands together, wrapping and unwrapping his legs until he resembled a nervous pretzel. "I thought you'd be *pleased*, really I did. *Especially* since it's Chuckie's new place. Remember, you *offered* to help. You said if there was *anything* you could do—" Izzy always spoke in italics when he felt strongly about something.

"I meant money," Tara snapped. "Like a loan if he needed it to enlarge his inventory or whatever you call a bunch of sex props. I did not, repeat, *did not* mean that I would appear in public with that—that pervert!"

"He's not a pervert," Izzy protested, but not too strongly. He was torn between loyalty to his lover and loyalty to his boss—and therefore his job. "My goodness, sugar, *everyone* who *is* anyone shops at Chuckie's. That's why he's opening a bigger place, business is so *fantastic*."

"According to his publicity man, it is," Tara said, glancing down at the open newspaper on her desk. "Just listen to this shit: 'When the jet set wants to know what to wear to the theater, they contact Dior, Givenchy or Balenciaga; when they need a kinky little number for an evening at the discotheque, they ring up couturiers Saint Laurent or Courreges—but when nothing will do but a sizzling, devastating, out-of-this-world creation for that oh-so-intimate rendezvous or very private soirée for two, there's only one place to shop—Paraphernalia from Eden.' God, what crap." She flung the newspaper to the floor and fixed Izzy with a sour look.

Daisy, who had been sleeping in a patch of sunlight near the desk, jumped when the newspaper struck her, meowing with injured dignity. She looked up at Tara with accusing green eyes, and Tara reached down and lifted her upon her lap. "Sorry, love," she murmured, stroking the ruffled fur and scratching behind the cat's ears.

"According to rumor, *everyone* from Garbo to Brando will be at the opening," Izzy pouted.

"Yeah, and I have a pretty good idea who started that rumor. Izzy, you could at least have consulted me before giving my name to the press agent. Now it looks like I'm personally backing this—this—"

"Boutique of erotic apparel," he supplied happily. "Don't you love it? It has such a classy but sexy ring to it, don't you think?"

She merely grunted and continued to stroke Daisy. She really was not that angry with Izzy. She knew she could simply not show up for the opening without going into such a tirade about it, but she had been feeling mean and off the wall lately. Ever since her "lost weekend" with Eric.

She had stayed overnight (as he knew she would), thoroughly enjoying the sumptuous dinner Maria had prepared, and they had made love countless times before finally falling asleep at dawn Sunday morning. She had awakened a few hours later and slipped away while Eric still slept and Marie and Benito were at church. She had left a hastily scribbled (idiotic) note thanking him for a wonderful weekend but suggesting that they not make a habit of it. In fact, that they not repeat it.

When Charley, Izzy and Mandy had bombarded her with questions as to where she had been and with whom, hinting that there might be a new man in her life, she had let them think so. She had told them that it was someone she had met at Doe's, a married someone, so she could not possibly tell them his name. Charley and Izzy had been hurt, as well as surprised. Tara had never been one to keep secrets. Not from her two closest pals. Mandy could not have cared less, once she saw that her sister was unharmed, and had charged outside to tell her horses that the hay winner was back home and all was well.

Eric had called many times, but Tara had instructed her answering service (and Hazel) to tell him that she was in New York discussing her new novel. After a few days, the calls had stopped and she was able to begin functioning again. She spent hours at the library, just browsing, looking for something, anything that might catch her fancy as the subject of a new book. *Seattle Slum* had literally written itself, and *Passion's Rogue* had been a story that she had always wanted to write. Now she had no idea what to do next. She had wandered aimlessly through book stores in Beverly Hills, Hollywood and the Valley, asking the clerks which type of book moved the fastest and had been told by almost everyone that Hollywood stories were still the most popular.

"Seems folks just love to read about movie stars and what goes on in the glamorous lives of millionaires and the like," the lady at Pickwick had confided. "I can't keep enough of 'em on the shelves."

Tara had spent another couple of weeks musing about it, wondering if she could tell about the world she had come of age in. She certainly knew, first hand, what it was like to be a celebrity, to move in the fast-paced circles of movie stars and rock kings, to have as a best friend the most famous blonde sex symbol since Jean Harlow and Marilyn Monroe. She thought about writing a novel about her life with Zock, but decided against it. He, as well as everyone else, would know it was about him and she did not want that. Did not want people to think she was using someone's personal problems for her own gain. But she had done that with *Seattle Slum,* and look what a success it had been. She had taken her problem to Jim Glasser and he had told her, "Write what you know about. That's the first rule of a successful writer. Hell, if you don't know anything about your subject, how in hell do you expect your readers to understand it?"

"But don't you think writing about my marriage to Zock would be sort of a 'kiss and tell' exposé?" she had asked.

"Shit, no!" the crusty Irishman had scoffed. "Writers do that all the time. Of course you change the names of your characters to avoid lawsuits and change the occupations just enough to stay in the clear, but otherwise I'd say go ahead and write it. Hell, you sure as shit went through enough crap with that prick to write two novels!"

Tara was not sure she wanted to rehash the horrors of those months with Zock, and so as yet had not decided to write the book. She knew she had to get busy soon. The long days of inactivity made her restless and short-tempered and she was anxious to get started on another project. Izzy had suggested a trip to Europe (with him going along as companion, of course), and Charley had suggested that she take Mandy for a month in the mountains—but Tara had rejected both plans.

She sighed now as she looked across the room at Izzy, his long face made even longer by his fear that she might seriously be angry with him. "I'm sorry, Izzy," she said wearily. "Let's not talk about it now, okay? If I decide to go, I'll let you know in plenty of time."

"It's in two weeks," he reminded her gently, a little sulkily. "And Chuckie's in a panic about the preparations. Please say you'll do it—for me, sugar?" he pleaded as prettily as a girl. "Chuckie" was the owner of Paraphernalia from Eden and Izzy's current lover. They had met the night of Doe's wedding when Izzy had gone home with the trombone player, only to fall in love with the musician's roommate—Chuckie.

"I'll let you know." She got to her feet, paced the length of the office and then stood gazing out the window at the rolling hills in the far distance. "God, can you believe it's almost winter when you look out and see a day like this?" Everywhere trees and flowers bloomed and there was the feel of a lazy summer day. With Mandy in school and Charley in her own private office, Hazel away doing the marketing, the house seemed unusually quiet. While Tara herself felt disquieted. It had been over a month since she had spent the weekend with Eric, but not a day had gone by that she had not thought about it. About him. She lay awake in bed at night wondering why she refused to accept the fact that she still loved Eric and wanted to be with him. Just plain stubborn pride, she supposed. She had made such a big deal of his fathering Mandy, having a year-long affair with her mother, that she would have felt ridiculous and embarrassed to just simply forget it all and go back to the way it had been before. But knowing that she was wrong did not necessarily make her want to admit it. Least of all to Eric. She felt she had to punish him for all the pain he had caused her as a child. The fact that he had no idea he was causing her pain did not even enter into it. As a raggedy ten-year-old child, she had sworn to hate forever the boy who brought her mother rum and stole her library books and brought so much sadness into her already pitiful life. Now she felt she still must reject him. Make him pay, somehow. And now that Mandy was almost grown, what would she think to suddenly find out that Eric, her sister's husband, her brother-in-law, was really her father? No, it simply would not work out. She could not spend the rest of her life living a lie. Seeing Eric and Mandy together every day, looking so much alike that sooner or later one of them was sure to notice.

"Sugar, what is it?" Izzy said softly, coming up behind her and putting his hands on her shoulders. "You've been uptight ever since Doe's wedding. Can't you tell me what's bothering you?"

"No. It's nothing, really." She turned away, causing him to drop his hands, and walked back to her desk. She stroked Daisy who now lay comfortably in her chair, purring contentedly and with no intention of moving. "I just have a lot on my mind. Trying to decide about my next project, you know, if I should write about my life with Zock the Cock—that sort of thing." She laughed a little but there was not any humor in it and she dropped her eyes when Izzy gave her a knowing look.

"Come *on,* sweetie, it's more than that. I *know* you, remember? You once said I was like a sister to you— and we girls have to stick together." He laughed, trying to get her to join him, but she merely smiled wanly and paced again across the room. "Is it a man?" he persisted. "Or the lack of one? You really haven't been yourself since that weekend when you disappeared with your married lover. That's *it,* isn't it? He can't get a divorce and—"

"Oh, shut up, Izzy!" She whirled on him, fists clenched and eyes flashing. "Jesus Christ, you're the nosiest son of a bitch I've ever seen! Questions, questions—why can't people just leave me alone and quit prying into my private life! If I do have a married lover, it's certainly my prerogative!" She stalked to the desk, jerked open a drawer and took out a joint. Daisy stared at her with a level green gaze, indignant at having been disturbed again.

"Well, *excuse* me, *Miss* Remington!" Izzy said with exaggerated injury. "I thought we were friends, that we could talk things out, try to help one another, but if you'd like to keep our relationship on an employer-employee basis, *please* let me know and I'll go back to answering your fan mail!"

"Oh, Izzy, I'm sorry, I don't know what's wrong with me." She went to him and hugged him briefly. "Here— get high with me, okay?" He took the joint with a little sniff of hurt pride, not ready yet to completely forgive her. "Christ, it just seems like everything is always the same and yet so different. Each day just sort of runs into the next and I don't feel I've accomplished anything, you know what I mean? I see Mandy growing and changing, but I seem to be standing still. Waiting. Everything stays the same for me, while it seems to change and grow better for other people." She took the joint and went to sit on the sofa.

330

"Mandy's in high school, and Charley and the Bear are in love and will probably get married and leave me. Doe, who used to be my very best friend and come over all the time, is now so busy being Mrs. Wesley Cunningham I haven't seen her in weeks. Even Hazel has her own life apart from me, and now you've got a new lover—and I seem to be the only one who just stays the same . . ."

"Oh, *sugar,* you'll *never* get rid of me!" He rushed to her and hugged her. "I *love* you, sweetie, no matter *how* many pretty little boys I take up with. You know that don't you?" He shook her gently, forcing her to look at him. "Don't you?"

"Yes, I guess so." She took another hit on the joint before passing it to him. "And I guess dear old Vince will always be around, but, damn it, that's not enough! I want more out of life than a love-struck starving artist and a—"

"And an aging old auntie?" he finished for her, smiling a little sadly. "You could have *anyone* you wanted, Tara. You're beautiful, successful, rich, why, if I had *half* of what you do, I'd probably *own* the world!"

"Sometimes I wish I didn't have it, Izzy. Sometimes I wish I was still working for Jim Glasser, writing my column, struggling to make it on my own. All this—" She swept out a hand, taking in the luxurious room and manicured lawn beyond the windows. "I didn't earn it. It was given to me in a divorce settlement."

"Now that's just simply *not true,* sugar. Why, the royalties on *Seattle Slum* have paid for this place twice over! And I *know* *Passion's Rogue* is going to be just as big, maybe bigger! What happened to your confidence? You used to say you had the world by the short hairs, remem-

She smiled. "Ah, yes, the good old days of innocence and wonder. Or as Jim would say, when I was full of piss and vinegar and nothing was impossible. Then I thought money was the answer to everything. Money meant a mink coat to keep me warm, though God knows why anyone ever needs a mink coat in California. And money meant caviar and escargots to fill my belly, and it meant not riding a bus but driving a Mercedes."

"It also meant bringing Mandy home to live with you," he reminded her gently.

"Yes, that's true, but now even Mandy doesn't need me anymore. She's always busy with her horse shows and her friends, going here and there with kids I don't even know."

"I think you're having a case of the feeling-sorry-for-me blues, sugar, and it's time you got out of the house and started living again. What about this married man you spent the weekend with? You must have *liked* him or you wouldn't have just dropped out of sight for two whole days and nights. Come on, sugar, tell me about it, won't you? It might help to talk about him . . ." He clipped the joint onto Tara's roach clip and held it to her lips while she took a toke. "That's the first time you've spent the night with a man since I've known you. Oh, I know you've gone to bed with other guys since Eric, but this one must be pretty special or you—"

"It was Eric."

"It was Eric?" he parroted incredulously. "You're kidding? How in the world did that happen?"

"I ran into him at Doe's wedding and, well—it just sort of—happened." She sighed and put her feet up on the coffee table, glad that the secret was out. Glad of a chance to tell someone. She trusted Izzy, for all his love of gossip, he was fiercely loyal to her and would not breath a word if she asked him not to. Besides, talking to Izzy she was able to get both a man's and a woman's point of view. "Why don't you make us a drink and I'll tell you all about it?" She grinned, for the first time showing a little humor. "It must be the cocktail hour somewhere in the world . . ."

"Sure thing, sugar." He went to the bar. "What shall we have? Champagne?"

"No, make it a screwdriver—mild. I need the vitamin C with all the cigarettes I've been smoking lately."

He rejoined her a moment later and she told him about her weekend with Eric, how wonderful his lovemaking had been, but how uncomfortable and embarrassed she had felt when she was not actually in bed with him. How their conversation, when they were sober, had been strained and awkward. How she could not forget the past when she was with him. "I suppose I'm probably the biggest ass in the world for not jumping at the chance to marry him. I know he still loves me, he told me often enough. But, damn it, I just can't forgive him, Izzy! What's wrong with me, anyway?"

"I don't know, sugar. You can bet if I had a chance at a hunk like Eric Marlowe, hell and wild horses couldn't keep me from him." He sipped his drink daintily, swinging one foot as he mulled over the problem. "I think it's because you've always felt so betrayed by your mother and then when you finally did find the man of your dreams, you discovered he was part of that betrayal. Does that make any sense?"

"Nothing makes any sense. That's the problem. God knows, I'm not the type to label people, blame them for my troubles. My life has been damn good since my mother's death. I've made it good. And I've worked hard to get where I am. I know that all I have isn't entirely due to Zock's generosity, that I did in fact earn most of it myself. I made almost a million bucks on the movie, not to mention the royalties on *Seattle Slum* . . ."

"That's *it!*" Izzy cried. "Your success was earned by the tragedy of your youth. You made your fortune by writing about the *very thing* that caused you so much pain as a child. You could almost say that every dollar you earned somehow paid for every tear you shed as a child. Or does that sound too dramatic?"

"It does sound a little dramatic, Izzy," she laughed. "I'm not sure I buy that."

"Think about it. *Seattle Slum* made you rich and famous—but the real Seattle slum you lived in as a child brought you shame and pain. Don't you see the correlation? You can't be comfortable with your success *knowing* that you used your mother and Eric and, yes, Mandy too to make it. You wouldn't have had a story without them, am I right?"

"Yes, I guess I see your point. I've never really thought of it that way. Maybe you're right—"

"Of course I am. Subconsciously you feel you wouldn't have had the success without exposing everyone you loved. You know, when I first met you, I used to wonder why you didn't seem more proud of your book. I mean, my God, it was a blockbuster, and you would just shrug off my compliments, almost as if you were embarrassed by it, and you'd hardly ever talk to me about it, remember? You were even that way on talk shows—embarrassed by your own success. I thought you were just being modest, but now I realize that you were ashamed of it. That's it, isn't it?"

"Oh, come on, Izzy, I don't think—"

"Yes, yes, it's perfectly clear to me now. You're actually ashamed of having told the story of Eric and your mother. And that's why you can't forgive him—because deep down you still can't forgive yourself."

"Okay, I think this conversation has gone far enough," she said in a tight voice. "If I wanted to spill my guts, I'd go to a shrink. Besides, you're way off base. I *wanted* to write the story—it had nothing to do with Eric. It was something I had to do for myself—to purge my soul, if you will." She said it facetiously, a little arrogantly.

"Maybe—but you haven't purged it yet, have you? Does Eric know he's Mandy's father? Does he know the book is really about him and his rather unnatural love affair with your mother?" He did not wait for her to answer. "Of course he doesn't. You're afraid to tell him. Why, Tara? Don't you think he has a right to know? Oh, I'll admit the book was very cleverly written, so cleverly written that unless a person knew the story as well as I do they wouldn't ever connect it to your past. But remember, we've had some pretty in-depth talkathons about your life when we were high—and you were honest with yourself." He got to his feet, took their glasses and went to the bar to mix fresh drinks. "That's what's eating at you now. You want to be honest, but you've lived with the lie so long you're scared to death of either Eric or Mandy finding out." He brought her the drink and sat

down again. "And if he was back in your life, both he
and Mandy could well discover the truth, couldn't they?
I mean, goodness, the older she gets the more she looks
like him. She's his spitting image, as my dear departed
mum would have said."

"Light another joint, Izzy," she sighed wearily. "If I
have to listen to this drivel, I may as well get high."

"Drivel it *isn't*, my dear—and you *know* it!" He
flounced to her desk and lit a joint, brought it back to
her.

"Okay, okay, so let's say it's true. So what? Now what
do I do about it? Knowing it's true doesn't change anything. I still feel the same way about him."

"What way? Tell me *exactly* how you feel about him."

"Like I never want to see him again—and if I don't, I
will never be happy again." There, she thought, I've said
it. As fucked up as it sounded, it was the truth. She did
feel betrayed, used, lied to, even though Eric had been
innocent, had never intentionally hurt her, the pain was
still there, still raw after all these years. And Mandy was
a constant reminder.

"Maybe I should go to a psychiatrist, find out why I
can't forgive him. I mean, I'm not totally stupid. I know
he didn't deliberately cheat on me with my mother—but
that's the way I feel just the same. And I feel like he ran
out on Mandy as well."

"Oh, come *on*, sweetie, how in the world could a
fourteen-year-old boy take care of a baby? Use your common sense, at least. Is that what you *wanted* him to do?
Take the baby and raise her? Be a father to her? *Surely*
you don't believe that would have been possible under the
circumstances."

"Then why did he have to keep coming back, week after week, taking advantage of a sick old woman, a woman
old enough to be his mother, for God's sake?" she cried
savagely.

"Because that sick old woman, as you call her, probably
gave him more love than he had ever had in his life. He
was a street kid, you said, orphaned, trying to just survive

335

in a world of adults with adult rules. Your mother was probably kind to him—"

Tara laughed shortly. "Oh, she was kind to him all right! She taught him how to fuck like a mink! He even bragged about it, told me he had learned everything he knew about sex from her!"

"Well, you should be thankful—you said he was fantastic in the sack."

"Shit, Izzy, who wants to go to bed with her mother's prize pupil? Prize stud, I guess is more like it." She drank, turning to gaze out across the rolling hills. How peaceful and untouched they looked. How inviting. A quiet haven for a weary traveler. Her head ached. Izzy was too close to the truth for comfort and she wanted to end this conversation. She had been a fool to ever admit having spent the weekend with Eric. She knew she would be opening the old can of worms by doing so, but had felt a great need to tell someone. Well, she had told someone and look where it had led. "Listen, let's change the subject, okay. I don't need to be psychoanalyzed—"

"Maybe you *do*, sweetie, but that's *your* decision." He smiled brightly. "Okay, the subject is closed. Let's think of something *terribly exciting* to do. You should get out of the house, go on a fabulous shopping spree, do something wild and crazy."

"Why? I have so many clothes now I can't shut my closet doors."

"So buy something else. Jewelry, a new car."

"I have two new cars and enough jewelry to make the Gabor sisters, Sammy Davis Jr. and Liberace green with envy."

"Well, really, Tara," he sniffed, "how can you expect to shake the doldrums with that kind of attitude?" His foot bounced impatiently and he recrossed his legs, slipping one slim ankle securely behind the other. She really was quite impossible.

"Look, why don't you take the rest of the afternoon off and go play with Chuckie-pooh? I'm in a lousy mood and really shouldn't lay it on you." She patted his cheek fondly. "I know you're trying to help, Izzy, and I'm being a bitch. I'd really be better off alone."

"Well, I like that!" He was clearly indignant. "Do you think I'd go off and leave you alone when you're feeling so down?"

"Hey, chum, it's not the end of the world," she laughed. "I've just got a case of the blahs. Probably going to start my period or some such female ailment. Go on—go help your friend take inventory of his erotic apparel."

"Darling, I have the most *marvelous* idea!" he shrieked, turning to her so quickly she jumped back, startled. "Let's take a ride and see Chuck. I've wanted you two to meet for some time. I know you'll just love him. And it will give you a chance to see his new shop. It's really quite elegant, you know."

"Oh, I don't think so, Izzy. I'm expecting a headache."

"Come on, sugar. It'll do you the world of good. It's a marvelous day, simply *too* gorgeous to stay inside." He jumped to his feet and danced across the floor to fling open the drapes. Strong sunlight flooded the room and he slid open the glass door, bringing the sweet, fresh scent of wild sage and roses inside. "Just smell that—simply heavenly, darling! Come on, what do you say? Let's go see Chuck's place and then maybe the three of us can pop into The Bistro for cocktails."

"I don't think so, Izzy. You go ahead."

"I simply will not take no for an answer. I am dedicating myself to cheering you up." He pranced back to her, pulling her to her feet. "Come on now, sweetie, trust your old Auntie Izzy, I swear you'll have a marvelous time."

"There'll be people around, and crowds—"

"There's not a soul around, except the carpenters. Chuck isn't opening for two weeks, remember?"

"How could I forget?" she murmured wryly. "You offered my services as mascot that evening."

"Well, this will give you a chance to tell him you won't be able to make it." He grinned mischievously, knowing how she hated to say no to anyone. "Come on, sugar, go upstairs and powder your pretty little nose, slip into something divine and let's set Rodeo Drive on its ear!"

She was weakening and he pushed his advantage. "His shop is just the *most*," he gushed, steering her toward the stairs. "He has the most outrageous paraphernalia—for the discreet consumer, of course. Who knows, maybe you'll find something to buy?"

"Oh, sure, I really need an erotic wardrobe and some new sex props. Why, just the other day I was thinking I should have at least a dozen dildos and french ticklers to round out my life."

"Ohhh, he has the most clever vibrators I've ever seen," Izzy whispered behind his hand, giggling naughtily. "And I know how *fond* you are of vibrators . . ."

"You prick," she laughed, starting up the stairs.

Izzy raised an eyebrow. "My dear, that's the first time anyone has ever called me *that*. A cunt, yes, to be sure —but a *prick*—really, Tara!"

"You idiot. Okay, you've talked me into it. But just for a few minutes, to meet him and have a drink. No dinner, no stopping by The Factory for 'just one dance'—promise?"

"I promise. Now get upstairs and change and I'll go tell Charley we're leaving."

Paraphernalia from Eden was like an oasis. Situated in the center of the block between two rather staid businesses, it was a cloister of shrubbery, trees and wildly blooming flowers. The front was solid glass, enabling one to see inside, up the curved staircase of polished mahogany and wine-colored carpet to the second floor. A huge crystal chandelier dominated the ceiling in the main room and a long, quietly elegant showcase hugged three walls. Several carpenters were busily painting, sawing, hanging wallpaper or peering at blueprints.

"He must be in the back," Izzy told Tara. "Wait here and I'll have a look."

She wandered around the huge showroom, surprised to find it done in such good taste. The decor was clearly expensive and the carpets, even though covered with white drop cloths, were soft and springy under her feet. The wall hangings and drapes were in quiet good taste and the whole feel about it, even though still empty, was one of elegance and sophistication. Not at all what she had expected from a "boutique of erotic apparel"—red velvet drapes and gaudy whorehouse gold trim.

"Sugar," Izzy called, "here he is!" She turned to see a slender young man in a ruby Pucci silk shirt, open to the navel, being led toward her. His slim hips were ajangle with gold chains that fell in graduating degrees over his cream-colored suede trousers and his dark, wavy hair was held back in a long ponytail by a wide gold ribbon tied in a perky bow. He was clean shaven and quite handsome, and when Tara looked into his face she could well have been gazing at her own mirrored reflection.

"Charles!" she gasped.

"Yes?" the man inquired politely, peering curiously at her suddenly white face. "Have we met?" Then he too blanched. "My God, it can't be! Tara!"

"What is this?" Izzy demanded. "Don't tell me you two know each other." He giggled, squeezing the man's hand and looking up at him adoringly. "And all this time I've been trying to get you together."

"I—I didn't know—I had no idea—" Tara stammered. She took a step backward, her hand at her throat, eyes wide with shocked recognition.

"I didn't either," Charles said, just as breathless, just as shocked. He turned on Izzy almost furiously. "You bitch, why didn't you tell me your famous boss was my kid sister?"

"What?" Izzy cried, his eyes going wildly from one to the other. "I didn't *know!* I *swear* it! Oh, my word, this *is* amusing, isn't it?"

"Amusing, my ass," Charles snapped. He turned to Tara, reaching out a hand to her. "Tara, you must believe me. I had no idea—the name Remington, you see —I didn't connect it." He dropped his hand when she took another backward step. "I'm truly sorry, it must be a hell of a shock for you."

"To put it mildly," she said, struggling to regain her composure. The workmen were all listening and pretending not to. "Ah, why don't we get out of here, Izzy, I mean—" She gestured toward the carpenters.

"By all means, a drink is definitely in order." He almost ran to open the door and hold it for her and she rushed outside, standing with trembling legs and taking in deep breaths of fresh air.

My God, my brother, Charles, she thought incredulously, the wealthy and infamous proprietor of Paraphernalia from Eden. She would not have believed it in a million years, so sure had she been that he would end up a derelict in some male whorehouse on skid row. Jesus.

"Tara, I really don't know what to say." Charles walked on one side of her, Izzy on the other. The Bistro was just a block up the street and they headed in that direction. "My God, it just never occurred to me that my little sister was the famous novelist Tara Remington!" He chuckled, looking her up and down. "You've certainly changed, sis, and how!"

"I might say the same to you," she retorted sharply, eyes raking over him. "It never occurred to me that my —brother—was a respectable merchant."

"Merchant! How wonderfully quaint," Charles laughed and Izzy looked dazedly from one to the other.

"Well, it seems I'm odd man out in this touching family reunion," he pouted. "Chuckie, why didn't you tell me you had a sister? I distinctly remember asking you about your family and you telling me that you were an only child, orphaned as an infant and raised by the nuns."

"He said that?" Tara hooted, unable to control her burst of wild laughter. "Oh, really, Charles, that's a good one! Raised by the nuns, huh?" She went into peals of laughter that caused passersby to pause and stare curiously at her.

"Well," Charles said huffily, his eyes suddenly frosty. "*Your* press release certainly didn't mention anything about our happy home on Fourth Street—" He broke off suddenly, stopping to stare at her. "Jesus, *Seattle Slum* was about you—about us, wasn't it? When I read it, I remember thinking it could have been my life story. I guess the joke's on me. It *was* my life story!"

"What in the world are you two *talking* about?" Izzy cried, tugging first at Charles' sleeve, then turning to look at Tara. "Will you please let *me* in on the joke?"

They were at the entrance of The Bistro and Tara opened the door for herself and hurried inside, wanting a drink badly.

Charles Woodhauser, alive and well and living in Southern California as he had threatened years ago. She wondered if he too had changed his last name. She could not recall Izzy ever calling him anything but Fuckie Chuckie or just plain Chuck.

They were shown to a table near the bar and gave their order to the waiter, and then Charles turned and took Tara's hand. She pulled back a little but he held on.

"Tara, there's nothing I can say to make this meeting any easier for you, but please, just listen for a minute, okay? You have every reason to hate me. I understand that now. But please try to understand me a little too. You weren't the only one who suffered as a child. It was hard as hell for me as well. Having a drunken hooker as a mother, a kid sister known all over the neighborhood as 'Ragpicker'—kids used to throw their garbage on me when I was walking to school and yell, 'Here, Woodhauser, give this to your sister for lunch!'—just little things like that. Did you know you had the nickname of 'Garbage Gertie' because you were always rooting in the gutters for that junk of yours?"

"I was looking for pop bottles and stuff to sell," Tara answered stiffly, taking a long swallow of her Harvey Wallbanger. The firey mixture of liquor burned a comforting streak through her belly, relaxing the knots there a little. She fumbled for a cigarette and Charles held his thin, gold lighter for her. She saw the initials C.E. in small diamond chips on the side and asked with a sneer, "Who'd you go to bed with for that?"

Charles looked hurt for only a second and then chuckled quietly. "Dear little sis, I don't do that anymore. I can easily afford anything I want now."

"What does the E stand for?" She hated to ask, did not want to show any interest in him at all.

"Eden," he shrugged, "as in Paraphernalia from Eden. If you can change your name, why not me?" He sipped his brandy Alexander, looking at her over the rim of the glass kindly, almost sadly. "I tried like hell to find you, Tara, a hundred times since moving to Los Angeles. I must have written every fan magazine in town asking for any information of your whereabouts, but I always got the same response: 'Sorry, we cannot give out our writer's home addresses.' I finally tracked down a secretary who worked with you at that local gossip paper, what was it called?"

"Beverly Hills Beat."

"Yes, that's it." He took his time lighting a cigarette, placed it between Izzy's lips and lit another one for himself. "But by that time you had quit or gone on to something else." He shrugged. "Then you just dropped out of sight completely, according to everyone I talked to. I used to see your byline sometimes, then suddenly, puff, even those vanished. I thought you had probably gotten married or left the state or something. There was no way of locating you."

"Why did you want to?" She said it sullenly, angry with him for being so gentle with her, so concerned.

"Because I had a lot of apologizing to do," he said softly, reaching across the table to take her hand again. She was so surprised she did not pull away, but stared into his green-flecked brown eyes so much like her own. "Tara, I was such a heel when you last saw me. I realize that now, but, Christ, I was just a kid then, a big dumb shit not knowing who was friend and who was foe. Do you think it was easy, being a homosexual? My God, admitting that was like asking to be burned at the stake. I was so confused and unhappy, and, yes, ashamed of my sexual—difference.

"So I went the other way. Instead of hiding in the closet, I flaunted it." He laughed wryly. "And got the shit beat out of me more times than I can count." He tapped his front teeth. "All caps," he said. "Compliments

342

of a bunch of so-called 'straights' in our old neighborhood."

Izzy's bright parrot eyes darted from Tara to Charles and back again, taking in every expression and gesture they made. He could not believe what he was hearing. His boss and his lover—sister and brother? It was *too* exciting for words!

Tara dropped her gaze from her brother's face and stared down into her glass. She did not know what to say. This was not the way she had expected to find him. She had hated him for years, had wanted to go on hating him, blaming him for her lack of family. It had been her hate for him that had given her the strength to get out of Seattle and make a life for herself and Mandy. She looked up at him, her voice sharp with pain when she said. "You haven't asked about Mandy. Don't you want to know what happened to your other sister?"

"Mandy? Is that her name? Sorry, I forgot, I guess." He grinned apologetically and ran a bejeweled hand through his fluffy bangs. "That's another reason I wanted to find you, to ask if there was anything I could do—to—to help in some way . . ."

"You're sixteen years too late," she said shortly, tossing off her drink and holding up her hand to signal the waiter.

"Sixteen years—it can't be possible." Charles looked at Izzy, as if asking him to verify it. "Sixteen years?" he said again, shaking his head. "Jesus."

"Yes, that's right," Izzy said gaily, looking brightly at both of them. "We're having her sweet sixteen birthday party next month, December eighteenth. Tara always says Mandy was the sweetest Christmas present she ever got. Right, sugar?"

"Where in the world did you get a name like that?" Charles asked, trying for lightness. "Don't tell me Ma named her. She went in for names from literature, like yours from *Gone With the Wind* and mine, she used to tell me, was from Dickens. She even changed her own name from Bertha to Belle because she used to say—"

"I named her," Tara said, cutting him off. She gave an embarrassed shrug. "Mom was too—ill for a long time after Mandy was born. And I was just a kid, you know, and I guess I thought Mandy was about the best sounding name I could give a baby. Rhymed with candy, right?"

"Yeah, you were always a real candy hound," Charles teased. "I remember you used to walk for miles, up and down the gutters picking up those crummy bottles, then you'd spend all the money you got from them on candy."

"Oh, I did not," Tara protested, but she laughed good-naturedly, remembering the better days (the few that there had been) when she and Charles had been close. "I used to buy groceries sometimes—and I *always* bought you that kind of bubble gum with the baseball stars in the wrappers. What was it called, Double Bubble?"

"Do you remember that?" Charles asked, his eyes soft and warm with memories. "Ah, the days of our innocence." He squeezed her hand which he still held. "Was it really tough on you, sis, when Ma died?"

"Yes," she said simply, honestly. "It was damn tough—but I was lucky, I guess. Remember that big Irish cop that used to drop in sometimes and check on us, see how we were getting along after Pa ran off? He used to bring us clothes and things from some charity center." Charles nodded his head. "Well, he took us in, me and Mandy, and found us a foster home."

She told him about the Davidsons, their fatal automobile accident and her flight to California with the money she had found in the house. How she had managed to pay for a year's care for Mandy while she went out to make it on her own. How tough it had been, a sixteen-year-old girl alone in a strange city, with no education, no skills to speak of.

"All I can say is, thank God for Jim Glasser. He gave me a chance when no one else would. He literally taught me how to write and convinced me that I was good. I think writing is the only occupation in the world that doesn't require at least a high school diploma."

"I should have known you'd end up a writer," Charles said. "You always had your nose in a book or else you were scribbling away in your diary."

"She's a *marvelous* writer," Izzy put in, trying to find

his way into the conversation. He was beginning to feel a bit like an eavesdropper, listening to their intimate recollections of the past.

"I know, I read *Seattle Slum.*"

"I'm surprised you didn't recognize me," Tara said. "My picture was on the dust jacket."

"All I saw was some foxy young lady, beautiful and sophisticated, far too glamorous to be my little ragpicker sister!"

"Tara a ragpicker!" Izzy hooted. "It's too, *too* incredible for words! My, wouldn't the gossip columnists freak out for that item?"

They talked and laughed through another couple of rounds of drinks and Tara found herself warming to Charles. Ready to forgive him for past hurts and slights. She felt she understood him now. It could not have been easy for him, either. A poor, abandoned homosexual, literally on his own from his early teens. He had obviously done what he had had to do to survive.

Sitting across from him, listening to his stories, she had to admit that she probably had not made it any easier for him either. Her own hostilities and fears had put a breach between them as children because she had not understood his life style, had not understood her mother's problems, had not really understood anything about the world she was trapped in. Charles, being older and more streetwise than she, had known what their mother was and why, and had acted accordingly. He had taken the responsibility of his own life into his own hands, leaving Tara to struggle along as best she could. And Tara had gone on dreaming, reading fantasy, hoping that she would wake up in a pretty world, an ordered, clean, happy world where no one would jeer at her and she would not find her mother sprawled naked beneath strange men.

It was after five when Tara finally said, "Well, we really should be going, Izzy. I didn't plan on staying this long and I'm sure Hazel is a nervous wreck, thinking we might miss dinner." She gave him an impish look. "She's making your favorite dish tonight, beef Wellington, just to prove that she can cook it as well as you can."

"No way," Izzy said firmly, lips pursed. "I'll admit that Hazel is an—adequate cook, but really, my dear, no one *but no one* can make beef Wellington as well as yours truly!"

"Izzy, you surprise me," Charles drawled, letting his gaze linger lovingly on Izzy's flushed face. "You didn't tell me you were a chef."

"You mean he hasn't taken over your kitchen and whipped up any of his famous dishes for you?" Tara asked.

"No, he hasn't—the bitch."

"Well, toots," Izzy giggled mischievously, "we've been far too busy *eating*—so there hasn't been any time for *cooking!*"

The drinks had mellowed Tara considerably and she heard herself asking Charles to join them for dinner. Now why did I do that? she asked herself, then answered, maybe it's not too late to have a good relationship with him. And he is Mandy's brother as well. She has a right to know him.

"Well, yes, thank you, I'd love to, sis." He seemed as surprised as she that he had been invited. "Now that I know who you are, I'd adore seeing this fabulous mansion you're reputed to be living in. Is it really as grand as the fan mags say it is?"

"Oh my, yes, it's simply fab!" Izzy gushed, squeezing Charles' shoulder affectionately. He could not seem to keep his hands off him, Tara noticed with a smile. She had to admit that Charles was very handsome, in an obviously effeminate way. "Acres and acres of land, stables, an honest to God groom, and the house is a virtual mansion —a palace! It's not to be believed, Chuckie, and my little sugar did all the decorating herself. Just wait until you see it!" He clapped his hands together in delight. "Oh, I'm just *so* thrilled, I can't stand it! My two favorite people, together again at last! It's the stuff dreams are made of. I should have known you were related. It's so obvious now, seeing you together. You have the same eyes, you know, and the same coloring, the same square, stubborn jaw—"

"And just possibly the same wardrobe at home in our closets," Charles laughed. "If you ever need some devastating little number for a special occasion, sis, I'll lend you one of my gowns!"

Izzy kept up a steady stream of excited chatter as they left The Bistro and walked the half block to where Tara had left her car. Charles raised his eyebrows at the shiny red Mercedes-Benz and quipped that it was sure a far cry from the days of walking the gutters in Seattle. Then he had moved a couple of cars over in the parking lot to his own automobile, a gleaming, cream-colored Maserati, and it was Tara's turn to chuckle.

"Not too shabby, bro," she said, looking at his initials in gold plate on the side of the sleek automobile. "How'd you manage these?"

"The salesman was crazy about me," Charles camped, preening comically and they all laughed.

"Izzy, why don't you ride with Charles in case we get separated on the freeway," Tara said, walking toward her Mercedes and waving away the parking boy who had dashed up to assist her. "See you guys back at the house."

CHAPTER SIXTEEN

"ARE YOU GAY?" Mandy asked, her direct blue eyes looking into Charles'.

"Mandy!" Tara gasped, and Charles laughed and reached over to tousle Mandy's hair.

"It's all right, sis," he said to Tara, then turned to Mandy. "Yes, as a matter of fact, I am gay—the happiest guy in town!"

"That's not what I meant," Mandy persisted. "I mean are you a homosexual?" She threw a mischievous grin at Izzy. "Sometimes you act as silly as Izzy."

"Well, thanks a lot, snooks," Izzy pouted and everyone at the table laughed, even Charley, who had been cool and reserved most of the evening. She had been shocked speechless when Tara had brought Charles home for dinner.

They had finished dinner (Izzy sighing ecstatically over Hazel's beef Wellington) and were now enjoying a light, airy chocolate mousse.

Mandy had casually accepted her brother, asking bluntly where he had been for the past sixteen years. And she had accepted just as casually his explanation that he had tried to find them but because Tara's name changed it had been impossible.

"Oh, did Tara tell you?" Mandy said. "When I was twelve she let me change my name legally to Remington, just like hers. Neither one of us liked our Dad's name—Woodhauser. Yuk!" She frowned slightly, looking Charles over carefully. "You must look like our Mom, 'cause you and Tara really look an awful lot alike. I guess I must take after my Dad." She shrugged. "But I never met him. He died when I was a baby."

Tara and Izzy exchanged glances and Charley quickly changed the subject, asking Charles about his business. He had kept them in stitches with his many amusing anecdotes of his life in the erotic apparel game.

"Yes, little sis," he laughed now. "I am indeed gay and am not ashamed to say so. One of these days the gays are going to revolt in this country, stand up for their rights as the third or alternate sex and be accepted just as the straights are."

"I don't know why everybody makes such a big deal of it," Mandy said, spooning chocolate mousse. "Gosh, you're just people like anybody else. I mean, you don't have two heads or anything gross like that."

Charles laughed. "I'm glad you're so understanding, Mandy. If more people thought the way you do, we could all come out of the closet."

"Why in the world do gay people live in closets, anyway?" she wanted to know, a frown furrowing her smooth brow. "I mean, gosh, you don't really *live* in one, do you? What does that mean, Chuck? Izzy never tells me anything when I ask him."

"And you should hear some of the things she asks me," Izzy groaned, rolling his eyes.

Charles explained what coming out of the closet meant and Mandy said, "Is that all it means? Just not being afraid to admit who you like? Gosh, what stupid laws." Then she giggled and said, "I just saw a big fat woman at the 7-11 store last week wearing a button that said 'Fat Power,' so I guess they want the same things that the gays do, right?"

"Right, honey," Charles grinned. "All any of us want is just the right to be ourselves and be with whom we choose."

"Well," said Tara. "I guess your time is coming. First it was Black Power, then Women's Rights—"

"And don't forget Gray Power for the over sixty-fivers," Charley laughed. "Hey, maybe I should start a movement for Secretary Power."

"Huh," Izzy snorted. "You have it so flipping easy it's not even funny. I don't know a secretary alive who wouldn't change places with you in a second!"

"Oh, yeah," Charley retorted. "And how about your cushy job, sweetie? Jeez, the fringe benefits alone are outrageous."

"*Please,* I look *atrocious* in fringe, darling," Izzy sniffed and everyone laughed.

"Gads," Charles said, "maybe I should give up Paraphernalia from Eden and get a job working for Tara."

"Good God, no," Tara cried. "I have enough freeloaders on the payroll as it is!"

"Someone mention my name?" Vince asked, ambling in from the kitchen. He stooped to kiss Tara's cheek. "Hi, honey—don't get up. Hazel let me in through the back door and said I might still be in time for dinner." He glanced around the table. "But it looks like I'm a little too late."

"No, you're not, Mr. Vince," Hazel called from the doorway. She pushed her ample hip against the door to hold it open and bustled over to the table, a plate in each hand. "Just sit yourself down. I found a little piece of beef left over that Mr. Izzy missed." Her eyes twinkled in Izzy's direction and he pulled a face. "And here's a little salad and a roll. Now you just help yourself and I'll see if there's a bit of vegetable left."

Hazel adored the dreamy artist and loved to fuss over him. She often invited him into her kitchen (a privilege few others shared) and would bustle about making bread or some pastry while he lounged at the table and sketched her. She just wished that Miss Tara would come to her senses and see that he was in love with her; his big dreamy brown eyes following her adoringly whenever she was in the room. And he was clearly enchanted with young Mandy. If Tara had any sense, she would marry him before he got tired of waiting around. Ah well, it was none of her business what any of them did, she supposed, clicking out of the room and bumping the swinging door open with her hip even though her hands were free.

Tara introduced Vince and Charles, and Vince raised his eyebrows a little. He too had heard about Tara's notorious brother and had certainly never expected to find him so comfortably seated at Tara's table.

"Oh, you're an artist," Charles exclaimed when Vince explained that he had been out back sketching. He picked up Vince's portfolio and glanced through it. "These are wonderful. I must get you to paint my portrait. You do people as well as horses, don't you?"

"Oh, did you draw a new picture of Midnight and Macaroni?" Mandy cried, snatching the pad from Charles. "Let me see."

"Yes, I do portraits sometimes. What did you have in mind?" He pulled up a chair next to Charley.

"Something terribly elegant. I've always seen myself in one of those marvelous old seventeenth-century poses, you know, with yards of lace at my throat and wrists. Perhaps a burgundy velvet frock coat, sitting in a Queen Anne chair . . ."

"The *Queen* Anne chair sounds good," Izzy murmured, ducking when Charles faked a punch at him.

"Seriously, Vince, can you do it for me? I want a *huge* one, perhaps five feet by three and a half feet. I want to hang it in my new store." He reached next to him to squeeze Izzy's hand. "Won't that be a camp, lover? Your truly bigger than life right on that wall facing the front door—you know, the one above the bar? I love it!"

"Yes, I think it would be good," Izzy said. "And Vince is a wonderful artist. You should see the sketches he does of Tara. I have dozens of them that he threw away."

"You do?" Vince asked. "Where did you find them?"

"I rescued them from the wastepaper basket. Goodness, you might be famous one day and then look at all the originals I'll have! I also have several you did of

352

Mandy on her horse, and a simply fabulous character study of Teddy leaning on his manure rake."

Vince laughed a little self-consciously. "Gee, I didn't think anybody'd want those. Guess I'd better be more careful where I throw things away."

"Don't you *dare* throw them away, dear boy," Izzy cried. "If you don't want them, give them to me. Signed, of course."

"Why would you want those old sketches of me?" Tara asked, clearly puzzled.

"Because you're so luscious, sugar," Izzy cooed. "And if I was straight I'd whisk you off to never-never land so fast it would make your head spin."

"I think you live in never-never land most of the time," Tara grinned, then turned to Vince and asked, "How would you like to be my escort for the gala grand opening of the Beverly Hills branch of Paraphernalia from Eden?"

"What the devil is that?" After she explained, he said, "Sure, why not? Do we get any free samples?"

Charles winked broadly. "Hey, big guy, for *you*—anything! I'll even demonstrate them for you free of charge."

"Why, you fickle bitch," Izzy pouted and Mandy looked from him to Charles in confusion.

"What are all you guys talking about, anyway?" she grumbled. "Chuck's new place is just a clothes store, isn't it?"

"Mandy, why don't you go help Teddy blanket the horses? It's supposed to get pretty cold tonight." Tara gave her a look that said, "Excuse yourself—it's the adult hour."

"I know what that means," Mandy sighed, pushing away from the table. "You're going to talk dirty, right?"

"Right, brat, now take a hike," Tara said, reaching up to hug her. She swatted her on the fanny and Mandy blew her a kiss and ran from the room.

"Tara, she's absolutely precious," Charles said. "You've done a wonderful job raising her. But she seems so, well, I guess the word I'm looking for is pure. Naive. Isn't she rather innocent for a sixteen-year-old? God, you should see the kids that come into my place on little Santa Monica. They can't be over fifteen, sixteen years old and they're buying vibrators, Joy Jell and French ticklers. Most of them are stoned out of their minds on something or other."

"Well, Mandy spent most of her life in a special school, you know. She hasn't been exposed to the harsher realities of life, thank God for that."

"Yet she seemed to accept my homosexuality so casually. Most people get pretty uptight or embarrassed by it."

"Well, I've always believed in being totally honest with her about things like that. People's different choices, you know. Like, we all march to the tune of a different drummer."

"Gads, I'm glad I found you, sis!" He leaned over to kiss her cheek and Tara found herself blushing a little.

"Look at them, Vince," Izzy said, beaming happily at his two favorite people. "Aren't they beautiful? I'd love to have a painting of them just like that."

"Uh-huh." Vince finished off the last of his salad. "I've been trying to get Tara to sit for me ever since I met her, but you know how she is." He reached for the chocolate mousse that Hazel had brought him and dug in. "Damn, this is good. I don't see how you people can eat like this every night without gaining twenty pounds at every meal."

Charley stood. "Shall I have Hazel serve coffee in the billiard room?" she asked Tara.

"Yes, please, Charley. Thank you."

"What does everyone want with their coffee?" Charley asked. She had served them all for so long she knew what each would have almost without asking, but did so from habit. And sometimes Izzy got fancy and tried something new. "Brandy, Charles, or a liqueur?"

"Oh dear, I'm stuffed," Charles sighed, leaning away from the table to pat his stomach. He was as lean as a cougar, his ruby Pucci body shirt showing not the slightest bulge. "But if you insist, I'll have a little Courvoisier."

They retired to the billiard room and Charley and

Vince shot a game of pool. A joint was fired up and passed about the group. Charles sighed, "I can honestly say I've never felt more relaxed and completely at home anywhere else I've ever been. You have a rare talent for making people comfortable, sis."

"Thanks, bro," Tara grinned over the rim of her anisette glass. It was a good evening. The conversation lively and the guests interesting. A fire blazed in the fireplace and outside the night was bright with stars. Even though it was only October and the days still sometimes felt like summer, the nights had been cold enough for a fire. Which Tara loved. She had always had a thing about fireplaces and had had two more installed when she had bought her house, making it now four.

"So, tell me what's required of me at your gala affair, Charles. I don't have to come out dressed in a black garter belt and carrying a cat-o'-nine, do I?"

"Marvelous idea," Charles laughed. "Why didn't I think of that?"

"Now that's the kind of painting I'd like to do of Tara." Vince said, turning to look adoringly at her and Charley sank the eight ball.

"Next!" she said and Izzy took over Vince's pool stick. "Rack 'em." She expertly chalked up. She had surprised many a cocky macho type who thought he could beat her, as she played the game almost every day. Tara had long ago designated her to the role of "keep 'em happy shooting pool until I get there."

Mandy stuck her head around the door and said goodnight. "Gotta study for a math test tomorrow," she groaned. "Bye, Chuck, I'm glad you finally found us. You'll come back again, won't you? I want you to come back in the daytime so I can show you my horses and ribbons and trophies and stuff."

"I'd love to see them, honey." He got up and went to her and kissed her goodnight. "And I'm awfully glad I finally found you, too."

Charley beat Izzy and challenged Charles to a game, but he held up his long hands daintily. "My, no I don't play anything more strenuous than checkers, my dear."

"Well, since I can't find a pool partner, I guess I'll go to bed. Tomorrow's a work day." She turned to Tara. "Oh, I forgot to tell you. Thorton called and wants you to meet him for lunch tomorrow. Something about promotion on *Passion's Rogue*. Hy Griffin's in town, staying at the Beverly Hills Hotel, so Thorton asked that you meet them there about noon. In the Polo Lounge."

"Thanks, Charley. Call him in the morning and tell him I'll be there."

Tara slipped between the cool sheets, thinking back over the day. What a surprise it had been to discover that Charles was the lover Izzy had been trying to get her to meet. But most surprising had been the fact that she had actually liked him. As if those awful early days in Seattle had never been. She turned off the lamp by her bed and snuggled deeper into the blankets, the chinchilla tickling her chin. She should have asked Hazel to build a fire for her. She often did her best thinking lying in bed at night, staring into the hypnotic flames of the fireplace.

Vince had said his goodnights soon after Charley had gone to bed, and soon after that Charles and Izzy had taken their leave. Hand in hand, giggling together like young lovers. She wondered how long this affair would last. Izzy was notoriously fickle and any pretty new face could turn his head. Charles certainly qualified as a pretty face. Had he been more masculine, he might have been called macho-handsome. He was built like a stud and acted like a dandy; not an ounce of fat on his six-foot frame, the shoulders broad, tapering down to a flat belly and muscled thighs. He held his well-shaped head high and rather arrogantly. He did not mince in tiny steps when he walked, like Izzy, but strode purposefully like a man who knew where he was going and wanted to get there with a minimum of fuss. Only the expressive fluttering of his long hands and the slight pout of his full lips gave him away.

She wondered if Izzy had told Charles about Eric and the part he had played in their early lives. She rather doubted it, as Izzy was devoutly loyal to her. But still, he loved gossip so much he might just spill it to see how Charles would react.

"Damn, why do I drive myself crazy with all this?" she sighed. Charles had never asked who Mandy's father was and probably did not give a fig who he was. Nobody really gave a damn about it except herself. She supposed even Mandy would simply shrug and say "Hi, Dad" if told that Eric was her father. The young seemed to take things in their stride so much better. Easier.

Why was it that somehow she always ended up thinking about Eric right before she fell asleep?

The Polo Lounge was already packed by the time Tara arrived at a quarter after twelve. Every booth and table in the Lounge, as well as the Loggia and the Patio, were filled with the Beautiful People. There was a waiting line shifting impatiently at the door and the luncheon maître d', Nino Osti, whisked Tara through them and led her to a booth near the bar where Thorton and Hy Griffin were already seated; Thorton speaking earnestly on a pink telephone plugged into their booth. He covered the mouthpiece with his hand. "Hi, honey, be with you in a minute."

Hy stood to let Tara slide into the booth between them. "Wonderful to see you, Tara. You look ravishing as always." He kissed her cheek.

"Hi, Hy," she laughed. "I just love saying that!" She kissed Thorton's cheek and silently mouthed, "Hi, darling."

"Would you like something from the bar, Miss Remington?" the waiter asked.

"Yes, I'll have a glass of white wine, please." She turned to glance idly about the room. "Well, I see all the regulars are here." She smiled and nodded at a dapper elderly gentleman, Eli Robbins, who at age ninety-four was the Polo Lounge's oldest and most faithful customer. He had dined here every day for the past forty years, always immaculately dressed with a dew-fresh white boutonniere in his dark lapel, sitting grandly at the number three table.

Elsewhere throughout the room was the usual spattering of movie stars. Dinah Shore sat across the room from Tara with a small party of friends, and Peter Falk and John Cassevetes laughed it up at a nearby table—to the delight of another table of flirting starlets. All the young women looked like clones of the typical California Golden Girl: long, straight pale hair, professionally sun-streaked by Sassoon or Shacove, big sunglasses pushed atop their heads, lean, lithe bodies encased in French jeans, knit tank tops or midriff-baring crop tops, high-heeled boots or five-inch wedgies. Their male counterparts were dressed almost identically, but they wore more jewelry than the sun-kissed blondes. Gold chains, beads, Oriental good luck charms, medallions, St. Jude and St. Christopher and whatever else the wearer deemed currently with it or "in."

Thorton hung up the phone and turned to Tara. "Hi, honey, sorry about that. I'm trying to put a deal together with Ian Starr, the Beverly Hills hair stylist, you've heard of him, haven't you?" She nodded. "Well, it could be a good thing for both of us. We're meeting this evening to discuss what image he needs. Hey, you look wonderful. How's the project coming?"

She acknowledged the compliment with a slight inclining of the head. "I'm still not completely decided about the Hollywood angle. I've been kicking it around a little but haven't gotten a strong feeling about which way I want to go with it."

"The hard-on for historical novels, romances and Gothics is at its peak," Hy said. "But there's also a trend now for contemporary novels with a female protagonist. A rich female cavorting about in lush backgrounds, the French Riviera, Cannes, Greece, like that one about Jackie Kennedy—can't think of the name of it."

"How do you think *Passion's Rogue* will do?" Tara asked, dipping a corn chip into a bowl of creamy guacamole.

"Should do as well as *Seattle Slum*." He was drinking a Jack Daniels and smoking a long, black cigar which Tara wished he would put out. He was a big man, lusty-looking and vital with steel gray hair that seemed to give his craggy, perpetually tan face an even more youthful look. He wore a diamond on each pinkie finger and, being a New Yorker, dressed in suits and ties at all times—while his California colleagues slouched about in denims and tee-shirts with slogans on them. He was barrel-chested, slim-hipped and boasted that he ran five miles every morning in Central Park before breakfast.

He was married to Molly Clahan Donnelly, a writer who had published stirring accounts of the conditions and rioting in Northern Ireland, but now seemed content to turn out a slim novella once a year in the old-fashioned tradition of Barbara Cartland. She was tiny, five feet even, with red-orange hair and a dusting of tan freckles on her upturned Irish nose. They were still in love after ten years of marriage, a condition that Tara envied.

"There will always be an interest in your books because of the enormous success of *Seattle Slum* and your writing ability will grow with each book. Just like Mary Stewart, Victoria Holt and Rosemary Rogers will always have their followers." He sipped his whiskey and took a puff of his cigar, momentarily obscured by the thick smoke. "By the way, Molly sends her love."

"Why didn't you bring her, you rat? You come out and bask in the California sun for two weeks and leave poor Molly in one of the worst snow storms the East has seen in ten years!"

Hy chuckled. "I did ask her to come with me, but she has a December first deadline on her latest magnolia and mint julep saga and you know how she is about deadlines." He helped himself to a carrot stick. "So I promised to bring her out during the holidays. We'll expect to be invited to Christmas dinner at your house, of course."

Tara grinned. "I'll have to check the guest list and see if I can work you in."

The menus were brought (even though they all knew it by heart) and they ordered lunch, then began discussing the promotion of *Passion's Rogue*.

Thorton had made the usual arrangements for the talk show circuit and had arranged appearances and autograph sessions in all the major cities from Houston to New York. Hy had already nailed down the serialization in a London newspaper, as well as excerpts in *Cosmopolitan* and other leading women's magazines. The Book-of-the-Month Club had not yet answered his call and Thorton was already using their name for the publicity layout, so sure was he that they would agree to his terms. Hy said that Swifty Lazar had sent feelers out about the possible package deal of hardcover, paperback and movie rights—the sum mentioned too staggering for Tara to comprehend.

By the time she left, two hours later, her head spun with figures, dates, numbers, towns. She supposed she would get used to the book plugging game someday, but for now just the thought made her weary. She wished writers did not have to demean themselves by trekking all over the country hawking their books like some kind of traveling medicine man. But the fact remained that it did sell books. Hy had shown her statistics where book sales had doubled and tripled when the author had gone on the road to personally plug it.

She sped along the Ventura Freeway, watching the brisk October wind snatch a handful of dirt and debris from the highway and spin it away in a tidy tunnel of gray. Trees whisked by, bent almost double by the strong wind, and she hunched up the collar of her Somali leopard coat.

She loved autumn. Loved wearing woolens and furs and tall boots. Loved the sound of brittle red leaves crunching underfoot as she walked with Mandy. But most of all she loved returning home and curling up next to a roaring fire, her family and friends around her. She always gathered everyone in her office at the end of the day for shared conversation, a period of relaxation before dinner when everyone could catch up on what everyone else was doing.

She took the Thousand Oaks turnoff and was immediately surrounded by rolling green hills and the calm of a country-day-in-the-fall feeling. Nothing was more peaceful, more beautiful. As always, the serenity of the country drove all thoughts of business, promotional tours and meetings from her mind and she began to hum as she drove toward home.

She thought again of Charles and how odd it was that they had liked one another. He obviously had done a good deal of growing since she had last seen him. He was gracious and charming, but with just the right amount of modesty and self-deprecating humor to save him from being vain. That Izzy was wild about Charles was obvious, and he seemed to return the feelings, so Tara could find no fault with him there. He clearly did not need to ingratiate himself with Tara because of her money—he was wealthy in his own right. That he must know movie stars and jet setters as intimately as she herself did, was obvious, so he was not trying to use her for publicity. He was not sexually attracted to her for two obvious reasons—so he must genuinely like her for herself.

"Jeez, put a lid on it, Tara," she said aloud as she turned into the mile-long lane that led to her house. Some of the trees had already lost their leaves and stood stark and bare against the gray sky, while others, the pine and orange trees, were still vividly green. She had to think of something sensational to wear to Charles' opening, now that she had committed herself to going. She did not usually show up at such public affairs, but the rare times she did, she figured she may as well knock 'em dead. If it stayed as cold as it was tonight, she could wear her new jumpsuit lined with Canadian wild mink or the evening suit in white broadtail she had bought the last time she had gone to New York. She had also picked up a wraparound bracelet in white gold with chunky coral knobs at David Webb's which looked great with the suit. Well, she would try them both and get Izzy's opinion—which was flawless in such matters.

She had decided on the white broadtail (Izzy had gasped, "It's *you*, sugar! Only someone as svelte as you could get away with wearing fur *all over!*"), the chunky coral bracelet, white kid gloves and a white mink hat. Vince was movie-star handsome (rather Warren Beatty-ish) in his tuxedo and camel hair top coat, holding her arm to guide her under the carved golden arches that spelled out Paraphernalia from Eden. Soft romantic music drifted to them as a handsomely clad butler took their coats. Tara recognized the song as an early Frank Sinatra number and remembered Charles had confessed to being a Big Band buff. The old-fashioned music, bringing back memories of more innocent days, lent a rather bizarre touch to the opening of a boutique of erotic apparel.

"Just a glass of white wine," she told Vince when he asked her what she was drinking. He ordered the same for himself.

Tara saw Izzy across the crowded room, waving his hands excitedly as he spoke with a group of richly dressed Beverly Hills matrons. Charles almost had not been approved in Beverly Hills when it was discovered what sort of business he intended to open. So he had gotten a list of names, the more influential and civically minded Beverly Hillites, and invited them for lunch at Au Petit Jean's to show them what he had in mind for Paraphernalia from Eden. He had naturally selected the most discreet gowns and such and skin creams that were more a naughty joke (so the matrons thought) than an actual sex cream to use on someone, and they had been charmed within the hour. He had presented each of them with a small gift as they left the restaurant and issued an invitation to attend the opening. From the awed expressions on their carefully made-up faces, they were still charmed by it all.

Vince led Tara to a corner of the packed room and they leaned against one of the handsome display cases, watching the crowd. Tara recognized the leisure set, the second-generation moneyed crowd who flew to Acapulco or the Bahamas for their winter tan and gamboled in the snow in springtime, in Gstaad, of course.

"I see the perennial tan set is here in full force," Tara said, nodding in the direction of a reed-slim woman who was as brown as a hazel nut, her wrinkled throat looking far too frail to support the weight of her diamond and ruby necklace. Tara recognized her as the ex-countess Incornado Maria Dicorato St. James, whose divorce from steel baron Charlton St. James had made headlines reminiscent of Tara and Zock, Taylor and Burton. She had complained bitterly to the press that her settlement of one million dollars a year was a tacky pittance, barely enough to keep her wardrobe up to date, buy her cosmetics and pay for her health farm trips. And of course there was the chauffeur, her personal maid, the butler, her personal masseuse, the divine cook who had just mastered the art of a flawless soufflé, her hairdresser and traveling charges when following the "season." It was simply disgraceful, she had claimed, meant to publicly embarrass her.

Tara saw the countess' face light up when she saw a famous European writer whose full and hedonistic life was often compared to those of the characters in his overblown novels. She was ready for him when he approached, slipping her hand possessively through his arm and cocking her head coquettishly to one side.

Vince, who did not know one celebrity from another and did not care to, gazed up at the portrait of Charles he had painted and which now hung above the bar. It was as impressive as Charles had known it would be. He sat imperiously on an antique chair of heavy, intricately carved design, his hands dangling languidly over the arms, long fingers opulently ringed. White lace drooped in an elegant spill over his wrists and the backs of his hands, and there was a froth of it at his throat. A large ruby stickpin glowed from his cravat, and his frock coat was a royal wine velvet. He looked like some aristocrat of long ago, proud, disdainful, cognizant of his position and wealth.

"I just love it, Vince," Tara said, looking up at the painting. "He fits that era so perfectly, doesn't he?"

"Yes, he does," Vince agreed. He looked around the room, twenty yards of elegance, at the masterpieces on the walls. There was an intimate little grouping of da Vinci sketches, a marvelous Rubens that fitted well with the store's line of merchandise, a Sisley. "Wow, he has a bloody fortune in paintings in here," Vince breathed. "What I wouldn't give to be able to come in here alone sometime and just look. Just spend the whole day, studying them."

"I'm sure you could talk Charles into giving you a private showing," Tara teased, reminding him of how coyly Charles had flirted with him during his sittings for the portrait.

"I said *alone*, smartass," Vince grinned. He turned to look again at the paintings and was grasped from behind in a warm embrace.

"There you are, dear boy," Charles cried, kissing him wetly upon the mouth. "I've been looking everywhere for you! Isn't this a crush? I love it!" He kissed Tara and drew her into his free arm. Turning to the man behind him, he said, "You must meet my sister, Ian, Tara Remington, the famous writer." He pulled Vince against him, beaming down at him like a proud father. "And this tender young morsel is the artist who painted my portrait, Vince Hollander. Say hello to Ian Starr."

They exchanged greetings and then Charles fluttered off into the crowd, leaving Ian looking solemnly after him. After a few minutes Tara realized that Ian always looked solemn. He was a slight, tragically handsome man who seemed to have some inner secret sadness. She knew who he was, of course, the men's hair stylist whom Thorton had just signed.

Ian Starr's clientele was impressive, consisting of movie stars, political figures, wealthy businessmen and titled Europeans who thought nothing of flying Ian from his Beverly Hills shop to their suite in London (or Rome, Paris, St. Tropez et al.) for a fast trim. His prices were outrageous, but he was a firm believer in Thorton's philosophy that the only thing the rich understand is money. Make it expensive enough and someone will have to have it. Ian's popularity with the ladies added to his reputation; he knew every gorgeous model, starlet, showgirl and call girl on both coasts and most parts of Europe. It was rumored that he was not shy about passing on their numbers to his more important clients.

"Nice place," he offered morosely, a wan smile just barely lifting the corners of his mouth.

"Yes, it is." Tara smiled down at him. He was at least

three inches shorter than she. "Have you known Charles long?"

"Yes." He did not comment further, but stood looking up at her with rather opaque eyes and an expression she could not read. He gave her the creeps. She saw Izzy making his way through the crowd toward her and sighed with relief. She certainly did not want to get stuck with sad sack Starr.

"Izzy, hi snooks, you look marvelous." She went into his arms for her kiss, then stepped back, holding him at arm's length. He had spent the last couple of nights with Charles, helping him with last-minute details, so Tara had not seen what he planned to wear this evening. He was stunning in an off-white tuxedo with a pale blue ruffle-fronted shirt and matching ascot worn high to hide his neck wrinkles. A sapphire the size of a robin's egg winked at her from his chest, and his cuff links were creamy pearls set in white gold.

"So do you, sugar. I told you fur would be just perfect for this affair. You're a vision, sweetie, a *rich* vision." He turned to Vince, his bright parrot's gaze almost undressing him, lingering on his crotch until Vince squirmed with embarrassment and tried to tug down his jacket. "And so do you, guy," he murmured suggestively, and Tara knew he had had his share of champagne already. "Simply yummy—both of you."

"Where is the proprietor of this establishment?" Tara asked. "He popped by to say hello, then flitted off somewhere. I have a little 'good luck' gift for him."

"Oh, what did you get him?" Izzy gushed excitedly. He adored presents, even if they were for someone else. "Let me see!"

Tara took a slim black velvet jeweler's box from her purse and handed it to Izzy. "I hope he likes it. What do you think?"

Izzy opened the box and drew out a narrow S-chain bracelet, a strip of gold as slender as a thread bearing Charles' name in lacy script, the clasp topped with a perfect diamond. "Oh, sugar, it's heavenly! Too, *too* divine! Chuckie will simply faint dead away!" He draped the slinky gold chain across his wrist, turning it this way and that, watching the glimmer of gold and the fire of the diamond catch the light.

"Do you really think so?" Tara asked anxiously. She always worried that the recipient of her gifts would find them ugly or in bad taste. "Do you really like it that much, Izzy? Tell the truth."

"It's only the most sensational bracelet I've ever seen. *Talk* about *thin* is *in,* my dear girl, you couldn't have *seen* it if it were a hair thinner. It's perfectly gorgeous— and I'm *green* with envy!"

Vince took the barcelet and looked at it. "Very nice," he said, thinking how perfectly useless it was. A little teeny piece of gold chain no bigger around than a cat's whisker with the letters so tiny and fancy you could barely read the name. He would lose it within the hour or leave it in some public rest room if it belonged to him. He gave it back to Tara. "Charles will love it. It's *him.*" His voice was slightly mocking and Tara wrinkled her nose at him.

"Yes, I thought so too." She finished her wine and handed Vince the glass. "Well, I'm for one more glass of wine, then we should pose willingly for the photographers so they don't catch me with my finger up my nose or scratching my ass."

She hated those awful, grainy close-ups of celebrities in those horrid tabloids, every pore showing, usually looking perfectly hideous. Whenever she could, she managed to control the situation by willingly posing when they asked her. At least she was sure of a good picture.

The hastily smoked joint she had shared with Vince in the parking lot had put an edge on her appetite and she was anxious to leave this boring affair and go to The Bistro for dinner. She knew that Charles and Izzy would not miss her after a few minutes, so busy were they basking in the limelight. Izzy's status as Charles' lover made him just as much a celebrity as the decadently handsome proprietor of Paraphernalia from Eden, and he was enjoying every shimmering moment.

"I saw Frank Edwards over by the lingerie," Vince

said. "Want to give him the shots?" Frank, a freelance photographer, had been a long-time friend; Tara had been running into him for years at this opening or that premiere. Since there were usually about fifty other photographers pushing and shoving for a shot of the arriving or departing celebs, mild-mannered Edwards was often forced to take the leftovers.

"Sure, why not? I like Frank." She looped her arm through his and they began making their way across the floor, stopping every few feet to speak to someone Tara knew. In this fashion it took them thirty minutes to get across the room, and Frank had left the lingerie department.

Charles and Gene Newberry, the owner of a new and very exclusive private club on Crescent Drive, were engaged in a discussion of fabrics near the gowns.

"Feel this—isn't this too much?" Charles let the pale mint green wisp of silk slip sensually through his long fingers. "I had the fabric brought in from Hong Kong, a raw silk as fine as gossamer . . ." Turning, he saw Tara. " 'Lo, luv, where have you been? Here, feel this marvelous silk. Isn't it too much? It would look sensational on you with your dark hair—simply super . . ."

"Oh, hi, I'm glad I ran into you. I have a little gift for —you know—for the shop and all. A sort of good luck thing." She was stammering, a little awkward at the first gift she had ever given her brother. "It's nothing, really, just a little something—I thought, you know—"

Charles gasped with delight when he opened the box and saw the diamond blinking up at him from its nest of pearl gray satin, the S-chain curved around it like a golden serpent. "Oh, my goodness, Tara, it's too fabulous! Oh my! Oh, my dear girl, thank you!" He kissed her cheek, then her lips. "Thank you so much—I know I should say, 'Oh, you shouldn't have'—but I'm just tickled pink that you did!" He held up his wrist, turning his arm over so Tara could clasp the bracelet. "It's only the most divine thing I've ever seen, that's all. Thank you so much, sis. I'll treasure it always."

"Well, you're welcome very much," Tara laughed, relieved at his effusive acceptance. "Wear it in good health, Charles."

He gazed at her a moment, tears coming to his eyes, which he dashed away with the back of his hand like Errol Flynn weeping quietly over a dead war buddy. He snatched the mint green silk number off the hanger and thrust it into her hands. "For you," he said, pressing it back when she would not take it. "You must take it. It would mean so much to me if you would please take it."

"Oh, Charles, you don't have to do that. I didn't buy you a gift because I wanted a free sample from Paraphernalia from Eden!" She looked at the puff of silk in her hands, as light and airy as a puffy green cloud. It was a beautiful gown and a color that she knew looked wonderful on her.

"Say you'll take it, sis. I really want you to have it. It's the most fabulous gown in the store, in all of Beverly Hills. You must have it."

"Well, I guess so—I—well, thanks, Charles. It *is* lovely." She held it against her white broadtail suit and the full skirt floated gently about her ankles.

"Charles, old cock!" said a sprightly British voice behind her and Tara turned to see the famous mystery writer Clarence Hubbard brandishing his gold-knobbed cane. "I say, dear fellow, this is a bit of all right." He waved his cane in an arc, almost beheading a mannequin modeling a straight fall of black satin from breast to ankles. "Yes, yes, 'tis a jolly wee shoppe, old pot, jolly, yes." He slipped in and out from Irish accent to English and Tara could not help smiling at his flamboyance.

"Clarence, luv, so glad you could make it." Charles threw his arms around the portly author and kissed him on both cheeks, French-style. "Don't you just love it?"

"Yes, yes, wonderful party, wonderful." He now sounded like Peter Ustinov as he leaned forward conspiratorially. "However, old cock, I dare say I would find it more to my liking if I had a bit of spirits in me hand."

"Mercy," gasped Charles, snapping his fingers briskly at a passing waiter. "What will you have, old man? Champagne? Or perhaps something hard?"

"I say, old cock, is that a proposition, what?" Clarence chuckled, winking broadly at Tara to show her that he was just having a bit of fun with the American lad; anyone could see that he was as straight as an arrow. There'd be no queers rattling around in his closets, by golly!

"Oh, I received my copy of your new book, Clarence," Charles said. "What a scream! I loved the character Rugby. Simply charming. But why did you have to kill him off? He was such an interesting and likable character."

"Yes, yes, old bean, that's why," Clarence harumphed, tapping his cane absently on the toe of his shoe. "You see, I do that on purpose, get the reader to really liking a character, then I bump him off." He cackled and winked again at Tara. She supposed he was winking, but he was doing it so often it could well be a tic.

She too had received an advance copy of Clarence Hubbard's latest mystery in a long line of mysteries. She had not read it because his novels were so predictable, like a Perry Mason or a Sherlock Holmes. She wondered if he had been sent a gratis advance copy of her book as well. He did not seem to recognize her and she was just ready to slip away when Charles took her arm.

"Clarence, you must say hello to my sister. She's also a writer." He shoved her a little toward the wheezing, rotund author. "Tara Remington—Clarence Hubbard."

"Yes, yes," Clarence murmured, his tiny eyes running over her in a brisk, professional, sizing-up look. Finding her to his liking, he leaned on his cane and said "Yes, yes" again, then lifted her hand and kissed it. "Enchanté, ma'mselle." He straightened and began tapping his cane on the toe of his shoe once more. "I say, pet, you don't *look* like a writer!"

Tara groaned inwardly. She would not have believed that a fellow writer would utter such an idiotic statement. Her old, often-used response, "What does a writer look like?" was on the tip of her tongue but before she could speak, Clarence cursed, "Blast, the bloody wench has spotted me again! I'm off, old cock." This to Charles. Bowing to Tara, he spoke in a soft drawl reminiscent of

369

Charles Boyer, "I will seek you out before the evening is over, mon amour, but now I must fly!" He glanced wildly over his shoulder and fled into the crowd.

"Charles, dear boy," the Countess Incornado Maria Dicorato St. James strode toward Charles, her hand outstretched for his kiss. "Simply divine party. Tell me, dear, wasn't that Clarence Hubbard you were just speaking with?"

"Why, yes, he was here a moment ago." Charles kissed the gloved hand. "Such a madhouse, it's impossible to keep track of anyone."

"That naughty boy said he would bring me a glass of champagne over an hour ago, now where do you suppose . . . ?"

Tara grabbed Vince's hand and pulled him quickly through the crowd and out onto the sidewalk, collapsing against him, laughing. "Whew, we made it. I was terrified we'd get stopped by someone. I couldn't have stood one more second of that desperate drivel."

"My sentiments exactly," Vince said. "Let's go." Hand in hand they ran down the sidewalk toward The Bistro.

CHAPTER
SEVENTEEN

TARA LAY on her stomach in front of the fireplace, reading the Sunday papers. She opened the entertainment section and saw a photograph of Doe and Wesley taken by the pool in their back yard. The caption read: "Still newlyweds after six months of marriage, the Wesley Cunninghams (just recently returned from an extended tour of Europe) say they are in no hurry to end the honeymoon but will admit that they are reading scripts, hoping to find a property they can star in together."

"Hey, Jim, look." She held up the paper. "The lovebirds are back on our shores. We should call and say hello."

Jim Glasser peered over the tops of his Ben Franklin glasses. "Humph," he said and went back to the sports section.

Tara smiled fondly at him. He had aged so in the past few months. His fine sandy hair was now almost white and his sassy Irish face was a bit gaunt. He had lost a good deal of weight and Tara found that she missed his little round pot belly, his round little fanny as high as a girl's. He sat near the fireplace in his favorite chair, the one he had years ago stretched into a comfortable sag to fit his contours. Whenever Tara had threatened to throw the disreputable thing out, he had cajoled her into having it reupholstered to match whatever new color scheme she was planning. It had changed color and textures a dozen times over the years. In fact, it was that very chair that had given away Jim's terrible secret.

He had been sitting before the fire, reading the paper. He had lately gotten into the habit of dropping by two or three times a week, just to visit, say hello and make himself at home on the patio, if it was warm, in the billiard room if it was chilly. He bothered no one, just sat with his tiny half-glasses perched on his ludicrously small Irish nose, reading. This particular night he had spent most of the afternoon in his favorite chair by the fireplace (it had been recently redone in a sprigged off-white fabric) and when he had gotten up to go to the bar he had left behind a bright red stain. A pool of red blood shockingly vivid against the off-white chair. The seat of his trousers was as red as the chair and Tara had screamed his name, staring in horror.

He had cursed and rushed into the bathroom, yelling through the door a moment later, "Hey, have you got any of those damn Kotex around? I'm leaking like a stuck pig. Again."

She had handed him a caftan (unisex style) through the door and was waiting for him in the billiard room. She poured him a scotch and demanded to know what was wrong with him.

It had taken some time to get the complete story, as he had grimaced, snorted and cursed, pulling faces like Wallace Beery and Lon Chaney in a mugging contest. She finally learned that he had been bothered for the past several months by occasional bleeding from the anus and recurring insomnia usually accompanied by severe low back pain. So painful some nights he could not fall asleep until he had downed a fifth of scotch.

It had started with a sort of rundown feeling, a weariness, a general feeling of malaise that had grown steadily worse. He had gone to the doctor when the pain had gotten so bad a fifth of scotch no longer numbed it. That's when he learned he had it. Cancer of the colon. The Big C.

"They wanted to operate right then and there, the next fucking morning," he had grumbled, scrubbing a hand over his face. "Fucking assholes, can't wait to get their scalpels in a guy."

"But, Jim," Tara had cried, "if they think it's that serious, why didn't you let them operate. Gosh, what if you die?"

"Hey, fair Tara, we're all going to die, didn't you know? It's a condition that's been around for some time now. It's called Death." He had laughed like Humphrey Bogart in *The Big Sleep* and taken a slug of scotch. "Naw, not me, baby—they won't get me. I'm not going to have some young schmuck just out of med school hacking around on me. Shit, the kid that examined me looked like one of the boys that Mandy's always dragging home." He grunted and lit a cigarette, coughed violently for several minutes and gulped some more scotch.

"Well, it's your life, you stubborn Irishman," Tara had said. "But if you had a brain in that cute little head of yours, you'd have it done before it's too late!"

What she did not know was that it was already too late. Jim was dying.

Tara had called Jim's doctor, whom she had known as long as she had known Jim, and asked him bluntly how serious it was. He told her, just as bluntly, that Jim could die at any time without the operation; could live for several more years with it. But when he had explained the procedure of surgery, Tara understood why Jim had refused. He would have to give up sex altogether as a result of the surgery, as it required the insertion of a soft rubber catheter into the penis and up the urethra to the bladder. It would be fitted with a clamp on one end which Jim would have to open in order to urinate. But the final humiliation would be the plastic bag attached to his side into which he would forever after defecate.

She had confronted him tearfully. "How can you be so selfish?" she had screamed. "Other people love you, you know. They may want you to stay around a few years longer, even if you don't want to! Why don't you think about them? About me? Oh, God, Jim I'd die if anything happened to you. Please have the operation—for me!"

"Now who's being selfish?" he had said quietly, more softly than she had ever heard him speak before. "Come here, little Tara," he said, pulling her onto his lap and holding her as if she were a small child. "Do you have any idea in that sweet young head of yours what a fucking rotten way of life that would be for me? *Me?* The oldest living lecher in the world today? No sex? Pissing through a straw? Shitting in a Baggie? No, not this kid, little Tara, not on your life." He rocked her in his arms until she stopped crying.

"Hey, cheer up. I've had the most fantastic life anyone could possibly have had. I made it to this age without getting shot by a jealous husband or thrown into the slammer for any embarrassing length of time. I've seen it all and done it all, honey. There ain't any more."

"Oh, Jim, there's always more! Dr. Bruce said you could live several more years with the surgery, and—"

"I'm dying, Tara. Face it," he said firmly. He stopped rocking her and took her by the shoulders, facing her squarely. "I'm dying," he said again, softer. "And I'll tell you how I know." He had sighed then, scrubbed a hand over his face and taken a swallow of scotch. When he had looked into her eyes, his were kind, sweet, almost like a father's. Or a grandfather's, he had aged so drastically in the last few months.

"I've been in love with you since the first moment I laid eyes on you, my little fair Tara. From the first day you walked into my office wearing that funny looking little plaid suit and clutching your little plastic purse to your chest like you were afraid I was going to eat you. Oh, you were beautiful that day, Tara, so fair. So very young. I only gave you the job so I could see you every day, but then you surprised me. You were bright and eager to learn. Like a greedy little sponge, just gulping in great chunks of knowledge wherever you could find it. Some good, some not so good.

374

"The more accomplished you became as a writer, the more I loved you and the more I knew I would never have you. I wasn't good enough for a girl like you, like the woman I knew you would become. You deserved some young stud with a future ahead of him, not already slipping away from him, living on past glories like I was. Oh, hell, I know I'm a good newspaperman, but the kind of reporter I used to be in the old days." He chuckled at the phrase, a mirthless sound. "Well, those days are gone now and so is my type of writer. A thing of the past. A relic."

He shifted her to his other knee so he could pour a little more scotch into his glass. "I used to lie in bed at night— no matter whose bed it happened to be—with a pain in my heart like a knife from wanting you. Loving you." His voice became softer still, a little dreamy and he was not looking at her but into yesterday. "Every morning for ten years I woke up with a pain in my heart, and then one morning I woke up and it wasn't there. And I missed it. And that's when I knew I was going to die."

He drank deep, closing his eyes, and Tara looked up to see his throat bobbing with each swallow. Lowering the almost empty glass, he had looked at her in that same grandfatherly way. "I guess just knowing that I'm going to die somehow frees me from wanting you. I'll never stop loving you, but now I can give up the wanting of you. Always before, even when I told myself it was futile. Impossible. Even then, there was always this small bright ray of hope that whispered, 'Yes, there's a chance—there's always hope as long as there is life . . .' "

He had pulled her face closer, tucking it beneath his chin as he started to rock her again. "So, now the life is going—and so goes my lust . . ." And Tara knew it was hopeless. Knew she would never ask him again to have the operation. He had a right to die the way he wanted to. With his dignity.

That had been a couple of months ago. It was now the first week in March, the typical blustering, chilly day that heralded warmer weather coming, and Jim was still alive. He had come early that morning for Sunday brunch, as had been his custom of late. He would spend the day walking slowly in the garden, his feet shuffling along the winding paths, stopping to chat with Teddy, who was now as gnarled and bent as the twisted oak trees he tended, and then come back into the house to read the paper with Tara —and sip a little scotch. He had cut his liquor intake in half, and Tara thought that he was looking better and was encouraged. Maybe the doctor had been wrong. Perhaps with a careful diet, he would have a little more time.

She found she enjoyed the quiet days with Jim. It was almost like spending the day with one's grandfather. Sometimes they would play Scrabble, Jim still as fiercely competitive as ever. Still beating her five out of six games. Sometimes they sat under the huge oak tree near the stable, cool in its shade as they watched Mandy groom her horses or put them through their paces. Mostly they sat in the billiard room, just talking, remembering. Then he would fall asleep, Daisy on his lap, both of them in a patch of sunlight from the open door, softly snoring.

"Two tired old pussycats, warming their bones in the sun," Tara would say, a great tenderness flooding her as she looked down at them. Lately Daisy had been limping stiffly about in the mornings until she stretched the cricks out. She was almost twelve years old, not that old for a cat, but no longer a kitten either.

Izzy, Charley and Mandy had accepted Jim's frequent, unannounced drop-ins nonchalantly. If they had some free time, they would sit down and play a hand of gin rummy with him. But no one except Tara would play Scrabble with him unless he spotted them fifty points. If they were busy elsewhere when Jim stopped by, each of them made a point of greeting him with a kiss (even Izzy, much to Jim's chagrin), which he would scrub off with a Lionel Barrymore growl.

"Let's do," Tara said, looking again at the photograph of Doe and Wesley. "Let's call them and invite them over for a drink." They looked tanned and relaxed, Doe much slimmer than Tara remembered. She was wearing one of the new string bikinis that were currently the rage and looked as sexy and luscious as a—well as a thirty-year-old. Doe's figure was much too lush to ever pass for a teeny bopper, but she looked damn good for forty.

"Ah, why not?" he growled, not looking up from the newspaper. "Maybe they'll give me a lead story for my paper." Even though he only worked a couple of days a week, he still owned the *Beverly Hills Beat*.

"Great, I'm dying to hear all about the trip." She dialed Doe's number and asked to speak to Mrs. Cunningham. "Doe? Welcome home! When did you get in?"

"Tara, love, hello! How are you?" Doe cried excitedly. "I've been meaning to call but, yipes, what a madhouse it's been around here. We stepped off the plane two days ago and have been giving interviews ever since. Everywhere we turn, there's a reporter and photographer. I'm ready to get right back on another plane and get away for a vacation!"

"Don't mention planes," Tara groaned. "I'm off next week for a three-month book-plugging tour. Ugh!"

They chatted a few minutes and Tara asked, "Have you made plans for dinner? No? Super, come on over and we'll catch up on all the gossip."

"Okay, sweetie, but nothing fancy. I'm too beat to even put on my eyelashes. God I hope those fucking photographers have left. They're hanging around outside the gate from the time we get up in the morning until we go to bed at night. Wesley thinks they sleep out there at night in case we decide to try to sneak out!"

"My, my," Tara teased. "The inconveniences you famous movie stars must put up with. How *do* you manage?"

"Fuck off, cunt," Doe boomed in her old familiar bawdy voice. "See you in an hour, love—bye." She blew a kiss and hung up.

"Great, they're coming to dinner," Tara said to Jim. "You're staying, aren't you?"

"Yeah, I'll stay. I'd like to see what a happy marriage looks like."

Tara knew that he had been spending more and more time away from home because of his wife, Frances. When she was not bugging him to go to confession so his soul would not burn in hell for all eternity, she was bringing priests home with her to talk to him. She had taken the news of his terminal illness calmly but had seemed to take it as a sign that she must save his soul before he died. Since she was not sure just how much time she had to accomplish this miracle, she threw herself wholeheartedly into the project until it consumed her every waking hour.

Jim had told Tara that there were so many religious statues and candles in the house he felt like he was living in a church. But when she had begun to burn incense that had been the final straw. He had packed a bag and checked into the Beverly Hills Hotel. Indefinitely.

"Shit," Jim had grumbled. "I believe in God, hell and all that crap. Jesus, what Irish lad didn't or he'd get his ass kicked by the nuns! But Frances is a fucking fanatic!"

Tara dropped a kiss on the top of Jim's head. His hair was as soft and fly-away fine as a baby's. "I have to go see what Hazel has cooking, love. Be right back."

"Yeah, go on." He shook his paper as if she had mussed it, peered over the tiny specs and went back to reading about the Dodgers' spring practice.

"Hazel," Tara cried, bursting into the kitchen. "Guess who's coming to dinner?"

"Who, Miss Tara? Sidney Poitier?" Hazel deadpanned. She was standing at the stove, stirring a big pot of chili. Tara could smell it from the doorway.

"You nut," Tara laughed. "No, it's royalty! The Wesley Cunninghams have returned, if you please, and have consented to sup with us this eve."

"Miss Doe is home?" Hazel cried, turning to wipe her hands on her apron, a sure sign that she was pleased. "Well, well, isn't that nice? Did she have a nice honeymoon?"

"Just super. Anyway, I was going to ask you what we're having for dinner, but I can smell it from here. Umm, and it smells divine. That's just what I had in mind, something simple and befitting such a cold, blustery day." She loved the word blustery and used it whenever possible. Since playing Scrabble almost daily with Jim, she had increased her vocabulary twofold.

"That's what I said to myself this morning," Hazel nodded sagely. "I said, a day like this, such a *blustery* day needs something warm and that will stick to the ribs." She replaced the lid, grinning at Tara. Every time Tara found a new word she was particularly fond of, she used it steadily for a week until everyone in the house began to mimic her. She had been so fascinated by "mundane" that she had used it for a week and a half before going on to something new.

"Let's see, what can we have with it? A salad, of course, garlic toast—what else, Hazel?"

"We can start with guacamole and some of those little quesadillas," Hazel suggested. "And what do you think about serving buffet in the billiard room? That way you can all sit around the fireplace and Mr. Jim won't have to leave his favorite chair." She laughed and added, "You do have to have your fire on such a *blustery* day, Miss Tara."

"Indeed I do, Miss Hazel, indeed I do," Tara laughed. "Well, I shall depart and leave everything in your oh-so-talented and capable hands. Shall we say chili around sevenish, hors d'oeuvres at six?"

"Very good, miss." She bobbed a proper curtsy as Tara swept grandly from the room. It was a game they played, lady of the manor and executive housekeeper. Hazel was chuckling as she went to the pantry for a loaf of French bread.

Jim sat in his favorite chair by the fireplace, leaning forward as he listened to Doe and Wesley tell amusing stories about their honeymoon. His gut burned like fire and he took a long swallow of scotch to quell the pain. Leaning forward took the weight off his rectum a little and relieved the pain in his lower back. He took another swallow of scotch, shifting his weight a little more forward.

Hazel passed around a tray of quesadillas and kept the mixer full of margaritas. Outside a light rain had begun to fall and the wind grew stronger, beating branches against the glass doors. Blusterier and blusterier, Tara thought. She took a sip of the frothy drink and smiled at Doe. She looked marvelous. Tan, slender, her long topaz eyes were, for once, without the thick tawny eyelashes that had become her trademark. She looked younger without them. She wore her hair in a simple, brushed-to-one-side style and Tara realized that it was the first time she had seen her without the big, teased, fluffy duckling hairdo.

That she was deliriously happy was evident. She clung to Wesley's hand or arm, looking up at him adoringly as if he had just said the most fascinating thing in the world, when indeed Tara sometimes found Wesley a bit dull. If one could be both dull and pompous.

Hazel set up TV snack tables in front of them, Doe and Wesley still side by side, Jim in his favorite chair and Tara across from him. Charley had had a date with the Bear and Izzy was with Charles, so it seemed a little quiet.

The chili was just hot enough, both with fire and spices, and the blustery wind and rain outside made it taste even better. Another batch of margaritas had been whipped up after dinner and Tara had passed a joint around. It was just like old times.

It was almost midnight when Izzy came floating in, making wisecracks about feeling like Cinderella forced to leave the ball before the clock struck twelve. He often spent the weekend with Charles and would stop by Tara's on his way to his bachelor home nearby. He had bought the house when he had decided that working for Tara was going to be a steady thing, he had kidded, which was partly true. He had only to drive ten minutes to work in the mornings, a blessing when he had been up half the night partying or making love with Fuckie Chuckie.

"Doe, you look simply marvelous, darling," he gushed, kissing her tanned cheek. "And, Wesley, my, you've lost weight. You both look divine. Do tell everything! Where did you go first?" He settled on some cushions on the floor, sipping his margarita and fixing them with his bright parrot's gaze.

So Doe had to repeat the stories again and Tara found herself yawning when she saw it was after one. Doe too yawned, glancing at her watch. "Yipes, Wesley, do you know what time it is? One-twenty, darling. Let's go and let these good people get to bed."

Tara walked them to the door, Izzy leaving with them, a tangle of arms as they all kissed and hugged goodnight.

"Come on, old darling," Tara said, going to Jim and helping him from the chair. "Hazel has the guest room made up for you."

"Thanks, honey, I don't think I could have made it back to Beverly Hills." He grinned apologetically. "A little too much party, I reckon."

She escorted him to the guest room and waited while he undressed and crawled into bed. "Sleep well, my friend," she whispered, bending to tuck him in.

"You, too, little Tara," he murmured sleepily, eyes already closing. "I love you."

Tara stood looking down at him for a long moment. "Goodnight, little Jimmy," she whispered and turned off the table lamp and tiptoed from the room.

Tara had been up since dawn, leaving her suite in the Dallas Hilton by chauffeured limousine to appear on the radio show The Early Bird Hour at seven o'clock. At seven-thirty she was driven across town to sign copies of her book at a breakfast given in her honor, and at noon it had been a luncheon given by some women's group, she had forgotten the name. She had appeared on a local television talk show, The Good Buddy Hour, where she had found herself in the kitchen while "Buddy" interviewed her between listing the ingredients he was tossing into his favorite recipe of stuffed tongue. She had just had time to rush back to the hotel, shower and change into a dinner dress for the banquet in the Hilton Dining Room.

She had just walked into her room when the eleven o'clock news came on. It had been a long day, she thought, as she slipped out of her black Halston gown, and five more to go before she got a weekend leave to go home. It was March seventeenth, St. Patrick's Day, and the boisterous Irish songs coming from the bar downstairs could be heard faintly in her room. She slipped into her nightgown and mixed herself a vodka tonic at the small portable bar near the television set. She took her drink with her and got into bed, clicking the remote control to turn the sound up.

"Tragic headlines from Hollywood this St. Patrick's Day," the voice of the newscaster said briskly. *"Writer Jim Glasser was found early this evening, dead from a shotgun blast to the head. An apparent suicide. Glasser was a famed ace reporter back in the Thirties, when he worked for the New York Times. He moved to Hollywood in the late Forties and went to work for Paramount Studio, writing screenplays for the super stars of that era—Alan Ladd, Errol Flynn, Gilbert Roland, Lauren Bacall, Victor Mature, Rhonda Fleming and many more. The list is endless—as is Glasser's endless novel and short story credits . . ."*

"Jim never wrote a novel in his life," Tara said aloud to the television screen. "And he didn't write short stories. He wrote articles." She raised her glass and swallowed until it was empty.

". . . family members say Glasser was despondent over his ill health which had worsened this past month . . ."

Yes, that was true. He had often sat so long in his chair by the fireplace, he could not rise to go to the bathroom and Tara had had to help him. Sometimes he had soiled himself.

". . . left a jaunty farewell note referring to Ernest Hemingway, and I quote: If Papa could do it, so the hell can I! I've always wanted to go out with a bang! End quote. Glasser is survived by his widow, Frances, 56, and their two children, a son, 26, and a daughter, 23. Now here's Marty with the weather. Well, how does it look for this St. Patrick's Day weekend, Marty? Fair skies ahead?"

There had been no fair skies the last time she had seen Jim. It had been a cold and rainy day. A blustery day.

She fell forward and buried her face in her hands, sobbing. Not willing to believe that her fiesty little Irish leprechaun was gone. Dead. Not her little Jimmy.

She had canceled all her appearances and flown back to Hollywood the next morning, arriving into mass chaos. Even though she and Frances had never pretended anything more than politeness, Tara had gone to the Glasser home to see if there was anything she could do. She had been met by a huge crowd of men, an angry mob, milling about outside Jim's house, crushing flowers underfoot and grinding out cigarette butts in the soft, well-kept lawn.

"Prissy bitch won't let us in," one of the men snarled at Tara as she tried to push her way to the front door. "Gonna have a proper burial for 'im, she says. Shit, lady, that ain't the way old James wanted it."

"Hell, no," cried another, taking a long pull from a pint bottle in a paper sack. "He told us how he wanted it —didn't he, men?"

A roar of agreement went up from the crowd and Tara heard high, angry female voices mixed in with the coarse masculine growls. She looked around and saw that there were almost as many women as men in the crowd, some well-dressed and rich-looking, others obviously from a harsher walk of life. She recognized several newspapermen, important screenwriters and actors, as well as every bartender from every saloon in Los Angeles it seemed.

After almost half an hour of trying to get to the front door, Tara heard the whole story. It came in bits and pieces. These people were all friends he had drunk with in the past; listened to their tales of woe, told them his; men and women he had worked with for over thirty years. People he had touched in some way during his life. Some had flown in from different parts of the world when they had heard about his death. Some had only to come from the East and many lived in Los Angeles, Jim's main headquarters for the past twenty years. They had wanted to discuss the ceremony with their old pal's widow. Find out where the cremation was being held.

"And that's when all hell broke loose," one blowsy red-head shouted. "That prissy-assed bitch in there with a poker up her ass says there ain't gonna be no cremation!"

"Yeah," a short, stubby little guy with a crew cut put in, jabbing the air with a well-chewed cigar as short and stubby as he was. "Says it's barbaric, that's what she says! Says her husband's gonna have himself a Christian burial, fancy funeral and all!"

"And we ain't even invited, how do you like that?" the redhead shouted, anger making her black-rimmed eyes bulge.

"He wanted to be cremated and have his ashes scattered at sea," a quietly handsome woman said close to Tara. She was in her forties, dressed in the latest fashion and sporting a diamond as big as a hen's egg. Tara worried that she would get mugged in this unruly crowd. "He used to say that he was born too late," the woman went on in a soft, cultured voice. "He said he was really a pirate, and, oh, the lovely poetry he used to read to me about the sea." She turned huge, grief-stricken eyes upon Tara. "Did you love him, too, my dear? Ah, well, didn't we all, didn't we all." She sighed mightily. "Goodnight, sweet prince. . . ."

Tara turned and stumbled back through the crowd to the sidewalk, gasping for breath as she leaned against an automobile parked at the curb. Jim, Jim, she cried silently. I don't know if this is a vulgar circus or if I'm touched by their love for you.

"He would have loved this," a voice said behind her and she turned to see Eric standing there. His hands were shoved into the pockets of his tan raincoat and he was grinning a little sadly. "Hell, he probably arranged it."

"Eric! What are you doing here?"

"The same thing you are, I guess. The same thing all these other people are doing here." He shrugged. "I thought I'd stop by and offer my condolences to the widow and see if there was anything I could do for her. I rang the doorbell and was promptly told to go fly a kite—or words to that effect. She did not, she repeated *very* firmly, did not want any of her husband's riffraff cronies around to blaspheme at the funeral service. Said Jim's soul was in enough trouble as it was without any sendoff from the likes of us."

In spite of herself, Tara giggled. Poor little Jimmy. "I can't believe it," she said. "I mean, I knew she was a little hostile toward Jim's friends, but—"

"Hostile is putting it mildly, baby. That lady in there is a real card-carrying barracuda! I was lucky I escaped with my vital organs intact." He took out his cigarettes and offered one to Tara.

"Thanks. God, I could use a drink. I flew in this morning from Dallas at some ungodly hour and just changed and came on over here. If I had known what was happening, I would have stayed home." She took a deep drag and leaned back against the car. "I tried to call several times but always got a busy signal, so I figured she just had the phone off the hook, you know. There must have been reporters calling all day—so I just drove on over and was met by this—this mob." She was talking too fast and knew it and could not stop. "All these people say that Jim told them he wanted to be cremated. Isn't there some kind of law that a person has the right to say how he wants to be buried? I mean, what right does she have to go against his wishes—his dying wish, really . . ." Tears blinded her eyes and she turned her head away.

"Come on, let's go get a drink." Eric took her elbow and guided her to his car and helped her in. She sat huddled in the far corner of her seat, like a small ragdoll with some of the stuffing missing.

He stopped at the first decent restaurant he saw on Sunset Boulevard and led her inside. The lunch crowd was just beginning to arrive as they settled into a booth and ordered drinks. Tara still had not spoken. At first she had not been able to shut up, and now she could not seem to utter a single word. What did you say to a man you had made love to for forty-eight hours, six months ago—and then just disappeared without so much as a "I'll see you around"?

By the time she had downed her second drink and was sipping her third, she had relaxed a little. The picture of the mob in front of Jim's house had mellowed, and she knew that they were right in wanting to give their friend the kind of sendoff he had wanted.

"Isn't there something we can do, Eric? He must have left a will saying that he wanted to be cremated, don't you think so, since he felt so strongly about it?"

"Yes, he probably did. Do you know his attorney's name, by any chance?"

"Sure, he's had the same one for years, Patrick O'Reilly. They used to go out every St. Patrick's Day and get so loaded, their wives wouldn't speak to them for a week!" She clapped her hand to her mouth. "Oh God, this is St. Patrick's Day—I didn't think about that. Oh, poor Jim!"

"It's perfect," Eric said gently, pulling her against him. "What better way for an Irishman to go than on old St. Paddy's Day, huh? Think of the wake those jokers will have for him." She smiled a little. "He would have loved it, baby, you know that."

"I guess you're right." She took a drink and glanced down at the menu. She did not really feel hungry, but when Eric discovered that she had not eaten since last night, he insisted that they have lunch. "Hey, I've got it! Let's call O'Reilly and see if Jim left a will. Then we can take it to Frances and she'll have to let him have his cremation and Irish wake, won't she?"

Eric had made the call, asking O'Reilly to call him back at the restaurant when he found out anything. They had finished lunch and met O'Reilly outside Jim's house, sitting in his car with him while he read the part of Jim's will concerning his burial. He had stated specifically that he wanted to be cremated, his ashes scattered at sundown over the ocean near Malibu. He further stated that he wanted two dozen cases of his favorite scotch, as well as two dozen cases of Irish whiskey, to be placed at the disposal of the mourners. And he wanted Shecky Greene to sing "Oh, Danny Boy" when the ashes were scattered to the winds.

The gang on the lawn had set up such a cheer when Tara, Eric, and O'Reilly had arrived to confront Frances that passersby stopped to stare. They had made a path for them all the way to the front door and when it was answered by a harried maid with two high blotches of angry red in her cheeks, they had broke into a loud, boisterous rendition of "When Irish Eyes Are Smiling."

Frances, the poker still up her ass, stood as if at attention while O'Reilly read the will and made it clear that he intended fully to carry out Jim's wishes. Then she had turned, pointed one rigid finger in the direction of the parlor and uttered five short words: "He's in there. Take him."

He was cremated the next day, and that evening a long line of mourners drove down Pacific Coast Highway to Malibu Beach and the cases of spirits had been brought out. A large fire was built in the center of the mourners, where they sat in a circle, telling stories about Jim. Each one tried to top the other with tales of the wild Irishman and his shenanigans. Glasses were clasped in both hands as they leaned toward the warmth of the fire, remembering.

Tara and Eric sat in the circle. The sad-eyed, well-dressed woman Tara had seen yesterday at Jim's house sat at her side, and a prim, trim, tiny little man (whom they recognized as a famous New York film critic) sat on Eric's left. The sad-eyed woman held a book of poetry in her lap, the pages dog-eared and much read.

Someone pointed to the sky and said, "Look, there he is." The small plane was just coming toward them, the sun a fiery ball of orange behind the silver wings as they dipped low along the coastline. It circled the group on the beach, swooping low and dropped several dozen white roses, their delicate petals shivering in the breeze as they sank into the ocean. Dozens of clover leaves spilled out with the roses, a gentle rainfall of green and white, dancing briefly on the wind, then disappearing into the black water. The pilot made a last circle, then headed out to sea where he deposited his last package—Jim himself.

As his ashes were scattered and blew crazily upon the

wind, the sun sank, coloring the sky and sea a blood red.

"Goodbye, little Jimmy," Tara whispered, half-raising her hand in a farewell salute. The wind whipped her hair across her cheeks, stinging her eyes as she stared at the small speck in the sky that was the plane. "Goodbye, my friend, sleep well . . ."

All around the circle, one by one, others raised their hands, saying their own special goodbyes. Tara heard the lady next to her cry out, fist raised to the sky, "Goodnight, sweet prince!"

"I want to go now," Tara said, getting quickly to her feet and pulling Eric up with her. She started walking briskly toward the parking lot.

Eric hurried after her, wanting to take her into his arms and hold her until the hurt went away. But he knew it was not the time. Neither of them had mentioned "that" weekend.

He looked over at her as he pulled onto Pacific Coast Highway. She looked so tiny and quiet sitting next to him. Tinier than he had ever seen her look. As if she had shrunk into herself. And she was more docile than he would have thought possible. She had agreed to everything he had suggested about the ceremony, his picking her up and driving her to the service and beach after. She had nodded her head dully when he had asked her to have dinner with him that night. Too stunned, he knew, to even realize what she was doing. He felt like a heel but knew he would use any advantage to be with her again. No matter how long or short that time may be.

They ate at the Albatross on the beach, talking quietly about Jim, trying to remember little things about him. Moments they had laughed together, trapped like yellowing photographs in an old album. Tara remembered every silly postcard they had sent to one another when either of them had been traveling. The late-night telephone calls. The lunches. The crazy parties.

Eric drove her home and she hesitated a moment before getting out. She knew she should invite him in for a nightcap. He had been so thoughtful to her for the past two days, taking over completely and gently leading her where she had to be, seeing that she ate and slept. "Would you like to come in for a drink, or are you too tired?" She hoped he would say he was too tired.

"That sounds like just what the doctor ordered," he grinned, helping her out and leading her up the wide steps to the front door. "Besides, I have to admit I've been curious about this mansion you live in. I think I've already seen just about every room in it between the layouts in *Women's Wear Daily, Vogue* and *McCalls.*"

Tara smiled a little as she unlocked the door and let them inside. Eric gave a low whistle as he looked around the tall, marble-floored foyer to the enormous crystal chandelier in the center of a stained glass skylight. "This is really something. And we're not even all the way in yet!"

Tara laughed, shrugged out of her ocelot jacket and took his raincoat. "Well, I call it home," she said lightly. "Come on, we'll go see who's around." She walked ahead of him into the billiard room and saw Hazel and Mandy sitting at the game table, playing Scrabble.

"Hi, Tara, how did it go?" Mandy said, going immediately to her to hug her. She looked anxiously into her eyes. "Are you all right?"

Tara nodded. "Yes, I'm fine, it went just great. It was really beautiful, wasn't it, Eric?" She pulled him forward. "Mandy, you remember Eric Marlowe, don't you? He used to come over a lot when you were a little girl."

"Eric!" Mandy screamed, flinging herself into his arms. "Gosh, I don't believe it! Eric!" She drew back to look at him, then fell forward to hug him again. "Wow, I just can't believe it!"

Eric was almost thrown off balance by her exuberance. "Hey, Mandy, hey—how are you? Boy, have you ever grown!" He returned her embrace, then swung her around and away from him, holding both her hands as he looked her over. He remembered her as a chubby little girl with big solemn eyes, clinging desperately to his hand and calling him Unca Eric. This graceful young woman with glistening black curls and level blue eyes could not be little

Mandy. Not this tall, willowy young lady with high cheek-bones and a bewitching, full-lipped mouth always on the verge of laughter.

"Well, well, Unca Eric," she teased. "You haven't changed a bit."

"Boy, you sure as hell have."

She blushed and looked down. "Come on, I want you to meet Hazel."

Tara just stared. This was not what she had expected at all. Then what had she expected? That Mandy would take one look at Eric and scream, "Daddy!" That Eric would take one look at Mandy and accuse Tara of keep-ing his daughter from him all these years? Jesus, Tara, she told herself, you've been reading too many Victoria Holt novels.

After being introduced to Eric, Hazel hurried off to the kitchen to make hot chocolate for everyone. " 'Tis a blus-tery night, Miss Tara," she said, winking.

"Indeed it is, Miss Hazel, indeed it is," Tara said auto-matically. She still stood stock still in the doorway, staring at Eric and Mandy. They had their heads together over the Scrabble board and Mandy was bragging that she had Hazel on the run.

"See, when she comes back it's my turn and I'm going to put this word on that triple space." She turned her tiles to show him the word "zany" which would give her another fifty points. She giggled at having the drop on Hazel. "Want to play a game as soon as I beat her?"

"Sure, I haven't had a good Scrabble game in years." He gave Tara a meaningful look. They had often played Scrabble together in bed, between bouts of lovemaking. And sometimes they had played strip Scrabble, making the inevitable coupling even more delicious with each piece of clothing they had removed.

Hazel served the cocoa, topped with a fat dollop of whipped cream, adding a generous dash of brandy to Tara's, and then Eric and Mandy got down to a serious game of Scrabble. Tara curled up in Jim's chair near the fireplace and watched them as she sipped her hot brew, letting it warm and relax her.

So engrossed were they in their game, they did not hear her when she got up and left the room. Returning a few minutes later, comfortable now in a loose-fitting, flowing satin robe, they were as she had left them. Eric leaned forward, chewing on his thumbnail, handsome face frowning in concentration. And Mandy, her straight black brows knitted together over her intense blue eyes as she stared hard at her tiles, moving them this way and that, searching for a word.

Tara went into the kitchen for another cup of Hazel's special hot chocolate. She knew she was going to have trouble sleeping, even as exhausted as she was. The brandy would take the jagged edges off.

Back in the billiard room she went to Jim's chair and fitted herself into the comfortable sag that had held her little Jimmy for so many years. Mandy and Eric were still at it, even though from the look on Mandy's face it was obvious who was winning.

"Is that a word?" she demanded, pointing at the board. "What kind of word is that, anyway? What does it mean?"

"Gnu," said Eric. "It's an African antelope." He couldn't help chuckling a little as he added up the score. "That's it, sweetcheeks, unless you can play that Q and Z you got stuck with."

"You rat!" Mandy cried. "Rematch! Rematch! Come on, Eric. Just one more game? Please?"

Eric glanced at Tara. She was sitting in the chair, a little smile on her face. He could not read her expression, and she sat so still he wondered if she had fallen asleep with her eyes open. "Tara?" he said. "How do you feel, baby?" He went to her and she smiled quickly up at him.

"Oh, fine, just a little tired, I guess." She stretched, rubbing the back of her neck with one hand. "Do you realize I've hardly closed my eyes in three days—all this business with Jim on top of a grueling three-week tour, and have to leave again in a couple of days." She sighed and closed her eyes briefly. "I'm doing the To-night Show on Tuesday and then flying to Philly for the Mike Douglas Show."

"Poor baby," Eric half-teased. "Would you like me to rub your back for you? Massage your neck?"

She drew swiftly back, even though he had made no move toward her. "No, thanks, I'm going right upstairs and soak in a hot tub. I've been hallucinating about a hot bubble bath ever since we first sat down on that cold, gritty sand."

"Well, toots," he said to Mandy. "I guess that kills the Scrabble game."

"Awww, Tara, come on," Mandy wailed, but at a sharp look from her sister, she began gathering up the tiles. "Okay," she said to Eric. "I'll let you off this time, but the next time you come out you better be ready to play some Scrabble, buster!"

"You're on, kid. The next time I see youse I'm gonna beat the socks off ya! Nobody challenges Rocky and gets away with it, see?" He made his voice Bogie-tough and Mandy giggled with delight. He helped her put the game away.

Watching them, Tara felt like a heel. She had to say something. "I'm sorry, guys, but I'm ready to drop. You can have a game another time, okay, sis?"

"Sure, it's okay," Mandy said. "I understand. You must be feeling just awful about Jim." She hugged Tara and perched on the arm of her chair, keeping a hand on her shoulder. "I feel just awful, too. But you know what I've been thinking? I'll bet he wouldn't want us to be all sad and everything. You know what a crazy Irishman he was, always joking and laughing, doing silly impersonations. Remember how he used to pretend he was mad at me? He'd grump and growl around the house, doing his Wallace Beery impersonation, and when nobody paid any attention to him, he'd go to his chair and put a lap robe over his legs and do Lionel Barrymore."

Tara laughed, tears filling her eyes. "Yes, I remember. He sounded just like him. He used to do Walter Brennan, too, remember? He'd recite the whole song of *Ol' Rivers* and I'd always cry."

"I did too," Mandy said. "But then he'd get up and

crow-hop across the floor in that silly gimpy limp of
Grandpa McCoy and make me laugh again."

They sat silently, both of them staring straight ahead,
and Eric began to feel like an eavesdropper. He cleared
his throat. "Well, if I can't get a game out of anybody, I
guess I'll mosey along."

"Goodnight, Unca Eric," Mandy said impudently. "I'm
awfully glad that you and my dumb sister aren't fighting
anymore. I missed you."

A lump rose in Eric's throat and he kissed her quickly.
"Goodnight, toots, sleep tight. I'll call in a couple of days
and we'll have us a Scrabble game, okay?"

"Okay, Eric, goodnight." She kissed him lightly upon
the mouth and bent to kiss Tara. "Goodnight, sis, see you
at breakfast."

Eric looked after her until she had disappeared through
the door and the sound of her lightly running footsteps
had faded away down the seemingly endless hallway.
"Well," he said grinning down at Tara. "Well, she's certainly grown up, hasn't she? God, the last time I saw her
she was just a little kid. Now she's a woman grown. And a
damn good-looking woman, too."

He stood awkwardly before her, looking down, she sitting calmly, looking up. Her marvelous dark eyes were
heavy-lidded, giving her a seductive look that greatly disturbed him. Should he try? He had a dynamite joint in his
pocket. He could get her high like last time . . . Jesus,
you bastard, he cursed himself. Poor kid is dead on her
feet.

"Yes, she's lovely." Tara rose and began walking in the
direction of the foyer. "Thank you so much, Eric, for taking over. I know I couldn't have gotten through it without
your steadying hand." She stopped at the coat rack and
lifted off his raincoat. "I really mean that, Eric," she said
slowly, looking him straight in the eye. "Thank you so
much for helping me say goodbye to my friend. I'm grateful."

"He was my friend too," Eric said gruffly. "Even though
I'll be damned if he'd ever admit it." They both laughed.

"Well, goodnight and, really, thanks again." She opened the door, stood holding it for him.

He slipped into his raincoat, taking his time about adjusting the collar, carefully tying the belt just so. He could not just walk out, say "Goodnight" and leave. Drive out of her life for another six months. Maybe longer.

Tara rubbed her hands together and licked her dry lips. Why was he just standing there? She would topple over any moment, she was so tired. Her temples pounded and she pressed cold fingers to them. "If there's ever anything I can do to repay your kindness, why—"

"There is one little thing," Eric murmured, sweeping her into his arms. "I'll consider the debt paid in full if you kiss me goodnight." Not waiting for an answer, he crushed his lips to hers, parting them with his tongue. She fought him for a brief second, then melted in his arms, her arms going around his neck, her lips opening like dew-moistened rose petals. Her body swayed against him, and his arms wrapped almost twice around her frail form. She had grown too thin, he thought, nuzzling her mouth, nibbling her lips, then kissing her closed eyes. He would have to fatten her up, get her back into that sexy, sassy form he so loved.

"Eric, don't—" Tara gasped. She drew back, opened her eyes and looked directly into his vivid blue gaze. The one that had always made her half-faint from wanting him. When his cobalt blue eyes changed to passionate black with desire . . . She saw his face coming closer, full lips parted, eyes boring into hers, and she moaned and closed her eyes and gave herself up to him.

"Tara, my darling, I still love you," he whispered between sweet kisses rained on her eyes, nose, lips, throat. "No matter what you do to me, I'll always love you." He kissed her mouth and she kissed him back with all the pent-up emotion in her body.

"You'd better go," she whispered shakily as they broke apart. She leaned against the door to keep from falling. "I—I'm so tired, Eric, really—"

"I know, baby, I'm beat, too. It's been a hectic couple of days." He hugged her, not trying to kiss her this time, but just held her against his body. "You get some sleep before you fall over, okay?" Tilting her chin in his hand, he bent and kissed her nose. Then her lips. "Go on in, now, before you catch a cold out here."

"Thank you, Eric," she said softly. He stood framed by the night at the top of the stairs. His broad shoulders seeming to fill the frame, his head haloed in stars, the moon just brushing his left shoulder. She raised on tiptoes and kissed him tenderly on the lips. "Goodnight, darling."

He stood looking at her a moment longer, then turned and ran lightly down the stairs. She watched him until he disappeared into the shadows near the garage, then closed the door and threw the lock.

CHAPTER EIGHTEEN

It HAD BEEN three months since Jim had put a shotgun in his mouth and pulled the trigger. Three months of hard work for Tara. She spent nine hours a day on her novel, researching, blocking, plotting, researching until her eyes crossed. *Passion's Rogue* had proved to be just as big a blockbuster as *Seattle Slum,* and the money was rolling in at an almost embarrassing rate. She still could not help but feel a little guilty about earning so much money for something that came so easily. That was why she had decided to really work on this one, the Hollywood Story, as Thorton and Hy were already calling it.

She had done her last talk show on May first and had taken a couple of weeks off to just flop in Lake Tahoe before starting the Hollywood Story. But mostly she sat in her office, gazing out at the spring days turning summer lush with each new bloom, each new leaf, plotting the Hollywood Story. (She hated saying it that way, capitalized, but that's the way it always sounded when Thorton and Hy said it.)

Tara stood, stretching on her toes and pressing her hands into the small of her back. She had been at the typewriter all day and felt it. It was a gorgeous June evening, just dusky enough to cast the garden and pool area in a romantic haze. Tara lit a joint and wandered outside, walking along the brick paths that twisted beneath towering oaks and wound around sculptured shrubbery. She paused for a moment by the side of a three-tiered fountain, each tier a shell, graduating in size from large to small, the water cascading over it sounding like Oriental wind chimes. She sat down on one of the stone benches that flanked each side of the waterfall, smoking her joint and listening to the quiet.

Mandy was spending a week with her best friend, Kim Monash, at the family cabin in Aspen, Colorado. Charley and the Bear had gone off to play in Big Sur, and Izzy and Charles were luxuriously cruising along the Caribbean shores. Poor Charles had pleaded fatigue after eight months of making so much money he could now open ten more stores. Thorton was dashing madly about, already putting together the tour for the Hollywood Story and she was not even on the second chapter yet.

She sucked in smoke, closing her eyes for the rush. God, wouldn't it be great to just take off, fly away somewhere and know you didn't have to get up every morning and sit down at that fucking typewriter and face a blank piece of paper and know you have to fill it (and four or five hundred more just like it) with something clever. Interesting. Socially significant. Witty. She felt strangely out of it. Thought about Jim and it didn't help. If he were here he would think of something insane to do or say that would make everything all right.

But Jim was gone, and Wesley had been killed two weeks ago in a small plane crash near Las Vegas. He had chartered a single-engined plane at two that morning and an hour later lay broken on the desert floor. The cause of the crash was still being investigated.

Doe had simply gone to pieces, refusing to see anyone but Eric and Tara (separately, of course; even in her grief she was always discreet) and her long-time manager, Manny Goldman. Manny had taken care of everything, and Doe had stayed under a doctor's care until the day of the funeral. She had attended on Eric's arm, Tara holding her other one, then had gone back home and locked herself in the house. She often called Tara late at night and asked her to come over to stay with her, and Tara would go. Sleeping in the big kingsize bed with her, holding her hand until she fell asleep. She whimpered and called Wesley's name while she slept, driving Tara out of bed and to the window seat to sit staring out into the night. To think.

She kept busy during the long days, days in which she thought about Jim and Wesley and Eric, thinking how funny it was that she had grouped Eric in with the dead.

She stood and began walking back toward the house, her eyes down, looking at the neat red bricks in the winding path. Like some great twisting snake winding away into the shadows. Her fingers trailed behind her, gently caressing the leaves and roses along the walk, catching a blossom now and then to crush between her fingers and scatter the petals behind her.

She entered the house and heard Hazel's muffled sobbing, then the housekeeper was putting loving arms around her, holding her close. "It's Miss Doe," she sobbed. "You're to call Mr. Goldman at once."

With hands that shook and turned cold as ice, Tara dialed Manny's number, knowing before he answered what he would say. Hazel pressed a large tumbler of brandy into her hand and she listened, not saying a word as Manny explained gently that Doe had committed suicide. "She just couldn't live without Wesley," he said, a catch in his gruff voice. "I'll let you know later about funeral arrangements."

"Yes," Tara said dully. "And thank you, Manny, for everything." Managers, she thought, they were always stuck with the thankless task of cleaning up the mess. She sipped her brandy and stared straight ahead, too stunned and heartsick to even cry. She wasn't surprised by the news. Doe was where she wanted to be—with her Wesley.

She curled up in Jim's chair, wishing it were cold enough for a fire in the fireplace. She always could think better staring into the flames. But the night outside was crystal clear, millions of stars twinkling as if their life depended on it. They did in a way, she thought. Didn't stars burn out awfully fast and plunge into nothingness somewhere out in space? And for every falling star, there's a new one born.

Eric paced the length of his den and back again, staring holes into the telephone each time he passed it. Willing it to ring. And suddenly it rang. He snatched it up, heart pounding.

"Mr. Eric? This is Hazel. I just wanted to let you know that Miss Tara is safe." He sagged with relief, sinking down upon a bar stool. "She just called to tell me that she was going to drive around a little while, then maybe get a room somewhere on the beach—you know, she just needs to walk it out."

"Thanks, Hazel, I really appreciate your calling to let me know." He lit a cigarette with hands that still shook

"Well, you know, when Miss Tara don't have her fireplace to stare into, then she's got to be walking along some beach somewhere."

"Yes, I know. Did she say when she was coming home?"

"No, just said not to worry. She was fine and just wanted to be by herself. I guess she'll be back in the morning. Do her good to get out of the house for a little."

"Well, thanks again, Hazel. I guess we can both relax now." They rang off after Hazel promised to let him know the moment Tara returned. He poured himself a Jack Daniels and turned on the television set, changing channels until he found an old Joan Crawford tearjerker guaranteed to put him to sleep.

Tara drove through Malibu, watching the moon play hide and seek among the clouds. She passed the Albatross Restaurant and remembered, with a jolt, the last time she had been to the beach. When Jim's ashes had been scattered at sea and Eric had taken her to the Albatross for dinner. She turned into the parking lot, made a U turn and pulled back onto Pacific Coast Highway, heading back the way she had come.

She could not face the memory of Jim's funeral. She couldn't go to the beach.

Instead of turning on Sunset Boulevard, which would have taken her back into the city, she stayed on the highway. She rolled down her window and let the summer breeze caress her warm face. She turned on the radio and tried to find a music station, but turned it off and slipped a tape into her eight-track beneath the dash. Barbra Streisand's soothing voice floated over her like balm and she leaned back in the seat and just drove.

An hour later she looked up in surprise to find herself approaching Disneyland. She had cruised along with the flow of traffic, not really caring where it took her. Just thinking.

Damn, why did every thought conjure up another one about Eric? Would he forever star in her memories? Think about Doe, and there was Eric. Remember times spent with Jim or Thorton, and there was Eric. Remember Wesley, and see Eric introducing them. Always Eric. Even when she thought of Mandy, she thought of Eric. Especially when she thought of Mandy.

She was stiff and suddenly very tired. The Disneyland Hotel was just ahead and she pulled in. She was given the Cinderella Room, all pink and white, frothy fantasy everywhere she looked. This is all I need, she thought wryly.

She ordered a bottle of brandy from room service, undressed and got into bed. She turned on the piped-in music very low, dimmed the lights and poured herself a drink. Leaning her head back against the pink tufted velvet headboard, she sipped the brandy. What she would not have given to have a room like this when she had been a child. It was like living right in the middle of a big puff of cotton candy. Maybe this was just what she needed tonight. A fantasy, a return to innocence when young. Just to close her eyes and go way back into fantasyland, to a time when people died naturally of old age, their families gathered about, instead of cancer caused by the poisons in our foods. Driving them to suicide.

She took another sip of brandy, heard the lyrics of the song and acknowledged them with a harsh chuckle.

401

"When you wish upon a star, makes no difference who you are . . ." She reached to the nightstand for her purse and lit a joint, glad that she had thought to bring them. She should be smoking with Doe. The two of them sitting together on the side of the bed, giggling like a couple of crazies, waiting for Wesley to come home.

Jesus. Eric again. She drank down the rest of her brandy and poured another. Push thoughts of Eric away.

And what about me? she thought. What will I do? The same bloody thing. Sit down at the old Iron Mistress every morning and face a stark white piece of blank paper that sneers up at me, "Okay, hot shot, fill me with something brilliant!"

She laughed mirthlessly, sucked in on the joint and held the smoke down a very long time. Until the rush swept wildly through her bloodstream and sent her spinning out of her body for a shimmering second, then returned her, lax and loose.

And what will Eric be doing? Will he have grown tired of waiting? Marry that redheaded anchorperson and have a dozen kids? Kids that look like Mandy? Jesus, shut up, Tara, she told herself sharply and took a big gulp of brandy. It burned a streak of liquid fire down her throat, but it warmed her belly and felt good.

She dropped the roach into an ashtray and finished the brandy. Snuggling into the soft blankets, she listened to the music, her mind a blank. Exhaustion beat steadily in every muscle of her body. She had held herself so tight for the last twenty-four hours, she felt as if she were tied in knots. She stretched under the covers, tightening and releasing the muscles in her calves and legs, shaking the kinks out. She must be getting old. Driving used not to bother her or make her as tired as she was now. She turned over on her stomach, hugging the pillow with both arms, making a little nest for her head.

Well, she thought sleepily, she supposed everyone was getting older. As Jim would have said, "It's a condition you can't avoid." He also would have said, "When you start thinking about how old everyone else is starting to get, take a look in the mirror!" She would have to do that. First thing tomorrow morning. Gee, maybe she *was* starting to look old. The thought momentarily jolted her out of her drowsy lull. She had been noticing movie stars on the tube lately and commenting to Izzy or Charley, "God, look at her [or him]—they look *so old!*"

And she was twenty-six. Or would be in August. "God, twenty-six years old." She said it aloud. Two and a half decades. The realization was a little startling. What had happened to the years? She sometimes felt as young as Mandy. She grimaced in the darkness. And then there were the times she felt at least a hundred and five. Her head pounded dully with her thoughts, the brandy, the long drive. She felt a little queasy but fought off the urge to throw up. She probably could not have gotten out of bed to go into the bathroom, anyway. Her limbs were so heavy, sluggish, even her brain felt turned off. Numb.

Tara slept late and had brunch sent up to her room. It felt pleasant to stay in bed and be waited on. She did not have to think about anything but eating the hot food and drinking the excellent coffee. She found that she was ravenous (how long had it been since she had eaten, anyway?) and cleaned everything off her plate—scrambled eggs, bacon, hash browns, three slices of toast. She drank a large glass of milk and another cup of coffee before getting into the shower.

She stood for a full twenty minutes under the strong, punishing lash of water, turned first hot, then cold, then back again, switching back and forth until her entire body tingled. She shampooed her hair and scrubbed away every vestige of yesterday's grime and fatigue. She stepped out, feeling exhilarated and toweled herself dry. Not wishing to put her soiled and wrinkled clothes back on, she called downstairs to the dress shop and ordered a pair of jeans and a tee shirt. "Yes," she laughed. "The Mickey Mouse one will be fine. But just plain blue jeans, okay. Size five, please."

She drove past Disneyland and saw the Matterhorn poking its head into the clouds and remembered the first

403

time she and Eric had taken Mandy there. She thought for a moment of pulling in, just to visit Fantasy Land. She did not feel like going home just yet. She was still deciding whether she should pull in when she was honked furiously out of her lane, forced over and a red-faced tourist shook his fist at her. "Have a nice day in Disneyland," she smiled at him.

Well, that decided that. She lit a joint, just flowing with the traffic, letting the faster more determined motorists cut her out or drive around her. She was slowly pressed across the freeway in this manner until she found herself in the right lane, heading for the Knotts Berry Farm exit. Well, she supposed one fantasy was as good as another. She slowed at the light and was pushed ahead in a surge of traffic going to Movieland Wax Museum. She was handed a ticket and motioned to a parking space. Unable to turn around, she shrugged and parked her car, a half mile from the attraction itself.

She was hot and sweaty by the time she had walked across the parking lot and into the museum. A cold blast of air struck her hot face as she gasped, shivering in the icy room. It was almost pitch black after having just come in from the sunlight and she stood a moment until her eyes became accustomed to it. She bought a ticket and stepped through the garishly painted door and was immediately confronted by the Keystone Kops, but she had been there before and knew that they were real.

"Good afternoon, gentlemen," she said. "Lovely day, isn't it?" She felt high, giddy, and in a surprisingly good mood from the joint she had smoked. Ridiculously, she felt like skipping down the carpet corridor. Then she was face to face with the Duke, big John Wayne in his buckskins and coonskin cap from *Hondo*, a shaggy dog at his mocassined heels. And a little farther down was Humphrey Bogart and Katharine Hepburn from *The African Queen*. Eric had done a Humphrey Bogart impression for Mandy the last time she had seen him.

She walked slowly, gazing into the glass eyes of people she knew or had known intimately. Vince Edwards, a tuft of black hair curling out of his tunic top, à la Dr. Ben Casey, his wax free face sneeringly handsome. Errol Flynn, swashbuckling fool that he was. Elizabeth Taylor, too beautiful even when cast in wax.

She stopped dead still, her hand flying to her mouth. There was Doe. She stood with her bare feet wide apart, a rifle held low, butted against her stomach. The buckskins she wore were in tatters and one lush breast was more than half exposed. Her blonde hair was a wild, savage tangle about her face and shoulders. There was a big rust-colored tarantula on her slim ankle. Harry the spider. From a scene from Eric's *Savage Desert*.

Tara stood like a statue herself as people walked around her, bumped into her to get a better look at Doe.

"Gee, she sure looks real," someone whispered and Tara stared up into Doe's magnificent topaz eyes, so life-like that they were eerie. The overhead lights warmed them, giving them a twinkle, and Tara almost expected to hear her say, "Hi, honey, how the fuck are you?"

She stood staring at Doe until the group that she had been trailing along with had gone ahead and another group now joined her to stare up at Doe and Harry the spider. She stumbled away, not able to look anymore. The group passed her, chattering, shoving, giggling and rough-housing, and she stepped to the side to let them pass. And looked up to see Wesley Cunningham smiling benevolently down at her. He was dressed in a tunic from his role as Julius Caesar, and behind him, richly garbed, was Susan Hayward. All dead, Tara thought, backing away. All of them dead.

She had to get out of there before she screamed. She started walking quickly down the wide corridor, trying not to look but drawn in spite of herself. Seeing dead, wax faces leering back at her. And she saw Zock McBain, resplendent in his white, diamond-studded tuxedo flashing like a myriad of mirrors in the sun.

Fake rubies and emeralds adorned his guitar and his boots were gold lamé with three-inch heels.

She turned and ran all the way to the exit, bursting

through the doors like the devil himself was after her, gasping in the hot, smog-filled air as she ran to her car.

It was after four in the afternoon by the time she got back to Los Angeles. She stopped to fill her tank and stretch her legs. She felt like she had been sitting in a car for a week. Back on the freeway she wondered where she could go besides home. With Charley and Mandy away, it would seem like a tomb. And she had had enough of that for one day. She could not count on Izzy popping by for cocktails because he was still cruising. Thorton was in New York. And Doe was dead.

She gripped the steering wheel hard, almost side-swiping another car. Sweat popped out on her forehead and she turned quickly off at the nearest exit.

She turned onto Sunset Boulevard and drove slowly down the wide busy street. Trees edged the sidewalks, towering overhead like hundreds of umbrellas open to the sun. She drove down the Strip, passing Stefanino's, where she and Eric used to go for late suppers after a screening or gathering of some kind.

Up ahead and to the right was the Beverly Hills Hotel, the fabulous Pink Palace that had seen more action than a mere mortal could ever comprehend. It was the last home Jim had known. Inside was the Polo Lounge, where she had made all three book deals, signing the contracts with Hy Griffin over drinks. The Crystal Room, where she had danced with Zock on Academy Award night—and looked over his shoulder into Eric's blue eyes.

She slowed and traffic behind her honked angrily, forcing her into the right-turn-only lane. Benedict Canyon. She slowed as soon as she made the turn, gazing at the beauty and serenity of this quiet tree-lined street. The lushness. How many, many times she had traveled this street, on her way to or from Eric's house. She bet if she closed her eyes and took her hands off the steering wheel, her car would find its way. With no help from her at all.

"Maybe that's what's wrong with me," she said aloud. She had never really had to put herself out to get anywhere. Publish a book? Sure, Thorton will arrange it.

Marry the biggest rock star in the world? It's as easy as saying yes. And so is divorce. Want a mansion with stables? No problem, all it takes is money. Like to see your novel made into a movie? Sell it to the highest bidder, kid. Want Eric back? Make him crawl—but not so he would notice. Pretend to be heartbroken, when it is really fear. Fear you will make an ass of yourself. Highly embarrassed because you were so very righteous and outraged. How can you take it all back without looking foolish? But that is what she wanted to do more than anything else in the world. Take it all back to 1973 and make up those lost years.

She stepped on the gas, driving fast now that she knew where she was going. She saw the fins of his Cadillac sticking out of the garage as she parked her car. Her legs were shaking so hard she could barely walk. She had to stop and catch her breath before ringing the door bell.

"Around by the pool," she heard him call. "Come on in." She walked to the side gate and with icy fingers pushed it open.

He was lying on a chaise longue in faded denims, no shirt, his feet bare. The sun caught on his hair, on his tanned bare chest, glinting on the tiny golden hairs on the backs of his hands. He was holding a script, his sunglasses pushed back on the top of his head. She would forever remember how he looked at this moment.

And she did not care what he had done. What he had not done. Only what he would do. He would love her and keep her safe. And then she was running, calling his name. Her hair came loose from the bun and whipped behind her, flying as she ran.

He stood, and then he was running too. Running toward her, his arms reaching out for her. Scooping her up like she weighed nothing at all and almost squeezing the breath out of her with that rib-crushing hug of his. She was home.

Bestsellers from BALLANTINE

No one who buys it,
survives it.

THE HOUSE NEXT DOOR

A terrifying novel
by
Anne Rivers Siddons

28172 $2.75

 BALLANTINE BOOKS

G-1c

Beauty is as beauty does...

The best
in modern fiction from
BALLANTINE